# MAKING PEACE

MARYLOUISE OATES

MAKING PEACE

WARNER BOOKS

A Time Warner Company

Warner Books, Inc., 666 Fifth Avenue, New York, NY 10103

**W** A Time Warner Company

Printed in the United States of America
First printing: October 1991

10 9 8 7 6 5 4 3 2 1

**Library of Congress Cataloging-in-Publication Data**

Oates, Marylouise.
    Making peace / Marylouise Oates.
      p.    cm.
    ISBN 0-446-51541-8
    I. Title.
PS3565.A82M35   1991
813'.54—dc20

90-43059
CIP

For my parents, Elinor and Ray, who taught me that politics have nothing to do—and everything to do—with love.

# BOOK ONE

# THE CONVENTION

Some things she knew then. She gave herself credit for that. Over the years she had put together pieces of the rest of the story. A few things she could still only imagine.

Like many others in her generation, Annie was a captive of her youth, her personal history. For the past month she had let her obsession have full rein, focusing on the Sixties, thinking of little else. She told her friends and colleagues that, in middle age, she'd found the perfect summer job: indulging in the luxury of her own past. She could click on random events and speed them through her mind like sections of videotape, but with a single odd discrepancy: all her memories were in black and white. When she began to run the news film from that era, miles of it from the network's tape library, what shocked her was not the turbulent politics, but the vibrant colors. In her head the colorful Sixties had somehow been reduced to poor-quality snapshots or a faded classic film.

Around her the political present was too colorful, intrusive, and the giant convention center streaked with the tarty tints of a Fifties musical. The hall had been chilled to a brittle temperature, but her palms were musty damp, as unpleasant as she remembered from high school dances. This story, her story from the Sixties, was too big. It made her nervous. It made her head hurt. She wanted to remember politics and protests, the cultural clutter of rock 'n' roll, free love, and being young enough to think you'd live forever. What kept getting in the way, she told her patient husband, were dark and dirty secrets, long-buried deceptions, and brutal deaths.

Annie paused on her way to the anchor booth, to watch the last scheduled hearing of the party's platform committee stumble along, the protagonists from both sides playing the voodoo game of parliamentary rules. Tonight, the opening night of the convention, according to the printed program, called for "Presentation and Adoption of the Platform...8:00 to 10:45 P.M." Not likely, Annie thought, since there was still no consensus on the "suggested platform" of the committee headed by Senator Mark Mulligan (D-Mich.), who, if he didn't muck it up with a messy floor fight, had a very big future. Mulligan was playing it smart right now, gracefully holding back and letting two committee members, a Latino woman and a black man, battle it out, do the dirty work.

Annie caught herself up short. That's all she'd need to do. Use some phrase like "do the dirty work" and immediately her motive in producing tonight's piece would be suspect. Then maybe not. Covering politics, the cynicism settled in quickly, uncomfortable but satisfying, like fast food eaten on the press bus. During a convention, the skepticism somehow subsided. Gone was almost everything about the everyday. Here in this great hall, like a secondhand spaceship, there was no day, no night, a political junkie's happiest time. Conventions were never needing the hotel room you fought so hard to get, seven days of seeing everybody you had ever met, having giant expense account dinners, and being part of the buzz.

Annie missed some parts of her "real" life, like her kids. Her network said the guys, at fifteen and sixteen, were too young for the coveted convention intern jobs. So Mike was taking a drama workshop, and Bobby was at camp. Maybe getting laid, she thought, immediately uncomfortable at her own nonchalance, worrying if he would be careful. Conventions were like summer camp, although at conventions nobody got laid much anymore.

Threading her way through corridors and over the wires, Annie finally got to the security guard at the entrance to the anchor booths. Her face would have laid lie to it, but a guess from afar, seeing her in slacks and Hard Rock Cafe jacket, lugging her two crammed canvas bags, would have put her as one of the interns.

She didn't feel like a teenager, hauling her stuff up the last killer flight of stairs to the anchor perch. Annie carefully placed one of her canvas bags on the anchor desk, then dumped the contents of the second one on the plywood floor. Spilling around her feet were bits of her own sloppy time capsule: a mint-condition button with a raised fist, a tattered brigade marshal ribbon, a mimeographed booklet, *March Manual, Fall Offensive Against the War.* There were a few plastic doves. That's how the world divided up then, doves or hawks, good or bad, for or against. In the Sixties everybody had politics. Her favorite campus headline had been when the Berkeley campus guides came out against the war: "Oskie Dolls Demand Peace." Annie picked up another button, a particular favorite: "Girls Say Yes to Boys Who Say No." Another ideological failure.

Enough of ideology, she told herself. This is television. Settling onto the anchor chair, she pressed a switch under the desk and asked Ralph in the trailer to please feed her backgrounder piece through to the anchor monitor. She needed to see it one more time.

Watching the opening minutes of the minidocumentary, she was pleased with herself. The nudging and whining had paid off. She'd begged the guys in New York to find her some original film, some footage that hadn't appeared on the air in the nostalgia trips the network loved to take: a speech by Dr. King that didn't say he had a dream; a clip of Bobby Kennedy in which he wasn't walking on the beach; JFK without his daughter and not saying, *"Ich bin ein Berliner";* black students before Afros, hair all slicked down with pomade; antiwar protestors who weren't from Berkeley or Columbia.

Some clichés couldn't be avoided. No matter how you edited the tape, they all looked too young. No getting away from it. And straight, too. How could these kids have scared the country, all looking like Sunday-school teachers, the girls demurely sitting in, with their long skirts and hats, the boys with crisp white short-sleeve shirts, straight from J.C. Penney's; cornflakes faces reflected in the candlelight at an antiwar vigil, a clapboard Congregationalist church dusky in the background? Revolutionaries? Hell, they looked like they would grow up and vote for Richard Nixon.

In the footage from 1964 and 1965 and 1966, the faces in the crowd had a soft innocence that still touched her, even after weeks of viewing and editing—like her kids, when they first woke up in the morning, forgetting for a few precious moments to put on their sophisticated smiles. Tender, these were tender faces.

The piece held together, proof that the romantic idealism of the time wasn't her particular craziness, although she didn't remember any poignancy or tenderness when she lived those days, unless it was some love-in or sensitivity group bullshit. Then everybody was trying to be sensitive so they could get laid. Funny the things you notice about people, the things you know when you're too old to do much about it.

The pile of Sixties stuff on the floor suddenly looked odd. Back and forth her eyes flicked, from the tape to the floor, no smell of madeleines or even of frying onions to speed her memory or stiffen her soul, just the slightly fuzzing gray-and-white images, the camera catching the four familiar faces.

Burnett and Bitsy, Kapinski and Tyler, all lined up behind a table, talking about the Offensive Against the War. There it was, her march, magically alive from more than twenty years ago, the one remembrance that could break her heart and her resolve. Annie flicked the switch and asked Ralph to freeze the tape. The image was too strong, with all of them moving and talking and being the way they were back then. The frozen screen was a bad photograph, blurry and slightly wrinkled, but even it was much too real. She looked away and stuck in an earpiece to catch the conflict on the convention floor.

If she strained a little, Annie could watch Elizabeth Clark, chairman of Forces for Change, brilliantly orchestrating her attack on Mulligan's platform. Bitsy looked good, Annie thought, solid and successful in a pretty pink print dress, although the sudden fullness of her friend's matronly body caught her off guard.

"Miss Clark." Mulligan was getting into the fray. Annie pulled a Diet Coke out of her second canvas bag and settled in for a little careful watching. "Miss Clark, we have held hearings on the platform, seventeen hearings, for the past six months, throughout the country. This document is a consensus of opinion in our party."

"I don't think so." Bits was not at the major mike. She had some effete little Harvard lawyer stationed there, reading off objections. But there was no doubt who was running the show. "I think you had hearings, but then I think, Senator, that you all went back to Washington and talked to the same old white men, and I emphasize *men,* and now we have a platform that says nothing. It won't attract one vote. It won't produce one solution."

Mulligan was short-tempered. Annie took a clean yellow pad and printed, "Cranky." The Dr. Spock words were almost invariably accurate in describing politicians. But he's attractive in his anger, Annie thought, getting better with age, his sandy hair turning a silvery blond, his big farmer's hands thinning into Michelangelo-style sculptures. He'd be great on TV, Bitsy was a worthy adversary, and, Annie thought happily, her piece looked better and better.

The backgrounder now frozen in the monitor had been entirely Annie's idea and project, an insurance policy that paid off no matter how the platform got resolved. No platform floor fight, and the piece would be a nostalgic reminder of past deep divisions in the party. But if the convention opened with a platform floor fight, as now seemed likely, her piece moved up from clever to brilliant. It was merely sensible when she'd thought it up in early summer. Looking over the preliminary reports of the platform committee, it hit her: the controversial planks were the same issues that had caused such violent and widespread reactions in the Sixties—race, war, civil rights.

The teams lined up this way: Mulligan and the party regulars wanted a platform that swept differences under a rug of generalities. Bitsy and her loosely knit coalition were pushing for hard stands on tough issues. Annie's piece looked at the crisis in the Sixties, focusing on several players, then caught up with where they were in the current scenario. The network was going to promo her piece all day: "A revealing look at how the problems of the Sixties have become the politics of today."

From a news point of view, it was great that the platform battle was this hot; otherwise the convention could have been a real yawner. The top of the ticket was decided. One clear front-runner had emerged early on in the multicandidate presidential race: a northeastern liberal with great speech-making skill and no inclinations to sleep with chickens or talk to outer space through his toaster oven. A few deals remained to be cut, but by tomorrow night only his name would be entered in the balloting.

Should have been a pretty show of party unity, but, as Pisano had put it last night, "the party will perform a little surgery on itself. Remove its guts and its balls and then bleed to death." Annie looked for Pisano on the floor and sighted him, seemingly intent on the heavy-breathing confidences of a stout state chairman, telling him a no doubt fascinating story about her delegation.

The second canvas bag sat fat on the desk. Annie reached in and came out with five blue chemistry notebooks, the covers faded, the pages thick from use. Almost reverentially she placed the pile on top of the buttons, a little shrine to the Sixties. Some clever professor had figured out the special copy books, the pages numbered so that a fledgling scientist couldn't ignore failures, couldn't rip out a mistake and start again. Every experiment had to be recorded. Nothing could be edited. Annie ran her hand over the books, rubbing her fingers back and forth until they tingled. Admitting to herself that it was too romantic, she nevertheless thought about when the books were new, when the journal keeper had bought them, one by one. How funny. One or maybe two of them must have been bought not very far from this convention, here in this southern state. She thought about the buzz each new notebook must have brought the author, no doubt echoing the remembered exaltation of first days at school with the smell of new books and freshly sharpened pencils.

A long time ago, when beginnings were new. And now she knew the notebooks by heart, the stories and subtleties of the Sixties drawn by one artist from a very special perspective. She missed the journal keeper. She missed her friend. She missed who she was and what they were.

Annie wished that memories were like old lovers. That they would show up at parties, married to the wrong girls.

The platform hearing broke for lunch. Pisano wasted no time. He squeezed the generous upper arm of the bubbly state chair and headed for the front of the hall.

Mulligan was wrapping up with the press: "This year the platform will not divide the party. That's the promise I bring to this convention."

The staff guy moved in. Pisano didn't know him very well, only his reputation, which wasn't bad. But he'd never replace Kelly. That was a landmark, tough old pol. Kelly was an original.

"Yo, Senator. How about one more question?"

The staff guy knew Pisano and his paper, so there was a second of hesitation before he shook his head and began to steer Mulligan away. "Mark," Pisano yelled. A couple of the radio guys looked at him as if he were crazy. You might play tennis, or drink, or even get laid with a U.S. senator, but in public he was "Senator."

Mulligan knew the rule. His head swung around like a Jesuit catching a freshman with a mouthful of profanity. When he saw it was Pisano, the look faded. "Joe, come on. I have to practice for the school play, run through the speech once with the TelePrompTer guy. But we can have a sandwich together."

"As long as I pay, Senator."

"Let up, Pisano. Or I'll sic my staff on you."

"But he's not Kelly."

"Joe, nobody's Kelly. And the last few years, Kelly wasn't Kelly anymore. But not a day goes by that I don't miss him."

"You could have used him these past six months. Maybe he could have figured a way for you to escape from the platform committee."

They were making their way down a deep canyon between the bleachers, but Mulligan turned to face the reporter.

"What are you talking about, Joe? Escape? What's that mean?"

Mulligan asked the question, then began walking ahead before Pisano answered: "You got a real mess on your hands. A floor fight over the platform. And yet you're completely relaxed. Come on. What's planned for tonight?"

Mulligan didn't answer until they reached one of the plywood cubicles built as holding rooms in back of the flashy podium. A standard staffer, spiffy enough to be going somewhere else for lunch, was parked at one end of a table, her cellular phone tucked firmly into a healthy head of blond hair.

"She's downright perky," Joe mumbled to Mulligan, who waved her off the phone, sending her to check on the sandwiches.

Mulligan sat down on one folding chair and propped his feet on another, managing to look comfortable. He still hadn't answered Pisano's question.

"You got a bloody mess on your hands, Senator, and you're sitting here, all happy."

"Joe, everybody will get their chance tonight. The loyal opposition will put up five or six or seven speakers to denounce each and every plank of the platform that they're unhappy with."

"And?"

"We'll take a vote. I'm relaxed because I know how to count heads."

"So relaxed that you supposedly told a bunch of other senators that tonight was just no problem at all. So relaxed, so confident, that you told them once you were through speaking, the platform problem was solved. Not settled, not decided, but solved."

"I don't know who your source is, Joe, but I'd never take anything for granted. And neither should you."

Miss Perky interrupted them, with a wicker basket crammed with sandwiches, fruit, bottles of Calistoga water, and a Thermos of coffee. She was sent on her way firmly, with effusive thanks.

Mulligan unwrapped his tuna sandwich and carefully transferred it to a gingham paper plate. He arranged his pickle and shook out a bag of barbecue chips as if they were part of an intricate, ancient mosaic.

"What's in the speech? And why no advance text?" Pisano asked, talking around the bite of sandwich in his mouth.

"Pisano, this is a major shot for me. I mean on national TV and everything. Now I know that none of you big-time reporters would break an embargo, but I also know that I want my speech to be a surprise, to be news, both to the delegates and to the viewers at home, not to mention you press types."

Pisano got a large grin on his face.

"You've figured out some way to fuck over everyone. You've somehow got this convention wired, and it wouldn't matter if Jack Kennedy and Martin Luther King showed up to speak against the platform. I haven't figured out what you're going to do, but it's big and it's not nice, Senator, I do know that."

"You are one self-righteous prick, Pisano. It must be great to be on the side of God and the American people." Mulligan put down his sandwich half and lit a cigarette. "Joe, you couldn't be more wrong. I haven't squeezed any delegates, not for a single vote for the proposed platform. You've got my word on that. What does the platform matter, anyhow? You and I know too well it's a piece of paper. With some nice words, which very few candidates want to remember the day after the convention ends. Heck, we can't ask some southerner to run on a platform that supports homosexual marriage or Commies in Central America. In the past, we pushed too hard on the issues, so we wound up with an honorable, principled, and very losing candidate."

Mulligan finished up half of his sandwich, then gave a small shake to his head and pushed the paper plate away, as if some unseen waiter had asked him if he wanted anything else. Goddamn patrician, Pisano thought, for some scholarship kid from a factory town in Michigan.

"Watching the old diet, huh?" Pisano asked, hoping to cut down on the tension.

"Pisano, I watch everything. A guy in my position has got to be very careful. An elected official with my history has got to be more than careful."

Mulligan had taken the white sandwich paper and folded it into a square, creasing the edges as carefully as an English tailor. Shit, Pisano thought, if this gets any more wired, Mulligan'll be washing the table.

"Hey, Mark, let's make this clear. I'm never going to use that stuff. I've never said a word. More than twenty years I've never told anyone. Only six people, counting you, knew anything. And three of the six are dead."

Mulligan tossed the paper down on the table. "For God's sake, Joe. I wasn't talking about that. You just can't forget, can you? That's all you think of, every time you look at me. That's what you see. What I was then."

Pisano tried to say something, but Mulligan reached across the table, grabbed Pisano's hand, and, ignoring the reporter's surprised look, said, "Joe, I gotta go. Sorry if I overreacted."

The senator bolted from the room.

Pisano sat alone in the cubicle, finishing his roast beef sandwich. Mulligan had gotten through the entire conversation and Pisano didn't know one thing about his speech. The son of a bitch had really turned into a politician.

The maître d' at Chez Kathy was so very happy to see Miss Clark. Bitsy hated it. The way people in good restaurants and the better hotels got extra nice when her black face showed up. Just can't do enough to show how thrilled they are that a person of color is eating and using the bathrooms in their establishments.

It also didn't hurt when she was meeting a star.

"Honey, you just come right over here and put yourself down in this booth. I just got here myself," Chloe Lewis announced. Bitsy was sorry she had missed the arrival of "one of America's living legends of rock 'n' roll, the blazing Chloe Lewis," as the deejays kept saying on the radio. No one would leave Chez Kathy today and not know who had lunched there.

At maybe 110 pounds, Chloe possessed an ability to nonetheless fill the booth—hell, maybe the restaurant, Bitsy thought. The massive kinky-haired wig swinging from side to side as Chloe chatted on, waving the jeweled fingers, the Chanel-red nails.

Chloe had news. She had a new manager. She had a new

lover. They were the same man. That was not new. She'd had the guy sign a prenuptial agreement. "He almost burst the seams on his Armani suit. But then, I had paid for the suit. I just wasn't going to pay for Italy."

Bits talked about her kids, about missing the time she was supposed to have them this summer, about how only something as important as the platform fight could keep her away.

"I don't get it, honey. Why the hell should you be so concerned about this platform stuff? Nobody gives a damn. They're just going to vote for whatever face they think is pretty. And us black folk are just going to vote for whomever Jesse and Teddy Kennedy tell us to. So what? We don't get anything after it's over."

The appetizer had arrived, some delicate teensy vegetable pâté. "Chloe, we're like two old churchy ladies, having lunch."

"Honey, no church lady ever had a prenuptial agreement in case of a possible palimony suit. But you know, Bits, much as I like all this visiting, you've never had time for lunch unless you were working on something."

"Chloe, I've known you for ten years, and you are one of my favorite people."

"And I know you. And I want to know what you want."

"I want help tonight."

The waiter had returned, also the captain and the maître d'. If the rest of the world ran the way French restaurants did, there just wouldn't be an employment problem, Bitsy thought.

Chloe tasted everything, pronounced it all perfect, rattled off a couple of sentences in perfect French—her second husband was a French film director—and sent the boys on their way. "Okay, what is it?"

"I'm nervous asking you to do what I want you to do. But here goes: How big a night is tonight for you?"

"Big enough that I bought a new wig and a new eighteen-thousand-dollar gown. Both, thankfully, tax-deductible. I gave up the Hollywood Bowl. Not major—but goddamn close.

There was no indication in my upbringing that I would sing the national anthem at the opening session of a national political convention or lead the delegates in the Pledge of Allegiance. And I figure it's kind of an audition. You know, I do well, the candidate does well, and I could be singing at the White House. I have, you know, been invited to sing at the White House in previous administrations, but the folks who were living there just weren't my style."

Bitsy picked at her fish. Chloe had ordered. Bitsy hated fish, especially delicate little white fish with some kind of pale sauce. She let Chloe talk.

"I'm not giving this up, Bitsy. I'm not boycotting or making some asshole Marlon Brando Indian maiden speech or pushing anything. I'm singing. The people who asked me didn't want my opinion on the World Bank or on Central America. They just want me to do what I do best—sing. And that is just what I plan to do." Chloe paused. Then she swung her wig and resumed her "honey chile" speech. "So don't favor me with asking me no favors, honey."

Bitsy began to slide out of the booth.

"Where you going?" Chloe's usual boom had dropped to a hiss, her bracelets rattling like some primitive princess as she motioned Bitsy to sit down. "Sit down, for God's sake. What are you trying to do?"

"I'll tell you what I'm not going to do. I'm not going to take away your dream." Chloe smiled, having no idea that Bitsy was just beginning to fight. "Only problem is, Chloe, the platform has a lot of dreams for other people. People who need jobs, kids who need education, women who need help because they've found themselves pregnant."

"Bitsy, I'm talented. God made me that way. He just didn't make me political."

"Chloe, you keep looking down your nose at people like me, political people, people fighting about issues. Well, let me put it this way: I got you your table reservation today. Me. Not your platinum albums, not your concerts. Me. Because if I hadn't put myself on the line twenty-five years ago, the only way you could have gotten into Chez Kathy would be through the service entrance. And you wouldn't be 'tasting dishes' here. You'd be washing them."

Annie ran into Mulligan as she headed down the anchor booth stairs to get a fresh Diet Coke.

"Aw, Annie. Where have you been? I thought I'd see a lot of you, here at the convention."

"Working too hard," she said, leading him back up to the anchor booth. Annie waved her hand around like a museum guide. "Not much to write home about, but for some million-dollar-a-year talking heads, it's home."

Mulligan stood staring at the pile of Sixties stuff. Annie thought she saw his face get pale under the tan.

"Annie, what is all this? Looks like you emptied your closet."

"Well, I'm doing this piece tonight, to set off your platform debate. How the Sixties questions are still around—abortion, women's rights, gay rights, military intervention, poor people, racism—all-American kind of live-or-die issues. And how the platform is the party's commitment to fight for those causes."

Mulligan took one glossy Church's loafer and tapped at a stray button, cautiously, as if the thing had a life of its own. Annie picked up the button and held it out to him.

"This isn't *our* button. It's from a later demonstration. Here"—she reached into the pile—"ours were better. A better fist."

Mulligan started to smile, but it broke on his face like a piece of long cracked pottery at Annie's question: "So what were you going to do up here, anyway, Senator?"

"Annie, why should I try to lie to you, an old and good friend? I came up here to see what I will look like when your people look down on me tonight. That sounds egocentric, in the face of all that's happening with the platform, but I just wanted to know how I would look on television."

My God, Annie thought as he finished, he's got his smile pasted back together, and I didn't even see how he did it.

"Mark, you'll look good. But don't dig this hole any deeper. I know why you're here. I got a call last week from someone on your staff, someone 'concerned' about my Sixties piece. 'Would the senator and his role in the Sixties be featured?' That kind of stuff. So you didn't come up here for the view."

Mulligan dropped onto the chair, smoothing out his slacks as he sat, as if he were readying himself for a photo opportunity. "Annie, as usual, you are exactly right. Just what is this minidocumentary all about?"

"About the Sixties. About us, the things we cared about."

"That's not very specific." Mulligan's eyes roamed the anchor booth, as if looking for a clue to the piece's content. He pointed to the pile of chemistry notebooks that Annie had shifted to the desk.

"Going in for science?"

"No. For history."

"I don't get it."

"They're journals. Somebody kept them during the Sixties. Somebody involved in a lot of politics. Civil rights. Antiwar stuff."

"Are they yours?"

"They're mine now. I got them a few weeks after the Offensive. For the first couple months, I couldn't read them. Now I've spent so many years with them, they're like a piece of me."

"Fascinating. But who actually wrote them?"

Annie's answer got lost in the blare of a Klaxon from the convention floor and the announcement that the platform hearings would resume in five minutes.

"Much ado about nothing," Mulligan muttered, standing up. "The party fights about the platform, the stands we take

---

17

get used against our candidates, and then, after the election, nobody mentions the word *platform* for another four years."

"What can you do, Senator? The platform is not going to go away. It's a rule of politics: 'Like death and taxes, the platform is always with us.'"

He hugged her, and Annie felt some of the old warmth. But his words took away that feeling: "Maybe not, Annie. Maybe not."

The southern August sun burned hot at noon, and Ed Kapinski's troops were getting tired leafleting against potential antiunion legislation in nine state legislatures.

Kapinski stood in the sun, his white baseball cap with the union logo stuck far back on his balding head. He was hot, his suit jacket stuck to his wash-and-wear shirt, which was stuck to his back. No matter the weather, Kapinski wore a suit. He believed it was important to the people he organized to have a union rep who looked like a big deal. Hell, if you were a working stiff, the only time you put on a suit was to go to wedding or a funeral or to show up in court.

Years—decades, really—organizing people meant that Kapinski was very good at what he did, which sometimes meant doing nothing, spending dozens of hours standing about, thinking about nothing. Past organizing victories. Defeats. Terrible vengeances that he would be able to exact on pigs who kept poor and black and brown people down. Memories of the Movement, with Edmund Kapinski, Jr.

Taken by his own memories, Kapinski almost missed Bitsy as she headed into the convention center. Shit, Bits was really stacking on the pounds. But she looked good—prosperous. Some delegate tried to corner her, and Kapinski watched appreciatively as Bits edged herself around to better make the break, somehow convincing the delegate that he was the most feeling and important person since Gandhi and it was only events that were tearing her away.

Kapinski motioned to his troops. "Let's keep up our spirits. Let's sing a little song. Let's do 'We Shall Overcome.'"

The first words caught Bitsy by surprise, and she used Kapinski's voice to find him, waving a hello, joining in, singing the song with his union guys. Kapinski knew she loved the lyrics and that it was the first "Negro" song she'd ever learned. He had taught it to her, on the Harvard campus, when he came recruiting students to go south. He loved the story, about how her very bourgeois mother wouldn't allow what she insisted on calling "nigger music" into the big house in West Oak Lane—no civil rights anthems, no rock 'n' roll. After all, the Clarks were one of the first colored families to move into the neighborhood, and there was no reason to reinforce stereotypes. So Bitsy had only a passing acquaintance with the Platters and the Temptations, little Stevie Wonder and the Supremes. She said she didn't feel very much like those skinny black girls on the stage with their crooked teeth and mops of processed wigs whipped into flawless French knots, their skinny, shimmery dresses that covered their skimpy boobs and little else.

Maybe that's why she thought she had no rhythm. She couldn't even dance until she was in her twenties. Kapinski taught her that, too, in a run-down house in Mississippi.

That was a memory all right. Bits was something else—smart, experienced, honorable...and probably the greatest lay Kapinski ever had.

Annie closed the notebook and held it tightly in her lap. This was always a period she had trouble with, reading about when they were in the South. So brave. All so brave and never realizing the depth of it all. She laughed out loud at her own pride.

"Funny? You made it funny. Wrong. It's supposed to be moving, sincere, extraordinary journalism."

Pisano's arrival in the anchor booth startled her.

"Did you eat?"

"No, but I'm not done. I keep tinkering with it."

"You been watching the platform go-round?"

"Sure. I saw you busily doing everything but covering the hearings."

"The hearings are not where it's going to be."

Annie started to shovel the notebooks, buttons, and paraphernalia into the canvas bag. "Mulligan showed up here. Mohammed to the mountain. Apparently very nervous about what I'm going to include—and what I'm going to leave out."

Pisano swung around to face her, but, backlit by the anchor booth window, his face was shadowed. Only when he spoke did Annie realize how angry he was.

"There's no question, right? I mean, you told him that we'd all keep our word!"

"I didn't tell him anything. He asked about the notebooks."

"Shit, Annie, you and I are going to have one royal fight. You told him about the precious notebooks, right? I'm surprised you didn't let him read a few pages. How dare you? Who the hell gave you the right?"

Annie hoisted her canvas bags over her shoulder. "I gave me the right. I paid my dues. And every time I deal with someone like Mulligan, see what he's become, I want to set the record straight."

"That's bullshit, Annie. You don't want justice. You want some more blood on the floor, some other dead bodies lying. If you can't kill them with a bullet, you want some magic to drive a stake into their heart."

Annie started down the stairs, seeming to take no notice of what Pisano said. Over her shoulder she said, "Anyway, I think Mulligan is going to do something weird tonight."

They walked slowly, making their way to the connecting building, where the massive convention operation for Annie's network was housed in a series of trailers. Neither of them talking until they arrived, checked in through security, and went to the temporary commissary set up for network staffers. The perverse convention operations manager had ordered not ordinary folding chairs and tables, but white wrought-iron sets with colorful umbrellas. The famous television news faces scattered through the crowd made the place look like a hot Washington bistro.

"I feel like I'm on planet Krypton."

"Joe, don't start. This is not the place to start in on television news."

"Okay," Pisano agreed, changing subjects. "You said you thought Mulligan might do something weird. What?"

"It's simple, really. What if there wasn't a platform?"

"Don't be nuts. There has to be a platform. Mulligan has spent six months on platform hearings all over the country."

"Even better. Six months and no consensus. The party splits." Annie waved to a familiar face across the tables. "What if he tells the convention tonight that he can solve all their problems? Just abolish the platform. I can hear it. 'Everyone in our party is committed to the same basic principles. A better minimum wage. Voting rights. Antiracism. The advancement of women. There are some differences. But let the candidates bring their own particular vision to the voters. Don't burden them with a platform.' And that's that."

"If you're right, it's a helluva story."

"It would mean no fight, no blood on the convention floor tonight. It would unburden the southern candidates. It leaves the party without an announced ideology, instead of twenty-one various sets of beliefs and special interests and warring minorities. And it means there is no standard to hold candidates to. It turns this party into a junior version of the other party."

Joe helped himself to the lavish buffet, barely remembering that he had eaten with Mulligan only an hour before.

"Okay, I get it. Safe, that's what getting rid of the platform would be. There would be no arena to fight out these issues.

And, unless some candidates were real champions, well, the issues wouldn't fade away. They would just die."

"And Mulligan would be the number one candidate for the vice-presidential nomination," Annie finished up. She watched Pisano silently finish his meal and knew that he wanted a cigarette. He always did after Italian food. "We could stop him," she said, leaning across the table. "We have the ammunition."

The months on the road, following the campaign, had left Pisano with a wintry pallor, as if he were still back in March in Iowa. He looks middle-aged, Annie thought, and smiled when she realized that of course he was.

"Wait a minute. This is crazy. You can't get involved. It doesn't matter how high the stakes are. It's one thing if you decide to use the stuff because you think it's journalistically correct, that it's the ethical thing to do. But you can't go nuclear with what you know. You're confusing justice with vengeance. And why bother? Nobody cares, you know. Nobody cares about politics. If we get a plane crash or Liz Taylor gets married or even gets thin, well, shit, that's the story that will be at the top of the page."

Annie spoke the words softly. "We could make Mulligan care. We know everything. Almost everything."

"We're a helluva long way from that time, Annie. We're a helluva long way from 1967."

"A long way from 1967? No, sweetie, that was yesterday, and this is only today."

# BOOK TWO

# THE MARCH

## MONDAY,
## August 28, 1967

Annie O'Connor lit a Camel, propped her sandaled feet up on the desk, and looked out the window at Vermont Avenue below. Almost time for the federal proles to start arriving.

Washington in August was too hot. The city smelled like a morning after sex, and people arrived at work rumpled like bedclothes. All summer long she'd kept track of the morning arrivals, finally figuring out the class system that had secretaries showing up at 8:00 A.M. and the heavies an hour later.

"Come de revolution," she muttered to herself, "and de bosses will be showing up early, too." No important leader of her particular revolution could hear any such seditious thought, since none of the Movement heavies showed up before ten.

"Everybody's a Star, and Most People Are Also Leaders," read the large, hand-printed sign hanging on Annie's wall. Nearby was a second, homemade announcement: "The Student Leaders of Today Are the Student Leaders of Tomorrow." Dealing with the egos of other people supposedly set on saving the world had turned her mild skepticism into rank cynicism, and she wore it like a hair shirt.

Outside her office door, in the vast open work space of the ninth floor, a dozen teenage volunteers were doing the slave labor that would make the march work. Annie insisted on calling them "teenies," and it was a mark of her control that they carried the nickname with pride. Two bookish boys stood with red thumbtacks, punching in the locations of the first-aid stations along the line of the march. The map of Washington, D.C., was starting to look like an overcrowded game board: green pins meant walkie-talkies, white stood for march captains. Some weirdo had figured out that brown was the perfect color for the portable toilets.

The march part was okay: the Sixties had taught her generation how to make a demonstration, how to put thousands of protesting people, peacefully, into the street. The problem with this particular event was simple: it was unclear who would to talk to the people once they were out in the street. Seven days until the Offensive Against the War—or "Off the War," as the buttons proclaimed—and the march steering committee still couldn't come up with an agreed list of speakers. What was needed was some magic formula that would satisfy the Left and the liberals (how long it had been since they were the same), those who believed in working within the system and those who wanted to blow it up. Annie had a particular dilemma: she couldn't keep telling the Washington press corps that this was the most important antiwar event ever and never have any details to back up her claim. Only the federal government could get away with that kind of misinformation.

Closing her eyes, Annie thought up the time, a trick she'd learned in high school, when the nuns had the clocks removed from the classrooms, the better to keep your attention. After a week she had figured out that she could tell time in her head and even now prided herself on not owning a watch or needing an alarm clock. Goofy, she admitted to herself, using her favorite adjective and one that deservedly got used. How could she worry about minutes passing by and have no sense of the years? All through college her life was such a known quantity, as if she had flipped to the last chapter of a novel and understood how everything would turn out. She had known what life was bringing her—finish her degree, teach, go to graduate school or into the Peace Corps. Lots of choices, but all producing the same predictable, measured ending. Now the immediacy in each day was so strong, so seductive, that it seemed unfaithful to think of the future, what or where one would be in a month, let alone a year.

Time. It was past nine, so Burnett and the other stars would be arriving shortly. The phone rang.

"Hello, honey. Need a date for next Monday?"

Nice. Joe Pisano. Annie liked Pisano. She lit another Camel and started working.

"No, Joe, sweetie. Not even for a nice boy from Newark. I got plans. Front-row seats for a very hot event. Largest-ever demonstration against the war in Vet-Naam." Annie had practiced LBJ's mispronunciation for months and proudly used it constantly.

"Who else is coming to your shindig?"

"Lots of people. Maybe even a member of Congress."

Burnett had warned her not to hint at the hoped-for appearance of a congressman at the march. But what was she supposed to do with a press corps that kept asking for proof that the Offensive was more than radical lefties?

"Okay. But is your mysterious speaker a United States congressman? Or maybe a legislator from a small Balkan republic?"

Pisano could get to her. He knew too much. He should. He'd covered civil rights in the South, and not just the beatings or the marches. Tough guy that he was, he'd figured out the infighting, the politics, the people who really made the decisions. He had a nasty trick he'd use to break big stories: he'd try to guess what the civil rights leaders would do next, then he'd spring the idea on one of them, as if he really had a source within their ranks. At least half the time he'd pick it right, and since he sounded as if he had the story tight, whoever he asked would usually fade and give him even more details. He had another powerful plus: only a few reporters stayed month after month, year after year, covering the demonstrations, so any Movement heavy wanted to stay on the right side of those who did.

Pisano's career moved fast, from line bureau staffer of a wire service—"covering cows, crime, and capitals"—to being the civil rights specialist for the number two Washington newspaper. And in a transfer that by circumstances turned out perfectly timed, his editors brought him back to D.C. at just the right moment to cover "the white kids coming home."

"Who else besides Congressman X is coming to your party, Annie? You got the steering committee members—Burnett, Ed Kapinski, Reverend Tyler, a roundup of the usual suspects. Sounds very pale, very white. And very left. Maybe Tyler, by virtue of his clerical state, is not a bomb thrower. But he's not a major player, not like a William Sloan Coffin or a Bishop Moore or anybody near that level."

"Joe, you think you can do a better job organizing for peace, come on by. We got plenty of room over here for smart guys like you."

"Annie, I just don't want you hung out to dry. You can't sell this march as being an all-American coalition against the war and then wind up with the usual crazies. Or with second-raters."

"Don't try to define this march, Pisano. Just cover it. And we're not having what you call the usual crazies. You really make me mad. Here I've spent all weekend trying to get Burnett to give you the name of the congressman first, and you're still giving me grief."

Annie took a long drag. She'd got him. Pisano said nothing. Too pissed to talk, Annie thought. Christ, I hope we've got some congressman, whoever he is.

"So?"

"Since your dance card is so filled next Monday, how about a meal today or tomorrow? I'll even take you somewhere other than the Astor."

"Really jammed. But I can meet you about one tomorrow." That gave her a day to come up with some concrete name besides the "usual crazies."

"Okay, Annie. And for a change, I'll have something to tell you, too."

Shit, Pisano was self-righteous, she thought, hanging up the phone. That's what she hated about reporters. They never took a stand, except on the sidelines—where they kept score.

What reporters called "objectivity," Annie thought of as "playing it safe." They sat out the moral battles of their time. Like Vietnam—the war was a moral question, not a political one. Principles, not politics, guided her actions, she would frequently assure herself, especially when she felt caught between a reporter and the Movement. She saw herself as a good person, involved in a struggle of good against evil, but increasingly she found herself forced to make up the rules to fit the Movement's actions. In the same way, she still called herself Catholic, only it had been months since she'd heard mass.

She found herself giving to the Movement the same empowering vision that she'd once deeded solely to Holy Mother Church. The main tenet of her new faith was that this was a special time when people were called on for unique sacrifices and powerful duties. If asked, she would have been hard-pressed as to which John of the Sixties should be credited with helping ignite this moralistic bonfire—John Kennedy or John XXIII.

Annie stared at the sign hanging over her desk. "Folklore Lounge. No smoking here." She'd stolen it from the University of Pennsylvania, which not only had a Folklore Department, but also a lounge where the folklore people could meet. For several years Annie insisted it had been summer session Folklore 102 that had forced her into political consciousness. "Sitting there, picking up education credits by discussing nursery rhymes and jump-rope songs, I found myself asking what meaning life held for me."

The story was a kidding half-truth, but folklore was what her job was all about: trying to sell America that fighting the government was American, that refusing to go to war was patriotic. Sometimes the biggest roadblock to her doing her job were the very people involved in the Movement—lefties who didn't want to "cooperate with the fascist press" or ego trippers who started making strange demands, like wanting to read the reporter's story before it was printed.

The Movement needed the press. And, as much as their objectivity irked her, the reporters increasingly were her friends, her supporters. She felt closer, more comfortable, with some reporters than she did with some of the ideologues on the steering committee. After all, she tried to explain to herself, it was the reporters and she who understood each other—the pressures of deadline, the competition, the need for constant grist for the news mill. She'd wound up here, in this office, in this job, in such a funny, offhand way.

Burnett had done it, really, just changed her life. When she went south in 1964, he was already an old hand. She had come, "just for the summer," as she kept saying, an English major from Manhattanville—"that's the Catholic girls' college the Kennedy sisters went to." She'd signed on not to make a revolution, or even to be political, but to teach black kids a little reading and writing. Up to then her biggest decision was whether she'd join the Peace Corps before or after getting her master's in education at Columbia.

Burnett changed that. He figured out that somebody with an English degree might be able to write a press release. Then, the third week she was in Mississippi, somebody had to make the press calls and nobody else had any time—and there she was. After the arrests, covered by the UPI, CBS, and the *Atlanta Constitution*, Burnett came up, hugged her, and told her someone else would take over her classes: "You've got a higher calling."

It happened so fast, like a 45 being played at 78. She could sort it all out if she had the time, but that was the joke—there just wasn't any time. There was the rush of being good at something, of being needed. The extraordinary high of wheeling and dealing with men who worked for *The New York Times*, of saying something "off the record" and hearing the words quoted that night on the network news from a "highly placed source in the civil rights movement." From her first news conference in the South, her judgment calls were solid, and "doing the press" became her singular and unique contribution to the causes she'd taken up, first as an easy adjunct to her Catholicism, then as a growing replacement.

Annie's worry about what she would tell the press boys later in the week got cut short when Burnett came in, wearing khakis and a washed-out workshirt, carrying an old Harris Tweed jacket.

"Don't you sweat?" she asked him. "Christ, don't you even get a little damp—" But he cut off the kidding with a curt nod.

"At the steering committee meeting tomorrow night, I should be able to announce that Congressman Mark Mulligan has signed on as a speaker." Burnett said it without feeling, like some conductor announcing the next train to Poughkeepsie.

Only this wasn't mundane. Annie shook her head. "That's a big score, Tom," she said. "I can't wait to tell the reporters who have been riding me all summer, especially Pisano."

"Not yet," Burnett cautioned. "This is so big—a real breakthrough. A congressman speaks out against the war, addresses a massive antiwar rally. One of Lyndon Baines Johnson's boys on the Hill breaks out of the corral, and says that others should follow. We want this story to get the major play it deserves, not be buried with the comics. We want enough time to encourage other liberals to join in the Offensive—but not so much time that the Administration has a chance to defuse Mulligan's actions."

Annie never had to fight Burnett on the value of dealing with the press. He'd fought battles that were won and lost by virtue of how the *Times* covered the story. He was a Movement veteran, but one who never wore fatigues, who somehow gracefully carried a special combination of old money and new politics, carried it as easily as he did the worn briefcase he was unpacking on her desk. That he was good-looking didn't hurt, with nice, regular features like the men in magazine shirt ads, his light brown hair falling into his eyes as he searched for some slip of paper.

"Only one big hurdle out there," he told Annie in a conspiratorial tone, but before he could continue, she chimed in.

"Don't bother trying to keep it a secret, sweetie. It is very noticeable that we have no one of the black persuasion on the speakers list."

"Annie, can you ever deal with a serious problem, a confidential problem, without being a smart-ass?"

"Only when it's news," Annie yelled after Burnett as he headed out the door.

And this was no news. Everyone connected with the Offensive had lived with the problem for several weeks. Just a fluke in scheduling, really, that put them in this bind, with no black speakers. Burnett had announced the plan for the Offensive, at a news conference with Kapinski and Tyler, in early summer. And then, just a few days later, the Conference on New Politics got called for Chicago—on this same Labor Day weekend. The conference people kept insisting that they had set the date first, but the Offensive steering committee said they couldn't back out of holding the Washington protest once it had been announced. So all the black heavies were heading to Chicago, Dr. King included.

Burnett kept the march going by arguing that the country was big enough, the Movement was egalitarian enough, and the Vietnam War grotesque enough that two events involving the antiwar movement could take place on the same weekend. Only now the speakers list could wind up as white as Wonder Bread.

Even if the scheduling screwup hadn't happened, nobody was sure that Dr. King or any of the main-line civil rights leaders would have come to the march or gotten on the speakers' platform. Annie knew too well that the civil rights leaders were like the Movement's royalty: they needed to know who else was speaking, how long would they speak, who would get top billing, who would pay their airfare, their assistants' airfares, the hotel rooms. And, in most cases, they and other speakers wanted to be sure that no one who was too left or too radical shared the platform with them.

"It's really *Catch-22*," Burnett had said at an early-on staff meeting. "No one will join the peace movement because it's nothing but left-wingers. And it's only left-wingers because no one will join it."

"Just like civil rights when white people could be involved," Annie had blurted out. What she'd said was true, only it was still too recent and too tender a hurt for many of the people around the table. Just at the moment when victory seemed at hand, when middle-class people, when unions, when elected officials, were getting involved in the civil rights movement—that's when the blacks told the whites to get out.

Burnett came back into her office, carrying a cup of coffee, which he put on the desk. "You want to help me with this, or do you just want to kid around?" he asked Annie, sitting down beside the desk. She said nothing, which he took as some kind of agreement, then started what sounded like his speech from the staff meeting.

"So we must have someone black. And not just anyone, but someone with a record in the South. And that's what you've got to do, Annie. You've got to help Kapinski recruit Bitsy to be on the committee and speak."

Annie laughed. "Yeah, and after that I'll stop by the White House for tea. You're stoned if you think that Bitsy is going to listen to Kapinski, or to me. She's going to tell him to screw off, stop bugging her, and shove the Movement. Bitsy's tough."

"Not so tough that if we just all bring a little pressure, we won't turn her around."

Annie picked up Burnett's cup and took a sip.

"You don't understand. She doesn't respond well to being pushed around. Last year, at some conference on tutoring projects, some guy started to give her a hard time about her name—you know, like 'Bitsy' is like this preppy, I-grew-up-bourgeoisie name. So he was giving her all this shit, about how she had to get an African name, and get rid of her 'slave' name, and finally, in front of like twenty people, she started in on this African shirt he was wearing, about how pretty it was, and how clean and beautifully ironed. And then she started to give him crap about who ironed his shirt—like, some woman was stuck at home ironing so he could be a big deal, and wasn't that just typical of the kind of black man he was, and that black women had two enemies—white men and black men. And she cut this guy off at the boots, so nobody gave her any more grief about being called Bitsy."

"I don't care if she calls herself Little Eva," Burnett said, making it clear that he had no time for Annie's joking. "Bitsy gives us credibility. Reporters know her. It's not such a bad thing to be written up twice in *Time* magazine."

"Dammit, Burnett. You and everybody keep using that like she was after the publicity. You just don't get a lot of black girls in the South from Radcliffe—getting arrested, getting harassed, and getting people registered to vote. And then, last year, that tutorial project in Philly, well, it's just amazing how many of those kids and their moms she's taught to read."

Burnett stood up. It was an annoying habit to Annie, dismissive, like when some adult announced to a kid that the conversation was over.

"No matter how you push her black consciousness, Annie, I know that you are on the phone with her all the time. And I know that Kapinski and she are still involved."

Without a second thought, Annie got indignant. "No, they're not. She hasn't seen him for a month." She stopped. "You got me. I talk to her. But she's not changing her mind, no matter who talks to her. She likes Philly and she likes her kids and that's that."

Burnett shrugged. It was years from Yale and the prep school that preceded it, but Annie believed that only boys who got Harris Tweed before their eighth birthday could shrug like that. More class struggle, she told herself. Burnett swept his papers off the desk, into his briefcase, and with a quick order that she should talk to Kapinski, he went back into the maelstrom that had grown outside her door.

Annie sat smoking and staring through the open door. Before the march, the offices were the D.C. headquarters of a giant life insurance company. Ironically, the way LifeCo had laid out the office space worked perfectly for the Offensive. The giant central open space, dubbed "the Pit," was crammed with desks and phones and people. At back was a small, closed-off space, with mimeo machines and kids painting posters. The windowed offices had been carefully allocated to Annie's press operations, to Burnett, to Tyler's clergymen, with the biggest space getting turned into a conference room for the steering committee, which, if it got any larger, would be capable only of steering the *Queen Mary*.

Everybody wanted to be a star, and everybody wanted a title. "March captains" were in charge of keeping the march moving along and were a bunch of old-hand Socialists who would kill rather than let anyone commit a violent act. "Logistic coordinators" rented portable toilets and set up first-aid stations along the line of march, hopefully in sufficient numbers to deal with sizzling weather and old peaceniks fainting and stealing the media's attention from the speakers. Transportation directors organized the buses from New York, from Philly, from Boston—and hopefully recruited at least a dozen people who didn't look Upper West Side Jewish with ban-the-bomb buttons. It was now past ten, so the Pit was filled with people busy screaming on the phones and at each other.

Kapinski had given her a credit card number to use. Somehow he'd gotten it from some guy on the Hill whom he knew from the South. It was supposedly one of the credit card numbers assigned to Dow Chemical, the makers of napalm, and Annie enjoyed a little shiver of happiness each time she cost Dow money.

"North Philadelphia Tutorial Assistance Center," one of the moms answered the phone.

"Miss Clark, please," Annie asked. She'd always found it easy to cut through the moms' barrier if she sounded official, like some War on Poverty flunkie or something.

But the gambit didn't work. The mom was insistent that Bitsy couldn't be disturbed, that she was meeting with two ladies from New York and that was that.

Since she couldn't think up anything else urgent to distract her, Annie was forced to start down her press call list. *The Washington Post*. The AP. NBC. The local television stations. Reassuring. Chatting. Just being her friendly little radical, flakking self. That's what the old guys called doing the press—"flakking."

Not just Pisano, but everybody, wanted to know the speakers' list. She kept pushing numbers—how many buses from New York, how many straight student government types—and all the reporters wanted to know about were stars.

It was all supposed to be so equal, this "participatory

democracy" shit. Which is why almost all meetings went on until three in the morning, because the lowest-level, dumbest, youngest people involved had to have their say. And all the heavies sat around and nodded and then did what they were going to do anyway. But the facade had to hold. Just like everybody had to share the same joints, even though some pigs got them real wet and then you got a mouthful of their spit.

Annie liked running her own little road show, here in the folklore lounge. Just her and the telephone, alone, which is why Annie had a rule. She had to have her own office, and it had to have a window. Finishing with the phone, she rummaged through the drawer of her government-surplus desk. How ironic that equipment deemed inferior for the government had been brought into service to smash the State. Whoops! Getting too close to the ideological nutzoids, she cautioned herself. Nobody really believed that the government took any of the antiwar protests seriously enough to see them as really subversive. Or that the government was competent enough to coopt the Movement. Shit, when the Agency wanted to subvert something, they paid off the goody-two-shoes, liberal National Student Association. Now that was out of touch.

She got distracted by her hand finding the familiar rectangular shape in the drawer. Great. First, a quick trip outside in the Pit to get coffee, light and sweet, and then she'd come back, put her feet on the desk, and get right down to her midmorning Snickers.

Life was made of moments like this. Getting on the phone and lying like crazy and convincing the Establishment that something was going to happen—and maybe it would. Having coffee and a Snickers bar and a smoke. Life was sweet, and she was only twenty-five.

Reverend Paul Tyler made his papers into neat piles and tried, as best he could, to avoid looking at Rabbi Sam Dersherwitz.

The rabbi annoyed him—never quite so much as when he was making a perceptive point, as he had been doing for the past ten minutes. Tyler had figured that the meeting of the Clerics and Religious Opposed to War (CROW) would be over by three. Lunch had moved along nicely enough, here in the private dining room of New York's Harvard Club. Tyler always insisted that they meet for lunch here, just as he always picked up the tab. He felt safe, comfy, coming home, with Frank the doorman always asking him how things were going in the church trade. When they began meeting almost a year ago, his CROW brethren were just a little ill at ease at the club, letting him slide easily into the catbird seat.

Marisa paid the bills. Marisa paid for anything and everything. That's what he would think about as the rabbi droned on—Marisa, his sweet, innocent bride. How clever he had been, Tyler congratulated himself, when at Mamaroneck three years before he'd spotted her at the club pool, lush as an Italian *pomodoro*. Her attractiveness grew when he found out her father was the largest olive oil producer in all of Italy. Tyler's WASP ancestors had spent too many generations in the pulpit and too few in trade, so he wound up with a meager legacy to finance a hoped-for marvelous life-style.

Marisa was so ready, with years of convent schools and finishing schools, on her first trip to America, eager to be carried off by the handsome preacher. The slight problem with religion got handled easily, since her father had three sons and two other daughters and knew the signs of a ripened body and a ready libido. Her innocence did bother Tyler in one way. As he kept explaining to her, in increasingly strong language, she simply couldn't say anything that popped into her head. And she had to be discreet about discussions outside the house—how they lived, what they spent, what they liked to do. It was private, just between them.

"Just between us," Dersherwitz intoned, "I would be happy if this march had never been scheduled. I know, Paul, that you are committed to the Offensive, but I wish that it could have been held back, held off. Maybe we can convince Bobby Kennedy to run against Johnson. Al Lowenstein's got this 'dump Johnson' movement off the ground. That's the way we should be going—working within the electoral system."

"That's not what we learned in civil rights, Sam-u-el." Tyler loved giving the full Hebraic intonation to the name. "We learned, and those of you who joined us even in the later years learned, that it was only when we made it impossible for business as usual, only then did we win."

"I'm agreeing, Paul. But what you and the Offensive are asking is that we give our full endorsement to the protest, although we've still got no guarantee of nonviolence. We still got no speakers' list."

"Agreed, we still got no speakers' list," Tyler began. There, he got the little ungrammatical Jew. "But you must trust me that I will make sure this week in Washington that the speakers' platform will be broad enough to hold all of us—even those of us gaining weight from our wife's Italian cooking." Tyler smiled.

The little twerp seminarian from Union Theological cut Tyler's glee short, shoving a magazine across the table, mumbling something about how Tyler's wife went other places than the kitchen. The article opened with a giant photo of a baby seal being battered to death—part of a long piece of the cruel methods used to obtain furs. On the facing page, standing outside the Plaza and looking beautifully sleek in a sealskin suit, was his wife, Marisa Pignelli, and her quote: "No, I don't think any seals were hurt for my suit. I bought it at Saks."

Marisa was nervous. She was always nervous this time of day, right before Paul was due home for dinner. In her head, she ran down the list. The dog had been walked, and he was shut off in the maid's room. She had left him water and cookies and had spent much of the day playing with him, so he should be quiet. She had searched the apartment for any dog hair and had Bessie and Janice revacuum the living room. Her father sent her plenty of money for staff, but Paul said it didn't look right for a clergyman to have live-in help, so the women went home at five o'clock.

Marisa wished that weren't so. Paul cared so much about things being perfect. Her knees still hurt from last week when he had come home and been upset at the marble hallway. Twice she had washed it, the daughter of Caesar Pignelli, on her hands and knees, and each time Paul had told her it was still smeared. Finally he'd said that the soap she was using was for the clothes.

Now she checked and rechecked the ladies as they cleaned. It was all right, really, since she had little else to do. All of her clothes she shopped for in Italy, except for furs. When she married Paul two years ago, at first she went to lunch with the women whose husbands were on his board or who had gone to school with him. But the conversation was too quick and the women older, most of them double her twenty-three years, and she just couldn't keep up.

So now she played with her dog, and she watched the ladies clean, and she read. At first she tried to tell Paul what she was reading—about Vietnam, about civil rights. Paul said she only got the words, that the meaning escaped her. But that's because he wanted her only as a decoration, beside him at dinners, wearing the lovely suits her father paid for when she shopped in Milan. Paul wanted her to smile at him and say how good he was in front of the politicians they met for lunch. And fuss over the old ones, he would say.

Now she was sure he would be mad about the magazine. It was months ago, really, that the picture had been taken, last February, when her English school friend Sandra Hopkins had hosted a luncheon at the Plaza. She had worn her sealskin suit. Then the woman from the magazine had called and asked her about the little seals, and she was sure her suit wasn't from hurt seals. And then she heard the door.

Paul was home.

"Marisa. I want to see you. In the bedroom."

He was already taking off his pants. She understood the signal but tried to avoid the inevitable. She quickly started to explain: "I'm sorry. I'm really sorry. I tried to tell you about the picture and then the woman called me and she sounded so nice, but really, mostly I'm just sorry."

"Take off your clothes, Marisa."

It hadn't worked. Sometimes it did, and then he just ignored her for a day or two, but this time, no.

"You have been bad. Sorrow is not enough. Repentance is what I seek. You have broken your promise to love and honor me. Your husband." It was Paul's church voice, the one that made everyone feel sacred, feel special. But now, alone here, the voice was mighty, and all she felt was fear. She knew what was coming.

"Piggy," he began to chant. "Piggy, piggy, piggy. Dirty piggy, fat piggy. Not a girl, but a piggy."

She stood still, as if the words were manacles.

Once, early on, he had quizzed her about her fears, about who was mean to her when she was growing up, and she had told him about the girls in boarding school, their anger and disgust when she was just eleven and started with her period and her great breasts burst forth beneath the uniform.

"Piggy," they had called her. It sounded almost innocent, even to the nuns, who thought it was just a schoolgirl prank, a play on her name, Pignelli. But Paul had given it real meaning, real evil, now, as he chanted, "Piggy, piggy, piggy," and she pulled off the shift, exposing her body, breasts pushing against the bra. He pointed to the strap, and she pulled it down, then the other, and her breasts fell free until he placed them in the bondage of his hands.

"Look at the pig's ugly breasts," he said, pushing them back and forth, faster and faster. He was careful in the summer not to bruise her, and only the masseuse at Elizabeth Arden had ever noticed the marks that he could leave behind.

He smacked her breasts, again and again, but only on the parts that her bra would cover. He pulled her pants down and pushed her face down, on the bed. He shoved her legs apart, and in a few horrible minutes, Reverend Paul Tyler, one of the true warriors for social justice, was done with buggering his wife, the beautiful Marisa Pignelli.

She lay with her face on the pillow, the tears from the pain drying slowly on her cheeks. The pain was quick, but the terror lasted a long time.

She would do better. She would be a better wife. And soon, after all this time, Paul would have sex with her as a man and a woman should. Soon she would be worthy.

And she fell asleep thinking of her father, of his questions about grandchildren and babies, and of how he would be so ashamed to know that his daughter was still a virgin.

Bitsy Clark knew how to run a meeting.

There wasn't a trick she hadn't picked up, as she added academic and forensic honors the way her sisters put gold charms on their bracelets. National Forensic League champion, student body president at Radcliffe, and, finally, a full-time staff member of the field organizing committee of Mississippi Summer. Bitsy always had her own agenda, which was not always the printed one that got handed out. And she made sure that by the end of any meeting, she'd hit all the points.

This particular meeting was not going well. The North Philadelphia Tutorial Assistance Center employed sixteen staffers—eight college graduates who taught and eight community aides who assisted. Except for Bitsy, the college grads were white, the aides Puerto Rican and black. Everyone on staff collected the same salary, no matter what their titles.

There were no problems at the beginning, in late 1965, when the first big federal grant came in and Bitsy started to hire. Women who had spent their whole lives either scrimping by on a husband's salary, or cleaning somebody's house for almost nothing, or getting a welfare check that never stretched to the end of the month—they were all thrilled to be taking home decent money, having health care and paid vacations.

Then Lida Jones began to date a Black Nationalist, Harry Spencer, only now he wanted to be called "Matuwa." Now Harry, or Matuwa, was happening. Harry was everywhere. And Harry had decided that the tutorial program violated its announced principles of community involvement, the community being Harry. So with a combination of lounge-lizard style and mau-mau techniques, he had raised hell with the teacher's aides.

They all wound up here, black and white together, sitting in the basement of the Friendly Baptist Church at Broad and Girard, black women in their best pastel polyester pant suits, the two Puerto Rican aides looking as if they were on their way to church, the white kids in sandals, tie-dyed T-shirts, and washed-to-a-lighter-shade-of-pale jeans. How hard the poor tried to look middle class, and how hard the middle class tried to look poor, Bitsy thought. And the rich just didn't give a damn.

"Bitsy, I think we should get the meeting started," Alan announced. Bitsy had arranged the chairs auditorium style instead of the usual informal circle. The whites had carefully sat scattered by ones and twos in the front rows; the others had arrived and sat in a bloc.

"Waiting on someone, Bitsy," Arlena announced. Arlena, Crystal, Chandelier. Why the hell couldn't her people give their children real names, real English names?

"Who are we waiting for, Arlena?"

"Waiting on Harry. I mean on Matuwa."

"Well, our wait is ended because here he comes."

Harry the Nationalist, Bitsy thought. Perhaps a new Marvel

43

comic. Matuwa and his flying dashiki. Only Harry wasn't in any comic mood.

"These are our demands," he said, putting down three typewritten sheets of paper. The bastard probably snuck in at night and typed the pronouncement on the project's Selectric. Titled "Give the Program Back to the Community," the non-negotiable demands stressed that every staffer be given the same title, "teacher," under the provision that life experience in the ghetto prepared one for life in the ghetto.

How right you are on that one, Harry, Bitsy thought as she scanned the pages, thinking how easy it would be for him to train the kids to repeat his own dead-end life. More demands. All finances for the program were to be turned over to a community board, which would decide exactly what supplies should be bought and, in the case of a job being open, who would be hired.

Harry's proposals were like a road map to destruction. He was going to have a field day with the program, now funded at well over $200,000 a year—unless Bitsy could blow him out of the water right now.

"Okay, Harry," Bitsy said after about a three-minute read. "It's all yours." She ignored the looks of shock on all the staffers' faces. "It's all yours," she repeated with an emphasis on the "yours."

Several of the women rose up to hug Harry, a few of the white staff whispered to one another, Bitsy gathered up the papers on the table in front of her.

"I'll be gone by Friday."

Silence. Bitsy continued to gather up her papers.

"What's that you're saying, Bitsy?" Henrietta Jordan asked. She had been the first black woman hired, her first time off welfare. She had told Bitsy at the beginning of the summer that it was also the first time in her life that her children had real respect for her.

"What's happening, Bitsy?" Harry interrupted. "We're not saying you gotta move out. We just gotta move in."

"Harry, I'm just giving you room, plenty of room to do your thing. I'm sure some of the teachers—that's 'teachers' by *my* definition—might stay, but I'm going to ask as many as want to, well, to come with me to my next project."

"Next project" was the magic phrase. Now she had them all. "What next project?" several staffers yelled out.

"Well, since we've been so successful here, getting government grants and getting such good reviews...well, I just thought we'd try to do it at another location. Here in Philadelphia. Not too far away, you know."

Harry was upset, waving his arms, his Afro hairdo suddenly looking lopsided as his face contorted. "I know you, bitch, you nigger bitch. I know you are just threatening this. I know you wouldn't really start up another program. I know your kind."

This was almost too easy. Bitsy had thought it would take hours of verbal bloodshed and then hours more of negotiations. But old Harry was just going to hand in the victory.

"Harry, let me share with you my views of the ghetto experience. Because I have been to Uncle Tom school and I know what Mr. Whitey wants, I know how to give it to him. In one month, the grant review board will be here, and if I, or someone equally competent, is not running this program—no, don't worry, they won't shut it down. They will just let it die on the vine, shrivel up and die like an old black bug."

Old Harry wasn't an academic, Bitsy thought, but he was street smart, and he knew that the next few minutes were crucial: now he had stopped talking to her and was fervently trying to keep his troops in line. "We can deal with these OEO people. We can show them that if they want our children to learn, it has to be our way," he exhorted the group.

"You're right, Matuwa," Lida Jones shouted, but the rest

of the aides were very quiet. The way the project had been run was working. The kids had been learning to read.

Bitsy knew it was all over, even before Henrietta Jordan said in a churchy voice, "Harry, I think we're fighting here 'bout nothin'."

Another hour of discussion, finally a promise that Harry would be talked to about curriculum and African history—that Bitsy would meet with him to discuss the program sometime soon. A small bone to save him just enough face to send him away forever, Bitsy thought. She smiled. Harry smiled. It was over.

One more extra warm smile for Harry, with Bitsy thinking to herself: I've been to Uncle Tom school. I know how to talk to Mr. Whitey—and to you, too, nigger.

Kapinski was nervous. He was always shaky when factors conspired against him. He'd set aside the hour from six to seven as the time to phone Bitsy, to convince her to come down and join the Offensive steering committee, to stop hiding out in that slum—and now she wasn't home to answer the phone.

It was all so easy when they started a few years ago. The back-and-forth was the best. Sure, there's problems in this relationship; sure, we come from different backgrounds. Sure, one of us is upper middle class and went to the best schools and is goal oriented. Only problem is, that one is the black one. Laughs. Lots of laughs.

Kapinski (that was always how he thought of himself— "Kapinski") was the first in his family to attend college. Roosevelt University in Chicago, where he managed to stay just three semesters. Then he heard a speech by Saul Alinsky, the great organizer. Alinsky talked about the failures and successes in putting together people organizations and the great power that came from such efforts. A month later Kapinski attended a meeting on campus of the fledgling Students for a Democratic Society, listening to several organizers who had come down from Ann Arbor with this new idea to change the world. "We are the people of this generation, bred in at least modest comfort, housed in universities, looking uncomfortably to the world we inherit," their manifesto, the Port Huron Statement, began.

Kapinski was a natural-born organizer. Other fancy boys might have to go and buy the work shoes and the jeans jackets that made the Movement uniform. He had them hanging in his closet, from the two summers he'd worked in the mills in Gary.

The millwork had been back-breaking, and it wasn't as if he were bringing the money home to keep the family going. His middle-class father had wanted him to understand how hard some people had to work for the wages they brought home. His father was like that, applauding his son's decision to go into the social-change business full-time.

But Kapinski, Sr., which is how Kapinski thought of him, was disappointed, too: he had always hoped that Edmund would follow him, first into his Skokie insurance business and then into the Communist party.

Kapinski, Sr., was a stalwart Party member, not letting his membership lapse even when many claimed that four out of five of his comrades were paying their dues thanks to J. Edgar Hoover. "So what?" he would ask with a shrug if a few times the FBI quizzed his neighbors. "They don't have nothing better to do, huh?"

His politics didn't hurt business, since Kapinski, Sr., had always gotten such great deals on life insurance for all the neighbors. Who could knock him? "Look, I'm a Democrat, the man next door is a Republican, and Mr. Kapinski is a Communist. This is a free country, right?" said Mrs. Weintraub, whose flippancy kept her in the FBI files until her death fourteen years later.

Organizing people, like his political bent, was as natural to Kapinski as fighting at the dinner table. If he learned his salesmanship from his father, he learned speech making from his mother, who always held the complete attention of her family by her unique approach to spoken English: she emphasized the wrong words. Her son copied her, making a singsong what-I-wanna-tell-you accent even more pronounced. Years later someone pointed out to him that the speaking style had been contagious, infecting almost every white organizer in the Movement.

What also came as part of the Kapinski package was his extraordinary impatience, his need to set things right, to make things better. People should cooperate, Kapinski believed, like being at home when he was trying to reach them on the phone. He had dialed the Philly number for the fourteenth time, and finally Bitsy answered, her voice as tired as it used to be after a day of door knocking in Mississippi.

"Bits, I'm going to make this short." He'd once suggested that she should use her full name, Elizabeth. But he'd only made the suggestion once. "Bits, I need you here. The steering committee needs you. The peace movement needs you."

"I don't need it."

A long phone silence. Bitsy used to wonder how two people who spent so much of their lives talking, convincing, pleading, and speaking could be so bad on the phone.

"You're not paying attention."

"No, I'm just tired. I had to pound Mr. Afro-American into the floor today. The actual battle wasn't tough, but I really got strung out before it happened, thinking about it."

"Maybe I need to come see you to explain."

"Maybe you need to cut bait and run. Look, find yourself another token for the March. This Negra is too busy in beautiful North Philadelphia. It's too touchy. If I get involved in anything political, well, the same Mr. Johnson who pays for the war pays for my tutoring project. If we turn off America on his war, he'll turn off our war against poverty in America."

"Bits, that is a great line."

"I know. I used it in a speech at Penn last week, recruiting volunteers for the fall semester."

"But do you believe it?"

"As much as I believe anything. I believe that I've got to get some sleep. I have a seven A.M. phone call from Merlee Brown in New York. You remember her. She's doing tenants' rights stuff. There is a major push to shut down one of the city's worse slum landlords, and I at least owe it to her to be able to talk strategy on the phone. I know you got bigger fish to fry, solving international problems and all that, but there is still poor folks out here."

"Bits, I know that. I would just like to save some of those young, poor black men from getting their heads shot off. Look, I'll come to Philly tomorrow night."

"I'll be here. But I won't be any more receptive to your idea."

"But how about to me, babe?"

"Kapinski, you are about as groovy as a green wool suit."

"I love you, too."

It was a luxury, being alone in the funny, triangular-shaped house at the corner of 20th and R, stretched out on the bed in her navy blue room. If Annie was going to be any one place for more than a month, she painted the bedroom blue. It made her sleep better, although she was getting very tired of sleeping alone. When Burnett had her come to work on the march, she'd thought he might have something personal in mind. She had slept with him once before. Just once. Annie O'Connor had slept with maybe a dozen men, but each man just once. "It's like doughnuts," she'd once told Bitsy. "I love doughnuts. And every time I eat a doughnut, I really like the doughnut. But do I ever like a doughnut as much as I think I'm going to before I eat the doughnut? No way. That's what happens when I sleep with a guy. Never as tasty as it looked."

She wished she had a book or something. A novel, maybe. All she had was some philosophical thing by Norman O. Brown and a Jack Newfield book on the South. She'd almost forgotten what to do if she had a couple hours off. The house she shared with two stingy teachers, a Legal Aid lawyer, and an actual congressional employee—a great living arrangement, since nobody was into ideological housekeeping. Collectives, communes, extended families—it was all too hippie-dippie. All this nonpolitical stuff floating in from San Francisco. "Let the sun shine in, shine in," she sang softly, then, in her best fake South Philly accent, announced, "I like the music. But I don't like the ideology. I'll rate it a seventeen." Daydreaming, she was more than half-asleep when Kapinski called.

"Okay, so how much did Bitsy scream when you asked her?"

"No, no, she wants me to come up there and explain everything to her. Looking good, looking good."

"Yeah, and Christmas is coming."

"Ah, wanna meet for a drink?"

"Meet for a drink? Have you lost your mind? Kapinski, I've known you for years, and the only drink you've ever mentioned is when I stand up in a meeting and you ask me to fill your coffee cup."

"Don't rag, Annie. I wanna talk to you, and in your house you never know who you will run into, either in the kitchen or the bathroom. Let's meet for a drink."

"Okay. Where?"

"I have to think of everything. I don't know. I never go for a drink. Where do people go for drinks?"

"I had a drink the other day with a reporter in the bar at the Statler Hilton. It was kitschy, but they had great things to eat. Like Polynesian things."

"Sounds awful."

"We won't meet anyone we know."

"Too bougie, right?"

"Naw, just too expensive."

■　■　■

A waitress in a wrinkled sarong served them Kapinski's double Scotch and Annie's Captain's Cooler, a frothy pink drink not embarrassed by its parasol stuck in a large slab of pineapple cut to resemble a surfboard. Kapinski shook his head at the waitress's offer of "munchies," but Annie quickly gushed, "Great. Just bring us the most fun thing on the menu."

"What is this, date night?" Kapinski snarled. Annie watched the waitress slither away. It was hard to walk any other way in a sarong, even if it was very short.

"You know, the miniskirt has probably really messed over cocktail waitresses. Now they really have to show a considerable amount of thigh to promote a good tip," Annie said.

"They're just trying to make their living. Just working girls."

"Spare me the class-struggle analysis. I'm here. Now why am I here?"

"Don't start, Annie. I've come to you because I don't know if I trust anybody the way I trust you. Not just that I trust you, but because you and Bitsy are such good friends and she trusts you, and, of course, there is no one I trust like Bitsy."

"Good. We all trust each other." Annie was getting nervous. Kapinski could talk, at any average meeting, at least an hour to set the stage for any ideological struggle that he thought was necessary.

The waitress had arrived with the munchies, a junior-size hibachi with pieces of shrimp and chicken and various fruits and vegetables cooking over the teeny open flame. Annie was charmed and began a thorough inspection of the various edible components.

"Please pay attention to me and not the goddamn meat," Kapinski hissed at her. "I was antsy about this march from the beginning. I get antsy when we start dealing with elected

officials—no, no, I know, we gotta have them signed on sometimes. But they make me shaky, and instead of feeling better
about the whole thing as we've been getting closer to the
march date, I just keep getting worse."

"Kapinski, when somebody has the politics you have,
you're always worried. You're paranoid. You don't trust anybody over or *under* thirty."

"But this is different."

"We're different. The South and the slums aren't messing
around with the federal government. I can tell the real difference by the kinds of reporters we're getting assigned to us.
The Offensive is big-time."

"You think it's going to come off. That we'll get big stories
this week, so big crowds will show up. There is something not
kosher about the way things are falling together. Like Tyler.
Burnett could have signed up any one of a dozen major
church guys. Instead he goes for this basket case. Treats his
wife like she was a retard. And he's a publicity hound. Remember when we'd ask clergy to go to the front of a line in
Mississippi, so their collars would show up in the photos and
on TV? We never had to tell Tyler. He was already there. And
how about no blacks, huh? How can we say that we have an
all-American march if everyone looks like Ozzie and Harriet?"

Annie chewed on the long stick that had held the pineapple and chicken. While Kapinski had been given his speech,
she'd worked herself through almost all the cooked meat, two
of the three egg rolls, two won-tons, and the fruit in her drink
and was now lighting a Camel.

If she felt she was on overload, it was Kapinski, not the
drink. One on one, he was like the giant mimeo machine that
day after day, in the back of the office, cranked out leaflets and
calls to march. Every once in a while the machine would go
crazy. And the papers just kept spewing out, some covered in
ink, others blank. If you talked to Kapinski, you couldn't

figure out which ideas were real, which pages had something on them, and which were blank.

"Look," she finally said, "you're just nervous because so much is riding on Burnett. He put it all together, came up with the money from that Yale professor married to the rich wife and the former Kennedy cabinet member, all money the peace movement's never been able to tap into before. This is not a cheap operation. Just building the TV camera platform is running thousands of dollars. And the city is insisting on portable toilets. And money for staff salaries, even though it's just subsistence. A couple of the peace groups are contributing in-kind stuff, but mostly it's Burnett who put it all together."

"Do you think I'm jealous of Burnett?"

"Sweetie, we are all jealous of Burnett. We are all jealous of each other. We've been together, on and off, for so long that we're more like a family than our real families. Who do I know better, you or my brother John? You, of course, Kapinski. I know what you believe and what you like and what you have said and what you have done. We live on a level of intimacy that none of our parents could ever imagine. We run around in each other's personal lives. We jump in and out of each other's beds. Shit, I never saw my father in his BVDs."

Kapinski didn't answer. Which, Annie knew, meant only that he was thinking about what she said. She waved the waitress over and ordered another Captain's Cooler. This was festive, like a party, or like the big shimmery ads in *Life* magazine for couples honeymooning in Bermuda.

"I don't get Burnett."

"Of course not. You're a Jew. No offense. But you are."

"You're not a Jew. No offense, but you aren't."

A guy at the next table who looked like a traveling salesman turned around and stared at Annie. She pretended not to notice.

"No, I'm a Catholic. That's what most of us are. Catholics and Jews, except for the clergy. We get a lot of Protestant clergy, but not a lot of Protestants. Except Burnett. That's why we don't understand him. He's a very classy WASP."

The waitress delivered Annie's drink, which, she happily pointed out to Kapinski, was precisely the same as the first one. He seemed uninterested, so she continued her explanation.

"Think about it, Kapinski, an entire movement made up almost entirely of Catholics and Jews. All the old Socialists are Jews. The Catholic Workers are Catholic. Who speaks out on the Hill? Gene McCarthy and Bobby Kennedy. We're the folks who are supposed to fit in, but we don't. We're okay—unless we do something wrong. Unless you talk too loudly, and then you are a kike. Unless I won't give in on an issue—and then I'm a stubborn mick. Bitsy's black, marked out, all her life. She's always ready to have people jump on her ass for anything. But you and I, Kapinski, we're nice middle-class Americans. Almost. We're Catholic-Americans or Jewish-Americans. We're hyphenated Americans. So every inch that really oppressed people gain gives us a lift. It's all self-interest. The more kids Johnson ships to Saigon, the more kids are going to be afraid of the draft and the more people are going to sign up to protest."

"Shit, Annie, you make it sound like none of us are doing this for bigger ideals, for bigger causes, for a better world."

"Sure we are. Sometimes. But the folks who really think they have God on their side are the people running the war."

"So what do you want, then?"

"I want to win. My father played soccer in Baltimore when he was growing up, with Ukies and Polacks and square-heads and you name it. Tough leagues. Guys who came from up the state, coal-mining towns. He said he learned one thing. Winning counts."

"Deciding to win means winning at any costs. Are you that committed? That radical?"

"Radical, schmadical. Nobody has those kinds of politics, do they—I mean, winning by any means necessary?"

Kapinski ignored her naïve question and responded with one of his own: "What do you really want?"

"What I would really love is another one of those munchies things. And, if you've got the cash, another Captain's Cooler. They are really something else."

## TUESDAY,
## August 29, 1967

The elevators in the Mayflower Hotel were notoriously slow, giving Annie time to survey the lobby people. At first she thought the woman near the elevator was someone she knew. Then she realized the woman reminded her of someone, but certainly no one from the Movement. The woman, even on this sticky summer morning, looked cool and comfortable, her loose Marimekko dress all crisp and full, her feet in white sandals, the nails on her hands and toes shiny pink against the deep tan of her summered skin. Sitting in the wingback chair, reading *The New Yorker*, she turned the pages at a quick, set speed that gave Annie the satisfaction of knowing that Miss Marimekko looked only at the cartoons.

Getting into the mirrored elevator, Annie saw herself full length—red hair pulled back, a fresh white blouse, a flowered skirt, her worn brown sandals. Measuring herself against the lobby woman, checking off the thinned cotton of her skirt against the rich depths of the Swedish pattern, her own feet grainy in the battered sandals, Annie suddenly realized why the woman seemed familiar. She's supposed to be me. Or I'm her. Or at least that was the way I was supposed to turn out—all fresh and crisp and waiting, patiently, in a good hotel in the right clothes.

Her father was a rigger, doing brutal construction work

that, as he liked to say, made him more money than the architect. He gave Annie and her brothers "all the advantages." No wonder he couldn't understand her life-style. How she'd just walked away from everything, staying in the South, not going to graduate school, and, now, becoming what her superpatriot father thought was only one degree less than a traitor. He stubbornly refused, Annie thought, to listen to the reasoned arguments she could so easily serve up and that would convert him to her beliefs. At Christmas and at visits home, he was warm and caring, as long as neither of them spoke the words, the arguments, that were the most important things they thought about each other.

The elevator door opened and Annie headed down the hall. She loved good hotels and, if anybody else she knew had been flush enough to stay here, would have cadged herself a room service breakfast. But not with Tyler.

She had come personally with his copy of the press kit, so that the good reverend thought he was getting special attention. That politeness done, Tyler would be less likely to scream when she directed reporters to interviews with other members of the steering committee.

Tyler was a pig—simply a pig. Impossible to deal with and yet, Burnett kept reminding her, crucial to the success of the march and a good speaker who could charge up a crowd. He was apparently fully charged up himself this morning. Even the thick wood doors couldn't block out the shouts from the suite. Tyler was letting loose, but not at Marisa. The exit of the bellman thankfully gave Annie a chance to enter the suite unannounced, after she realized that Tyler was too engaged on the phone to notice her knock.

He stood in his striped boxer shorts and a black shirt edged with a cleric's collar, holding the phone receiver and shouting, "I want it handled, John, and I want it handled now! This is not *pro bono* work that you are doing for the church. You make a great deal of money off these contracts. And, let me point out, as a member of the vestry, you took part in the decisions that got us into this mess."

John Whoever must have been shouting back, Annie thought, since Tyler got redder in the face, puffed up like a balloon in the Macy's Thanksgiving parade, his features bloated against the halter that was his cleric's collar. Annie tried to keep the pleasure at Tyler's discomfort off her own face, although she wouldn't have felt badly if he noticed that she looked a little smug.

"I'm listening. I'm listening," he finally spurted out, and it was only at that moment that Annie noticed Marisa, curled up like a frightened child on one of the two flowered sofas flanking the fireplace. Annie walked across the room to hug her, hoping to give Marisa some feeling of warmth. Movement people were always hugging hello and good-bye. Annie once explained the practice to a reporter by saying that when you hugged someone, they felt more real, and if they were real, you were real. But what she felt from Marisa was fear and nothingness.

Tyler noticed Annie and spoke quietly into the phone: "Just hold on while I get this in the other room." He walked across the room, nodded to Annie, and slammed the bedroom door behind him. Marisa just shook her head. "It's very bad," she told Annie. "I don't understand the happening of it, but it is very bad."

Marisa's boarding school English carried only a touch of accent, but she must have been missing the weeks they taught syntax, Annie thought. Everything she said was just slightly out of kilter, charming, but out of kilter, like the look on her face. Her feet drawn up under her thin cotton shift, she looked like Sophia Loren in one of those postwar movies about starving, skinny teenagers or like one of the Klee children that the department stores sold as art. Annie had always written her off as a bead brain, someone to hang clothes on. But that hug had hurt Annie, made her feel Marisa's hurt.

"So, the Rev is in a little bit of a mood, huh?" she asked, trying to lighten the situation. But Marisa's thick eyebrows just seemed to move closer together, underlining the furrows that had bent her brow. Obviously her husband was no joke to the Mrs. Reverend Tyler.

"My husband, well, you know he is so important and the church matters and the peace matters put his wits to the end," Marisa finally said. "And how is the marching coming and going, Annie?"

"Good, good, very good. You should come over to the office. You are always stuck in these hotel rooms, although it's not such a bad place to be stuck, right?" And I know who's picking up the tab, Annie added to herself.

"I would come, but I have not the facility to perform any helpful activities. You understand." Marisa looked right in Annie's eyes, and it was like the hug. "I have not the facility to be as a helpful person."

"Sure you do, sweetie. You just come by, come this afternoon, and you can help me, help me..." For one moment she faltered. But then it came to her. "Help with the general official tasks." Shit, now she was talking like Marisa. Next thing she'd be saying, *Où est la bibliothèque?*"

The invite to the office was obviously the right thing to say. Marisa lit up like a strobe. Click. But one especially loud shout from Tyler in the next room turned off the light.

Annie caught Marisa's look and caught on that what was happening here was no domestic quarrel. Poor kid, she thought, then said conspiratorially, "Let's not tell Paul. He's such a worrywart. Probably would think the work was too hard."

"Yes, yes. A little secretive thing."

"Right. When you get it together, just show up at the office and I'll put you to work."

"Cool."

"Yes, that's it. Cool."

■   ■   ■

Kapinski wanted to meet Pisano near the office, even though Joe had insisted that he was buying breakfast and they could meet somewhere fancier than the place the Offensive staff called the Dirty Drug.

"I'm going to get a bad stomach from covering you," Pisano said, settling into the wooden booth, handling the menu gingerly, as if it were as greasy as the food. The plastic cover on the cardboard sheets had long been cracked and torn, but each day the owners of Cy's Coffee Shoppe replaced the slip of paper that, clipped to the front, announced the daily specials. The regulars knew the specials never changed: corned-beef hash and Wimpeyburgers, with cheese, either for eighty-five cents.

"My mother says all wops wind up with delicate internal systems," Kapinski countered, then ordered the hash, which was seconded by Pisano. Kapinski insisted he wanted two eggs on top. "I try to stay far away from the dietary laws," he said.

"Did you grow up Jewish?"

"Pisano, that's like asking did I grow up a boy. We were Jews. You're Italian. Did I grow up religious? Sure, but not Jewish religious. I grew up Commie religious. I am the original red-diaper baby."

"And now?"

"Now I am New Left. That's as far from Commie as you can get these days. The New Left is so busy making sure that it's not Old Left that, before you know it, we're members of the Republican party."

"You are mildly religious about this stuff, Kapinski."

"No, I am simply very smart about it. I know I'm going to sound like some flower child, but this country is on the cusp of a new era. Kennedy, the Pill, civil rights, airplanes, television. Every night people in the suburbs get to sit in their living rooms and watch the Vietnam War. See napalm at work, see yellow babies burning, and before you know it, you've got a revolutionary right there, watching the tube."

Pisano dumped a spoonful of sugar into his coffee, then stirred it absentmindedly. "So what am I supposed to write about the Offensive, huh? What about you? I keep waiting to see you in a leadership role. I keep waiting for you, in your own special style, to grab that microphone and take over. What's holding you back?"

Kapinski took a few seconds to finish up one egg before starting the second. He ate his food in order, one item at a time. With the hash, it was hard to separate, so he ate the food in a clockwise approach, starting at twelve and moving around. His second egg was right about four.

"I'm here. I'm on the committee, Joe, although I'm on the committee with a few folks that I've had a bad time with in the past. And I'm sure for some of the more liberally inclined people, well, they don't like being on the committee with me. Little nervous about us rads and what tactics we'll want to use next. But it's all going to work. This march could make the difference. Not just radicals or freaks, but straight people against the war. Burnett believes that if one tame congressman speaks out against the war, it's a success. Of course, that congressman stuff is off the record."

"What happens to you in all of this? You told me last year, at the Mississippi reunion, that you were going to plug yourself into international peace organizing, that this 'new day' of politics means old boundaries get forgotten."

"I did some international stuff, but I don't want to talk about it right now. And also, I've got a little problem with my li'l ole Selective Service classification. I'm not quite twenty-six, and some right-wing Neanderthals back in Illinois want my ass in fatigues. I'll probably go to jail. I mean for a while. There's a lot of talk about organizing guys to resist the draft. Just say, 'Hell, no. We won't go.'"

Pisano swung around sideways in the booth and lit a

Marlboro. He'd turned twenty-seven in June. His draft problems had been dealt with by a stint in the North Carolina National Guard, arranged for by his wire service employer.

"Going to jail for a principle always seems fine—in principle. Nobody is going to get behind this resistance stuff. Everybody's father was in World War II. It's John Wayne. You can't go that far, Kapinski."

Kapinski finished polishing his plate with the last quarter of toast, then reached over for Joe's plate, where half the hash still sat. His fingernails were broken and grimy, and the middle knuckle stood out like a sentry, a souvenir of a hefty toss into a police car in Jackson, Miss. A white scar underlined Kapinski's left eye, from the same meeting with the Jackson authorities. Pisano admired his courage, while doubting that Kapinski had any practical politics.

"What Americans don't know, Joe, is that the Vietnamese people don't want this war. They just want us out. They want to decide their own lives."

"And how do you know what the Vietnamese people want, Kapinski?"

"I know, Joe, because I've been there. I've been to Vietnam. I've been to Saigon. And I've been to Hanoi."

Kapinski's mother would have been proud. He let the words hang over the table, like exhaust fumes over Pittsburgh, heavy and dark. Mrs. Kapinski rarely used the technique, the best in her conversational arsenal, saving it for important occasions, like the death of a close friend or when Mandelblatt the butcher ran off with his sister-in-law.

"And just when did you do all this jet-setting, Kapinski?"

"Several months ago, right before I signed on for the march. I went into Saigon on a minister's passport. Then I went to Laos. From Laos, I took Aeroflot to Hanoi."

"I find this hard to buy."

Kapinski slapped his left hand down on the table, spreading the fingers, the better to display the silver-looking ring. It looked something like a cereal box prize, Pisano thought, with its simple drawing of an airplane and the numbers "2700."

"A gift to me from the Vietnamese people. This ring, and thousands others like it, were made from a downed American plane. I don't know what the number means."

Pisano took a long time to say anything, but his face told the whole story.

"I think you are one sick son of a bitch," he finally said. "Some American kids went down with that plane. Or else they're in some rice-paddy prison. And you're telling me that this is a 'gift of the Vietnamese people.' You're screwing around with the enemy."

"Cool it, Joe. What if my trip helped me do something so big that it really went a long way toward ending the war? People'd soon forget I was 'with the enemy.'"

"The goddamn ring makes me sick."

"I also got some women's hairclips made from the same plane, beautiful things, with pictures of butterflies. The North Vietnamese people are struggling to show that they can create beauty out of death."

"Hair things? Beauty out of death? For God's sake, Kapinski, tell that to some lady who shops at Sears and whose kid is getting drafted next Tuesday."

"That's it. That's the lady I want to get to. She's one of the people who can end the war."

"If you want to get her, then lose the ring. And what the hell can be so important, anyway, to justify a trip to Hanoi?"

Pisano pushed, but Kapinski played a seesaw game with him, refusing any details, just saying that he had decided to take Pisano into his confidence only this much. If there was any attempt to search out his secret, Kapinski warned, Pisano would be endangering what could be a coup d'état against the war. That was the way it was left.

■　　■　　■

Kapinski left Pisano at the pay phone in the Dirty Drug. He knew the reporter was unhappy with the meeting, but there wasn't much he could do about that. He walked down Connecticut Avenue and stopped in front of Martindale's bookstore. What the hell did Pisano know about any of this stuff, anyway? What did he know about history, about ladies who shopped at Sears?

Kapinski knew. He knew from life, from books. He knew from rewriting history.

In Skokie, other people showed off by having an Oldsmobile or Florida vacations or an Autumn Haze stroller mink for the wife. Kapinski, Sr., had books. He remembered his father, fresh from the frustration of an unsuccessful two-hour selling siege, pushing open the kitchen door, already in full diatribe as it rocked to a close: "The son of a bitch. He's shopping around. He's a phony. He's in a big house, with a big car. And a big mouth. And he's a schmendrick. What were on the shelves? Let me tell you. *Reader's Digest* Condensed. And they weren't even cracked. Never opened."

Money was often tight, since Kapinski Sr.'s causes and commitments kept outdistancing even his salesmanship. But for books there was always money. The junior Kapinski got in trouble for three things in high school: reading a book while class was being taught, refusing to say the Pledge of Allegiance when Eisenhower inserted the words *under God*, and fighting with Mr. Steve Peterson about the factual inaccuracies in *America: Our Country Strong and True*.

"But where are the Russians?" Kapinski asked, innocently at first, but then repeatedly as History 3 trudged its way through World War II. "It's like the Russians weren't even in the war." It was in his escalating fight with Mr. Peterson that Kapinski made two crucial political discoveries: one was that his mother's way of singsonging her way through an argument was as arresting to the rest of the world as it was to the family around the kitchen table. Second, the most enlightening, was the realization that being right didn't equal victory, if the person who was right had no power. He could drag in any number of histories—real books, written by people at Harvard and Yale and not just for high school kids—but Mr. Peterson and the Skokie school system were always going to have the last word.

Kapinski, Sr., talked with him long into the night, finally convincing him that the two-day suspension Mr. Peterson imposed was a moral victory for his son and one that he should accept, since no other victory would be coming.

"After all these years, some people wonder why I still belong to the Party. And I know you and your mother are two of those people," Kapinski's father had told him. "Someday you'll know what it's like to play the game under your own terms. Maybe what I do will never be respected or respectable. But I do what I believe in. It's not important for me that the world judge me as right or wrong. It's important how I judge myself. That's enough for me."

But is it for me? was Kapinski's thought, both then and now, as he walked into the bookstore.

Although some actions wouldn't bring success in the short term, it was always the long term that Kapinski was thinking about. And he always played to win, even though he was his father's son.


Burnett could have soloed past the maître d', but Representative Mark Mulligan (D-Mich.) was delighted to give his old school friend the assist into the House Dining Room. Being able to help his Milton Academy roommate made Mulligan feel just great. Burnett had been so good, so welcoming, so warm, to the scholarship kid from nowhere.

A decade later, Mulligan, almost on a fluke and certainly on Lyndon Johnson's coattails, had become the youngest member of Congress. No wire or letter brought him more pleasure than the note that came from Burnett in rural Mississippi: "I knew you were slated for great things. I know your presence in the Congress is a hopeful sign for all oppressed Americans. This is just the beginning of an extraordinary career."

Following Burnett to a table by a window, Mulligan thought about the note, about the formal phrasing. It was the kind of letter that one kept in an upper desk drawer; a reminder that beyond the daily grind of politics, there was a bigger game, bigger stakes. The letter was precise, ordered, like the tables spread out before them, crisp and white, garnished with silver and the easy grace that practice brought.

Mulligan thought the House Dining Room perfect, especially at breakfast, the meal that was forgotten or at best an afterthought in homes like the one he grew up in. His mother rushing off to teach at the junior high, his father, before he left, coming in from the night shift at the auto plant, his sisters screaming about the prizes in the cereal boxes—that was the Mulligan breakfast. Not until his first debate tournament at Milton, his first visit to New York, his first night in a hotel, did the realization dawn that even the ordinary occurrences, like breakfast, could be stylized and socially significant. His other realization concerned the wonders of money and prestige and power.

His first weeks at Milton, screened from any too blatant display of cash or cache by the New England refusal to show off, he still couldn't forget that he was different from the other new boys. The difference wasn't the money they paid for tuition while his came free. On that first New York trip he learned how deep the difference was—it was style and knowing, a sense of ease, not just at home with maids and cooks, but out in restaurants, where waiters and busboys bustled about, bringing rashers of bacon and strong coffee and cream that dripped glop-glop out of the heavy silver pitchers, elegant in excess.

In the ritual was safety, the security of doing things by the book. Only if you were the people who wrote the book—people like Burnett—could you carelessly toss it away. Hey, you might say you don't need it, but the safety net was still there. Look at Burnett, in a wrinkled, too heavy sports jacket and rumpled khakis, the long-sleeved Oxford-cloth Brooks Brothers shirt giving him a touch of class. Burnett was as piss-ass elegant, as luxurious, as the heavy cream that still pleasantly amazed Mulligan when it appeared on the table. Yet to Burnett the cream was mundane, as predictable as the silver pitcher that held it.

Some formalities had to be observed.

"Your family, Mark. How are they?"

"Good, good. And yours?"

"My father is the same. Always the same. Working now on some book about English maritime law and colonial expansion. He had a sabbatical last year, and he and Mother went to England, to the Cotswolds, and he said it was really quite glorious. Which is exactly how he said it."

Mulligan smiled. Burnett always knew how to put him at ease. Here he was talking about his father, the much honored Sterling Professor of History at Yale, Brevard Burnett, and he could joke about him. Like we were on the same team, on identical wavelengths. Burnett's father and his father before him, master of Jonathan Edwards College at Yale and eventually secretary of the university, were the wing of the Burnetts who taught and studied. The other Burnetts ran the successful real estate business in New York that provided vacations and the summer home on the Vineyard and the other "goodies," as Burnett's mother would say. Visiting the Burnetts, as Mulligan had during two spring breaks and one summer vacation, was like being in a play. A clever British play, with talk by Noel Coward and big floppy furniture and cheese and butter left out so the icebox wouldn't kill the taste.

Mulligan could never understand how Burnett could walk away from it all, until he finally realized that anytime he wanted to, Burnett could walk right back in. Rules for boys like Tom Burnett were made to be bent; he could spend a term finishing up his undergraduate degree, have his father write a gracious, explanatory letter, and somehow slide into graduate or law school. It would all be very smooth and nice, the not-too-prodigal son coming home.

Not like himself, Mulligan thought, watching Burnett read the lengthy menu as if it were the front page of the *The New York Times*. Mulligan performed without a net and knew too well that one slip would put him out of the game, just another hotshot who'd burned out fast in D.C.

Mulligan also knew the purpose of this breakfast reunion, and he was ready, for once with Burnett, to keep control of the agenda.

"Before you give me your pitch, let me tell you why I want to step up to the plate. And yet I just can't," the second-term congressman began. That was how he thought of himself: the second-term congressman, determined to be the third-term congressman.

"Kelly, my AA, ah, my administrative assistant, had the staff run a phone survey in the district. Nothing big. And certainly nothing foolproof. But the results are overwhelming. People are beginning to question the war. Now let me stress that the operative word is 'beginning'. It's especially true with mothers of teenage boys."

Mulligan reached over and poured some of the cream into his coffee. Burnett said nothing, holding his menu as if he might resume studying the breakfast selections at any moment.

"But most people, and I stress *most*, no matter how much they question or are even opposed to the war, well, they are simply not going into the streets to raise hell. Maybe a prayer vigil. A teach-in? Well, as long as it's peaceful and the professors wear ties, it's probably okay. But not a full-fledged protest. And certainly not a march and rally that involves radicals."

With a slight wave of his left hand, Burnett brought the waiter to the table. He ordered the full breakfast, starting with fresh raspberries, "the eggs over easy, a rasher of bacon, potatoes, a side of the thickly sliced tomatoes, and coffee immediately, please. And throughout the meal."

Once again, even on Mulligan's home field, Burnett stole the play. Mulligan opted for the most graceful loss, nodded to the waiter, and said simply that he'd have the same. The waiter poured the coffee, Burnett lit a cigarette and, in his carefully modulated tones, brought Mulligan to heel.

"I am not interested in surveys, even ones that support my position. You should not be interested in surveys," he began. "You should be interested, committed, to having a real impact on the crisis facing the country, concerned about duty and about patriotism. You are a patriot, Mark. But patriotism is not about playing along with Lyndon. It's about hearing the different drummer, walking in step with the moral heartbeat of the country. America is catching up to its visionaries, Mark. And those who are not visionaries, those who refuse to sign on—they're not just going to be congressmen who went wrong. They are going to be ex-congressmen who went wrong."

The waiter interrupted, trying to bring more coffee, but Burnett sent him away with a shake of his head.

"Let me put it this way, Mark. You have a future that can take you far beyond"—Burnett paused and waved his hand across the House Dining Room—"far beyond this. But not if you play the politics of the past. And that's what Lyndon is, and Hubert, and the Party establishment. You can be their acolyte, or you can be the first to break free, to move in the direction the country's inevitably going to take."

"Tom, when I hear you talk, everything sounds good. It's like we were back at Milton. There wasn't anything you couldn't convince me of, nothing." Mulligan paused, a slightly sad look on his face. "But this is different. I have my district. And I try to represent them."

"Mark, you have to lead. And you have to believe me. Every day we are getting more and more people calling, volunteering. Look at the news magazines, for God's sake. And I think Bobby will challenge Lyndon. This 'dump Johnson' thing is not just a half-ass idea. People want a president to get them out of Vietnam."

"But how do I know that some left-wing idiot won't get up before me and say something really inflammatory, like 'Let's trash the White House' or something? How do I know that?"

"Congressman Mulligan..." Burnett leaned slightly back to allow the waiter to pour more coffee. "Congressman Mulligan, I give you my word as a friend that you will not speak on any platform on which any inflammatory or radical statements are made. You can speak last, and if you have any problem with what has been said before your turn, you can walk off the platform. And, if you had to do that, even that's not such a bad thing, showing the folks back home that you are opposed to the war, but that you won't have any truck with any of these peace nuts or hippies or long-haired rads."

"You make it sound so easy."

"Mark, I guarantee it. This speech will not come back to haunt you. With Bobby and the rest of the Senate just sitting there, some elected official has to speak up. The one who does it first—that person is history. You will be history. You, Mark Mulligan. You'll probably get to give the speech in 1970 at the Milton commencement." Burnett smiled, and so a split second later did Mulligan.

"So all I have to do for that singular Milton honor is to give this speech first?"

"Oh, I think you'll do a lot more, because that's the kind of person I know you are. And you know who I am. And you know I'm not going to betray you."

Burnett reached out and pressed—no, he squeezed Mulligan's arm in a brotherly gesture of intimacy. Mulligan said nothing, just nodded his agreement as the waiter brought their breakfast.

Burnett could make him believe anything, Mulligan thought

a half hour later as he and his old friend parted company to go their separate ways at the Rotunda. Mulligan still believed that Burnett held that power over just about anybody. He watched the tall man he knew so well stride down the hall. Charismatic, noble, some strain of New England Puritan still pacing his stride—an original, but too original to be understood by the assembly-line families in Mulligan's district.

For one moment, watching Burnett capture whatever piece of the hall he was passing by, for that moment Mulligan wanted to trade places. Not for the security that Burnett's breeding brought, but for the journey that Burnett had set himself upon. But just for a moment, as Mulligan checked the typed index card that outlined his schedule. It was almost ten, and he had to hurry or he would be late.

The representative from Michigan turned and strode purposefully to the Capitol's "members only" barber shop. He certainly didn't want to look like some long-haired hippie.

Annie was starving. So she was standing, in the heat, in front of the Offensive offices at 1029 Vermont, waiting for Pisano to show up in his Volkswagen convertible. It was really goofy, Pisano buying a car like that, something some San Diego surfer coed sweetie would like. A convertible with air-conditioning—like an old man who wore suspenders and a belt, just in case.

And he'd probably set up some fancy-dancy lunch, or at least gotten reservations at some "in" place, like the Peking or the Occidental. The "Accidental" was how Annie thought of it, since you never knew who you would run into. Pisano had made such a big thing about lunch that she'd been tempted to go home and change from the yellow shift she was wearing, only there really wasn't anything much better in her closet.

"Get in, get in," he yelled.

"I'm moving." Annie wasn't terribly tall, maybe five feet five, but between her boobs and her hips, getting into a small car became an act of great skill, as she crumpled up like an envelope. Pisano, of course, had the top down, and the leather seat seared the back of her legs where the shift didn't reach. Something from *Sergeant Pepper* was on the radio, and Annie reached over and turned it off without a word.

Pisano teased her: "Do you think you should try to be more aggressive, push a little more, not shrink like a violet so much?"

Annie looked out the window as though she weren't listening, then turned to Pisano with a clipped, "Where to, Mr. Gallant? And, by the way, the haircut is terrible. What are they, junior muttonchops? You look like a Brit rock 'n' roller."

"We're going somewhere exclusive, a special hideaway, m'dear. And many people at the paper complimented me this morning on my look."

Pisano must be getting sloppy and weird in his old age, she thought. This car reeks of garlic, which wasn't so bad since it blocked out the city smells, the exhausts, all fading away anyway as they made their way out Rock Creek Parkway. When they finally turned into a wide driveway, the steep side of Rock Creek Cemetery was pristine and glistening in the summer heat.

Annie was thrilled. "Pisano, this is just what I needed. Now where you should turn—"

"Thank you, I am running this little tour. Where we should turn is right here, then a left here, and look, look behind the trees. Do you see that little bump?"

Annie nodded excitedly. She loved cemeteries, almost as much as funereal monuments, the vast carvings, baroque and complex, that lined the walls of European churches. On her one trip abroad, the summer after high school, she'd photographed dozens of them, like the massive Shakespearean tribute in Westminster Abbey and then, just a glance away, the modest slab listing all three Brontë sisters.

Nothing about a current death much appealed to her, nothing about funerals or even reading the obituaries, which her parents did as a matter of course every morning. But stone angels and carvings and the dates on some baby's monument that showed "This Tiny Angel of God Was with Us So Briefly," that was enough to put Annie into a state of euphoria. Some people collected stamps, Annie gathered inscriptions, taking an occasional photograph of some unusual intricate monument, but mostly committing to memory the long, lavish, lingering inscriptions to loved ones dead a dozen or a hundred years. Burnett had told her once about the cemetery that abutted the Yale grounds, with the wrought-iron gate and inscription "The Dead Shall Be Raised." She'd gone there and drunk take-away coffee and eaten a doughnut sitting beside Eli Whitney's grave.

But this was wonderful, Pisano obviously making a special reconnaissance trip, walking through the cemetery looking for something to please her. Now, standing beside her, he pointed to a tall monument beneath a tree. A large obelisk rose high, and the wide base carried the name of John Patton Linder, 1886–1917. The inscription read:

*Do they miss me at home, yes they miss me.*
*It 'tis an assurance most dear*
*To know at this moment, some loved one is saying*
*I wish our Daddy was here.*

"Must be the Great War, Joe. When was the big flu epidemic, in 1917 or '18? But if it was the war, why isn't John Patton Linder in Arlington?"

"I can't believe this, Annie. I bring you to one of the great tombstones of our time, and you've got a picky quarrel with it."

"No, no. I love it. It's perfect. John's family must have had a little money, or at least Mom and Dad did. Hey, you want to see something interesting? Look at the placement of his name on the base, off to the side. There was supposed to be another body that eventually rested here. Mrs. Linder. I bet he wishes Mommy was right here with him. But wait, let me think. Okay: 1886. That means she was probably a couple years younger or the same age. Hey, Mrs. Linder could be still floating around somewhere, just waiting for the day that she gets to be with John. I love it. The poem is great, obviously home-grown or cut from a magazine. You are great, Pisano."

"Now that we've satisfied the spirit, let's go for the body."

Pisano ran down the hill, opened the car's trunk, and brought out a large cardboard box. It was lunch—Chinese food, all steaming and smelling like garlic. He spread out a bedsheet right next to John Patton Linder and, handing Annie a pair of chopsticks, proceeded to open the little white containers, showing her the contents of each one. "I thought you needed a decent meal," Pisano finally said as they ate slowly, directly, from the boxes. Annie mused that the Washington heat was okay, as long as you were outside, under a tree, and eating Chinese. "I would have gotten some fruit for dessert, but the Farm Workers are picketing the Safeway, and some guy in Bermudas and a cleric's collar kept breaking up watermelons and screaming that they had puss in them."

"Big guy? Beard? Reverend John Tutweiller. No kidding. Used to be a WASP but is now 'of the people.' Delightful. But then the Movement is big enough for everyone. Even you, Joe."

Pisano stretched out his khakied legs, still carrying a hint of the fresh press he'd begun the day with. His Weejuns were shiny, his sports jacket was in the car, laid carefully over the backseat. He reached over and pushed strands of Annie's hair back off her face and announced that they could either have an interesting conversation about sex and whether they should try it—or she could begin her Jesuitical interrogation about his lack of involvement with people like the strange Reverend Tutweiller.

"Joe, the Movement isn't handing out membership cards.

We don't choose who's going to help make a difference," Annie said, shaking her head and wishing that she looked like Julie Christie.

"I'll give you something to like about me, if you want to. Something that will make you jump for joy about my lack of involvement. You remember my friend with the FBI, the guy who told me the truth about the bomb?"

Annie remembered. There had been an agent who'd befriended Pisano in the South. She'd assumed he was young and maybe even Italian, if only because Joe seemed so close to him.

"Well, I called him the other day, just to try and figure out what all the FBI boys thought about your Offensive. And you know what? They don't seem worried one little bit. Now that's crazy, because if this protest comes off even halfway successfully, it should really shake things up. Putting together the not-too-rads like you and Burnett along with the rads like Kapinski, that should be one helluva combination. Only they're not scared one damn bit."

"That can't be true. The New York Fourth of July protest had everyone jumping through hoops. Before the Fourth, the FBI and the cops were pushing reporters about who was going to speak, who was actually putting up the money. How can the Offensive not get the same reaction? What are we about if it's not making the feds nervous?" She smiled at her quip, but Pisano didn't.

"This is serious. There is something not kosher about the government being able to shrug off a big antiwar demonstration. Especially since these FBI guys earn their way by keeping an eye on you crazies."

Annie let her head wander for a moment, thinking about the Marimekko woman with the nice pedicure. She looked on her now sweat-streaked feet, pieces of grass coming out from between her toes. Why wasn't everything neat and clean, like room service, where they brought you everything you wanted, and then they took away the mess that was left at the end?

"So why aren't they worried, Joe?"

"That's what I have been trying to ask you. I don't know. But I am going to know more this week. Remember Harold Sams, the fellow from World News Service in the South? He's in D.C. I talked to him, and he says he's got an interesting line on why everybody is so relaxed about the Offensive, people who should be running around with wet pants."

"How do these FBI guys know so much, anyway? Do you think the Movement has agents? I feel like a fool even asking that question."

"Yes, insurance agents, FBI agents, motion picture agents. Yes."

"No, do you think people we know are agents? I know that some Movement types think that, but it always seemed both paranoid and self-important, like, Hey, we're so heavy the government's running scared."

"Agents or not, you peace people are playing for big stakes. So, clean up your Chinese boxes and let's go back."

"Now I'm worried."

"Okay. Here's a deal. I will take you out tomorrow night. I know there's the steering committee every night this week, but you, I also know, are not invited. So we can have a real dinner, and we can get drunk. A good Irish Catholic girl like you loves to drink. And I can make the prerequisite pass, and we can have some laughs."

"That's what I need, sweetie. A pass from an Italian and some laughs."

Annie hated not being invited to the steering committee meeting. The boys, she thought to herself. The damn boys. The representative from Women's Strike for Peace was due in D.C. Thursday and would add one female voice to the all-male chorus.

"I'm pissed. Really pissed," she told Bitsy on the phone. "Maybe the reason you should really come down here is not as a black, but as a woman."

"Honey, it is hard for me to be either one without being both," Bitsy said.

"I always feel I'm doing well running my little project here, since I am in charge and I have men working for me who are not black. But no way are those white boys going to let any girls get in that room unless they have to."

The "boys" were a constant conversation between them, usually centering around complaints that as soon as someone who was not one of the boys got any power, she became a ball buster.

"It's nuts. I'm the one who has to face all the reporters. I'm going to be the one who will have to coax and cajole and wheedle and please. And I'll get everything secondhand. I have to remember my place. I'm a girl and I'm staff."

"Annie, you got to always 'member what my mammy told me," Bitsy started. Annie smiled. She knew this routine. "My mammy sez, 'Lizzie, all these boys want is one thing. A place to bake their loaf in. A roll to put their sausage in. An envelope to hold their letter.'"

"More, more," Annie pleaded.

"'All deese white boys wan', dat's even clearer, honey. Dase jes' wanna package for dere present.' Or, as we might say at Radcliffe College"—Bitsy's fake mammy-mouth fell away—"an attaché case to hold their brief. And some of them, my dear, are very, very brief."

"More."

"Chile, I ain't had some in so long, I can't even remember what to call it."

Annie laughed. Bitsy could always do it, make her laugh. Especially when she'd felt like a second-class citizen, like today— do the work, but don't get to make the decisions.

"Seriously, Annie, do you think I should come down and get involved in this madness?"

"Yeah, sure. But I'm saying that partially because I'm involved. It's like I want a partner for the third-grade recess line. I gotta go now, sweetie. Burnett is banging on my door."

"Burnett does not bang. He enters," Bitsy finished up, and hung up the phone.

Burnett certainly did know how to enter. Even knowing what trouble was brewing at his dinner meeting of the steering committee, he looked calm and centered.

"Okay, Mulligan just called me, and it looks like he's in. He wants some conditions, wants to wait to formalize it until he talks to his staff guy who's coming back tomorrow."

"That's great. Let me get the news out right now."

"No, we have to do this pro forma. His invite to speak will come from the steering committee for the Offensive. I want to make sure that this platform doesn't get 'liberated' from the left, or the right, so every member of the committee who's already in D.C. gets to be part of Mulligan's invitation. I just wanted to be sure what his answer was before we asked him."

"But what if one of these characters, in an attempt—I know you will find it hard to believe any of them capable of promoting themselves—but if one did, and talked to a reporter and leaked this stuff."

"I'll lay down the law tonight. But, Annie, no leaks yourself. Especially to Pisano. I know how close you are."

"No, you do not know how close we are. We are not that close. We are friends, and he has been very honorable with me, in every piece of work I've done in the past three years. But no, we are not 'that close,' and we never will be."

"Never say never."

"Thank you, Dr. Hippocrates. Call me at the house when you get done with the animals."

"I'll call you when I've got them trained."

■　　■　　■

When the insurance company owned the building, the conference room was where the widow found out just how much the deceased really loved her. Kapinski's father always said such moments required the "three S's—solace, sadness, and the stability of a paid-up policy."

Any illusion of stability had been obliterated by the signs and banners piled against the walls, left by the volunteer teenagers who had been pushed out at a couple minutes past six. "Flower power," psychedelic art, all a product of what the media was calling the "San Francisco summer of love," were beginning to push into politics. Kapinski critically examined the bright-colored signs with the wispy lettering, pencil drawings of robes curving into faces, the triptych within a circle, the peace symbol itself, tripping out into starkly Eastern faces.

"Great artists, these kids," Kapinski said to the American U. fine arts student in charge of putting together the hundreds of posters. The student smiled. It was great to be appreciated.

"Now get rid of every one of these hippie-dippie masterpieces. Burn them or sell them at a love-in. Tomorrow I want everybody on staff to spend two hours in the morning painting signs. Use big block letters. They are to say one of the four following things: 'Peace Now.' 'Get Out of Vietnam Now.' 'Bring the Boys Home Now.' And, and, ah, 'Mr. Johnson, We Don't Want Your War.'"

The AU student had pulled back from her precipice of tears as Kapinski reached over and hugged her. The only thing good about this hippie-dippie shit, Kapinski thought, is that arguments get ended fast, with a hug or some touchy-feelie bullshit slogan.

The sandwiches from Art's Deli were brought in by a delivery boy with an Afro and the general appearance of H. Rap Brown. Kapinski targeted the one chopped liver on rye and turned to Tyler, who was spreading mayonnaise on his corned beef.

"Let's get this delivery kid to give the 'black' speech

Monday. Sure, the real Rap would still be in Chicago. But, what the hell? One black activist looks just like another, hey?"

Tyler did not get the joke, if it was a joke. When Rap Brown had taken over SNCC a few months before, he made a quick call for revolution his main agenda. Everybody on the Left had his own agenda—Black Power, Student Power, fights about Israel, fights about Arabs, South Africa, Northern Ireland, Hungary.

It was this fragmented world that Burnett was trying to patch together to make the Offensive—plus factoring in the liberals, who were always afraid that the Left was going too far. When he signed on, Kapinski had told Burnett he was equally frustrated about the balkanization of the peace movement. And Burnett had invited every single antiwar, civil rights, or church group to participate. Some hung back, some signed on. So what, Kapinski thought. After he pulled off his own special action, who would care who was there?

Burnett started the meeting. In addition to Tyler and Kapinski, Harry Kaplan representing the Socialists, Frank Langusto representing the New York Mobe, and David Preston representing the academics sat around the table. By Thursday the committee would grow from its executive size to an unmanageable dozen, so it was crucial that Burnett get as much accomplished now as possible.

"I have an agenda. And I have some announcements," he began, but Tyler cut him off.

"What I'm worried about are news stories that have nothing to do with the policy of the Offensive. Every day I'm seeing things in the papers that have not been approved by the steering committee, and that I don't think are proper for press speculation."

Burnett piled his few papers into a very tidy display. "I think you've got it wrong, Reverend. There's been so little advance publicity that we shouldn't be worried about what's in the papers, but what's not. Like the fact that it's happening next Monday."

"Maybe our press operation isn't doing its job," Tyler said, almost biting his tongue in anger at his own slip. He had wanted doubt about Annie to percolate through the meeting, finishing up with a dark brew that would color the steering committee's confidence in her.

Burnett started to tap the worn conference table with his pen, just tapping and not saying anything. He was right. Tyler was pissed that Annie had somehow placed short profiles of several other march leaders in *Time*.

"Ah, so wadda ya think, Reverend? Ya think we shudda hired like, ahhh, Doyle Dane and Burnback? Or what, huh?" Kapinski singsonged, knowing that the mill-hand grammar would get Tyler even madder.

"I don't need you to start your smart-ass stuff, Kapinski. What I do need, and what this march needs, is decent press representation. Not someone who plays favorites, who focuses attention on certain members of the steering committee, who feeds stories to press people who have a special relationship."

"So you do have problems with Annie?" Burnett broke in, bringing Tyler's anger to a head, probing like a teenager trying to extract a blackhead. "I don't. But if you or any other person around this table has a problem, let's hear it."

This was not what Tyler wanted. He wanted others to come forward, to witness against Annie, and then he wanted to be the mediator, not exactly accusing her, but bringing the group to the consensus that the operation was beyond her skill. Some cigarette-puffing hussy, some two-bit Movement whore being in charge of the press operation—Tyler hated it.

"I don't have problems with Annie," Tyler finally responded, he hoped appearing reluctant to pass judgment. "But I do have questions about her professionalism. She seems to have a very close relation with Joe Pisano, whom we all remember from the South, and even though he was a generally fair reporter, such an entanglement can only mean that eventually she will give him information that is either helpful to him and not to us, or that should be available to all the news media."

"This is a very good point," Burnett said, surprising Kapinski so much that his head snapped up. At most of life's crucial moments, Kapinski managed to look like what Bitsy had called him years before: a kosher Golden Retriever, his kinky hair hanging in earlike lumps down the side of his face, his prematurely receding hairline allowing a full view of his massively wrinkled and frequently furrowed brow. He looked worried. He couldn't figure out Burnett's response.

"Paul," Burnett said, "you also have made a point you don't realize you've made. We've got to be sure that as far as the Offensive is concerned, we speak with a single voice."

Aha, Kapinski thought, wishing for a moment that he was his father, knowing that the senior Kapinski would have "ahaed" out loud. Now this pompous ass is going to get his.

"I have here," Burnett began, opening one of the several ragged file folders on the table, "some newspaper clips from the past several months, starting with three days after we announced the Offensive. Here's one from the *Times*, which quotes you as saying, 'We're going to bring this Congress to its knees, even as Moses brought the Pharaoh and the Egyptians.' That's a helluva quote, Paul."

Tyler was too busy keeping his anger in check to even hear what Burnett's second reading was, but the third one brought him out of his terrible trance. "Here's a real killer, Paul. A blind item in *Newsweek*, saying that the national church folks, with only a few exceptions, were too concerned about their midwest congregations to get involved in what one un-named prominent clergyman called 'the fight against the Philistines of procurement.' There's another terrific line, Paul. You sure can keep the pressure up. Only I'm not sure, and I don't think anybody else around this table is sure, that what you are saying in any way reflects what we want with this protest."

Outside the frosted-glass conference room there was an argument over who hadn't cleaned the mimeograph machine, and someone was standing in the center of the Pit screaming that the portable toilet people were refusing to show up unless they were paid in advance. Kapinski could take full note of these conversations, since nobody, but nobody, was talking around the table.

Tyler shook his lionlike head and, pushing back his hair from his forehead, managed to wipe away the globs of sweat with the same graceful motion. This guy is great, Kapinski thought. Too bad the bastard is so rotten, because he could really fake out the world.

"Tom," Tyler began, showing the seriousness of what he was about to say by granting Burnett the rarity of his Christian name, "I didn't come to this meeting to be put on a rack. There are questions I had, and have, I might add. And I won't have my sincere and honest questions turned away by attacks on me or by carefully documented diatribes that are at best misleading."

Burnett flipped open another folder. Kapinski strained his neck but could only make out that the few sheets of paper in this file were typed, not newspaper clips. Burnett did little to help either Kapinski's or anyone else's view, since he covered most of the top sheet with his hand and left the salutation exposed, which he read out loud.

"To Senator Eugene McCarthy. Dear Gene, I want to write to you today to make a proposal, one that will touch—"

Tyler let him get no further, his face puffing above the pink sport shirt, a large spot of spit finding its way to the corner of his mouth.

"I'll not have that. I'll not have you invade my privacy. I'll not be the victim of an inquisition. You have no right, no right to probe my life, you fascist little scum."

Finally, in the silence that followed Tyler's outbreak, there was the sound of Burnett closing the folder. As he had begun the meeting, he began again: "I have an agenda. I have some

announcements. In just a few days, when these farcical elections in Saigon are over, when Thieu and Ky become the
democratically elected despots, the antiwar movement better
have something going on. I'm not going to stand up in front
of the Lincoln Memorial like some goddamn hobbit next
Monday and not have the most representative group we can
muster behind me. And all of you feel the same way, or you
wouldn't be here. So let's drop this penny-ante stuff and get on
with making the Offensive happen."

Kapinski nodded, and even Tyler gave a reluctant nod of
the head. And the meeting finally got to Burnett's agenda.

The people who turn up late at night in Philadelphia's
30th Street Station, Kapinski was thinking, were a lot fancier
than late night railroad people in most other cities. Bitsy had
once explained to him how many of them were going home to
fancy places in Ardmore and Haverford, how they all took the
train, and how the train, which was the main line of the Paoli
local, was so much a part of their lives that they were even said
to live on the Main Line. Bitsy always knew shit like that, nice
stuff, how it all falls together. It was near midnight, and
only a few people were in the station, looking as if they'd been
to the theater or to dinner, now walking along, with women
holding their husbands' arms, some of the younger women, in
their skimpy shifts and hair bunched up on the top of more
hair, looking like the models in *Blowup*. Kapinski was not one
for movies, but he had become addicted to the David Hem-
mings film and went to see it maybe half a dozen times, trying
to figure out the existential meaning of the tennis match
finale.

This is a classy city, he thought, going into the still open
bookstore. Bitsy loved presents, especially presents she could
give away, and Kapinski asked the salesman to point out the
kids' section even though the guy seemed reticent to come out

from behind the counter for anyone wearing a workshirt and a "Peace—A Non-Negotiable Demand" button.

He found a sweet book, with a bedroom lit only by the moonlight coming through the window. Bits would like it, especially since no child, just possessions, was pictured. She went nuts about books that only showed white kids, so she was very big into bunnies and lions and puppies, as Kapinski knew from past, not-so-fruitful gift-buying ventures.

It took him six tries, but he finally got a black cabdriver— three whites and two other blacks had turned him down—to take him to Bits's apartment near Broad and Girard. Once these giant brownstones had rivaled New York's as the residences of note, but long ago they'd begun their downward ride, like the whores who lived on the first floor of Bitsy's building. Those ladies, she'd once told him, had started in their profession in beaded gowns, seated in the luxury of hotel dining room booths, but now they worked out of the neighborhood bars or the blind pig, the one that sold illegal liquor all night long.

Bits took almost two minutes to get all the security stuff unhooked, then locked again, all the while buzzing away about how she couldn't believe that Kapinski would lug himself all the way up to Philly, and didn't he realize that she was too committed to her project to do anything else, and why the hell couldn't they get some of the big black boys to come in from Chicago and make an appearance, and why, anyway, did she have to come to the rescue?

Kapinski interrupted. "You are too hyped up. Something good is happening. Tell Daddy."

"First tell me how your meeting went. Especially how was the good Reverend Tyler?"

"Shit, Bits. How did you hear about it? Annie can't have heard already."

"I don't know anything about your meeting, but I know that the reverend is going to be in a very hot place in the next couple days—and I know that it's going to seem mightily like hell to that lying bastard."

Kapinski sat there, in the heat that was Bits's apartment. She refused to have an air conditioner, since none of the families she worked with had air-conditioning, and she wanted to know just how tough the summer nights were for the people she had to deal with the next morning.

He loved her story. It was too good, he thought. What a schmuck Tyler was. To let his church buy up blocks of slum housing. To do nothing about the conditions of the apartments, nothing about the rats, nothing about the utilities that worked some days and didn't work others.

"Kind of like this manor, huh," Kapinski kidded.

"No, this apartment is a mansion, with windows that work, and electricity and doors that lock and no addicts in the entire building. This is heaven, Kapinski. Not like New York. Merlee Brown has been keeping me in touch. Tyler had his lawyers hide the church ownership through a series of holding corporations. A bunch of college kids were trying to track down who really owns the buildings, and a young guy in the tax offices— either so turned on by one of the girls or so turned off by the way it was all hidden away—pulled files he wasn't supposed to, and so there is Tyler, who's scheduled for some egg on his face in the next few days."

"But then we wind up with egg on us, too," Kapinski said. "The Offensive, that is. We look like the only church guy we could get was the one rotten one. Isn't there something we can do to screw Tyler, get what the tenants want, and yet keep him clean enough publicly that we can use him to give the protest the necessary credibility?"

"I don't know. I'm not running this show in New York. Merlee only called me because we did that tenant thing here last year, but what she has on her hands is a much bigger deal. There have got to be four or five buildings, all owned by Tyler's church. We're talking hundreds and hundreds of tenants, lots of families, and conditions that make it look like Alabama."

"It does pleasure me, as our Quaker friends would say, that Tyler is going to get his. But why can't you, or Merlee, approach him with an offer to get everything you want—and, in exchange, you won't fry his ass in public?"

Bits was pulling wineglasses out of the closet. She'd refused to do any dope, even to smoke a joint, in the two years she'd been in Philly, saying it wasn't worth getting busted and losing all the federal money for the project. So she'd gotten into red wine, good red wine, and since she spent practically zip on the apartment, she bought herself several bottles a month, reading about French versus Italian versus the new wines that were coming from California. She'd even gotten one of the two-pronged little openers the waiters in good restaurants used and four crystal wineglasses, which she brought from her parents' house in Germantown. The wine had been opened an hour ago, she told Kapinski, "to let it breathe." He sat back on the bed that doubled as a couch and broke out laughing.

"Bits, you get more and more like your mother every day. Here we are, in the middle of one of America's great ghettos, and you're acting as if Princess Grace were coming by to pay a call."

"Cut it out, Kapinski. The one person I don't need to be reminded of tonight is 'my mother.' She called me twice today to announce that she was never going to speak to me again unless I stopped making a mess of my life. I was going to get killed or raped or worse—I couldn't figure out what she meant by that line. According to my mother I'm now supposed to get some nice suits and go to law school. She just doesn't get it. She wants to separate herself out from the welfare moms in my project. And she doesn't get that, until their lives get changed, everybody sees her and them the same way. Colored women. That's what we all are."

"Does she know about me? About us? It is weird, all this time we've known each other and you talk about her and yet I've never seen her."

"Know about you? You're probably the fate worse than death or rape. Radical Jewish boy from Skokie. You'd be the final straw. Heck, Kapinski, *I* have problems with my being involved with you. I used to tell myself I was here in Philadelphia because there were a couple kids I could change things for—they would go to school, get ahead, break out. I still believe that. But I'm really here because I'm black and I'm fighting back, not letting my people go off to an existential Auschwitz. I know that the black power boys see all of this as a sop, a sellout. It's dirty. We use government dollars. Let me tell you, it's better to use the government's dollars to feed these kids and make sure that they can at least tell red from blue than it is to say, 'Hey, I'm pure. I won't touch that tainted money. I don't need Whitey's hands on my soul.'"

Kapinski sat on the bed, watching her walk around the spartan studio, a wistful look on his face, the same tone to his voice as he asked, "But what about on your body, Bits? How about this white boy putting his hands on your body?"

She laughed so hard at the white boy she called her sometimes lover, laughed so hard that she fell into bed beside him, which, Kapinski thought, was well worth a train ride to Philadelphia.

## WEDNESDAY,
## August 30, 1967

The room service man took the brunt of his anger, but Marisa knew that he wasn't the real reason for her husband's screaming. She thought about it, speaking softly to herself in English. In no language did the outburst make sense. Or maybe it did.

It had to be the apartment buildings that had so made the problem for Paul, she told herself, having him shouting to the phone and for many hours. He surely was not jolly coming back from the meeting of the steering people last night. And, for once, even before she made the discovery, she was clever, thinking up the temperature for herself, a sickness, and him so fearful of catching the sore throat and being unable to do the speech. And then the shouting, even in the good hotel it came through the walls. If only she understood better. But Paul said that he didn't want the people knowing how he was now having the buildings. It would hurt the image. He couldn't be doing the ripping off of black mothers.

Marisa Pignelli Tyler sat on the brocade chair in the sitting room of the $105-a-day suite and thought about her husband, but only in Italian. She knew he couldn't read her mind, but she felt more comfortable doing this kind of thinking when he was away from her, or sleeping, or safe in the tiled shower with the pouring water. Why? How can this be, that this good man, this minister, has done something he has to be ashamed of? she thought, staying in Italian. The "why" was a new question. Never in the time of their marriage had she looked at her life and her husband and tried to see the pattern.

Sometimes, as her father would say, one had to step away to see. She remembered as a child, about six years old, going with her father to Siena on a business trip, how driving there, he told her about the cathedral. The magic floor, with beautiful pictures. She ran up the steps, through the doors, into the cathedral. But when she looked down at the floor, she saw nothing, just pieces of black and white. Where were the pictures? she cried to her father. He picked her up, put her on his shoulders, and, from high up, she could see the biblical scenes, inlaid on the floor in black and white marble. Her child's mind thought they were giant photographs. The first one they stood on had a dog, a spaniel. It looked so real, she wished it was and that she could touch it. Her father laughed and squeezed her leg, then walked her through the pictures, telling her Bible stories, leaving out plagues and deaths and Job, telling only happy endings. He showed her sometimes one had to stand back, to look from many angles, to see everything the artist showed. And never lean too close, or all you will see, Marisa, are the pieces. Never the picture.

Marisa opened her eyes wide, staring at the painting of flowers across the hotel room. Carefully, slowly, she pulled the pieces from her memory: the tiny bits of fear that Paul showed when she bruised; the time she'd asked him why he hid the books he copied from for his sermons; the angry outbursts the first few months of their marriage, screaming that stopped only when she stopped asking why they didn't have the kind of sex that brought babies.

Sorting through her broken memories, Marisa didn't hear the shower stop, the doors open. She gave an involuntary jump as Paul entered, buttoning his shirt. But he was too preoccupied, his eyes hungrily on the telephone, perhaps waiting for the receiver to rise up and greet him. She made a slight noise, and he turned to her. Funny how Paul hated dogs, and yet, at this moment, he was so doglike, fearful, showing the tops of his perfect teeth in a smile that was a snarl.

"Yes, what is that you're saying, my little dumb wife?"

"Nothing. I was just happy to see that you were arriving here, in the room."

"Well, if things keep going like this, you're going to see my departure. I'm going to be dead from this pressure."

Marisa knew this mood, knew what was required. A quick hug, a reassurance. But some newfound stubbornness kept her on the couch.

"Explain to me the crisis about the buildings. So I will be careful to avoid saying anything of a bad nature."

"Say nothing. Just say nothing. It is nothing that you would know about. But if anyone asks you, then call me or find me immediately. Don't delay."

"Are these people in the buildings who are having some injustice? You are always so helpful when people are in trouble. Perhaps you could make the committee or the newspaper ad?"

"You stupid wop bitch. These are people who refuse to pay their rent on time. Who throw their garbage into the halls. Who have children to stay on welfare. If any injustice has been done, it's by these people to themselves."

"But are they not poor and black? Like the ones you worked for in the South?"

"No, no, no. You sound like some lousy community organizer. Negroes in the South were oppressed, beaten, refused any help. This is the North. There are jobs. These people could get off welfare and do something. Instead they live in filth and squalor."

"But, Paul, if there is the filth, why are you not cleaning it? My father, he is the landlord for many buildings, and it is always the landlord's duty to make sure the buildings are safe."

"You can't be that dumb. This isn't the Spanish Steps and these people are worthless, shiftless blacks. Not like southern Negroes, these are troublemakers. What do you know, anyway? You do nothing to help anyone. You do nothing but shop and eat and sleep, and you are getting fat, Piggy. You will be more than just a piggy soon. You will be Superpiggy. Ladies and gentlemen, my wife, Superpiggy."

Marisa was close to the door. Maybe it was her proximity, the temptation of an occasion of sin. Maybe it was the escalation of the marital war that she sensed in Paul's tone. Whatever prompted it, all that was needed was one spurt of bravery.

She ran out the door, down the hallway to the elevator.

There were people waiting, and Marisa played out a happy little domestic tableau, waving to Paul in a cheery manner and leaving him standing alone in the doorway.

The people on the elevator smiled, and Marisa smiled back. By the time the elevator reached the lobby, she was more excited than scared, like a child on a roller-coaster ride who knows the car is soon to pull into the station. Out the revolving doors and onto Connecticut Avenue. She could shop. She had a checkbook in her purse, which she had grabbed from the table beside the door.

The windows of the Little Jewel Box shop were filled with pretty things, and only as she caught herself in the antique mirror did she realize the tears were running down her face like baby diamonds. No, no shopping. Paul was right. She would do something. She would find her way to the march office and she would find Annie and she would help. Of course, it was early in the day, and she would take her time and look in all the store windows on the way.

Mark Mulligan did one very smart thing, the old Hill hands would say. He didn't know much. He didn't know a damn thing about being a congressman. But he did know someone who knew. And that's how he hired Jerry Kelly.

Kelly was a bit of a dandy, liking to think that what he lacked in stature he made up in style. His shirts were custom-made and always had double starch in the collars and in the cuffs, which framed his soft, pale hands and shone like his buffed nails. He'd come to the Hill the same week that Franklin Roosevelt went to the White House. Just for a year or so, he told his friends, and then he was going to go back to Boston and maybe run for something himself. Days and eras had passed. The New Deal, World War II, Joe McCarthy, and Ike translated in Kelly's life to the political careers of the four congressmen he had served and managed. Every once in a while, in his long Hill tenure, some new honcho over at the

National Committee or a hotshot senator wanting the White House would approach Kelly. They'd sing some siren song of power, telling the old mick that he could really be powerful, really put his experience to good use. Kelly would get a hot spot of pink on his soft cheeks, making him look like a greeting card leprechaun when he would say simply, "No, thanks. I've found a home in the House—and a good Irishman like me never leaves home."

A fatal heart attack by the chairman of the House Appropriations Committee during his hometown's Jackson Day dinner had left both his congressional seat open and Kelly at loose ends when Mulligan approached him almost three years ago. The kid was a "'64 Wonder," carried into office on the broad coattails of Lyndon Baines Johnson's trouncing of Barry Goldwater. But, as other landslide wonders had been grandstanding and would soon drop by the wayside, Mulligan had been busy serving the folks back in the district. He had a decent victory in a bad Democratic year in 1966. Kelly foresaw no problems with Mulligan's next reelection in fourteen months, and as a survivor of the congressional class of 1964, his boy was certainly entitled to some new and better committee assignments.

In Kelly's mind elected officials were just the window dressing of what he saw as the reality of the Hill. They allowed the real running of the government to be left to professionals like himself. Kelly arrived at work every day at eight, coming to the office directly after mass. And he stayed until six, when he would have two drinks and a lot of talk at the Carroll Arms on the Senate side of the Hill before heading home for dinner. It was a very powerful lobbyist or a national crisis that would keep Jerry Kelly from his dinner table—and only a national crisis that would force him to reschedule one of the two times a year that he left the government in other people's hands. One would be August, when he went to Maine to join the family, and then again when he and the wife took the family to his mother's for the Christmas holidays. He had never even taken a junket. He kept telling people that he was going to get to Ireland one of these years, but politics had a stronger pull than his native land, although Kelly believed that his inheritance had given him the blarney necessary for his profession.

It was "with a firm hand" that Kelly ran the show. He had yielded to the symbolism but not the substance of Mulligan's insistence on an office run by what the new congressman called "participatory democracy" before Kelly had him drop the phrase. There was a regular weekly meeting at which all staff members, no matter their title or job, were invited to have their say on pending legislation. Or how the office was working. Or how to end the war. Or who wasn't making coffee. But, as one veteran explained it to the new receptionist, "Everybody has a say. Then Kelly decides."

It took him, Kelly would estimate, about three terms to know a congressman. Then, as with two of his three former bosses, would come the glory days, when they could work together like bread and butter. His second Hill job had been murder, when Kelly prayed that the son of a bitch he was working for would fall down drunk in the streets and wind up with his picture on the front page of *The Washington Post,* his hand up a whore's skirt. Then it got so bad that Kelly pictured him drunk all right, but with his hand on some faggy boy's ass. That would have served him. Revenge came in another way—a bad piece of advice here, a dropped hint there, and the senator from the congressman's state suddenly had an election-age son who wanted to run in the congressman's district. And the congressman was persuaded to run for governor, with the senator's help, and Kelly gave a very fine speech at the newly elected governor's going-away dinner.

Kelly knew well the Washington rule that almost all important business took place over food or drink. He made sure to meet with his congressman at least once a week for breakfast off the Hill—a long way, at least psychologically, from the House Dining Room. The usual agenda was only a pretext.

Kelly's real purpose wasn't to go over the calendar or talk about fund-raising back in the district, but to set together the pieces of a relationship. This morning he and Mulligan were having their regular Wednesday meeting in a coffee shop on Pennsylvania near Foggy Bottom, a few blocks from the Department of State, "the Fog Machine," as Kelly called it. As he glanced around the coffee shop, tapping his finger softly on the Formica table, he thought how different it was from eating on the Hill, where you had to keep looking around to see who was in the next booth. Part of the strategy of these meetings was to get Mulligan to open up and tell Kelly what was on his mind. The young congressman was thinking too much about issues, "all that blazing substance—it only gets you in trouble," Kelly grumbled to his wife after a long day's work at stopping Mulligan from reforming welfare, "at Lord knows what cost, to the taxpayer and to his career."

At times like that, Kelly yearned to say to the congressman: "Who do you think you are—president of the United States?" But, of course, part of Mulligan thought that's exactly where he would wind up. So Kelly would content himself with some pushing, a little pulling, to steer the congressman past potential pitfalls: "So much easier, Mark, if we don't take on this problem at this time. Save yourself for one you can win."

Today was different. Today was more serious than usual. Today's cockeyed nonsense was the peace demonstration these nuts had organized for Labor Day. Kelly thought the phone survey of the district would have discouraged Mulligan's getting involved in this antiwar nonsense. And he was angry that his own absence in Maine had left the boy alone; but then who ever thought that anything important would happen in August? He wasn't upset that Mulligan's sudden need for his guidance had forced him to cut his vacation short. The grandchildren seemed to fill up the house with noise and toys a lot more than his own kids ever did, and, since the grandsons slept in the next room, his wife, Ellie, just wouldn't let him do the things at night that Kelly thought men needed for good health.

So he had one daughter drive him to Boston for the plane, and now he was smiling at his young congressman across the Formica. The kid was really revved, Kelly thought, someone had really hit the pedal.

"The stuff I sent up to you, the printed 'call for action,' well, it might not show just how broad-based support for the Offensive is," Mulligan began.

Kelly nodded. Every once in a while the glaze that prep school and Amherst had put on Mulligan wore a little thin, and the good stuff shone through, making Kelly more hopeful that his congressman was more than a smooth, Irish Sammy Glick. It was clear to Kelly that he had to kill off any plans Mulligan had to be part of this crazy protest, but he was relieved that at least the kid was approaching the argument in political terms, pressing the idea that he could hold the Democrats in his district while opposing the war and pick up a lot of moderate Republicans who didn't like the prowar politics coming to dominate their own party. "For the Republicans," he told Kelly, "it doesn't work when the Nixons and the Reagans say Lyndon's real problem is that he hasn't bombed enough."

"Reagan," Kelly repeated, diverting the conversation. "Only in California."

Mulligan pressed on, trying a new tack: "And I really am against the war, which carries more weight with me and should with you than anything else I can say. I'm really opposed to this involvement—our young men dying...." Mulligan was slipping into his oratorical mode. "Our national reputation is being tarnished, while the dissent over this war is ripping apart the national fabric."

Okay. Enough, Kelly thought. He smiled his lopsided smile. He knew people thought he looked like Barry Fitzgerald, but he liked to think of himself as a Spencer Tracy, he's-not-heavy-he's-my-brother-style guy.

"That's great, Mark. But you've got no control over this show. You have no idea what some long-haired crazy is going to say before you have your chance to speak. Think about the photographers. We wind up with your picture running in the *Detroit Free Press*. Only problem is the story is about some half-ass Negro saying we should burn down the White House. TV will be there, so while a Commie is talking, it will be your face that's getting broadcast. His rhetoric goes up in flames— and so does your future. Nobody's going to remember who said what. They'll just know that it's too radical for them. It won't be American."

"Shit, Kelly, people are speaking out against the war every day. Gene McCarthy spoke out several months ago at a Clergy Concerned About Vietnam meeting."

"Right. And Gene knew just what political pew to put himself in. He wasn't down in the street with hippies. He was talking with God's people."

"Well, I *am* a congressman. I'm elected to talk to everybody, not just God and churches. And I sure as hell can't keep making decisions that have as their primary purpose my staying in office. What good is the job if I can't do something with it? Why bother to be a congressman if I can't affect change?"

"You been reading *Profiles in Courage?*" Kelly asked. "Just remember—the guy who wrote it didn't crusade for civil rights until *after* he was president."

"Well, I'm already in Congress." Mulligan purposely missed the point.

Kelly looked up at him. "Let's hope you stay there." Then he picked up a sugar cube, dropped it into his lukewarm tea, and just started nodding as he slowly stirred the liquid, clinking his spoon against the side of the cup like a metronome. Mulligan interrupted the silence to ask him what was wrong.

"Nothing. How could anything be wrong? In the thirty-five years I've worked on the Hill, in the four congressional offices I've worked in, never, really, never have I heard anyone so clearly take a moral stand. Not a political one, but a moral one. Even for a hard-hearted old bastard like me, well, it does my heart good."

Now he had stopped stirring and instead was building a little tower of sugar cubes, lining up the edges carefully.

"Kelly, I want to use this office to fight the war. What good is this sword of government if I keep it sheathed?"

"Now that's a great line. I think you should have a lot of important-sounding rhetoric like that in your speech."

"I know you're just talking me down. Okay, Kel. What do you really think?"

"Not think. Believe. Believe that you will have an impact on just one group of people—the voters who will come out against you in your district. Believe that you really do care about ending this war, but that you can do a lot more as a congressman than you can as an ex-congressman. Believe that no matter what the issue is, it's not worth giving up this seat—or what comes after it. And then, after that. No congressman has been elected president directly from the House in a hundred years."

Kelly'd said it now. The magic "p" word. It could make someone like Mulligan freeze in his tracks. Everything else was playground ball, kid stuff. Lot they knew, believing the White House was the political pot of gold. There had been thirty-nine presidents in a hundred and seventy-eight years—but every moment there were two or three hundred presidents-in-waiting in the Senate and the House. Maybe all 535 of them in some way believed that it was their particular prize, but Mulligan...this kid actually has a chance, Kelly thought.

"You could go all the way," he said. "But first you have to go to the Senate, or the governorship. You just have to line up your ducks." Kelly spread out the sugar cubes in a diamond pattern. "You have a good shot for Senate. Phil Hart's not going to want to work this hard forever. Or for governor.

Romney will be out soon, one way or another. I don't think he can win the Republican nomination, though; he hasn't got Rockefeller's money or Nixon's meanness. Not a bad place for you, although I think you're a Washington kind of guy."

His congressman's face was all expectant, Kelly thought, like the kids down in front in the line for a department store Santa Claus, or the slightly older men who watched aging strippers from the stage-front tables.

But Kelly had misread him, or at least Mulligan refused to reveal himself.

"What you're saying is that I should forget my principles, forget that I believe that protests like this do matter, and simply turn my back on the whole Offensive?"

"Jeez, how the blazes can you want to get yourself tied up with something called the 'Offensive'? Yes, maybe you should turn your back on this march."

"And line up what ducks? The prominent Democrats who meet with the president every day and get this country deeper into Vietnam? Aren't they war criminals? Aren't they guilty every time a baby gets napalmed?"

"This year they might be war criminals. I guarantee you that in ten years, if this war proves a mistake, they'll all be writing books about how they were the voices of reason, how they tried to turn Johnson around. They won't be war criminals then. They will be the grand old men of *our* party. And if you still want a role in this political party, and if you like the job the folks back home elected you to do, then we will have to figure out some way for you to be against the war without you napalming all your bridges behind you."

"All you are telling me, Kel, is that compromise is the only way to get political results."

"No. That's what you're telling yourself. What I am telling you is that the next time we have a discussion like this—and there will be many next times—remember that the bottom line is you like being a congressman. You want to continue to be a congressman until you can be something better. You put that on the table"—Kelly had moved the ketchup bottle into the center of his sugar cubes for emphasis—"you put that personal agenda on the table, and then we'll know how to make our decisions. As far as this antiwar Offensive is concerned, let Burnett and his buddies sit for a day or two while we figure out if there is anything at all that could come out of it that would be good for you."

Mulligan reached for the bill. Usually Kelly put up a fight, even though the chit just wound up on one or another of their expense accounts.

Today, though, there wasn't even a mock battle for the check. Kelly sat still, smiling his Spencer Tracy smile and thinking that for help like this, the kid could pick up the tab. That was a Jerry Kelly principle: You didn't get something for nothing.

The three-story mansion on 21st Street was once the home of Rusty Randall, built when the cattle baron came east to buy his way with Congress—which he did. His blond wife could not match his success. Her attempts to enter the magic circle of Washington society were blocked by what she told Rusty were "ugly old women who aren't half as rich as we are." Rusty was intent on making his bride happy, so he packed up his congressional favors, including the grazing rights to large chunks of several western states, and the Randalls set off to become the dominant force in St. Louis society.

Rusty's success on Capitol Hill had been due in no small part to a Harvard lawyer he'd had the luck to hire, a young man who accepted the overdone manse in payment for the swollen bill he was still owed by the cattle king. Appropriately, he converted the mansion into his law offices.

That clever young man was T. R.'s father, patrician and mustached in the portrait in the private reception room, once the cattle baron's "small library." The painting was carefully suspended with wire from the crown molding, so as not to disturb the ornate silk damask fabric covering one wall. Mrs. Cattle Baron might have been judged to be lacking in social graces, but she did have money, and with the passage of time, the expensive furnishings, no matter how garish or gauche in their original incarnation, became increasingly valuable. "Most antiques are born in bad taste," T. R. liked to say. "Someone, someday, will probably prize an Edsel."

The other reception room walls were crammed with the black-and-white photos that Burnett thought of as "T. R. with" pictures—T. R. with presidents, with Gandhi, with Nehru, with Chiang Kai-shek, with Churchill. In other Washington law offices, photographs of senators and congressmen provided the proof of power; T. R.'s wall was too exclusive a club for most mere elected officials to make the cut.

Burnett was early, as he always was for his meetings with T. R. The day was already sticky, but he'd walked the dozen blocks from the March headquarters. It was a habit, really, one he'd picked up at Milton, walking everywhere even in extreme weather, not for exercise, but for the time alone.

Walking wasn't physical, but spiritual. Not that he was religious. No, Burnett was by birth Episcopalian and would probably stay that way, since it required no faith, no religious conviction, just an intermittent repetition of ritual. That was Burnett's way, defining things not for what they were, but for what they were not. The walks became spiritual because they were not material. He chose Yale because he didn't like Harvard. Vanilla became his favorite ice cream because he had no taste for chocolate. Reactions grew where preferences should have flourished.

Big decisions were saved for the walks—world problems, the struggle between good and evil, racism, poverty. Burnett would stride along, his angular face resolute. At Milton and then at Yale, Burnett thought of politics. McCarthy had really fouled things up. Joe, not Gene, of course, but that, too, he thought, was probably coming up. Joe McCarthy, an evil, reckless clown who beat the drums about communism and in the end did a better job than any of his adversaries of convincing the America public that the witches he hunted were mere figments of his fevered politics or his paranoia.

Burnett himself became a stringent anti-Communist not because he was conservative, but simply because he was not a Communist. He watched the anti-Red paranoia of the Fifties as his father's university colleagues became either the accused or the juries that judged them. He believed there was only one successful alternative to international communism, and that was a liberal alternative, although the great Red Scares of McCarthyism had stupidly colored liberals along with the Reds.

Like any adolescent, he believed that all discoveries were personal and unique, so he was pleasantly amazed in the late 1950s by the realization that his developing worldview was shared by a society of elders. The Liberal Establishment, mostly refugees from public service, then lived in the private world of law firms and corporations, a tiny remnant secreted in the few insulated agencies where the level of security would keep nosy senators from asking political questions.

Burnett's discovery of this most elite secret society came slowly, with T. R. peeling back each layer, a sailor working off ancient waxes. T. R. Simpson's liberal cohorts resumed public lives at the start of the Kennedy presidency. Johnson was hardly their ideal president, although many of them had known him and dealt with him during his long tenure on the Hill. "A rough-cut diamond," T. R. said of Johnson when he emerged during the Roosevelt years. A little too rough for the D.C. social circuit, even when he became vice-president. But many of the worldly-wise liberals had appreciated his skills despite what they termed his "earthiness." Now they were part of his presidency, and Vietnam was their kind of war: measured, a metaphor for containing China, a conflict that didn't aim to conquer the North, only to preserve South Vietnam, a minor image of their earlier war to preserve their half of a divided Korea. It was, in their phraseology, a "limited war"—limited, unless you were a soldier called up to fight.

Burnett, then only nineteen, had met T. R. at a seminar at Pierson College, one of the twelve Yale undergraduate residential "colleges," each with its own architectural and scholarly bent. Pierson was "political" and so had invited Theodore Roosevelt Simpson, former assistant secretary of state, former aide to FDR, former special emissary to De Gaulle and the Free French, and former Yalie to speak on why involvement in government and public service was not just a duty, but a right, especially for the Sons of Eli.

After Simpson's speech the undergraduates ringed him, each earnestly trying to impress him, knock off his over-the-calf black socks. Finally Simpson turned to Burnett, who looked him right in the eye and asked if they could have lunch. "I have some thoughts I'd like to bounce off you, sir, if it wouldn't be a problem with your time." No bullshit questions. Just a simple request for Simpson's attention and experience. Simpson took Burnett not to the refectory or to Mory's on the edge of the campus, but to a Wooster Square Italian joint, where there was privacy and time and a legendary antipasto diablo.

And that was how the friendship began, rich and flavorful as the sauce. From the beginning it was all of a piece, the shared worldview, the background of quality, the personal touches, and, finally, that most intimate of exchanges, those of intrigue and secrecy. Although initially Burnett had never realized the depths and heights of trust it would reach, he now accepted as fact that T. R. had known, had guided the whole venture.

A buzzer signaled, and T. R.'s secretary, Miss Sager, gave him a signal to go on in. T. R. had a worn dowel oak table that he used as a desk; with no drawers, he told clients, he had no place to put papers and so had to finish his work by the end of each day. But this time T. R. was seated on the corner of the chintz love seat, on the phone, and motioned Burnett to one of the wingback chairs that flanked him.

Burnett sat down, feeling shabbier than usual in these plush surroundings, forgetting for a moment that it was T. R. who had dressed him in his costume of dissent. Hanging up the phone, T. R. smiled, pressed a button, and asked Miss Sager for coffee "and something sweet for my two friends."

Perhaps the dog really could understand everything T. R. said, which is what his owner claimed, or maybe it was just a terrific sense of timing, but T. R.'s request brought Homer's head up from the floor under the coffee table. T. R. had once told Burnett that basset hounds were a perfect dog—they weren't supposed to hunt or protect or do anything except be faithful, be consistent, be true. That was Homer, who drove with him to the office each day in the black Lincoln, sitting beside Harry, the driver, in the front seat, waiting patiently if sleepily for the end of a breakfast meeting, spending the day in the office moving ponderously from a spot of carpet in front of the window to one closer to the door. It was not true, as was rumored and once even printed, that the younger associates in T. R.'s firm were rewarded for good work by being permitted to take Homer on his twice daily constitutional.

T. R. made small talk just long enough for the tray to arrive, then told Miss Sager they should not be disturbed. He sat parceling out bits of a sweet roll to Homer while Burnett served up his choicest pieces of gossip and analysis.

"It's all holding, although Tyler scared me last night. He's furious at Annie, who ignored him with the *Time* piece. I felt like slapping his simpering face."

"How do you control him?"

"I didn't bring up the wife, although I came close. I used his own words against him, quoting from the clips you'd sent over, with his tacky use of biblical allusions. Then I just put him out of bounds for conducting his own press operation. Told him he had to stop. By the end of the meeting, he was totally on the defensive and should be a little lamb for the rest of the week."

"Tyler's got other problems. Seems as though the good cleric has been playing slum landlord, and now the fat's in the fire. Big demonstration planned for tomorrow in New York."

"Are you involved?"

T. R. stood up slowly from the love seat and settled himself on one of the Windsor chairs. His back was bothering him again.

"No. I'm only interested because I'm wondering if the Black Nationalists who are meeting in Chicago will want to move in on it. Could be happening too fast to be taken over by anyone."

Burnett nodded. T. R. was always thinking several steps ahead, trying to judge who would gain what advantage from what maneuver. It did help that his "government friends" provided him with the kind of information that made for astute guesses.

"And Mulligan?"

"Mulligan will sign on today. We're down to the wire. I think we can get him on the *Today* show tomorrow morning, and he can do a news conference right after on the Hill. He's got to announce soon, if we're going to get the biggest impact on what follows."

"What's holding it back? You told me two weeks ago that he was ready and eager. We have no time now to make a different plan."

"It took me until yesterday to get him face to face. I have a long history with him, and he knew that once we were one on one it was all over. Now the only barrier is his goddamn aide, Jerry Kelly. Mulligan is afraid to move without Kelly's okay, and didn't want to make it urgent, and so we are all stuck because Kelly was up in Maine."

"Tom," T. R. began, emphasizing it so that it became two syllables, "we only have Mulligan. There is no one else with the particular credentials and the special background that fits the requirements. He's a mainstream comer, not a liberal nut, so that his signing on to speak at the march will bring out the press."

"He's very nervous. Damn, I had to promise him that if anyone too crazy spoke before he did, he could just get right off the platform."

"I don't care if you tell him you'll lift him off in a whirlybird. It doesn't matter what you promise him to get him to announce that he'll speak. He just has to announce."

"Do you want to hear the rest of this stuff?"

"Yes. Of course."

"Most of the black leaders won't make it. Still too busy with the Conference on New Politics in Chicago."

"The only difference between Old Politics and New Politics would be that old politicians are out and new rascals would be in. But it's good that they're tied up. When I first found out about that meeting, I knew it would be just the drain on the Offensive that we needed. We have to keep the representation broad, but only with second-level speakers. Present company excluded. We want Mulligan to be the keystone to what is important about the march."

Homer moaned, and T. R. rubbed his wingtip along the dog's tummy. Even that slight move caused T. R. to arch his back, so Burnett knew how bad the pain must be.

"How about Kapinski? You know, you and I have spent so many years discussing Mr. Kapinski, Jr., that I feel I know the young fellow. The only time I've ever seen him is when he disrupted the secretary of state last March. Hell, Rusk was so dull that I was ready to disrupt it myself, on aesthetic grounds alone."

"Kapinski is good. He's Left, but carries a lot less baggage than other radicals. He'll probably be able to bring a black on the platform. Bitsy Clark."

Simpson nodded.

"I know her. How many Movement people do I 'know'? Has to be dozens. More than a hundred? I know their background, politics, personal lives. I know what brand of cigarettes they smoke and whether they like their sex straight or a little strange. I know them—and have never met one. Funny, seeing someone, even seeing him every day, does not mean you know him. Conversely, it is not necessary to ever see anyone to know all about the person, to know him—except, of course, in the biblical way."

Simpson waited until Burnett smiled at his little joke.

"You detest my jokes, don't you, Tom? Worse than the puns, are they? I'm too much an old poobah to be fooling around with such nonsense, that's what you think. You want everything serious and straight. Well, that's not life. You must laugh. It's what the Jews and the Irish have known all along. We might have ruled them, but the people below us got the final trick. Their laughter trumped us, trumped our aces. Not everything is funny, Tom, but everything is absurd. Politics is absurd. Look at Hitler, look at Mussolini, laughable in their katzenjammer uniforms. All these Saigon generals look like something out of a Marx Brothers film, tiny little men with rows and rows of ribbons, self-declared heroisms lining their chests. Welcome to Fredonia."

Burnett motioned with his hand that he'd had enough of Simpson's teasing. Hand signals and nods and single-syllable answers continually proved how intertwined their lives and minds were. Once, Simpson had told him that he was like a son to him, and Burnett was moved to answer that Simpson was more than any father could be. Like kids afraid to step on a sidewalk crack, before and after that time they avoided talking about their relationship. It simply was, like tomorrow or a good martini.

"So I should laugh more?" Burnett asked softly. "Do you know what makes me laugh, what gives me pleasure? You sitting here, 'tinkering,' as you call it. I know the pleasure you take in what you accomplish. But I take great pleasure that you sit here with Homer, in your Sulka tie and a Bond Street suit, happily interfering with the protest movements of America. Or at least trying to."

Now Simpson did laugh.

"And what would your radical cohorts think, if they found out about my 'tinkering'?"

"They'd think you were one tough old dinosaur. Which is true. What they wouldn't know is that you're a lovable old bastard, T. R. They just wouldn't get the lovable part."

Marisa Pignelli Tyler turned out to be one champion collator, even though she had never heard of the activity when Annie announced that would be her first job at the Offensive. Annie led her past desks overcrowded with people yelling into the telephones, about buses and toilets and permits and marshals, past the bulletin board with the Jules Feiffer cartoons and the notes about sharing apartments or getting rides to Berkeley and UCLA once the march was over.

In the back room, Annie put her arm around Marisa's shoulders and gently pushed her closer to a table, piled with stacks of paper, with several people walking around it.

"This is Marisa," Annie announced, "and she's helping us out this afternoon." The line stopped. Marisa got placed by Annie close to a pile of papers, one of which read "March Manual"; she followed the others around the table, taking a paper from each of the eighteen piles, then handing her packet to a boy standing next to another table, who stapled it and put it in a box. It was a simple, effective system: four walkers and a stapler.

The music on a radio was loud, with a heavy beat, and only the kidding interrupted the step-and-stack motion of the collators. Marisa loved it—so regular, so neat, so ordered. For an hour they danced their pickup rhythm around the table, then the boy with the stapler said it was time for a break.

With the work removed, Marisa was suddenly wobbly; with her dance step taken away she didn't know where to walk. But the nice stapler boy asked if she knew where the coffee was, and she shook her head no, so that she wouldn't have to show her accent. He grabbed her by the arm and took her back through the big room, holding her arm gently and telling her that there were also some of the rottenest doughnuts he had ever eaten.

"You listening to me, huh, talking. This is South Carolina, and this is the way we talk. I'm Jefferson Talbot the Third. And you..."

"Marisa. Marisa Pignelli." For some reason she didn't bother to add her husband's name.

They talked very little, drank their coffee, went back to the room with the piles, which had shrunk toward the table-top. Their short stacks made Marisa nervous about whether there would be anything to do when the collating was done, and she asked Jefferson about it. He didn't answer, just walked to the metal shelving lining the walls, picked up bundles of paper in each of his big hands, and started replenishing the workload.

"We got like fifty thousand people coming here, and when they get here, we want them to know what's happening. So we gotta give them the manuals."

The dance continued. Her only break in the rhythm was to go to Annie's office, to ask this, her one friend, if she could stay with her that night.

Annie asked no questions, just hugged her and said, "Of course. You will have to fight for clean sheets, but I have an extra mattress in my closet and it's all yours."

"And you won't be telling Paul? Promise?"

"Honey, you are the one who married him. Not me. If you don't want to tell him, he's untold. How is your work?"

"My work? I must hurry back. It goes very well."

Marisa was not the first activist to find solace in shit work. It was shit work that fueled the revolution, Kapinski would have told her, citing his own practice of trying to do at least one hour of collating or stuffing envelopes or sticking on address labels every day, just as in the South he always spent one or two hours on the phone, calling up the local Negroes about voters' registration class or a special Sunday meeting speaker.

Kapinski could have told Marisa that he thought this work was the barn raising of the new politics, that the joy of something completed, even if it was just a tabletop of mimeo sheets, was a feeling often absent in the day-to-day struggle to change society. And that people couldn't sit on their elite asses and let someone else do the nitty-gritty for them.

Kapinski could have told her all of that—the only thing was, Kapinski had bigger fish to fry.

The sun was just starting to set when Kapinski left the Adams-Morgan storefront, banging behind him the door with the painted emblem, "PEACE—BY ANY MEANS NECESSARY." Two hours of mollifying yet another peace-and-politics group that wanted to take over the Offensive. It was aggravating. Kapinski liked the slogan of the D.C. Committee Against Fascism and Repression, but he didn't like the committee, a malcontent group of boys from Queens College with Trotskyite wire-rim glasses and coordinated out-of-fashion politics. His father was more relevant to today's struggles, Kapinski thought, walking down 17th Street to the Mall, the strip that ran between the Lincoln Memorial and the Washington Monument.

Kapinski once knew a girl whose fantasy was that the Monument, an obelisk, would fall, raping the Memorial. But he also knew a young black guy from Georgia who came to help work on the 1963 March on Washington and who shared quarters with Kapinski in the guest house of some ritzy Georgetown couple who were strangely committed to the civil rights movement. The third night or so they were walking home, and the red lights at the top of the pristine white monument were lit, to ward off planes, and this kid, Edward Moreland, just kept staring at the monument, finally telling Kapinski, "I don't care what anybody sez. It looks like a big Klansman to me."

Moreland was a good kid who graduated from Talladega in 1965 and was dead in Vietnam just about eighteen months later. The war had to end. Black boys from Georgia didn't get much of a chance, even when they did go to college.

No matter what Moreland believed, Kapinski thought, these are our monuments. Kapinski saw Washington as a vast battlefield, with hawk villages falling, one by one. The National Press Club building was under siege—more and more reporters questioning the war, the U.S. involvement. Tiny revolutionary cadres were infiltrating the Hill, and every time a senator or a congressman hired a young staffer, and that staffer was against the war, another beachhead. The Lincoln Memorial was once captured when King announced his dream and everybody, if only for that moment, shared it.

Young couples and old ones too were strolling down the Mall, headed for the Watergate bandstand and the outdoor concert, or maybe nowhere. Kapinski thought that heading nowhere was a great luxury. Only better, maybe, was heading home for the weekend, even if home was one thousand miles away. That meant you had a good car or, even more likely, the plane fare. Kapinski, Sr., was not poor, or cheap, but he would never understand leaving your job, your commitment, to come home. "To do what?" he asked his son the first time the question came up, several years ago. "To perhaps go to the country club? Your mother and I love you. We will come next week to Selma and visit you. It will be good. Perhaps we could do a little door knocking, a little voter registration, while we are there."

Kapinski sat on the steps of the Lincoln Memorial, waiting, loving the luxury of ten or even twenty minutes without a plan. The sun was setting behind him, he was as distracted as he could permit himself to be, relaxed enough to seem startled when the long-haired Asian kid with the UCLA sweatshirt sat beside him and mumbled the opening line.

"I like sitting here at this time of day," the kid began.

"Only place that's better in the world..." Kapinski answered, leaving the phrase unfinished.

"Is Saigon at the end of winter, and..."

"We know that winter doesn't last forever."

Kapinski felt his eyes filling up as he finished. The two had never met, and yet, like star-crossed lovers in a Shakespeare play, the world and the fates had conspired to bring them together on this vast marble stage. Maybe it was his sense of melodrama, or maybe he just wanted, in later years, to be able to say that he met this "friend" at this patriotic shrine. Anyway, they were here together, and for a few minutes, neither spoke.

"You have any problem, at least any problem since Friday?"

"Nothing. The people at Berkeley were wonderful, and I came across country in a large mobile home. Now I know what America is fighting for."

Only his preciseness marked his English as foreign, but Kapinski knew that was why he had been chosen for this special mission. He had spent all his growing-up years surrounded by Americans, the kitchen in the back of his family's restaurant churning out not just native specialties or the frenchified leftovers from colonial days, but also the cuisine of America, of Kapinski's country.

"So would you please tell me, as they say, 'where it's at'?" he asked Kapinski.

"Everything on my part is moving along on schedule,

although a couple times I thought this whole thing was going to fall apart. There will be a congressman. I think. That would be great for us—and one helluva surprise for him. The few people you know in this town, or who know of you, are not near the platform. I've finagled to 'disassociate' them from the march. My more important question is, how do you feel?"

"I feel strong. I feel that this is something I have to do, and that it is an honor that I have been chosen to do it. As we say in rock 'n' roll, 'Don't think twice—it's all right.' "

"Are you okay here?"

"Yes, but I am not to tell you who is keeping me. Then there is no chance that you could be tricked or pressured into telling my whereabouts."

"Okay. I don't get this extra layer of mystery. But okay. I'll call you at the pay phone every day, at six. Is that right?"

"You got it, babe."

"Please try to keep the groovy phraseology to a minimum on the big day."

His friend laughed, the first time Kapinski had seen or sensed any emotion. Troi Van Dong put his hand on Kapinski's shoulder in a sign of affection. And that let the boy from Skokie see that the boy from Saigon had no nails on the end of any of his fingers.

Annie O'Connor loved the phone. It kept people both near and far. It kept one from being alone, from being single, from being a solo act. That was near. But far was the quality harder to perceive. No one really got to know you on the phone. Phone talking was like being in a play, but the only audience was you. Sure, the person at the other end thought you were talking to him or her, but you were talking to yourself, sorting out the pieces of your life as the scholarship girls at college did, selecting what mail slot would get the invitation to the sorority and which would get the letter from home.

The mailroom girls were odd ducks who wore deep

brown stockings and would make any boyfriend they managed to get use condoms and never screw when they had their periods. Of course, Annie thought, footnoting her own commentary, she had never screwed with her period, either. That would be liberating, like the few women who were saying, "Off our backs," and wanting part of the action. But this analysis was digression from the phone analysis and phone analysis was merely digression of the first order—putting off calling her mother.

The phone, an ally on all other calls, became a weapon against her when dealing with Jennie. Mary Jane O'Connor knew every nuance of conversation. "Every little movement has a meaning all its own," Annie hummed to herself. Even that song was a point for Jennie, some "cultural clutter." That was her mother's phrase, but Jennie could call it whatever she liked, since she had invented it, force-feeding it into an innocent child from an early age. When the girls at college said how thrilling it was that *Casablanca* was at the Brattle Theater in Cambridge and they should all go up and see it, Annie was able not only to say she'd seen it, but also to recite whole scenes from memory.

Credit it to the fact that Jennie never slept. Oh, a couple of hours most nights. But not like regular people. The rest of the family, her father and three older brothers, had given up on Jennie's nocturnal habits long ago. Annie, as the youngest child, had a cocker spaniel eagerness to please, and fetched up for her mother the one attribute necessary for admission to Jennie's secret society and special friendship—she stayed up with her. And what wonders, indeed, opened up, as Channel 10, night after night, played the "Syncopated Clock," and George Sanders and Ronald Colman and Edward Arnold were there, in the living room, as Annie's feet touched her mother's under the blue-and-white afghan Jennie had won at the Medical Mission Sisters luncheon and card party.

Years later, in late nights with college roommates and in

the South, someone would always say how politics got formed by a professor, by a book, by JFK, by rebelling against JFK. And Annie would want to say that her politics were formed by the movies—by *Back Street* (so unfair that missing the boat should corrupt Irene Dunne's life) and *Tale of Two Cities*, with the true poignancy of sacrifice. Right was right, and wrong was wrong, and if everyone else had signed on to save the world because they believed the fifth-grade civics book, Annie figured she had been just too tired to read it.

When she was older, like her mother, would she have the same coloring process on her memories, like the MGM musicals in which the teeth were too white and the lips too red? When she had a real past, would everyone be beautiful, all memories tinted, spotlighted with special effects, the days moving by like ordered sheets of the calendar? Perhaps her past would become like her mother's, movieized, all predictable and positive, and even the tragedies, like when Beth died and Kate Hepburn had to go on and marry the professor, turning out just perfectly. Jennie loved happy endings, perfect endings. When Bambi's mother died, it was Jennie who explained to Annie, who then told the entire third-grade class, that of course the mother didn't die. It was a movie. Walt Disney had simply hired a deer to play the mother's part.

"You are avoiding calling her, you know," said Annie out loud, looking into the frosty window that separated her office from the Pit. "Yes, I know," she answered herself, and quickly opened the door. Jennie might have managed to make her who she was today, but that was no reason that she had to call her mother and once again go through the personal inquisition on what a mess she was making out of her life and how every girl she went to high school with was now married, with a perfect happy ending.

Joe Pisano knew a good bar, like one in the movies, Annie thought. Joe did everything to show that he knew stuff, dressing in Brooks Brothers and always having lots of fives and singles so if you had to borrow money, it was there.

Everyone was allowed one particular hate in life, she was telling Joe over her third drink, and hers was General Westmoreland.

"'We are winning it slowly but steadily.' That's what the lying bastard said. Yeah, we win if we pave the whole damn country over and make a parking lot. Or we lose and these guys in black pajamas make fools out of the U.S. Only a lot of dead soldiers won't be able to laugh."

"That's what I like about you, Annie. Always a good time." Joe called the bartender over and ordered two more Scotches, Johnnie Walker Red for him and Dewar's for her. Both were products of Catholic private schools, so both could drink Scotch for several hours as well as differentiate between an Elizabethan and an Italian sonnet, a mark of learning that they had discovered in each other in Selma several years back.

"It's not a good time at my shop this afternoon," she said. "Only the proles are left. Burnett is gone on one of his mysterious errands, probably up to the Hill to shore up a faltering voice. Kapinski is playing with the other rads, a bad trip that I don't want to handle. The Young Socialist League twerp who is supposed to do the marshals has spent the entire day trying to convert the kids in the mimeo room to his way of thinking. And then we have these damn druids who have camped in."

"Damn what?"

"Druids. You know, like Stonehenge. We had them once before, early in the summer. They're from Berkeley, and they are spending the summer on the East Coast trying to bring their message. Only trouble is they are so tripped out that I sure can't understand what kind of god they are selling. So they do a prayer meeting action in the hall. Here it is the hottest day of the month, and they are in these massive woolen capes, like nuns, only they are pagans. Think about it. We've now got pagans for peace."

"So who is watching the shop?"

"You won't believe this, but Marisa Pignelli—you know, the wife of the good reverend? She's been there all day with this kid from the South. Seems like he dropped out of the Citadel and now is thinking of going to Canada or burning himself up or something. The two of them are having a great time stuffing envelopes. I wish I could be happy stuffing envelopes. I always want to decide what goes in them and who writes it and how they should be stuffed."

"Speaking of stuffed, how's Burnett? Where do you think he's off to, anyway? A little secret liaison or what?"

"What bugs you about Burnett, Joe? You and Kapinski. I think you're both jealous. A little too much natural tweed when placed against you, a Newark boy? Look, he's pulled together this march, and we might be able to pull it off. Sometimes he's on his own trip, got his own drummer. But who cares since he cares?"

"You care, Annie. And that's great. But I'm not so sure it's contagious."

"Wrong. Look at this mimeo room kid. Jefferson Talbot. Just about as all-American as you can get. He went to the Citadel, like his good father and grandfather before him, and he was supposed to spend a couple more years learning how to kill people and then go do it for a living. Only trouble is, during summer school, some smart-ass graduate officer showed up on campus with actual footage, right from the Army of the Republic of Vietnam. And while all these guys are sitting around the rumpus room, screaming about killing gooks, this one kid sees the babies getting napalmed and women getting bayoneted. And then this joker, some major or something, tells the students that, sure, the Saigon government is corrupt, but who cares? It's a good little war, a good chance to fight, a great chance for promotions, and a lot of gooks for target practice. And when they get over to Saigon, there's going to be a lot of slanty-eyed poontang waiting for all of them. So Jefferson Talbot goes back to his dorm and packs and he's read about the Offensive so he comes here and now he's living on somebody's couch. First time the guy hasn't looked glazed over was when he met Marisa this afternoon. She's more naïve than he is, so he's turned into a real southern gentleman, showing her the ways of the world—how to take a stencil off the Gestetner, how to collate, how to make coffee."

"Why is Tyler letting her out of his sight? Usually he's got her bound to him with chains."

"Well, maybe I shouldn't be saying this, but the reverend has a real mess on his hands. Bitsy tells me that the rev's well-intentioned, liberal church has invested zillions in Manhattan apartment buildings so decrepit that the rats have moved out. And the ladies who live in the buildings got themselves organized into a tenants' committee, and they are going to raise hell with the reverend."

"Annie, are you telling me this on or off the record?"

"Ah, I knew this question would come up." Annie started rustling around in the Indian cloth bag that she thought passed for a purse, searching for matches or maybe cigarettes, anything to delay the decision.

"As a staff member of the Offensive, I really should protect the rev, but as a thinking, breathing human being, I think the creep should get tacked to the wall. I don't know what the hell he's done to Marisa, but there is something terribly scared and sad about her, and he's done nothing but try to screw me over since I started with the march. So Joe, throwing aside all caution and knowing I'm going to have to deal with the firestorm, I'm telling you that you can print it—but of course, not for attribution."

Joe sprinted for the back and the pay phones. Annie watched him, thinking he was just like every other man. You give them what they want. They take it and run away.

# THURSDAY,
# August 31, 1967

Tyler screamed at the maid, and she ran from the bedroom. The night before, the stupid bitch had left the heavy curtains not quite closed, and he was awakened by a slit of light. A slit of light just in time to see that the slut of night had not returned.

At midnight he had called the desk and demanded that he not be disturbed—no calls, no messages slipped under his door, no visitors. The evening had been brutal, with first Stevenson and then three other members of the vestry committee calling and complaining. The ninnies. They had wanted the income from the buildings. They had come up with the idea of the church investing in them. They had complained that his prophetic preaching only attracted a young crowd who came in their bright, hip clothes and merely smiled as the plate was passed.

Tyler stuffed the fat down pillows under his head. A night of tossing had left them wrinkled, and they in turn had left their lines on his fair skin. He was uncomfortable and sat up on the edge of the four-poster bed and stared at the mirror, all gilt and ornate beauty above a marvelous bow-front commode. His stocky body, his broad face, his now no longer prematurely graying hair, all looked fuzzy in the reflection. He had asked specifically for this suite for Marisa. The carved posts on the bed, the mirrors, could have provided so much pleasure—if the little slut hadn't run away.

She was like all women, just as his father had told him. That great light of modern American ministry, another lionlike figure with an even greater growl, had ministered to the same church that was now Tyler's. Only, so many of the more pristine and prestigious names had now drifted out of the city, while the filthy flotsam washed up on his marble steps. His father would have done something, Tyler thought, turning on the TV as he headed to the bathroom. His father would have known how to curb these animals who daily made his life hell, these pagans who crashed through life with their drugs and their music. His father knew the difference between good and evil, understood the base natures of man and woman, recognized the serpent of physical desire.

The Negroes in the South—what a difference. Gray-haired grandmothers ambling their way to church, with their grandchildren tagging after them. So grateful, so respectful. Respect was due leaders. And if it was not given freely, it had to be demanded.

The reverie was broken when the woman on the *Today* show starting talking about the Offensive Against the War. He couldn't believe it, they were going to have some march spokesman on network TV, and he had been told nothing about it. And there was Mulligan, in NBC's Washington studio, announcing that he would be joining the others who were speaking out against the war.

"You little prick!" Tyler screamed at Mulligan's face on the screen. "You were supposed to wait until we all could announce it with you." It was that O'Connor bitch. Like the rest of the Irish, she just didn't know her place. Now that they had Grace Kelly and the Kennedy family, there was no holding them back.

The screen changed, and there were tens—no, hundreds—of Negroes walking, singing, holding signs. For a moment Tyler thought that some new civil rights strategy had broken out, but that illusion lasted only a moment.

"It's my church!" he screamed, the shout ricocheting off the brocade curtains. "You are desecrating my church."

The picket signs were brutal: "Let Your Tenants Go," "Sow Love, Not Disease," "Remember Jesus Said Love the

Little Children." The reporter was interviewing a Health Department official who kept stressing the number of violations, "and, in this, church-held property."

"This can be handled," Tyler said out loud. "I can handle this. These are not the worthy poor. These are welfare mothers and their pimps. I can tell people that."

The camera zoomed in on a large toy rat, a photograph stuck on the rat's head, a photograph of the Reverend Paul Tyler. He didn't listen to what the woman carrying the rat said. He didn't care. He just put his bare foot through the television screen in his $105-a-day suite.

The regulars who picketed the White House were a hearty bunch. Most of them carried signs protesting the war, but two older women today were holding large and graphic photos of napalmed babies, and three others held placards announcing, "There's blood on those grapes."

Several of the antiwar leafleteers recognized Jefferson and waved him over. But he shook his head no and, taking Marisa's hand, led her on to the tourist bus. He made her feel better, even when she made a mistake, like trying to pay the two-dollar fee with a check.

"My treat!" he announced. He looked so cute, Marisa thought, in his short-sleeved plaid shirt. Even though it was hot, several of the boys in the office dressed in fatigues all the time, shirts and pants from army surplus, or else in jeans and wrinkled denim workshirts.

But Jefferson dressed, or at least he dressed in the two days she'd known him, in neatly pressed clothes, his reddish blond hair only slightly longer than military length. Marisa thought sideburns and mustaches wonderful, but Annie had explained that, for the march, both hair and rhetoric would be cut short.

Annie was so nice, so generous, this morning, lending Marisa a pair of cotton culottes and a blouse, "and please take care of them, since it is my one 'date outfit' that I keep if anyone actually asks me out." No one had asked her about Paul and the fight. The office, Annie had said, was a "sanctuary," and she was Marisa's friend, giving her the "date" clothes.

A date. Maybe this is a date. Crazy, no, a married woman on a date without her husband? This is perhaps an assignation, a rendezvous. But she and Jefferson were not in a dark bistro, but on the "See Washington Top to Bottom" double-decker tour bus, Marisa pressing her nose against the window to wave at the leafleteers.

"Maybe we should not be playing the truants," she half asked Jefferson. "Maybe we should be in the office making more leaflets about the march and the war."

"No," he said slowly, not looking up from the brochure they had gotten when he'd paid the fare. "It's just three hours. And there are things I want to see. The Supreme Court, the Capitol, the FBI."

"But Jefferson, if you are so angry at the government, why do you want to see the government?" Marisa asked, surprised at feeling his pants against her bare knee. "You should turn your back to them, ignore them."

"Marisa, I don't hate my country. I love my country. I don't understand why we're supporting a bunch of killers and crooks. So I thought if I could have a closer look-see, then maybe I would understand it better."

"I am pleased you asked me to accompany you. I am excited for knowing so much about all of this, too."

The morning got served up in tasty little pieces, like a breakfast spread at a resort hotel. Out of the air-conditioned bus and up the steps of the Capitol, stand in the Rotunda, hear the guide speak, then back on the bus and to the Supreme Court. All around her everyone looked so American, like Jefferson, really. All fresh and looking like magazine ads for refrigerators. Not fashionable, not stylish, but proud and feeling good that this was the building of their Congress.

The FBI part of the tour did not include going inside, just driving past the Department of Justice building. Somewhere within the gray stone walls was the fiefdom of the granite J. Edgar Hoover, and Jefferson was disappointed that the tour passed it by, telling Marisa that the target range and the gangster stuff was supposed to be terrific. But Marisa pointed out that now they could have lunch, and it would be her treat.

They went to the Jockey Club, the dining room in the Fairfax Hotel, where the maître d' gave Jefferson a jacket and Marisa simply pulled the scarf from around her hair and tied it around her neck in a single, glamorous move. Jefferson had only seen one woman do anything like that with a scarf, and that was Audrey Hepburn in *Breakfast at Tiffany's,* which he saw when he was eleven years old and got his first hard-on.

The maître d' came by the table and, in rapid-fire Italian, asked Marisa about her father and why she was in Washington and how was her husband. Marisa was astounded how easy it was: she told Piero that her husband was busy, and this was a nice young man who was the son of an old family friend of Paul's, and they had promised to take him to lunch and now it fell to her to make the party. And of course, Piero, don't give us a check at the table because it might make him uncomfortable. And, switching into English, "Maybe you would select something which could be going along with the lunch. And, Jefferson, do you mind if I am making the order. Please?"

Her "date" nodded. Marisa felt the little buzz of happiness long before the wine came. She had taken the morning and had had a wonderful time. She had fooled both Piero and this adorable young man sitting beside her. Paul was not coming here and finding her ("I hate the goddamn place and the fawning waiters," he had announced on their last visit), and she was running the show.

"Do they all know you here?"

"Piero does. He's been knowing my father, who stays with

this hotel. That's how it is most places. They are knowing my father...or my husband. My father would like to be knowing you, Jefferson. He would."

"How about your husband? I don't think your husband would like me."

"That's silly. He would. You are so very nice and so dedicated against the war."

"And having such a nice time with his wife. Marisa, why aren't you with your husband? I know he's here in Washington, and I know you spent last night at Annie O'Connor's."

When she had removed the scarf the pins held the side pieces of her hair away from her face, and, whether from nervousness or style, Marisa found herself loosening the clips. Her hair drifted past her cheeks as she shook her head.

"We must not talk about Paul. I am not sure what is happening, but our marriage is not really such a marriage after all, and I am trying just to be having this day as enjoyable."

Slowly they ate. She pulled a scallop through the white sauce, and carefully spinning the fork so as to avoid dripping, she held the bite out to Jefferson. He held her hand so as to steady the fork, but then refused to give it up, and so they sat for the rest of the meal, talking little, drinking a little more, smiling a lot. Marisa was forced to use her fork American style in her right hand, and Jefferson clumsily made do with his left, their other hands wrapped tightly together under the white linen tablecloth.

Some days are gifts, tied with ribbon, protected with tissue, smelling of good stores and old leather and rubbed polish. This day had layers and layers of wrapping, each prettier, more intricate, hand-painted Florentine, and it was Marisa who took off the final piece, simply by announcing, at three o'clock, when they left the restaurant and were standing in the hotel lobby that she was tired and she was going upstairs for a nap.

"How will you do that? You haven't any money."

"Jefferson, I have my father's name. He is known here. And I found out today that's just all I require. Now I asked Piero to open a room for me, and, when you were in the bathroom, he brought to me the key, and we must go now, immediately, or I will cry in the lobby."

"But, Marisa, don't you—"

"No, Marisa don't anything. Marisa's going upstairs, where it is very cool and the sheets are cool, and you should take a nap, too. We Italians know about these things."

Jefferson nodded and followed her into the elevator, down the hall, to the door of the room, inside and to the edge of the bed, where she pulled off Annie's date clothes. She watched Jefferson, his body so pale it was translucent. Like the angels in paintings of the Annunciation, Marisa thought as he took off his shirt and then his trousers, taking the time to find the creases and hang them over the back of the chair. His back and his chest were hairless, baby smooth, but his legs were covered with thick yellow hair, which grew in a great clump around his cock.

"Oh, my God, Jefferson. What is that? But it is gigantic." Like a child caught by surprise, she gasped, the surprise taking away her breath.

"Marisa, don't laugh at me, or it won't be there anymore."

But she did, the nervous excited burst from a bride.

Jefferson Talbot suddenly knew that all was not what it seemed. The product of four generations of Citadel-trained men, he prepared to do his duty. He touched, gingerly, softly, Marisa's great breasts still bound to her chest. He ran his finger along the line, near the top of her bra, where the summer tan met her winter white. But even his gentleness brought a tremor to her body—not one of excitement, but of fear.

"We don't have to do this, you know. We can just get dressed and take a nap or go for a walk or anything. We can stop right now." Jefferson had used that line maybe half a dozen times in his life, putting that little wedge against a girl's self-control, that nudge against her pride. It was like saying, Well, honey, it's not that I'm so hot, so turned on by you.

But before Marisa could answer, he retreated.

"No, that's not true. I don't want you to stop, and I don't want to stop. I want to touch you and do a lot of wonderful things to you and with you."

"I do not like my body, and I am feeling also ashamed. It is too much."

"Aw, Marisa, it's never too much. It's wonderful, and you are wonderful," Jefferson announced, surprised at his great good fortune. This woman was beautiful and he worshiped her and the wine ran down his body, which he pushed against hers.

"Let's dance," he said. "Let's just dance."

"You are crazy, Jefferson. I am here with almost no clothes...."

"No, you are here with no clothes. You must take off the rest of your clothes and then we will dance. Let me do it," he said, unhooking her bra, and, in a motion practiced in dozens of backseats, pulling down her panties with one gliding swoop.

"Woke up, got out of bed..." he began, doing the slow, lazy dance steps that southern boys and girls did. Marisa looked at him as if he were crazy, and then she began to dance, her naked body joyful in the afternoon light, her ebony hair bouncing up and down to its own rhythm. He pushed his face into her hair, his hands between her legs, face on her breasts. Since he was fourteen years old, Jefferson Talbot had fooled around, gotten pussy, been laid, and had his ashes hauled.

But this time Jefferson Talbot, with southern grace and military precision, this time he made love. He followed a plan that was designed to keep her in a high state of torment, letting her think that he had tired of one part of her body, then suddenly rediscovering it, going back with new vigor, new determination. His plan led him to what in his adolescent mind he had thought of as the "buried treasure." And it was only when he reached the treasure that he found the biggest surprise was his, when he realized he was the first to follow the map to Marisa Pignelli's secret place.

Even Kapinski seemed happy. He balanced his skinny ass on a chair that was missing one leg, leaning half of himself and all of the chair against the one unused desk in the crowded room. The kids working the mimeo had the Doors playing, and Kapinski hummed. He could never remember any words to any song, except "Moonlight in Vermont," which his mother had taught him and which had no rhyme.

Around Kapinski, the staff and volunteers did the piece-work that would put together the march. It was a factory, Kapinski thought, churning out social change, turning out the revolution. Almost all of these kids, a couple like Burnett excepted, were just a generation or two away from the sweat-shops. That's the American way. One generation in the factories, the next one in the offices, and the third one anxious to get done with college so they could begin tearing down the whole system that got them there in the first place. Of course in this factory of revolution, he, Kapinski, was a boss, he added to himself, his smile broadening, his ass giving a little happy wiggle that almost sent him sprawling.

"Don't smile, Kapinski," Burnett warned. "It makes me uptight. What happens if the professional worrier gets relaxed?"

"Never relaxed. But I gotta tell you that the Mulligan production is enough to make me believe in the tooth fairy. Just put your broken beliefs under your pillow, little man, and the next morning there is a full-blooded, all-American congress-man to carry out your commands. I love it. It's quite a trip."

"One very short trip if everyone is not conscious of what they say before Mulligan gets to the platform. Now he's coming by the office today to meet the crew. If there is one picture of Mao, no personal offense, but if there is one piece of graffiti or stuck-up posters or anything that could be interpreted as radical, you can kiss Mulligan good-bye."

"No problem. Miss O'Connor, in her dual role as mother superior and thought police, went on a sweep of the entire office this morning, removing any telltale Marxist material from the bulletin boards. She is relentless. Even made a couple of younger kids with really long hair pull it back into pony-tails, so they look totally all-American."

"I have a more serious problem, really, with Bitsy."

"Look, in more ways than one, I've shot my wad."

"No, no. You did it. But now there's a bigger hassle. It's Tyler. She wants him off the steering committee."

"That makes it unanimous. The guy's a prick."

"He's our prick. He's our one religious member, and as much as he makes my skin crawl, he can make a crowd of athiests feel that they've got God on their side."

Kapinski wiggled on his unsteady perch, turning his attention from Burnett to the chair and back to Burnett again. It was one of his most annoying and yet most effective conversational habits—sitting in an unconventional way, playing with a briefcase that would not snap, fiddling with his watch. Kapinski forced the other person in a conversation to make what they were saying so interesting that he, Kapinski, would have to pay attention.

"If Bitsy says he's out, then he's out. And anyway, Tyler should be out. He's running a goddamn plantation up there on the streets of Manhattan. He's got these poor black folk living in slums and handing their welfare checks over to him."

"Just be careful. His wife is working around here some-where, and I don't want this more messed up than it is already."

"He is a beauty. All he wanted to do in the South was hold news conferences or get into this damn touchie-feelie bullshit."

Burnett was getting impatient with the conversation. The last thing he needed was to have Kapinski start to fight through years-old battles from the South and civil rights. Tyler was an ass, a pompous ass. And if he wanted to, Burnett could blast him right out of the Movement waters forever. But that's not what he wanted right now.

Having Tyler's church explode was the one thing he and T. R. hadn't imagined in their dozens of "might happen" scenarios. And having Kapinski go after Tyler right now, rather than letting the blacks do him in, could be dangerous.

"I'm a lot more concerned about another member of our happy little team." Burnett was casual as he laid out his ploy.

"Whadda you mean?"

"Annie. Tyler wasn't all bullshit when he questioned her involvement with Pisano the other night. It's too close. Girls just can't keep it separated. Once they sleep with you, they just want to tell you everything. Every little thing. Every other guy they've slept with. Every time they've come. They get laid and they want to lay it all out. Annie's no different. If she's sleeping with Pisano—and if she's not, then I'm crazy—then whatever we talk about, whatever we decide, will be talked about in bed."

"So what if Annie tells Pisano something about the Offensive, what the hell can she tell him that won't be known by everybody in a day or two? You can't be this hard on people. I'm supposed to be the ideological idiot, not you." Kapinski stood up, leaving his chair swaying on its three legs. Another Kapinski tactic: Make a good argument, then end the conversation before the other guy can take his shot.

In her office, with a full ashtray of Camel butts, the object of Burnett's concern was sorting through the same problem, furious at herself for letting "some boy" so invade her head. All of her friends, all her life, had been boys. Her mother believed, as did Annie, that a woman could trust another woman—but only if one of them was truly ugly.

Even at school Annie became a buddy to any man she thought really sexy. When somebody came along—and it happened a few times, someone who was really beautiful, who could talk or just sit there and just break your soul—those guys got assigned immediately to be good friends. There would be long "coffee dates" or an occasional lunch at school; Annie would probe, offer advice, get to know the intimacies of whatever girl they were dating, or had dated, or wanted to date again. Always play it safe. Always play it with a net.

Pisano had sneaked up on her. He was funny-looking, really. He seemed to have picked the worse traits of his Italian heritage: the large Roman nose of his father and the pale, wintry coloring of his Venetian mother. Pisano's mother really was Italian, a war bride.

"My father kept her barefoot and pregnant—until a stack of boxes with Campbell's soup cans fell on him, crushing his leg, breaking his arm. Then Mama suddenly had to step in and make sure his two brothers didn't run off with the whole grocery store. By the time he was on his feet, she had become 'strictly American.' Sure, we had pasta and meatballs on Saturday. My mother made her own gravy. That's sauce to you. But the checking account she'd opened when he was in traction just never got closed. And by the time I wanted to go to the Jesuit high school in Union City, my father's objections meant nothing. Mama had the cash squirreled away. And for my three brothers, too. There are only four of us, since a neighbor got hold of her while Papa was laid up and told her about a priest who would give you absolution even if you were using birth control. So that was that."

That was that, Annie thought to herself. For days she had played and replayed every conversation of any depth she'd had with Pisano, like a moody teenager listening to some 45 of Frankie Valli, over and over. Pisano had just crept up on her, just like the goddamn Viet Cong, he had infiltrated before she knew what he was doing.

How could she be this dippy over a guy who called his cock "Mr. Penis"? She only knew about "Mr. Penis" because two years ago she and Pisano had gotten blasted together after he covered this fancy fund-raiser at a Central Park apartment. He took her to the Algonquin for a drink. For tequila, it turned out. Annie loved the measured drinking of it—licking the salt off her hand, belting down the burning liquor, then biting into the lime. Smoking, drinking, talking about stuff. A rhythmic time, with, of course, the topic getting around to sex.

Pisano had split with a girl from New York six months before and was supposed to see her for a late date that night. But as he and Annie got more and more loaded, he realized he was going to stand up his former honey. He talked more and more about the sex he might be having, finally announcing, "I don't feel badly that she rejected me. She was mixed up. Even if I was some kind of a shit, how could she turn down Mr. Penis?"

Annie had drunk a fair amount of tequila, so it took several minutes to fully comprehend that Pisano had actually had a name for it. The waiter had to come over and hit her on the back when she figured it out, she was laughing so hard.

How terrific. She could take Pisano home to Jennie and say, "Hi, Mom. I want you to meet Joe Pisano and his great friend, Mr. Penis." It really was adorable. He really was a sweetie.

"If you want to blow your whole head open, just come with me right now," Mr. Sweetie announced, bolting into her office. Caught in her daydream, Annie felt embarrassed, as though Pisano had caught her with her hands in her pants. But he seemed to notice nothing, waving his hand at her as if he were summoning a cab and repeating, "Just come on. Just come on."

"Just hold on. What the hell could be so important that

you're like this?" Annie was scooping the stuff from the top of her desk to her green bookbag as she spoke: cigarettes, lighter, yellow legal pad, green phone book, sunglasses, house keys.

She was pissed. This is what happened when you started fantasizing about guys. They came in and just took over. The only thing that required this kind of urgency was the march, and she'd be damned if Pisano knew something about the march that she didn't.

Pisano pushed past Burnett, who covered the mouthpiece of his phone to say hello and got a curt nod back. Annie shrugged and followed Pisano out the door, catching up with him at the elevator. Their progress past the dozen-plus people in the Pit would, no doubt, be a conversational topic for the next several hours.

"I really don't like this, Joe, I don't like you presuming on our friendship and just coming in and pulling me around. In fact, I am going back to work now and you can run off on your bullshit urgent thing."

"My bullshit urgent thing is, believe me, your bullshit urgent thing. Just try to play along and not take control for once in your life and you might find out something."

Annie stood there quietly by the elevator, her face quickly turning the color of her strawberry hair. She and Pisano had certainly had their arguments, but this was a fight, a real fight.

Maybe she should hit him, wallop the son of a bitch over the head. Great headline: PEACE MARCH STAFFER ASSAULTS REPORTER.

"Look, if I'm going to let you pull me out of the office, make us the cause célèbre for the next several days and almost make me cry, then I at least deserve to know what the hell is happening."

The elevator door opened.

"Oh, honey," the owner of Mr. Penis announced, "cry? I would never make you cry. Never. That's a promise."

■     ■     ■

The National Press Building was not unknown turf to Annie. Just in the lobby she'd run into two reporters who swore they had been trying to reach her for days.

No, she wasn't sure what Tyler was going to do about his church. Yes, it was brave of Mulligan to speak out, but she didn't have any idea what he was going to say at the march, nor did she have an advance text. No, she hadn't heard what had happened that day in Saigon, so she wasn't going to say anything until she'd read the wires. Yes, they were going to build a camera platform to the right of the podium, and, yes, the television boys were not going to get all the good spaces.

"How do these kinds of reporters wind up in Washington?" she asked almost rhetorically as she and Pisano got out of the elevator.

"Washington was made for 'those kinds,' honey," Pisano began, with Annie almost losing the rest of the sentence after the "honey" hit her. "Just like they ask you to explain things, they ask the government flacks, only they ask them a lot more questions and they give them a lot more space. Now, the federal government has been around just a little bit longer than the Offensive, or even the Movement, so 'those kinds of reporters' have had time to get dependent on what the government employees tell them. There are very few real reporters in this town. A guy over at the AP named Seymour Hersh started a whole shitload of trouble when he asked real questions at the Pentagon. This guy we're going to see, whom you know about from the South, this guy is a real reporter."

As he spoke, Pisano pushed open the door marked World News International and asked for Harold Sams at the reception desk. When Sams came out a few minutes later, Annie wondered if D.C. hadn't turned Sams into another "that kind" of reporter. He wore the D.C. summer costume of seersucker striped suit and a flimsy white shirt, his spotted tie knotted halfway to his neck.

"Let's get out of here. Go for a drink," Sams announced,

then, picking up on Annie's somewhat critical look, added, "It's three o'clock to you, but it's eight at night to me. I've been working since five A.M."

Sams said no to the bar across the street, and the one upstairs at the Press Club was closed to women. So they walked a couple of blocks to a place called the Paradise Pool. If Annie hadn't been sweating so much, she could have found the walk almost interesting, with Pisano and his buddy talking newspaper gossip.

The red leatherette booths were torn, but the air-conditioning worked and the bar was surprisingly crowded for this time of the afternoon, or maybe not so surprisingly, considering the neighborhood. Pisano ordered a beer while Sams asked for "7 and 7" and Annie made do with a Coke, ordering it with the unsolicited announcement to the waitress that drinking in the afternoon made her sleepy. Pisano stared at the waitress's apron, and Sams just shrugged.

Then Sams took a large manila envelope from his jacket pocket and unfolded it carefully, smoothing it out on the chipped top of the table. Nobody talked, with Pisano and Annie staring at the envelope as if it were the most interesting thing they'd ever seen.

"Did you tell her anything about what I have?" Sams asked Pisano, who shook his head no.

Sams then carefully opened the envelope and slid out a pile of newspaper clips, a few photographs, and a bunch of wire copy. Pisano started to talk.

"Harold Sams, you might remember, Annie, was sent South by his wire service in 1963 to write about collusion between the Klan and various local law enforcement types. Harold's series should have gotten him a Pulitzer, but JFK's assassination knocked him and everybody else out of the box."

For once in her life Annie sat there, dumbly, nodding her head. Sure, she knew the story about Sams, a great tenacious reporter, a guy with a killer instinct and a great sense of drama in his writing.

"So there is Harold, in 1964, with all this knowledge about the South, and he's looking for something to write about. Not about the Mississippi Freedom Democratic party. Not about the separatist move within the Students Non-Violent Coordinating Committee. Not about the SCLC. No, Harold Sams decides to write about how certain dramas in the South are written by people who never step on the stage. He wrote his story, but his editors were the only people who got to read it."

Sams began to nod and pulled a photograph from his shabby pile of stuff.

"Now let me tell you, Annie, that Harold here is currently covering the Department of Agriculture for World News Service. He got that job only because the top brass at WNI would have looked crazy to sack a Pulitzer Prize nominee who never had to backtrack on a story."

Sams interrupted Pisano, rapping his knuckles on the table like an impatient parliamentarian. "And I am not going to have to backtrack on this one," he said, leaning across the table to make sure that Annie got his message. "I had to stay with the wires, even after they screwed me, because I needed to pay the rent. But two weeks ago I signed a contract for a book. Not a big contract, but one with an advance, and I've given my notice and I'm going to do the best story that I've ever come across. A little piece of which I'm going to tell you about today."

He pointed to the photograph of a man who looked vaguely familiar. "This, kiddies, is T. R. Simpson. The shot you are looking at was taken at JFK's funeral. You will notice how close he is standing to members of the cabinet. Simpson, though, is no ordinary appointee. He's a free-lance adviser, an ambassador without a portfolio. He's the calm voice that an unseasoned senator, or even a president, turns to when the waves get high. He's a very, very important man."

Sams motioned the waitress over for another round, and Annie took the chance to quickly switch from Coke to beer.

"My story keeping you awake?" Sams asked her with an ugly snorting noise. He had a mean, curt way about him, a man who had left civility and kindness somewhere in his past.

"So I'm trying to piece together, and this was in 1964 and I was writing about that year and some other years, I was trying to figure out just who was really making the decisions. I mean you had Bobby on the phone and you had Doar and you had Siegenthaler. But there were missing links in whatever story I picked up, whether it was on or off the record. And all of a sudden, in a casual chat here in D.C., right after Johnson's big win, there it was for the first time. I'm talking to a Kennedy type who can't find a place in the Johnson administration, and he says that for him, the choice is either to go with a law firm or to go to Simpson and have help finding what he called a 'more interesting job.' So like what? I asked him. It turns out that Simpson can arrange a 'transition grant' from one of the big foundations or see that he gets a one-term appointment at Harvard or Yale. Not bad, I tell him. So then he tells me that Simpson and he became old buddies because when he was a White House staffer, like a minor player, Simpson was in and out of the place all the time. Simpson is a really important guy, this kid is telling me, really important. And then, confidential like, he tells me that Simpson was the one who persuaded JFK not to send the marshals in right away in Mississippi. Simpson is big buddies with the southerners on the Senate Armed Services Committee, and he carried their brief to JFK—a little quid pro quo. At first it seemed crazy, but then I started to really look into it, to really try and figure out what Simpson had done."

Sams took a long swallow on his drink and shook his head, as if he couldn't believe what he knew to be true. He waited a second, either for the drink to take effect on him or his words to take effect on his two listeners, and then paged through his papers for a second picture. He held it but did not share it with Pisano and Annie.

"So I became interested in this guy T. R. Simpson. He never ran for office, but he picked up a lot of powerful positions and more powerful friends along the way. He had a couple of just-out-of-law-school jobs in the 1930s, when FDR brought William O. Douglas and some of the whiz kids down from Yale Law School. Only thing is, for Simpson, it was like coming home. His father was a big deal, but everybody says that Simpson did it on his own. Then, at the start of World War Two, he's picked to head up the Latin American division in State, where he's so goddamn clever and diplomatic that when they start having trouble with de Gaulle, they ship Simpson over as an envoy to the Free French. By the end of the war he's out of sight. Very OSS. One fellow even insisted that Simpson had done the on-ground reconnaissance for D-Day. And then he comes back to D.C. and he goes to work in his father's law firm, and never, never does he ever do anything 'formally' with the government again."

Sams finished his paragraph, finished his drink, and sat there, staring ahead. Annie was ready to say something and, leaning across the table, had just started when Pisano jabbed her leg under the table.

"By the mid-1950s Simpson is everywhere—and nowhere. Every time there is a fingernail puller from some South American country—you know, the guy who is the 'liberal alternative' to the left-wing rebels—well, you can bet that Simpson or some young guy from his firm has General Dictator in tow. Taking him around the Hill, making sure he gets his picture taken with some important senator so that the *Post* has to run it. Hosting a little cocktail party at their fancy offices so that the general hangers-on can come by for a little snack and half a dozen drinks. All very classy, mind you. No broads or anything like that. Just Simpson selling his brand of democracy."

Annie was confused. What did this have to do with the Offensive?

Pisano took up the story, "I called Harold last week, just on a fluke, really, trying to beef up a story I was doing about how the civil rights leaders of yesterday were the peaceniks of today. We had a couple hurried conversations, but I didn't want to tell you anything until I was sure, really sure. So Harold and I met this morning, and Harold showed me what he's got in his hand."

Sams looked at the photograph he'd been holding. He was nursing his third drink, but the expression on his face was cold and sober.

It must have been a lot like the look that passed over Annie's face when Sams turned the picture over to her. There was Simpson, in what looked like a white hunter outfit. There were several guys who looked Mexican, so Annie figured that it was Central America or maybe the Philippines. Anyway, where it was wasn't important, because standing by Simpson, dressed as though he were heading across the Yale campus for an early autumn class, was Tom Burnett. He looked just like himself, with a short-sleeved shirt and a pair of khakis and a serious look on his face, the set-in-stone stare he would get when trying to figure out something important. One piece of his hair dangled in front of his left eye, and Annie could just imagine that the second the photograph had been snapped, Burnett would have taken the back of his hand and pushed it back, as he always did.

Pisano said something that Annie didn't quite catch, and then Sams was shaking his head.

"No, for me, the big story is Simpson," Sams said. "Simpson is one of the guys who keep advising this administration on how to handle the rest of the world—the Russkies, the Chinese, this war in Vietnam. So what was your guy Burnett, the antiwar leader, Mr. Anti-Establishment, doing palling around with a guy like Simpson? That's your story, Pisano. Now, I don't think you're going to get away with using Simpson's name in a story. Your paper doesn't have the balls. The editor won't get to the right dinner parties. But you can certainly build a case that Burnett just ain't what he seems. Shit, the group he was with in Santa what's-its-name was funded by a foundation that turned out to be a CIA front."

Annie waved to the waitress, then made a little merry-go-round motion with her hand, signaling another round. Pisano and Sams just kept on talking, like trains racing down a track.

Sams took a deep gulp of his new drink, hitting the ice cubes against his teeth so loudly that Annie felt the chill. Then he continued his story: "I spent months working on a real bell-ringer piece on Simpson and his influence in the South. And then, when I had it tied up, ready to run on the 'A' wire, Simpson moved in. He's got many friends in the news business, an impressive list of editors who want to stay on his side. They're hopeful that he'll do them a favor in the future or thankful that he's done something in the past, like get one of their reporters into a country where the borders were shut down or set up an interview with a particular banana republic *el presidente*. Simpson had friends at my shop. My editors got antsy. Called me back to Washington. Killed the piece on general bullshit grounds, but who cared, the piece was dead. I complained. Now I'm covering pig futures. Once I stopped feeling sorry for myself, I sat down and started on my book. It'll be a good read. T. R. Simpson is the best-connected man in this town. He has people working for him here and everywhere else. He is bound and determined not to let my story out. But a book is a harder thing to stop."

For one uneasy moment Pisano got the same feeling he'd had when he'd been assigned to the State House in New Jersey for a summer job. The State House was a magnet for crazies, at least a dozen of them waving their papers in the hallway every day, coming up to you, their breath stinking of garlic, flourishing their cause, their petition. People with lawsuits against the state, people who thought that a dump was poisoning their well, people who believed that someone was sending radio signals to control their minds. Sams had the same obsessive attention as the State House paper wavers, but maybe that particular craziness was what allowed Sams to stalk this prey so long, to risk his job, to almost kill off his professional future, to get this story.

"So why is Simpson so connected? What makes him so powerful?" Annie asked Sams.

"He's the Agency. He's a spook. He works for the CIA. And he's got a lot of little friends, like your buddy Tom Burnett, who help him get the job done."

Mulligan was glad Burnett called, really glad, even though he was ready to go to sleep after a long evening with his two younger staff members. There had been a little too much celebrating, toasting Mulligan's signing on to speak at the Offensive Against the War. But now, Burnett was coming by and would get a chance to see Mulligan's apartment, his home. Here, even more than on the Hill, he would see what Mulligan was, who he was, or at least who he was becoming.

Mulligan was proud of what he had made of himself, both his career and the family background he was filling in, piece by piece. In Washington, everyone wrote their own histories—a little exaggeration, a touch of false modesty, a mild interpretation all combined to paint a prettier picture. It was style, not substance, that he had learned as a scholarship boy at Milton. It was the secret paths to his own and others' hidden agendas that he had uncovered: the bringing of a hostess gift, the writing of a thank-you note. What Milton, and then Amherst, gave Mulligan were not just the credentials, but the secret passwords. He learned not to mimic, but to interpret. Nowhere was his annexation of another life-style more telling than in his apartment.

Here was his history as Mulligan was learning to tell it,

getting a slightly worn patina, like the front of his apartment building. The apartment had been a real find, up on Connecticut, a building with four floors, a large one-bedroom flat in the rear looking out over the zoo. He was trying to decide whether or not to use the word *flat* when talking about the apartment. Maybe it was a little too pretentious. But it did have a shabbily successful ring to it, like a good piece of family hand-me-down furniture.

His background, his scholarships, were too well known, and too appealing to the voters in the blue-collar part of the district, to lie about. But his life story was easy to enlarge and enrich, and that was where Aunt Nell came in. Who, of course, was real, if anyone bothered to check. His father's aunt, who died when Mark Mulligan was in the third grade, had lived her entire life in the same small Detroit house. Aunt Nell bounced into Mulligan's life quite by mistake, when he purchased his first piece of china from the Little Jewel Box near the Mayflower.

He'd been down interviewing for a Hill job, late in the spring of his second year at Amherst, and bought the floral cup and saucer on a whim. When he took it back to Amherst and put it on his desk, thrilled at the grace of it but making it okay by using it for paper clips, his suitemate actually gave him the idea. It was so natural, really, when Spencer admired it, asking whom it had "come from." Not where, but who. Like the Boston lady who, when asked where she bought her hats, replied, "My dear, we don't buy our hats. We have our hats." Of course Spencer couldn't image that someone would buy, not inherit, something old, so Mulligan, in a moment of pretentious panic, reacquainted himself with Aunt Nell. Once she was back in his life, she stayed there, becoming the source of the mahogany secretary in the corner of the room (doubling as a breakfront for a few really special pieces), the small Persian rug in front of the desk in his little den, even the almost matched set of Blue Willow that he used for his everyday dishes. "She really was a funny old thing," Mulligan would say when someone admired one of his possessions. "Quite amazing, really, to have had such taste and flair in that time."

Waiting for Burnett, he wondered what piece, what object, his old school friend would seize on to admire. He wished he'd gone ahead with the painting, that the walls had been done the planned hunter green. Then the leather couch—his one new acquisition—would really look comfortable, like the headmaster's study at school.

Mulligan had only been abroad once, on a trip arranged by his French teacher between his junior and senior years at Amherst. He had spent the whole two weeks wondering how to spend the $50 extra he had stuck in his back pocket (some fund from some dead old grad had paid for the trip itself). Finally, on the next-to-last day, he'd bought two prints, two good prints of Paris, which, reframed last year, hung over the couch. They were always a good conversation piece, because then Mulligan could say that he'd bought them in Paris "several years ago" and what a pity it was that with the pressure of congressional duties he just couldn't get back to Europe this year. He hoped Burnett wouldn't comment on the pictures, since he would remember the trip to France. It had almost ended their friendship. Burnett was set to go, too, and in fact had pushed Mulligan into applying for the travel grant. But then Burnett had heard about the Encampment for Citizenship, some Eleanor Roosevelt–inspired summer program on politics, and, with no warning to Mulligan, had dropped out of school and into changing the world. No, let him ask about the secretary or the rug, Mulligan wished, putting ice cubes into an old pewter flower pot that he used as an ice bucket, putting out two of the cut-glass tumblers he'd bought at a junky secondhand shop at 16th and T.

The pewter pot was yet another piece, another little layer of belonging, of having, of being. If his apartment, like the ones at Pompeii, was frozen suddenly in time, Mulligan would

have fooled even the cultural anthropologists. Here was someone who came from a family that might have fallen on hard
times but had been something, had known things and ac-
quired things. This was not the social residue of plastic tablecloths and meat-loaf dinners, the longed-for, worked-for TV
drowning out the petty squabbles at dinner. This was a fresh
fruit cup or a grapefruit with the segments already separated
from their casings, and lamb chops with mint jelly, and desserts that were never advertised on *I Love Lucy*.

So lost in his contemplation of his possessions was Mulligan that Burnett's banging on the door gave him a sudden
start and then a chill down his back. His Irish grandmother,
the real Aunt Nell's sister, would have said that the chill meant
someone had "walked over his grave," but Mulligan had aban-
doned such handed-down wisdom in his acquisition of a
different history.

Burnett looked tired. He was tanned from hours in the
sun walking the march route, but the summer color emphasized the beginning age lines around his eyes, and Mulligan,
looking for the boy he once knew, saw only the man he had
become.

"You look worn out," Mulligan said, walking over to the
improvised bar he'd set up on the secretary. "Let me get you
something to drink."

"I'm not tired, Mark. I'm beat to shit. I could use a vodka,
on the rocks."

Not gin, but vodka, Mulligan thought. Who drank vodka,
except in screwdrivers? But maybe Burnett's ahead of the
curve again.

"I just couldn't handle gin tonight," he said as Mulligan
poured the vodka for Burnett and then the same for himself.
"This latest explosion, with Tyler and his goddamn housing
problem . . . I've had to field more phone calls on it than on the
Offensive."

"But it's coming along, the Offensive is coming along, isn't it?" Mulligan asked. Sipping, he found the drink strangely tasteless.

Burnett sat directly in the center of the sofa, allowing Mulligan only the option of one of the two club chairs, both of which he'd redone in a washed-out tapestry. "This is really nice, Mark, really quite pleasant. You've really done well for yourself—here, and up on the Hill. You've got a big future, and we've got to be careful to do the right things to keep you moving along."

Mulligan heard the words, words he knew were correct, but somehow they put him a little off base. This was his house, his place, but Burnett, just by coming in the door and sitting down, had made himself in charge. Judging him, maybe, which was what Mulligan wanted, but judgment from a peer, from an equal. Mulligan tried to take another sip of his drink and realized that somehow he had emptied the glass. It was almost like not drinking at all, he thought, but suddenly he was light-headed. "Would you like another?" he asked Burnett, getting up to pour himself a refill. Burnett clinked his ice to show that his own glass was still almost full and shook his head no.

"I'm looking around here, and I'm really liking what I'm seeing, Mark. This is really a beautiful place. You really have great taste, a great style."

Afterward, when he replayed the conversation in his head, Mulligan would always wonder what would have happened if he had let the remark pass, had let Burnett spin out his conversation and follow the designated plan. But the vodka and the more potent brew of Burnett's approval rushed to his head, puffing him up, setting his thoughts and words slightly out of kilter.

"You keep praising me, telling me how wonderful I am. Be careful, Burnett, or I might think you're making a play for me."

Wrong. God, that was wrong. Mulligan would have given

anything to take the words back, edit and correct what he had said, as he could do with the speeches in the *Congressional Record*. But explanation would just make it worse, so Mulligan simply grinned and shrugged his shoulders, smiling at Burnett, looking at his old friend for sympathy, for understanding. "Faux pas. A little faux pas," he finally mumbled, and downed most of his second vodka in a single gulp.

"A false pass? You got it. That's your game, not mine. Although this week I have helped you make a false pass. Not like in sex, not my game. But I've left you out on the field, with the ball. And you've got nobody to throw it to. Nobody."

Mulligan had lost the conversation, lost it. Couldn't figure out for a damn where Burnett was going. He might be a little high, but it was Burnett, not he, who was now sounding strange.

"So listen. I saw you on the *Today* show. Terrific. Lots of coverage on the local TV news, and a minute each on NBC and CBS."

"Great, huh? That's what I thought. And even Kelly, who was nuts about my screwing up in the district, well, you can't argue with being on national television."

"And you're going to get that shot again, Mark. Right up there for the whole country to see you, on network TV, in a bigger way than you have ever believed you could."

"The speech. I know, the speech. I want to have the text by tomorrow afternoon, and maybe we can go over it tomorrow night. I've got hold of a White House fellow, maybe you remember him, Tom McBride, who is really pissed at LBJ and the war and all, and he's going to give me a lot of help on the speech."

Mulligan watched while Burnett took a long, slow sip of his drink. It was so relaxed, all so very relaxed, that Mulligan was now thinking about offering his old friend a joint. Mulligan himself wasn't a big doper or anything, but a boy who had been at the apartment a couple weeks ago had left a few joints, and Mulligan had wrapped them up carefully in Reynolds Wrap and stuck them in a box of frozen spinach. Sure, Burnett had to smoke dope. All these political types did drugs.

Instead, he looked at Burnett and blurted out: "Sorry. The past two days have just been so intense with Kelly and everything. Making my decision. I'm just wiped. I keep getting lost in this conversation."

Burnett leaned forward, his elbows resting on his knees, his hands clasped in front of him, suddenly looking again like the leader and athlete Mulligan admired, tagged after from his first day at Milton. "Okay. You're probably getting lost because I know where we're going and you don't. It's not the speech. That's not what I mean. You're going to make a much bigger statement, be a much bigger deal, than anything that could have happened from speaking to the Offensive."

The "could have" hit Mulligan like a blast from the air conditioner, and he was suddenly getting very sober. "I don't get it, Tom. What's the 'could have'?"

"Look, this should be a long, involved conversation, and as I said, I'm beat to shit. I'll make it clear. I haven't been totally honest with you. But I've always been honest about having your best interests at heart. We're friends. And I have other friends. Good friends, people like you and me. These are people concerned, worried, no, who are scared that the Left in this country is going to use the peace issue to start a revolution."

Mulligan forced himself to be sober. "Burnett, you sound like LBJ. This is no revolution. This is a protest, a demonstration."

Setting his glass on the table, Burnett looked around the room. It had been a long time since he had been in a friend's home with nice old pieces and a feeling of permanence. Mulligan must be some true believer to have risked all this and promised to sign on with the Offensive.

"Revolution is the word. And the losers are going to be people like you and me, and all the people we've been trying to help. Social change, social justice, are just going to go right out the window. The country's going to react to the Left, and we're going to wind up with a right-wing, conservative government. Nobody will care about blacks or farm workers or kids. Nobody."

"I care. That's why I said I would sign on. You pressured me, you pushed me. You said it was important."

"It was important for you to sign on, and now, now it's important for you to drop out. You know, tune in, turn on, drop out. Just like the druggies say. Now you're with the Offensive Against the War. Now you're not."

Burnett stood up and walked over to the bar, shaking his head as though Mulligan were the one who was telling this fantastic story.

"Now this country has a peace movement. Just like we had civil rights. Only trouble is, just like in the South, crazy people are starting to really take over, to push it in ways it should not go. You remember, Mark, before we distracted people from the sit-ins and the freedom rides, before we rechanneled energies to voter registration, hell, we had a potential revolution on our hands then. You can't allow people, especially young people, to move outside the well-established channels for social change. There is one way to do things in this country: that way is through the government. The government is us. We are the government."

Now it was Mulligan shaking his head, finally managing to blurt out, "But you were like a hero. You spoke out. You pushed for change.

"You've pulled me in. Why make me do the news conference announcing that I'd speak? I trusted you. Now you tell me the Offensive is too radical. Burnett, it's your fucking march."

Burnett sat down, on the other chair this time. He sipped at his replenished drink, and with the same quiet, deliberate smoothness, he started in again on his lecture.

"So we have to make sure that all this antiwar sentiment gets channeled in the right way. And, Mark, let's talk politics. I guarantee you that in the next several months somebody is going to run against LBJ for president. Somebody's going to emerge as the antiwar presidential candidate. When he does, he's got to have troops. The antiwar feeling can't get sucked off by these crazy protests, drained off by kids going to Canada. We've got to make sure these young people stay in the system, keep them from signing on for a movement run by radicals and nuts. And that's what the Offensive Against the War is all about."

"I don't get it."

Burnett smiled at Mulligan and then said softly, "You're a smart boy, Mark. You, like many other people, just a few years younger, thought this protest was one thing. But now you realize it's something else. That it's too far to the left. That the people running it don't understand how America works. So you are going to pull out, tell the American people that the radicals running the antiwar protests have it wrong. Americans don't have to destroy the system to get out of Vietnam. No, the way to end the war is by working within the system. We just have to make it work."

"I get it. You bastard! I'm some sacrificial lamb that you are now going to serve up on network TV. I'm now supposed to look like some goddamn fool who first says he's going to speak, and then backs off after finding out what he should have known before he signed up."

"No, you are going to look like one loyal American, who, after the steering committee meeting Saturday morning, goes home to his tastefully furnished apartment, searches his soul, and decides against—I repeat, against—having anything to do with these leftist crazies. You're still against the war. You're still going to do something about it, you'll say at your press conference. But you, Representative Mark Mulligan of Michigan, are going to be absolutely sure that protest gets carried out in the American tradition. Sure, people can gather to oppose the war, and you are heading to Michigan Labor Day morning to participate in a silent vigil. But after seeing this group close up, even your old school chum Tom Burnett, you now realize that the Offensive Against the War is not the kind of protest that you, or any American, can feel comfortable with."

"Tom, this is nuts. This is really nuts. I feel like I'm on some goddamn bad trip, like I've taken acid or something and my head is going to burst open and everything is going to be lying at my feet. Maybe you're the one who's really crazy, who's really nuts. You're the one who can't figure this out. There's no reason for me to go along with this half-ass plan. You're nuts. I'm the congressman. I believe that my signing on for the march will make a difference, and nothing you say is going to change that."

Burnett didn't try to argue. He leaned over to the couch, to the large sloppy pile of papers he'd walked in with: folders, newspaper clips, and one manila envelope, which he pulled from the pile with a little flourish, a never-spoken "Ta-dum."

Even before Mulligan took the envelope, touched it, opened it, and saw the photographs, he knew what it would be about. Not who, or where, but what.

"A little faux pas, my friend. A cute one, although a bit on the young side. How old? Sixteen, seventeen? But wonderful reproductions, huh? Bring back the whole week in Puerto Rico? Those long, luscious nights with your young friend?"

Mulligan's rosy face drained to white, then turned red again, fiery red. He stood up, leaning over Burnett, his hand on the chair back, making the two of them into a slightly deranged portrait of a happy couple. "Why? Why me? I was your friend. I was more than your friend. I was your lover. You were the first. You were the one who showed me. Why? Why me?"

"Don't get sentimental. We all did each other. For God's

sake, Mulligan, nobody told you to turn into a goddamn pansy. Just because you had one drink didn't mean you had to have the whole bottle. Kids experiment. Boys try things out. You were so new, and so innocent. And you looked at me with all the admiration anybody could want."

"So you fucked me in the ass then. And you are fucking me in the ass now."

"No, I'm saving you. I'm letting you be part of something important, letting you play a role that is much bigger than the one you would have written for yourself, when you pull out."

"And when is that pull-out supposed to happen?"

"Saturday afternoon. That allows the story to get carried on the network news and run big in the Sunday papers. Then you go on the talk shows on Sunday, and your comments get played up against my statements or the statements from the steering committee."

"Look, Burnett, this is too much. I'm falling apart. The pictures, the back and forth . . . I just feel blown away."

"Mark, you have a very definite job. You need to come to the steering committee meeting Saturday morning, about ten. Then you head back here. I'll call you about noon. You're going to tell me on the phone why you are pulling out. And then you are going to have an emergency news conference, up on the Hill, at about two-thirty, three o'clock. You'll get the second-string weekend team, and they'll give you a big play. Do you get the plan?"

"Yes." Mulligan had curled into the couch, a child seeking shelter. Burnett walked over, stood beside him for a moment as if deciding whether or not to go this far, but finally rubbed his hair in a big-brother gesture.

"Have another drink and get some sleep. And, shit, don't do anything dumb like talk about it with anybody, or go out to pick up some kid. You've got a great future in politics. Count on me. Do what I tell you. For the next few days, you're mine. Just like at school. You're my boy."

## FRIDAY,
## September 1, 1967

"Early mornings are good. You have a lot of time to do things before you do anything. Like read the paper or something."

Pisano was yelling, rummaging in the bottom of the giant stove that filled up half his apartment kitchen. The big buzz of a coffee grinder was followed by a loud, unexplained noise.

"Now I'm making coffee," came the next announcement. Annie opened her eyes just a crack and watched as he put together a complicated, upside-down-looking coffeepot. She must have dozed back to sleep, since the smell of the coffee was the next thing that hit her. She curled her toes hard toward the bottom of her feet, pulling back under the Indian bedspread, snuggling into a corner of the couch. The apartment was a giant studio with a kitchen and bathroom stuck on, architectural afterthoughts. Trust Pisano to luck into one of the old Georgetown carriage houses, just a few blocks west of Wisconsin. The lawyer who owned the three-story house in front had permitted his two teenage sons to "move" to the carriage house when he'd brought their new stepmother home, and now that the boys were safely tucked away in good colleges, daddy rented the apartment, cheap, with the sole proviso that the tenant put in a kitchen. Pisano had hunted around and found an old bulky and blackened restaurant stove and a big pastry table. Together they'd filled the "kitchen area," exiling the refrigerator to the main room, where, Pisano hoped, it looked discreet with its camouflaging layer of black paint.

All the time she'd known Pisano, Annie had never been to where he lived. They had met in various and always temporary offices, in the South and in D.C., or in coffee shops and bad Chinese restaurants. So it was strange, looking around, to see that Pisano lived in a grown-up place, with real bookcases, not the ubiquitous bricks and boards. The couch was old, but it still had all the cushions it had started with. The Museum of Modern Art posters were framed, not just stuck on the walls with tacks or tape.

Two dozen or so framed photographs crowded the fronts of the bookshelves: Pisano with his family, Pisano getting various prizes, with a group that looked somewhat familiar at the NCAA finals, and a blurry snap of Pisano with her, at the Fourth of July demonstration in Atlanta two years before. She was laughing at the camera, but Pisano was looking at her, and with such tenderness that the memory of finding the photo-graph, of realizing his look, would rob her of a piece of her heart forever.

Annie had covered her feelings with a lot of bustle about unpacking dinner. She and Pisano had stopped at the Little Tavern on Wisconsin Avenue, where the air conditioner had blown out about three hours before. So they got take-out, Annie giving a long discourse on why southerners called it "carry away." They took the bags of teeny hamburgers she loved, stopped at the liquor store near 34th Street for a couple of six-packs, then walked to Pisano's apartment. It was gloriously cool, like a movie theater, since Pisano was running the huge air conditioners that blew at each other from opposing walls. The landlord's sons, it turned out, were allergic to everything, so Daddy had put in sufficient cooling power to do Capitol Hill. All the utilities were included in the monthly rent so, Pisano explained, "I live like I was on a government-funded project. I work hard at keeping the costs up all the time, or Uncle Sam will figure out that I can economize and get upset if the lowered bills then go up again."

Annie laughed and ate and drank her brews and smoked half a dozen Camels, and, funny, they didn't talk much about the talk in the Paradise Pool, or even about the Offensive, and sitting here, this morning, she couldn't really remember what they'd talked about. At two-thirty she announced she was heading home, Pisano shaking his head, going for the closet, pulling out the cover and telling her as an afterthought that Kapinski was coming for breakfast at eight, and she might just as well catch a couple of hours on the couch. It didn't take much to convince her, and at the sight of her nod, Pisano went back into the closet again, coming out with a new "guest toothbrush" and clean towels. "Like my mother," she told him.

Well, not quite, he confessed, his purpose being so different: "I won't go to a girl's place. I just won't sleep anywhere but my bed. It's okay if it's just my bed for the night, like a hotel, but it has to be mine. The girl has to either spend the night or go home alone. And if she stays, there's always a toothbrush and towels."

The conversation made Annie uncomfortable. How had she never thought about Pisano screwing around? Did she think he was some sort of a virgin or a fairy or something? she asked herself in the bathroom mirror, brushing her teeth. She'd never seen Pisano with anybody, she thought, coming out of the bathroom and realizing that he was already in bed, reading the *Times* with a funny gooseneck lamp beside his bed pressing down on the paper like a futuristic monster. "This story on George Lincoln Rockwell and his Nazis is really something. Imagine getting your head blown off by one of your converts who doesn't believe you're pure enough. This is a very good death for you to collect, Annie, since the funeral arrangements will really be something. They'll probably have German shepherds shredding children as the choir sings Wagner."

For one moment she thought about going over to the bed, for a quick little hug or a kiss—or something. It was sweet of Pisano to always remember her death collection. A little kiss? No. Instead she climbed under her Indian bedspread and, squashing the pillow under her, turned on her stomach and fell asleep.

She slept soundly until the noise and then the coffee smell woke her. Pisano loved to cook, and even breakfast had him doing a busy little two-step, putting together omelets with fresh tomatoes and feta cheese, spiced by a running commentary with Annie, stationary on the couch, relishing the air-conditioned icy feeling.

"The thing about the newspaper biz is that the people who work for papers care too much about everything, while the people who own papers don't care about anything at all. That's why publishers get together behind closed doors for their pow-wows. No reporters allowed. Shit, we might see that their concern is the bottom line, and ours is the byline."

Pisano was now telling reporter stories. Annie had once heard a joke, from a reporter, that sports reporters didn't like sports. They just liked other sports reporters. All reporters were like that, and everybody who ever worked for a newspaper knew at least half a dozen good tales.

"Once there was this guy," Pisano was saying, "who had covered cops and stuff in Philly for years. He's about four months past doing this big series on corruption in the police department and trying to get back part of the downtime he figured the paper owed him. But he's working for the *Bulletin*, which has like seven editions a day, so about two P.M. every day he goes to his favorite watering hole and the bartender tells the editors that he's not there. It's great. No chance that he'll get pulled in doing a killer deadline story for the four-star final. The punch line is that he gets the Pulitzer for his cops series, only he's the last one in Philly to know it, because his editors can't find him. He won't come to the phone."

Pisano was now gently edging the eggs from the sides of the pan to the middle. The doorbell rang, and he stuck his head out the window, yelled a hello, and told the ringer to come upstairs. "It's Kapinski," he explained unnecessarily to

Annie. "So this story," he continued, "doesn't mean that I'm saying it's a good business or anything, but it is the most interesting business around. I get to do everything. I get presidents. I get whores. I get some who are both."

Kapinski hit the top of the stairs as Pisano finished and clapped at the smell of breakfast cooking, although the hollow place created by the air conditioners' hum turned the claps from applause into thunder. A nod to Pisano allowed him to continue the monologue, while never breaking stride with the eggs. "It's like the first guy I worked for said: Know everybody, see everything. Get the front seat at the parade and never worry that the elephants will shit in your face."

Pisano waved them to the kitchen with his spatula and slid one fat omelet onto a platter, where it nestled beside its twin, flanked by broiled tomatoes and cottage fries. A basket piled with toasted bagels was already on the table, and Pisano filled their cups from the upside-down-looking coffeepot.

"Marry me," Kapinski yelled after the first bite. Annie simply ate, her fork marching relentlessly across the plate, as she leveled with great even-handedness the puffy eggs with fat rivers of yellow cheese slipping down the plate toward the piles of tomatoes and potatoes. Pisano finally sat down to his own omelet, but only after tediously spreading jelly on toasted bagel halves and pouring coffee refills.

"You living here now, Annie?" Kapinski asked, working on the last of his eggs. "This is nice, but a little too cozy for some of the members of the steering committee."

Before she could explode, Pisano started on another story. "See, there was this guy, named Denny O'Brien, who's been around a long time in Philly. Worked for Movietone News. So the queen of some Nordic country is coming to Philly, and he gets hired to shoot for the city, the inside guy, because if nothing else, O'Brien is the consummate professional. Never misses a shot. And Denny, he's briefed on protocol like he's going to have a date with her. Let's admit it, Philly gets turned on when Princess Grace comes home, and this was better, a real queen with a real country. Her plane arrives and she's standing at the top of the stairs, reporters and photographers all down below, near the red carpet, and she's saying something to her husband. Who knows what. Maybe did he remember to piss before he left the plane. And suddenly there is O'Brien. He's gotten himself onto the roof of the hangar. It's a great shot, with the queen at the top of the stairs and the carpet and all of us, only she keeps looking straight ahead, so to hell with protocol. He yells, 'Hey, Queenie, flash a big one over here. How 'bout a right profile?'"

Annie roared, while Kapinski smiled politely. Pisano got up to get more coffee. In a pair of jeans and bare chest and bare feet, he looked like his own kid brother.

"That story is what we call in the news biz a blue-ribbon lead, like it sneaks up on you. 'The dog was howling in the distance,' you know, and then ten graphs down you find out the story is about a mass murderer. So my blue-ribbon lead to this conversation is about how a good photographer, or a good reporter, will go to any lengths, break any rules that aren't written by the journalistic profession, so that he gets the picture or the story that he wants. And there's a story about the Offensive that I'm about to break."

Annie knew the look on Kapinski's face. She could remember once, when dozens of them were getting arrested in the South, when she was standing at the side with the lawyers and the bail money, watching Kapinski be dragged into a police car. That was the look, she thought. The look that kept anybody from figuring out what he was thinking or feeling or being afraid of. She shivered in the air-conditioning but shook her head no when Pisano asked if it was too cold.

"Look, Pisano's just playing straight with you, that's all, so you understand there's going to be a story, and that what he says here today doesn't mean that he's not going to do the story," she said, getting up to get her smokes from her bag.

Kapinski stood up, turned his chair around, and sat down again, straddling it, his hands holding the posts so tightly that the blue veins stood out, looking as if another word, another phrase, would burst them.

"Annie, you're supposed to be working for the Offensive, and now you're messing around with this reporter." Kapinski stopped suddenly and shook his head.

Before Annie started yelling in response, Pisano interrupted. "Okay, that's it. Whether Annie is 'messing around' with me or not has nothing to do with this. What's important, Kapinski, is that you're a relatively honest and honorable person. And it made me really mad when I figured out that your own honesty and commitment were getting turned against you."

Slowly, now, with great attention to detail, Pisano outlined the story that he planned to run Monday, the morning of the march. He began with Simpson, whose very name brought a snort from Kapinski. The reaction startled Annie, who was shocked not that he knew who Simpson was, but that he greeted the name with such knowledgeable contempt.

Pisano went right on, putting together the bare bones of his story as he talked, figuring out just what he would still need to flesh out the piece, how far he could go with what he already had. "I'm pretty sure I can't get Simpson's name in the paper. But I can write about him as the unnamed Washington power broker who sees Vietnam as the next possible domino to fall to the Commies. And he's not too happy with what's happening with the Left here at home. The Left is the Left is the Left, is how Mr. Unnamed would describe it. So given this world outlook, there's no chance he'd sit down with the likes of you and plan a peace demonstration. Right? Am I right?"

Kapinski simply nodded. Annie got up to get herself more coffee, and, holding up his hand like a traffic cop to stop the rush of information from Pisano, Kapinski followed her to the stove. "Annie, I'm sorry. I want to say it now, before Pisano finishes. I had no right to question your commitment or anything. That was bull on my part."

Annie shrugged and led Kapinski back to the table, where Pisano resumed his story: "Now suppose Simpson sees the antiwar movement getting so strong that the government can't let it go along on its own, can't let it be like water finding its own level. So he and his friends, who always think they know best, want to take it over. They think of themselves as liberals, but their politics is not the same as some guy in Connecticut who joins a peace vigil every Saturday in the town square."

Pisano reached over and took one of Annie's cigarettes, lit it, and watched as the air conditioner spun the smoke to the ceiling.

"The guy in Connecticut, and a lot of people like him, are becoming opposed to the war. Simpson wants to make sure that these people, his troops, don't get ahead of him and the other policy-making generals. It's too threatening to have you antiwar types in the streets. First, you're not under his control. Second, he's not sure how far you'll go in changing the world. Third, it doesn't look too good to other governments around the world to have U.S. foreign policy getting decided in the streets. So Simpson and a bunch of other heavies get together, and they know that they can't move in on what's already marked off peace territory, like the Fifth Avenue Peace Parade or the Mobilization. So instead they set up their own game, a temporary coalition of a lot of people and groups, and they invite all you activists to play."

Kapinski had released his death hold on the chair, but his voice was tight as his fists had been.

"Hey. Hold it. Simpson couldn't come near us. This guy left footprints all over the South. When the civil rights movement started, everybody was welcome. Then, as King and others started to pile up more victories, the Simpson types showed up and started judging everyone by their own political yardstick. 'Don't let anybody too left decide the strategy. Don't move too fast. Don't push too hard.' "

Pisano was still amazed at the gaping chasm between radical and liberal, between the New Left, as it was beginning to call itself, and the Liberal Establishment. Students for a Democratic Society, Students Non-Violent Coordinating Committee, Congress on Racial Equality, Mississippi Summer—all saw themselves as getting screwed by big-time liberals.

"When some people in the South wouldn't take their direction from these self-appointed leaders," Kapinski continued, "then the Red-baiting started. Suddenly a lot of the northern money just stopped coming. And when there were meetings, well, it wasn't with us. It was with the conventional liberals, who were moving at the 'correct' pace."

Kapinski stopped, some of that disappointment showing on his face, his chin resting on his hands on the chair back. He looked suddenly old and bent, Annie thought, like the little Jewish men with skullcaps and baggy sweaters who sliced lunch meat. Kapinski raised one hand and pushed his glasses back on his nose, leaving a deep red gash where they had been sitting.

"So we're agreed on Simpson," Pisano picked up. "But let me provide the missing link. Let me show you how this all ties together like a term paper on betrayal."

With great drama and pacing, Pisano pulled the photograph of Simpson and Burnett out of a folder. He laid it down just to the right of the plate. The remains of the omelet had dried quickly in the air-conditioning, and Kapinski chipped at the dried egg with his thumbnail as he stared at the picture. He never touched the photograph, just kept looking at it and hacking away. He didn't say anything for a long time, then he began to jiggle his chair, like a kid who had to go to the bathroom. Jiggling, jiggling, rocking back and forth. Finally he looked up.

"Where was the picture? Santa Marita, where Burnett was

supposedly working with the progressives on stuff like voter registration? Son of a bitch. I'm going to wring his neck. I'm going to make sure that nobody, but nobody, ever goes near him again. He's dirt and he'd dead. He wants to know what it's like to be marked. He'll have it. He's a pariah. Nobody will touch him, talk to him. Dead."

Pisano laughed. "Great. Now you sound like the boys at the State Department. The murder-for-peace plan. 'Let's blast them out of the water. Let's napalm 'em.' Or better yet, 'Let's blacklist the bastards.' That's what you sound like, Kapinski. Like some Saigon cowboy or like some Mississippi sheriff or some Joe McCarthy in reverse. Or, better yet, like Simpson himself. 'Let's make sure these kinds of people don't get in the way of what we think is good for America.'"

Kapinski just kept jiggling. "Yeah, right. But what about the Offensive? What's going to happen to everybody's credibility? If these bastards want to co-opt the peace movement, take it over, let me tell you with the Offensive, they've got what they want. Burnett is running the show, really. We've listened to Burnett and kept it safe. 'Let's protest, but let's not yell too loudly. Let's get people to sign petitions, but, heavens no, let's not go to jail.' It's pansy politics. And I can see where it's leading. It's playing it safe, so next year, in some Podunk congressional district, some good guy will win. I don't want to play it safe. I don't want this war to end someday. I want it to end now."

Pisano reached for another of Annie's cigarettes and got nothing but the empty pack, which he crumpled up and tossed on his plate. No one spoke as Annie dug around in her bag for another pack of smokes and Pisano went through the complicated ritual of making more coffee in his intricate pot.

Finally, with cigarettes apportioned and coffee poured, Pisano resumed. "I'm running this story the day of the march, not the day before or the day after, because I'm hoping that Simpson will pull back on whatever he's planned as a march follow-up. Let me bring up one other item. What about the Agency? Don't look shocked at the Simpson-CIA connection, Kapinski. You rads are all the same. You can't believe it when your suspicions are proven right. Here are the Agency people, fresh out of messing up with the National Student Association and pulling stunts using kids, and just months after the big exposé and all the publicity, now it seems like they are sticking their fingers into the peace movement. I can't come right out in the story and say it's the Agency. I can finger Burnett as being tied for a long time to well-known D.C. types who meddle in foreign policy. I got a lot of detail from a friend of mine, so I can run Burnett's résumé and it sure looks like he's always lived in spook city. Before he came south, he attended both the domestic and international 'summer camps for student leadership' that NSA was running as a CIA recruitment front. His time in Santa Marita was funded by one of the foundations linked to the Agency this past spring. But I can't come right out and say Agency."

"What you are saying, Joe, is that you are going to fire a lot of bullets—and everyone is going to get hit except the guy you are aiming at?"

"No, no. What the story does is put the government on warning—the Agency, the Hill, the White House—that they can't send in their men to do a boy's job. They can't both run the war and run the antiwar movement."

"And what I am supposed to do, Pisano, for the next three days? I've got to go over to headquarters right now, meet with Burnett, discuss strategy. How am I supposed to do all this, knowing that the bastard is working for the government?"

Annie wanted to close her eyes. This was why she never went to horror films, or even scary movies. Here was the scene with the knife coming through the curtains, the creak of the step on the stair. Simpson and Burnett really were the bad guys. Sure, their intentions may be great, but these were the guys who were pushing governments around, running their own little government, their own little foreign policy. James Bond guys, the by-any-means-necessary guys. What she'd learned last night finally hit home, and as much as she tried to push the dead feeling away, it sat like a weight on her stomach. Of course, on her stomach, and the only way to relieve that pressure was with another piece of toast, she thought, reaching over Pisano's outstretched arm.

Pisano reached out and took Annie's hand as he spoke. For a moment she didn't listen to him talking about the future of the Offensive and the Movement. Instead she was trying to figure out what was going on, what Kapinski was thinking, and if her palm was as damp as it felt to her. Pisano gave her hand a hard squeeze and said, clearly to both of them, like a nun directing first-graders, "Go back to the office. Do just what you would have done if we hadn't had this conversation. The Offensive has to go on as planned. Don't worry about it. Worry about what Burnett is going to do when the Offensive is over, who is going to be the voice of peace. Just remember that on Monday morning, I pull the rug out. Instead of Burnett taking bows, he just becomes some spook-related schmuck who was trying to horn in on the peace movement. The Offensive goes on as planned. And, who knows, Kapinski, maybe you end this war. Eventually."

Bitsy was angry at the meeting place. The dean of the National Cathedral had offered his "study," and despite Bitsy's protests, that's where the face-off would be held. Bad enough that the ladies had to come down from New York. She'd made damn sure that the money from the church office covered hotel rooms for them and had ridden the train down with them yesterday afternoon. Merlee, confident that Bitsy would protect the ladies in the meeting, stayed in New York to keep the daily pickets and protests going. That's all Tyler and his guys would need to see, the leadership leaves and the action ends.

The small Georgetown hotel where the ladies were staying catered to lots of lower-level European and African diplomatic types. There had been one minute when Bits was going to take them over to east of Capitol Hill, to an all-black hotel, but, hell, they were in the big league now, and some of the newness of operating in this white power world might get worn off between the hotel and the restaurant. So she got them settled in a two-bedroom suite with lots of squeals and general bullshit about the size of the beds and wouldn't they just know what to do with some big man in this layout, hey.

And she dragged them down N Street to the "1789," a block from Georgetown University and named for the year it was founded. The atmosphere was Colonial, and the building looked several hundred years old. A nice touch, Bitsy thought; my people never sat in this front room back then, and now Tyler's paying for it.

Grace Henry was in full control of the dinner table, as she had been in control of the protests in New York. Grace, in her massive powder blue pant suit (the way Grace said it made it "power blue") and her lopsided wig, was the treasure that every community organizer, every door knocker, searched for: a natural leader. For twenty-one years Grace had worked as a laundress in the Waldorf-Astoria. She never missed a shift but was unable to push herself forward in the ranks, leashed to the children at home and to her husband, Hubert, with one leg already gone to diabetes and the other fat and covered with sores. It was only when her daughter, Natalie, a full-time student at Hunter, thank-you-Jesus...well, Natalie had come home and told her mother that in Government 101 it was clear to the professor and the whole class that the Henry family was paying a lot of money for an apartment with what Natalie called "hot-and-cold running rats." When Grace went to the local Democratic leader, he said he had no pull with the Health Department. Besides, she'd already been there, and to the minister, and even called Mayor Lindsay's utilities hot line.

"Hot line, damn. It felt just about as hot as the water in my tub, which is damn cold." So Grace told Natalie to go back to class and figure out what could be done. Then Grace Henry put on her best flowered summer dress and went to knocking on doors in her building and three other buildings.

As soon as they had some organization going, she explained to Bitsy on the train ride down, "every two-bit leader of the people, with tight jeans, who had ever knocked on a door wanted to come in and take it over." But no, no boys were getting in to mess it up, and Grace made sure of that from the beginning. The welfare checks, the Aid to Dependent Children, the food stamps—all of that comes to the moms, so Grace said it was the "Mothers for Better Housing" who were protesting.

Grace found Merlee and other community organizers at the nearby Harlem Advancement Council office. Merlee helped her work out a strategy and round up enough Vista volunteers to put together a decent enough demonstration around the management company that ran their buildings.

But the best thing Grace had going for her was Grace. She just didn't stop. Picketing the management company just wasn't going to work, Merlee told her. The management company got paid to take shit. "Grace, honey," Merlee had said, "you have to find out just who owns the buildings, who holds title." So Grace got Natalie, who got a handful of other students, and they pressured their government professor into saying that it could count for credit in the summer school class, and after days of researching records and phone calls, it was clear that the famous Reverend Tyler himself, and his church, and his rich white elders, were doing the "po' black folk dirty," as Grace told Gabe Pressman on the five o'clock news. "We think it's wonderful that he wants to help Negroes down there in the South, and to keep people from getting killed in Vietnam. But we've got babies dying here, with no water and rats, and most would be better off in Mississippi."

After a week of phone calls that got nowhere, on Wednesday the picket lines had gone up around the church itself and two days later, here they were in D.C. to meet with three men from the Council on Social Justice from Tyler's church's national office.

Grace was really something. Like at dinner, in her glory. After all, she'd been around good china and linen tablecloths all her life: she'd washed them and polished them and ironed them. Her two "lieutenants," Joanne and Betty, had been a little uncomfortable, but Bitsy was convinced that going first class was going to help them; especially reassuring was seeing that Grace knew her way around. When Grace gently called over the white waiter and asked for more salad dressing, he carefully motioned the busboy; Grace waved off the young black man, then beckoned the waiter and asked him to serve the dressing: "Don't know that the young boy would know how to do it."

As the pink glop was ladled over her hearts of lettuce, Grace told the table about her first job, working on the Upper East Side for a young couple with two children. "I was there ten years—from the time the older boy was born until the young one went to school. From the time I was seventeen. They loved me, those boys, and their momma couldn't tell me enough how much I was part of the family and how much they were thankful for what I was doing. Of course, when both the boys were old enough for school, she went out and found a cleaning service that would come in three days a week, and then I was sent on my way with two weeks' pay."

The women laughed. They all knew about white folks, who didn't want you living in their neighborhood—unless it was in the back bedroom of their house. You could kiss and hug their babies, but don't you let your son touch their daughter.

Now, sitting in the anteroom, waiting for admission to the meeting, Bitsy thought about stories of her own, stories she had refused to share last night with the ladies at dinner. Maybe she didn't want to have the ladies lose faith in her. Maybe she thought she was better than they were. Maybe she was getting uppity. "An uppity nigger," that's what Donna Sue McCallum had called her. She would never forget Donna Sue, or her blond hair, or her fine Georgia accent, rising sharply behind the closed door of the resident adviser's room her first week at Radcliffe. "Negras are different. They smell different and I'm not going to share no bathroom with no Negra and I have talked to my Daddy and he's real upset and wants me to come home." The college sent Donna Sue exactly where she wanted to go, Bitsy remembered with a smile. But the experience shook her, and the first weekend home, she talked about it incessantly with her mother and father. "She's just ignorant. What does she know, a girl like that? White trash. You just shake off those comments," said her mother in her most proper Morehouse College accent.

What Bitsy never told her mother, what only went away after months and years, was the shame that had her in the bathroom late that night, sniffing at the towels of the other girls.

"Smell differently!" her mother had pronounced, dragging out each syllable of both words. "That's some crazy cracker talk. Never, never, even think about that again."

But her mother was wrong. In the South, Bitsy discovered the bitter smell of sweat—from people who had worked fourteen hours in a field, then come directly to a church for a three-hour meeting on how to register. She learned the smell there, leaning over some natty-haired man old enough to be her father, looking like he was her grandfather, pointing to each place on the form, showing him how to make his block letters fit in the space.

Bitsy only wished that she could confront Donna Sue now, for just about two minutes. "Yes, we smell different. We smell like slaves, with no time to wash or freshen up and no running water to do it with if we had the time. We smell like work—like *your* work. Woman who spent all day in your mother's wash house, so that all your linen and cotton was just perfectly pressed, then walked two miles home to wash feed grain sacks and press them, walking in the heat, and, if they were lucky, carrying the leftovers from two-nights-ago dinners at your house. Not last night's—that might still make some lunch or snack. But two-days-old leftovers, and thrilled to get them."

Sitting in the reception room outside the canon's office this noontime, Bitsy looked over her trio of ladies. A long time ago, when she first went back to Philadelphia and started taking mothers down to the welfare, she got angry at the way they dressed. Not that they were poor or raggedy. Far from it. They all had on their best. Here she was, trying to convince social workers that families that lost their checks couldn't make it through the week—and she's got a bunch of women with her who look as if they're on their way to Saturday night clubbing. It sure would be better if they looked, well, poorer somehow, which is what she came out and said to one of the teacher's aides, how maybe she could gently suggest to one of the moms not to get so fancy. It wasn't a party or anything. At which point the aide took her head off, telling her that if you were trapped in an ugly life, and you were trying to be like a person, you needed people to see you like a person, not like some dirty beggar. Just because you were on welfare didn't mean you didn't care. So Bitsy gave in and was now amazed, but not angry, at some of the getups the ladies would show up in to meetings. Today's outfits were mild, with Grace in her powder blue polyester and Althea in a pink-and-green-striped shift, enough material to cover a small couch. Betty's skinny legs stuck out from under a too large black dress, and there were bright red high heels on her long narrow feet. Why, she's pretty, Bitsy thought, having never before seen the third, more quiet officer of the mothers' committee dressed in anything but a pair of shorts and a ratty shirt. Bitsy herself was in her "lady lawyer" outfit. She'd figured out, as the lawyers eventually would, that in the South, dressing like a field hand made people treat you like a field hand. Overalls and jeans only looked great in Harvard Yard. Today she had on a navy blue linen suit (an old one of her mother's), and she nervously patted the short haircut that curled above her collar. Her hair wasn't kinky enough to style a real "natural," but she'd stopped processing it—"I've given up Dixie Peach forever," she'd kidded Kapinski—and the tight curls felt existentially light on her head.

The door slammed open to the reception area, and Tyler entered, nodding graciously to the ladies, just in case, Bitsy thought, a television camera happened to be hidden behind the oil painting of Saint Sebastian, tied to a tree with arrows in his pasty white chest. What Tyler hadn't been prepared for was Bitsy's presence, but his quickly composed and condescending welcome was just the kind of emotional pop to send her into the meeting with flags unfurled.

It was all very civil, Bitsy thought. Grace was well prepared after spending all morning in the hotel room with Bitsy practicing, talking out her story. With the members of Tyler's National Church Board listening, Grace outlined the tenants' problems, the concerns, their needs. There was a good deal of nodding from the three wise men, and when Grace finished her presentation and the ladies flanking her nodded their approval, Althea going so far as to mutter a quiet "Amen," the silence was roaring in Bitsy's ears. This was the hardest time, she knew from the years in the South and the months at the welfare office. This was the time you wanted to take your self-righteous cause and ram it down the throats of the old goats sitting on the other side of the table. But this was also the time to be quiet, to let Tyler fire his volleys, to see how the enemy was armed, what firepower he had brought into the meeting. Kapinski was the first to explain it to her: the strategy of silence.

Tyler had apparently never heard of it, so in only a decibel softer than his Sunday voice, he began his tale—the pressures of the urban church, the crisis in the city, his knowledge of the horrors of being poor and black, the need to make incremental changes and improvements.

Bitsy was scared. Tyler could make a grocery list sound like the Sermon on the Mount, but Grace caught on and caught him up. "Well, I can guarantee you, Reverend," she interrupted, "we ain't had none of those incrementals, or any other kinds of improvements, since I been in that building, and that's now eight years."

Shaking his head at Grace's naïveté, Tyler took a moment to explain how "incrementally, little by little, things are going to get better." He and his church, he insisted, felt a responsibility to the neighborhood. "We care, ladies, and perhaps we should have been more vocal in our plans for those buildings— but you should have come and talked to us, and we would have been happy to work with you."

Now, Bitsy thought. Now I got you, babe. "Reverend Tyler, I think you are laboring under some false information." She leaned forward from her position at the left of the ladies and, keeping her elbows on the table, forced the church officials to lean forward, too. "I know that you and your national denomination are concerned about the bad publicity. And I, as one who has worked with church leaders in the civil rights struggle, I could not be more in agreement that it is tragic to blot such an impressive church record." Bitsy waited, the voice and source of reason. "But you must understand that Grace and her neighbors didn't know you owned the buildings. You and your church board made every effort to keep that information from coming to light: a series of informal and formal holding companies and committees, along with a management company, guarded your identity like the family silver. No, Reverend, there was no way Grace and Althea and Betty could sit down with you. They had to find you first."

Bitsy began to skim through the papers in front of her, allowing the silence to sit on the table like a big, ugly pile of uncollected garbage. These church people were fat and happy; they would never move, never do a damn thing, unless they felt uncomfortable. Bitsy pulled two sheets of paper from the pile and reached into the briefcase at her feet for a handful of photographs. She dealt them out to the three church officials, leaving Tyler empty-handed. Then, picking up the sheets of paper, she began to read: "This is a survey taken of the building known as Tennyson Arms on August 27. The survey was conducted by thirty students from Union Theological Seminary under the supervision of Professor Arnold Schrader. Teams of students spent an average of forty minutes in each of the apartments surveyed, and at least one member of the team personally tried the utilities." Big breath and a look around the table. "So, here's how it works. Or doesn't work. At least fifteen percent of the toilets were inoperative. Not slow or anything. No, just plain broken. Just nowhere to go to the bathroom. On floors two and four in the rear apartments there was no hot water. None. At least ten percent of the bathtubs were unusable. And at least one-half the apartments had a serious problem with the electricity. Exposed wiring or switches that just didn't work."

Then, the bomb. "Gentlemen, let me also point out that samples taken from peeling walls in at least six apartments show the paint to contain lead. These are apartments that are home to children, babies, who stand a good chance of permanent brain damage if they eat that paint."

The conversation became a seesaw, Tyler talking about the plans for the future for the buildings, admitting some guilt but pointing to his years of service to civil rights. Bitsy going back, again and again, to the merciless exploitation of mothers and children, several "Amens" coming from the ladies whenever rats or the plumbing got mentioned. After almost two hours, the Reverend John Dough (Bitsy loved the name) announced that he and his committee members would ask the group to step outside while they discussed some possible remedies.

Now, Bitsy ordered in her head. Now, Grace.

"Reverend, I don't believe that we are going to wait outside while you ministers discuss our lives. We have a plan for the buildings the reverend and his rich church owns. Let me tell you this plan, gentlemen. My daughter, who is a student at Hunter College, found the papers showing how much the reverend paid for the four buildings. Here is the total."

The amount had been circled at the bottom of the recorded deeds. As Grace spoke, Bitsy dealt out the copies.

Grace paused. And then she flashed her big smile. "We want to buy those buildings from you. We want you church people to help us buy them. We are going to make those buildings into cooperatives, and we are going to pay you what you paid for them."

Tyler snorted. Grace looked at him: "Why you making that noise, Reverend? It's possible for us to buy a building. Your very own church is helping people do that in other cities."

"Yes, yes. But we've owned those buildings for seven, and in one case ten years. Prices have skyrocketed in New York. We would have to charge much more than we paid."

"No, Reverend," Grace intoned. "You wouldn't have to do that at all. Unless you think you should make money on the sweat and blood of poor people. You don't need no profit. You bought the buildings for this many dollars—you sure ain't put no money into repairs. Now you can sell the buildings for the same dollars. We are going to corporate into what Bitsy here will explain to you."

"A nonprofit corporation," Bitsy interjected, but slowly enough to make it clear that she wasn't trying to correct Grace. "We, that is, Grace and the committee, have spoken to several lawyers at Legal Aid here and in New York, and it is possible for a nonprofit corporation to be set up to run the building, with the tenants as members of the corporation. But, gentlemen, details can be worked out. And, now that we have told you what an acceptable solution for this problem is, the committee and I will leave you to your deliberations. The ladies need to catch a train back to New York. And they expect to hear from you in the near future."

The members of the committee sat stunned, but not Tyler. Bitsy had to give him credit. He'd lost, but he wasn't leaving the table empty-handed. He was going to walk away with his reputation.

"Ladies, Bitsy..." He smiled, somehow aligning himself with his protagonists, not his committee. "Your case is undeniable. My church deacons and I. Never. Meant. Any. Harm." Bits just loved the way Tyler could speak in capital letters.

"No, the business of a church is not to make a profit, although as membership dwindles we are dependent more on good investments than on good intentions. But, no, this situation is indeed unbearable, both for the tenants and the church. And"—God, he has changed sides, Bitsy conceded—"it is a losing battle for my congregation and for my national denomination. I will go back to New York—no, better, I will call the members of the deacons' group tonight, and we will obviously vote to help the tenants and the tenants' organization work out a legal transfer of the properties. And one last thing. My father invested forty years of his life in my church and in this neighborhood. I know that somewhere in this process, new names will be given the four apartment buildings involved. I would like to submit my father's name for one of those honors."

Tyler sat back, the church committee smiled, the ladies looked stricken with success. Bitsy hadn't had many wins in her career, but she had thought long and hard about how she would act in the face of an overwhelming victory. Gracious, pleasant, modest—she was all those things—thanking the committee, getting the ladies out of the room, setting up a time for the next get-together. "Your lawyers or ours?" she kidded. Just a gentle nudge. Not too much, just a reminder that under these polyester pant suits beat the hearts of real fighters, real winners. She wanted the ladies to understand, from the very beginning, no matter what Tyler's attitude was, that this was not a gift, but a victory. Not a present, but a prize.

And, she thought, walking down the steps, under the arches of the heavy-hanging trees and out into the late summer heat, she would also explain to the ladies just how some kind of victory always can be salvaged from a defeat. Tyler had done that, in his one simple suggestion to name the building for his father. Bitsy wondered if any of the trio of church officials remembered, in the heat of the moment, that the Reverend Paul Tyler's full name was the Reverend Paul Tyler, Jr.

Tyler didn't miss a trick.

Kelly loved the late afternoon in late summer. Just about now, a little after four, the "heat would break" as his mother would say, and even if it was just a small dip, to eighty-five or eighty, there was that promise of fall, of the too few and, Kelly thought, perfect days of autumn. He had an old record at home, of Walter Huston singing "September Song." Must have been cut in the early 1930s, and Kelly couldn't think of another record he'd ever heard of Huston making. But, by God, Kelly loved the song, loved the idea of "days dwindling down to a precious few," loved the fact that his own age had finally caught up with his beloved season. Kelly looked over the summer to the waiting autumn. Like every Irishman born in the States, he thought of himself as possessing, through ethnic selection, the soul of a poet, hidden though it might be under an expanding girth put on by too many expense account lunches. In his poetic moments, he saw his own autumn as bright and golden, with only a few leaves dropping in the heavy breezes that whipped through the corridors on the Hill.

Six or seven years back, Kelly had taken up cigars. Longer than that, he corrected himself, looking at the photograph on the wall: him and old Joe and young Jack Kennedy. Kelly had a large cigar in his hand, probably a Cuban. Like Pavlov's dog, he reached into his upper drawer and pulled out the wooden box. "And now, Kelly my boy, celebrate the end of the day with something from the fields of Mr. Hauptmann, now in the hands of Mr. Castro." What a joke. No Cuban cigars, according to the laws passed by the good senators and congressmen. And yet, up and down the halls, nothing seemed to be as prized as these contraband cylinders. Kelly had a stewardess bring his in from Europe. He had half a dozen good cigar clippers in his drawer, gifts from various lobbyists and even a previous president. But Kelly preferred to use his sharp, tiny, even teeth. Everything about him was ordered, top to bottom. He had served in the navy and still wore his hair with a military brush, and his shoes, Florsheim wingtips, were polished every morning before he headed off to mass.

Kelly lived, and felt, like a rich man. He'd been married thirty-two years, and except for a drunken slip at the 1948 convention, he'd never touched another woman. In his marriage, he played by the book. On the Hill, he played by rules, but they were often rules he wrote.

A long time ago, an old hand had told Kelly how politics worked. A city was like the Roman Catholic church. The pope ran the Church, but he lived far away and didn't even speak English. It was the parish priest who represented the Church, who baptized and married and buried. To a voter, the most important man in his city wasn't the mayor, it was the ward leader down the street, who could get the mayor on the phone, get somebody's brother put on the Streets Department payroll, or get a kid out of jail. The average voter wanted something concrete, close at hand, like a regular trash pickup, or a number to call when it didn't happen. Good politicians knew how to take care of their constituents.

Kelly's business, as he saw it, was the trade of politics. Discreet. Smarter than he'd ever let on. A pol's pol. As his friend Jack Kennedy once said, "He wouldn't tell you if your pants were on fire—and he wouldn't tell anyone else when your ass got burned."

Once, just once, his Ellie had questioned him about the ethics of trading of favors. Kelly told her his ethical code was "short and sweet. You need something, you have to give something. It's like the Church, Ellie. You want a favor, you make a novena. It's all quid pro quo. And if it's good enough for the Church, it's good enough for me."

But Kelly wasn't thinking about trading this afternoon. He'd even put the goddamn peace march out of his mind. He was puffing on his Havana (the stewardess was the girlfriend of the young lawyer he'd had put on the Appropriations Committee staff) and enjoying the view.

Until Mulligan came in. The kid looked awful, Kelly thought. Like someone died. Or maybe someone had told him he was going to die. In the corner of Kelly's office was a faded leather couch that he'd had somehow squeezed out of the sergeant at arms's office. Mulligan threw himself down on it, as if he were in a shrink's office or something. And he just lay there, staring.

Everything Kelly ever saw or learned was somewhere in his persona. For other old hands on the Hill, with age came experience that had been edited. People normally modified themselves, and no one was as self-correcting as a professional politician.

But not Kelly. Sure, he might switch tactics or an approach, he might decide that for six months the legislative aide would deal with the lobbyists and not the staff director, but everything with Kelly was an option. And he never let any option go. It all got filed away, like the numbers from close elections that the real political junkies traded late at night.

So when Mulligan stumbled into his office that afternoon, as close to tears, Kelly later told his wife, as anyone he'd seen since their grandson broke his leg sliding into third, he was met with the best bag of tricks anyone could hope for.

Not that Kelly wasn't rattled at the sight of his congressman teary. And when Mulligan started, not from Burnett's conversation, but with a full-fledged confessional about sex in boarding school, Kelly, who thought he'd heard it all before, didn't know what to do but listen. Frantic at first, Mulligan slowed down, focused in on the story, with Kelly sitting, dragging on his cigar, hunched over like a priest in confession.

"What's crazy about it, Kelly, is that Burnett kept talking about how it was important to end the war—but how it was just as important not to let the radical peace movement end the war. And I just wanted to slug the bastard, but then he pulled out these photographs. How the hell could he get these photographs?"

Kelly had known a lot of congressmen, or senators, who got messed over by a foolish thing like sex. He knew that with some men it propelled their lives, but both the rudder and the engine on his boat was politics, not a pretty face. Besides which, what Mulligan was talking about was a mortal sin, a political disaster, and as worldly wise as he liked to think he was, this thing with boys just turned his stomach. But he had to deal with this, because whatever else, Mulligan was his congressman.

The kid had said "bastard." For Kelly, that was a safe place to start.

"Remember, never say bastard," he instinctively reminded Mulligan, following the personal rule that kept his own language clean. Then nobody wound up at a party picking up the grandchild of a contributor and saying, "What an adorable little bastard."

For a while Kelly said nothing else, just sat there thinking, looking out the window. The first thing he thought was how angry he was. Here were all these plans for this basically decent kid—and now they're scrapped. Finally, he looked at Mulligan. "Okay, now you've lost your virginity. No, I don't mean the fooling around with boys, although, blazes, how can you do things like that?"

Kelly's instincts were now kicking in, the practitioner starting to sort through his bag of skills and tricks. The equation was simple. Quid pro quo. Mulligan pulls out of the march, and the pictures stay in their brown manila envelope. Backing off now wouldn't create a crisis in his district. There was no ground swell for or against the war, just some polling numbers that anybody could interpret any which way. Heck, Kelly knew that a clever pollster could phrase a question to make motherhood and apple pie lose big. Since Mulligan announced his intention to speak at the Offensive, the UAW was hanging with him, as well as a good number of the protestant clergy, although Kelly was never sure if they voted or just prayed that everyone else would. And then there were the students, at least those registered and over twenty-one.

So if Mulligan pulled out from the protest, still insisting he was against the war while saying the Offensive was radical, he could hold on to most of the antiwar bloc and make those who were undecided feel as if he had answered their complaints and worries. Maybe Mulligan could have it both ways— against the war, but also against the people who were against it. Kelly calculated that might be exactly where the American people were, or would be by the next election.

Or, Kelly found himself saying out loud, "We could face off the bums. We could just tell them that we're going ahead and doing what we think is right."

Even in his shock, Mulligan realized that the "you" of earlier conversations about the Offensive had become a "we." He nevertheless shook his head. "What about the pictures?

The two I saw were, uh, explicit. There's no question what was going on. Who the hell would have pictures like that? Who would be that interested in me?"

"Take your pick. It's the Agency. Or it's Mr. Hoover. We've only got two kinds of people out there taking pictures, and they both work for the government that you supposedly run." Kelly took this opportunity to emphasize what was coming next by a long drag on his cigar. "Now I can almost assure you, Mark, that these people are never going to use these pictures. They're going to shake them at you, and the next time they need a pet congressman, it's likely they'll pull these photographs out of the hat. But as far as releasing them, no, that's not their style."

"Kelly, if I could believe that, I could just tell them to go to..." Mulligan paused. "I could just tell them go to blazes."

"Yeah, well, the doubt is the power they have over you. Even a tad of doubt, and you know you've got to protect yourself. Only thing is, Congressman, I'm not sure that doing what these guys tell you to do is any way to protect yourself."

"And this is nuts, too, Kel. But when I showed up, here in the office, there's a message for me from Burnett. Like nothing had happened. Telling me that he'd be by early this evening with the press girl from the march, Annie O'Connor, and the two of them would meet with me about the speech."

There were too many ifs: if Burnett was really working for the spooks or the FBI; if the kill-off-the-lefties agenda he'd announced to Mulligan was honest; if Mulligan could hold up to another day of pressure, while holding off Burnett. Kelly needed a few hours on the phone. He had people to call to check on Burnett and on the girl, Annie O'Connor. Somebody knew something that would help his congressman. He just had to figure out who it was.

"You know, Kelly, this isn't the first time. I mean, they could have other stuff on me from other times."

Using his best Holy Name Society timbre, Kelly answered

his young boss. Short and sweet, as he would tell his wife later: "But it's sure going to be the last, Mark. We're just going to make this the very last. We're just going to sit tight. The two of us. And one of us is going to make a few phone calls to a couple of friends. And we're going to try to figure out what the game is, so we know just how high the betting's going to go. If they had more pictures, more 'incidents,' Burnett would have hit you with them too. None of these guys are subtle. And I'm not going to be subtle with you. That time is past. Some fellows grow up more slowly than others. We're just going to take your 'incidents' as a phase you were going through. And we're going to find you a nice little girl with very little tits, and you're going to learn to have a wonderful time screwing her."

Kapinski kept trying the number, getting angrier at each busy signal but unable to keep his finger off the dial for more than a minute. It was getting close to eight in D.C., seven in Skokie, and his mother would soon be spooning her famous chicken in a pot into the white and blue-edged bowls, stuffing big chunks of carrots down beside "this wonderful bird. Let me just get in one more potato." His father, Kapinski knew, was on the phone, trying to sign up another hot prospect. Kapinski, Sr., always liked to finish up a week's business by the end of the week, just as his mother always served a Shabbat dinner on Friday night. Jewish was Jewish, even in this, the least observant of households. Just like Kapinski himself, who, from his first summer away at Camp Fern Lock with the dozens of other little progressive, red-diaper babies, always managed to call home at dinnertime on Friday night. This time, Pop, you're going to miss my call, and you'd be interested in what I've got to tell you, because in about fifteen minutes I have a very special guest showing up, right here, in my furnished, month-to-month studio apartment.

Kapinski had a rule: Live by yourself. Alone. Kapinski

slept odd hours, if at all. His mother was also an insomniac and could ring him up on a whim at 4:00 A.M. His paranoia during 1965 was so great that he suspected that anyone who wanted to share his apartment was spying on him. All these were good reasons he gave for his solitary existence. But Bitsy believed the reason Kapinski lived alone was because he was a screamer.

She knew his habits only too well. Three nights ago in Philadelphia, despite the easy kidding around that had preceded the sex, she'd warned him that one yell and she would cross her legs into a yoga pretzel that wouldn't untwist until morning. So Kapinski, with a reasonable amount of carping, relented, monitoring his own joy, muffling his own moans of ecstasy. Not that his roars were a hidden asset. In the early Sixties, Kapinski got lucky and wound up sharing a sleeping bag with a tall girl from Ann Arbor at a church-sponsored international peace conference in Illinois. Whether it was the bottles of Almaden Mountain Red drunk after dinner, or the joints the girl provided as a nightcap, Kapinski didn't know, nor did he care. Neither did he know or remember that some seventy other conference participants were scattered in their sleeping bags, generally solo, around the big church hall. When Kapinski and the girl (he simply couldn't remember her name, then or now) came back in from their joint jaunt, they pulled her fancy bag up behind the organ. And then the girl, Kapinski could remember this, hugged him and said, "I've always liked organs. Let me play with yours." That did it. He was on, and when he came off, the screams jolted most of the conference participants, at least those who hadn't gotten joints from the same girl, out of their sleeping bags and into their own screams of fear.

"It's just too weird," Bitsy told him years later, after particularly noisy sex. "It's too primitive. I like it, but it's like seeing somebody in *National Geographic* and thinking she looks like you." When Kapinski thought about sex, which was often, he figured that his scream was an announcement, that he, Kapinski Jr., was about to shoot his wad into yet another waiting woman.

Not that he'd done much balling around in the years since he'd met Bitsy. At first he thought it was a turn-on because she was black. Sure, he criticized himself for that kind of prejudice, but he also changed his opinion on orgiastic and not just dialectic grounds. He loved screwing her. Bitsy standing up was just about two inches taller than Kapinski, even before his hair started thinning out on top. But lying down next to each other, or on the floor, which they did for one period because it made it all the more rudimentary, Kapinski and Bitsy fit together just right.

"You are black, you are beautiful. Arise, my love, and come with me," he intoned from the Song of Solomon one night. He had gone to the library on the Benjamin Franklin Parkway. Bits had been in Philly about two weeks, and he was nervous that her move there signaled an end to their relationship. So he went and looked up a little biblical come-on and, in his most cantorlike style, socked it to her. Bitsy stood up and ran around the room, arms flailing like a windmill, her hysteria overflowing.

"Look. I'm sorry that you think I'm a fool. I went and looked it up. I just figured that I didn't know how to say it, and…" Kapinski started to smile himself and then to laugh. Later he would believe that this time was maybe the best sex they ever had, and they always had great sex, but the best had started with a joke. As if they were loosening up before working out, shaking off the tension and the knots in their muscles. And getting Bitsy wet. Not a difficult thing to do, Kapinski would frequently tell her, his head bending over her face, his hand in some secret position inside her.

God, Bitsy was something else, Kapinski thought, redialing the phone, finding his cock hard and pushing against the cold zipper of his jeans. About six months ago he'd given up underwear, not for any political statement or anything, but because the last clean pair had more holes than cloth. Bits was shocked and really got on him about it. She was so middle class, so straight and proper. She even talked proper, except when they were in bed. "Snatch" and words like that came out of that sweet Seven Sisters mouth so quickly. Girls from fancy schools loved to talk trash, "bitching" and "screwing" and "fucking." But Bitsy in bed was real clear that the words were more than country club curses. "Just put your cock right inside me," she'd say. Or, "Why don't you put your mouth on my pussy?" Of course, Kapinski told himself, that was all his doing. She'd only done it with two guys before him, and they must have been like clowns in bed because when he first took her to bed and they started to fool around, well, she was like ready to do it and get it over with. "Hey," Kapinski told her. "This is not a race. The game is not to get to the finish line, but to see how much fun we can have getting there." So as he did each thing, and encouraged her to try some stuff on her own, Kapinski talked about what he was doing. "Now I'm going to eat you out. Spread your legs and let me see your sweet pussy." On other nights, Kapinski figured out that he could turn Bits on just by talking about what he was going to do. Like if they were walking back to the apartment or room or wherever they were staying, he'd simply start, in the Mrs. Kapinski singsong voice, about "when we get there, I'm going to lick your nipples for about five hours. And then when you can't stand it anymore, maybe what I'll do is just rub your snatch for about three or four hours with my hand."

It took Kapinski about six months to realize that arousing Bits was like the greatest turn-on of his whole life.

And thinking about it distracted him so much that when he came back to reality, he realized his "friend" was almost thirty minutes late.

Congressional offices always reminded Annie of convents. Lots of dark wood and dimly lit rooms filled with women devoting their lives to a man they thought of as the Messiah. Spinsterhood to these women came early, a special kind of virginity that had nothing to do with sex. Some of them had long-running affairs with their bosses, others preferred to work out their fantasies on the younger male staff, while still others were happily married and totally faithful sexually to their spouses. No, it wasn't sex. It was devotion, the undying devotion that belonged solely to "the senator" or "the congressman," as in "The senator is so busy today. Perhaps you could call again tomorrow." Or, in dealings with lower staff, "The senator has never done it that way."

The division of duties and distribution of power was the same on congressional staffs as it was in the Holy Roman Catholic church, Annie was thinking. Longtime staffers were just like nuns who ran the parish, educated the children, preserved the faith, nurtured the sick, lived a truly communal life with vows of obedience, poverty, and chastity, and bowed and scraped every time the pastor could take a measured-off hour from his golf game to give them a hand with first communion classes. Sitting on the worn chairs in Mulligan's reception room, waiting while he and Burnett finished a private conversation, Annie was so busy watching the gray-haired secretary, still loyally at her desk at eight on a Friday night, that she missed the older man who sat down beside her.

"I'm Jerry Kelly. And you're Annie O'Connor." She nodded. "With names like ours we should be running for aldermen in the South Ward of Boston."

"Boston doesn't elect women, unless they're racists. Nobody elects women, and women just don't seem to run for office. Just to run the government for the men who get elected."

Annie's sharp reply surprised her more than it did Kelly, and she quickly apologized. "Sorry. I was just thinking how most of these offices are run by women. I know, the congressmen are men. And the AA's are men. But women handle the day-to-day stuff that makes this all possible, and yet only a handful of women are actually in on the decision making. It's like the Holy Mother Church."

Kelly didn't answer right away, taken off guard not just by Annie's frankness, but also by the statement itself, facts that he had simply never thought about. Women came to work for a candidate, they stayed if they were committed, and they did the kind of work that women had always done. Another one of these beatnik ideas, Kelly thought, but he had to admit he liked the girl.

"And?"

"And I'm waiting to meet with Representative Mulligan and Tom Burnett about the Offensive Against the War. I do the press."

Kelly was about to reply when the door opened to an inside office and Mulligan waved Annie inside. Apparently the signal was also for Kelly, who bounced out of his chair with the lovely grace of those portly men who dance light-as-a-feather jigs on St. Paddy's Day and never move the rest of the year. Mulligan's office was small and simple, tastefully put together. Mulligan had turned his desk against the wall, not just to give himself more office space, but also so that he could meet with visitors as equals, with no desk as a barrier. Only a few photographs were on the wall, along with several plaques. Like funereal monuments from live people to live people. The thought made her smile, but Burnett's look froze her face. He immediately moved to take control of the meeting like some Boy Scout who was teenage mayor for a day. Watching him operate somehow made Annie feel better. She'd never again be taken in by him, but she could give him his due.

"Annie, Mr. Kelly, sorry. Jerry. The congressman and I have been talking about his speech for Monday. I've asked Annie to be here because I want her spending some time on the phone tomorrow morning, making press calls, pushing the fact that the congressman's appearance Monday is so very key to the Offensive having its full impact."

Annie gauged the congressman's appearance today at about one step this side of the grave.

"Even without a speech, Representative Mulligan's a star, huh, Burnett?" The question came from Kelly.

"We want to work on the speech with you, help out in any way we can," Burnett responded. "We want to help you staff the congressman's appearance on Monday. Annie will help advance it with the press."

Like a priest collecting for a new rectory, Kelly oozed charm. He opened the large wooden case on the banged-up coffee table and pulled out a fat cigar. "I wish we'd kick Castro the hell out of Cuba so I could get some decent smokes. How do you feel about Castro, huh?" he asked Burnett.

"Never met him."

"Think he'd like to come speak at your march on Monday?"

"Castro would like to come speak in Washington anytime he could get the invite. But no. I think that what people will be saying on the platform is not what Castro wants to be part of. He's got a different agenda than us pulling out of Vietnam, of pushing for free and open elections before we go."

"You think you're a patriot? Pushing this peace stuff? Is that patriotic?"

"I think I care about the future of America, and I don't want to see an entire generation of men become a generation of graves."

Mulligan cleared his throat. Annie felt sorry for him. It must be tough if your own staff was second-guessing you.

"Let's get on with this, okay? Jerry, what do you think we should cover, as far as background on me for Annie to start getting it out?"

"Just one thing first. As you can probably tell, I'm not happy about this decision. I think it's a mistake for Mark, at this time of his career, to go out on a limb. Especially since that crazy Texan down in the White House takes great delight in sawing off limbs and watching his enemies break their necks on the hard ground below. But since we're into it, and since he's so committed, and since I always try to do right by my boss, what I want to push to the press is Congressman Mulligan's courage in taking this stand."

"That's not what I'm talking about," Burnett interrupted. "We're interested in Mark's history, background. That kind of stuff."

" 'That kind of stuff' means nothing. No offense, but any seasoned Hill reporter will simply pull up his *Congressional Record* and check Mark's voting record and go from there. No, I think what we want Annie to stress is that it takes a lot of guts for a congressman to oppose his own president. And I want Annie to point out that other senators and congressmen who dissent just won't take the step to really criticize Johnson. A lot of these so-called doves have entire office staffs that do nothing but call up *The Washington Post* and *The New York Times* and tell them all how painful it is that their senator is caught in a moral dilemma, being against the war but not wanting to oppose the president. And to that I say 'Nonsense,' because if people are against the war—and I'm not, mind you—but if people are, then it is their duty to stand up and say it."

Burnett looked silent and somewhat unhappy. Annie was simply confused. Mulligan had stayed out of the discussion. Kelly was pouring on the pressure to make Mulligan the star of the Offensive, even though Kelly was opposed to his congressman being part of the march program in the first place. Electoral politics were turning out to be crazier than the Movement.

"We all understand how important the congressman's appearance at the march is to the success of the day. But I have a lot of constituencies to satisfy, and I think I'd have to check with the steering committee about generating this much focus on one speaker," Burnett said in the crisp way that usually let his opinion stand as analysis.

"*We* have only one constituency," Kelly responded, "but it's a constituency that actually went to the polls and elected this guy." He pointed at Mulligan. "Congressman Mulligan, when he stands up to speak, actually speaks *for* someone. So I think you better just handle your 'constituencies' as best you can. Because I'm not seeing him hang himself out to dry without at least some recognition that his act is more courageous than that of some minister or some self-appointed leader or some left-winger."

"I agree totally, Mr. Kelly. And it's a much better story, anyway." Annie spoke out, breaking the pact she and Pisano had struck earlier that day for a strategy of cooperation with Burnett. They didn't want to make him suspicious in any way. But Kelly's argument was too compelling, too true. And anyway, she thought with a mental shrug, she could act on her own without Pisano bird-dogging her every move.

"I don't want to sound like a glory hog or anything," Mulligan said, finally getting into the conversation that was deciding his entire future, "but, heck, if I'm on a limb, I want people knowing I was brave enough to climb out there."

"Of course, of course," Burnett said. "But we're just trying to give you the maximum protection from the White House. We don't want to make you the only target of LBJ's rage."

"Son," Kelly began, and at that moment everyone knew the argument was over, "none of you have to run for office next year. And none of you will go back to your district in the next couple weeks and face people who will think you are a traitor or worse. By God, if Mark is going to get hung for a horse thief, he's going to be the biggest, best-known horse thief we can promote."

No one responded to Kelly's argument, so he answered it himself, with a dismissive, "So we're all in agreement, right?" as a wrap-up. Annie shot a glance at Burnett, who was not happy, but Kelly was up on his feet, his arm around Mulligan's shoulders, pulling the congressman off to the side, and then turning, as a second thought, and asking Annie if she could stay for a few minutes; he'd pull out some not-so-standard bio stuff so she'd have it in front of her when she called the reporters.

"Why do I get such a strong feeling that you're not very happy?" Annie asked Burnett, standing in the hallway outside the main entrance to Mulligan's offices.

"Because I thought we had the same plan for this meeting. Then I get into it and it turns out you're working not for the Offensive, but for Congressman Mark Mulligan. It's not very loyal, Annie."

"You're crazy. It's much better for the Offensive to get as much prepublicity as possible, and Kelly's right. Pushing the fact that Mulligan is courageous, brave, and true is one way to get space in Sunday's papers. Get a positive twist on the Sunday night news shows."

"That's a bad call on your part. We don't need the wrong kind of publicity."

"What's the right kind? Holy Ghost appears over head-quarters? I know something about this press stuff. And just because someone suggests an idea that's not yours, well, you just can't shoot it down, Burnett. Once in a while even a leader like you has to lose a little. You can't decide what's best for everybody."

Later she would tell Pisano that in the four or five years she had worked and known and liked, and yes, maybe even loved Burnett, she'd had no idea how angry he could become. Until this moment in the hallway. Like a reporter, Pisano tried to pick apart what she had said to Burnett, to see what key phrase had set him off, and finally decided that it wasn't Annie's statement or action. No, Burnett must have had some gut-level feeling that it was coming apart, that somehow he didn't have his hands on the strings.

"You don't know who your friends are, Annie. You don't understand that I had to battle to get you this job, fight to keep it for you. We'll see in the next few days if you have any idea how this town, or this pack of reporters, works. You missed the boat in that meeting we just left, and that boat isn't coming your way again."

Later she would tell Pisano that at this moment she almost blew the whole thing, she almost began to scream about the spooks and Burnett's betrayal, of people dying in Vietnam and his victimization of boys he was supposedly committed to. "'How could you, how could you?' is what I wanted to scream. I wanted to hit him with my bag and yell and stomp him," she told Pisano.

But just at that moment, Kelly stuck his head out the door and, with a big smile, motioned Annie back into the office.

Something isn't kosher with the little Lefties, Kelly thought, sitting back with his feet on the desk, pulling out a fresh cigar, going through the short but practiced steps of smoking, of smell and cut and light. He watched Annie, settling in on the sofa across the room, and then it hit him. "I'm sorry. But here I am going through my little smoking ritual and I look across the room, and you're doing your little smoking ritual. I wish I could give the damn things up!"

"Not me," Annie answered defiantly, her attitude reflecting not what she was saying to Kelly, but what Burnett had said to her minutes before, "I love smokes. I love the stuff you carry around with you and put on a bar, the lighter, the matches, the case you carry your cigarettes in. The only time I don't like a cigarette, and this is probably sacrilegious, but I just don't like them after sex. Now I've shocked you, Kelly!" she finished up, not knowing how she'd gotten to this place in the conversation.

He shook his head. "People in my generation do it. Or did it. We just didn't talk about it."

He dragged long and softly on his cigar, watching a trio of secretaries in their short skirts and sun visors rushing to their cars to race out to Virginia Beach and the summer's last weekend. Kelly liked this girl across the room, liked what he had found out about her in the past four hours. She's an attractive girl, he thought, the kind of girl who was never very pretty but might turn out, in another twenty years, to be handsome. His wife, if she could know his thoughts (and he was glad she didn't), would say that he just liked the girl because she had red hair, an Irish name, and was obviously hand-raised by the nuns. That was probably right. We all feel familiar with what is familiar, Kelly thought.

"So here we are, a couple of micks, a pair of chowderheads, right here, in the halls of power. Hey, not bad, huh?"

Annie looked up from the pile of papers that explained just how important the young congressman from Michigan really was and looked at Kelly as if he were from another planet. "I think of myself that way, but it's fading."

"How about the Church? Guess that's old hat, too."

"I go to peace masses. I know this Jesuit at Georgetown who is very good at getting guys out of the draft, and I think he's a real saint. But like go to parish masses? Never."

"I'm a daily communicant myself."

Annie was ready with a quick comeback when she realized he was serious. So instead she said, "So's my father. Not my mother. She's certainly Catholic. But not religious like my father."

"Not that I believe everything, mind you. I have the same doubts that any rational person would have. And some of these Vatican Two things, well, I just can't understand why we have to give up the Latin mass."

"Why are we talking about this? Or, maybe I should ask,

why are you talking about this? This is the weirdest conversation I've ever had with any politician."

"I always talk like this. Maybe not about the Church. But about something that I think is personal between me and another human being. We're going to have to do some work together in the next few days, and we should know a little about each other. What rings my bell. What rings yours. That kind of thing."

"Look, that's really a nice sentiment, but we're not heading out on a crusade or anything. I'm going to read this stuff, and in the morning I'm going to be on the phone selling the risk your congressman is taking, his courage in signing on against the war. And by noon tomorrow, I'm going to be dealing with at least seventeen television people who think they've been screwed over in the allocation of platform space."

Kelly stood up and walked to the front of his desk. "Very mundane stuff, right versus wrong. All philosophical questions really come down to very mundane ideas: good versus bad, life versus death. Truth and untruth. And honor."

"You know, Kelly, in a million years I couldn't have imagined having an existential conversation with anyone today."

"But it is a matter of existence, my congressman's existence."

"I think he's taking a big risk with the Offensive. But, hell, look at the way people are turning against the war. That means that Congress is going to get turned around, and he's just going to be in the front line."

Kelly took a long pull on his cigar. For the first time, Annie wondered if he inhaled the giant rolls. She put out her Camel at the pause in the conversation, but not until she'd lit another from the hot butt.

"This is not philosophical existence. Or even political survival. No, it's his very existence. How long have you known Tom Burnett?"

Annie choked on her own cigarette. "Kelly, I'm beginning

to feel like one of those guest stars on *Laugh-In*. Like in a minute, I'm going to get a pie in the face."

"No pie. Just Tom Burnett's idea of just desserts."

Kelly came around the desk and sat beside Annie on the couch. He looked her right in the eye, like movie tough guy, and slowly, quietly, dragged her into his confidence.

"I need someone I can trust, Annie. Someone whose politics I don't agree with, but whose soul I admire. Now I wish I could tell you that I can make this kind of a guess about a person just by looking at them. But then, that wouldn't be true. And I plan to be very true with you, Annie."

Kelly stood up and began to pace the space between the couch and the desk. All these years, all his different offices must have had the same layout, since he walked out the area like a longtime convict who knew the exact dimensions of his prison cell.

"I had a quick check run on you this afternoon. Sure, the standard FBI stuff. But I have a lot of friends around the government, and even though we keep telling the public that we don't know very much about them, in truth we do. So I know about the O'Connors, your mother and father, down in Margate on the Jersey shore. I know your background. No drugs. Not too much sex. Your family's tax records, father's navy service. And I know just how Catholic that background is. And it doesn't matter if you've been receiving the sacraments lately or not. What I'm interested in is whether any of that took, the stuff about truth and about giving your word."

Annie could do little more than shrug. Her arms seemed pinioned to the side of her body.

"So now I'm going to ask you to swear a solemn oath. Kind of like a loyalty oath, but it's just between you and me, that you will be loyal to your principles and keep what I am going to tell you between us. I need an ally, a friend, Annie, and you're my only applicant for the job. You put the icing on it when you stood up to Burnett in the meeting. You believe in what you do. And so I'm going to believe in you."

Kelly had stopped pacing and looked directly at her. "Annie O'Connor. I'm asking you to swear before God that what I am going to tell you will not be repeated. I give you my word that what I will tell you will do you no harm and that I am telling you with the best of intentions in my heart."

Afterward she couldn't believe she had done it—raised her arm and said yes, that she so swore. It was all so Irish and movielike and dramatic and scary, although once Kelly began to talk, she knew she had done the right thing.

In detail, Kelly laid out to his new cohort what had gone on between Mulligan and Burnett. Years of briefing dulled-out Hill reporters on the real meanings of legislation had made Kelly a brilliant storyteller, and he pulled Annie along with lots of adjectives and a lot of suspense.

"And then your friend Mr. Burnett pulled the pictures out of the envelope, and there was my congressman, with a male friend of his, in what we called a compromising position. And that's when Mr. Burnett made his ultimatum."

Annie listened, knowing the words made sense, coming one right after the other, just as in every other series of sentences. But she felt the way she had when she was five years old and Bobby Redican had told her there just wasn't a Santa Claus. It was too much to handle, too much to hear. So Kelly finished up his little tawdry tale; she sat there for a long time, smoking her Camel and playing with the fringe on her bag. It had been one thing that Burnett was working with the Agency, one thing that he was screwing over the peace movement by giving control to the same old boys who made the war in the first place. But this was something else. This was trying to destroy a person, a friend. This was betrayal of another magnitude because it was so small and so intimate and so deadly.

"This isn't politics," she finally said out loud. "This is just vicious and cruel, and I don't know what else to say."

"You said it all, Annie. This is one crazy person. Now what I can't make out is what Burnett's talking about when he tells Mark that there are people who are in charge and who know what's best for the country."

Kelly had pulled a chair over nearer the couch and was leaning over the coffee table at the girl, like Perry Mason breaking it to the jury.

"Is he talking about the Communist party? Is this Burnett a real traitor, or what?" Kelly read his line straight. This girl was totally hooked up with Joe Pisano, who, one source over in the Pentagon had told him, was hitting everybody in town with questions about young Mr. Burnett. Kelly told himself he didn't want to prejudice her answer by letting her know too much. And he didn't want her to know how much he knew for other reasons.

"The Commies? Boy, are you off base, Kelly. Do I have a little story to tell you." Annie began to lay out the pieces of the puzzle that she and Pisano had picked up so far. Kelly's approach had worked. What he told her was much more intimate, more a "secret," than what she was telling him; he trusted her, and she was proving his trust right by telling him what she knew.

Her only omission was leaving out the fact that they had told Kapinski about Burnett. Maybe it was Kelly's reaction to "Commies," or maybe she didn't want him to think that Pisano ran around telling the world everything he knew, or just maybe she didn't think it was important. Anyway, she left it out as she told her story.

Kelly lighted on a familiar name. Simpson.

"Simpson, huh. I knew it had to be someone used to screwing around with the spooks to come up with those photos. Never let it be said that the Agency was doing anything that had anything to do with what it is supposed to be doing."

"But why, if Burnett wants to burn Mulligan and make him back down on his commitment to the march, why then didn't he want us to push Mulligan forward as a star? Hell, Mulligan falls much flatter on his face if we first say that he's the great white hope, then he pulls out."

"Just the opposite, Annie. The news media tells America that Mulligan is a courageous guy. It doesn't matter if America agrees with his politics on the war: it will admire his principles. I never get over just how much a congressman can believe in his own good press. Look at Lyndon Johnson. He had to figure out some way to make his mark, make his place in history against Jack Kennedy. So one of those little Harvard twits he keeps in the White House came up with the idea of a Great Society. I've known Lyndon a long time, and believe me, he didn't have any inkling of changing the world for poor people. But it's his key to history. When he announces it, the press loves it. And they love him. And they believe in him. And, shit, before you know it, he believes in himself. He *is* the Great Society. That could and probably would happen with Mulligan, or at least that's what I think Burnett is worried about. Mulligan makes the speech, he could be the new darling of the antiwar movement, and suddenly Burnett and his buddies are more out of control than they were before the Offensive."

"Is Burnett smart enough to have figured that out, just in the few minutes we were meeting?"

Kelly relit his cigar before finishing his lecture.

"Burnett has known this theory for a long time, if what you are telling me about him and his friend Simpson is accurate. These guys are masters at playing around with other peoples' lives. They're like good campaign managers. The managers get their candidates to perform by knowing all about ego. That's what politics is—an ego game. Why the hell would one human being decide that he knows how to lead and govern and watch over hundreds and thousands and millions of others? Just ego, Annie. Just thinking you're a little bit better than your fellow man."

Annie and Kelly sat there, like a couple on a retreat, keeping the vow of silence while going over the mysteries of the faith that had just been revealed to both of them, a funny kind of faith, in which you meet someone for the first time, and there is a spark of understanding. Annie had it in the Movement, had it in the South, but never thought that she would have it with some fat old Boston Irishman whose pants were too tight under his belly.

Kelly instilled a feeling of confidence in a lot of people. It was his talent and his job. It was often, if not always, a sham, his giving off the feeling of best friends, but always holding a little of himself, of his knowledge, in reserve.

Like with Simpson. Kelly knew that in a few hours he could know more about that man than his mother herself. With a few phone calls, he would have more pieces of the puzzle than Annie could imagine. All those G-13s out there who had needed jobs, references, a special line in a special bill, now all wanting to return the favors.

"So, my girl, let me think about this a little. I'm going to release you from your vow in one instance. I know you'll want to tell your friend Pisano what's going on. And you can. As long as he agrees never to write about Congressman Mulligan's private life. He's got to give you his word first. I'll assume he'll do that, since I still believe that journalism is the last refuge of an honorable man. Besides which, Annie, it's an unwritten rule in this town that all congressmen and senators are celibate before their wedding days and faithful all days that follow."

Standing up, Annie was trying to scrape together her bits and pieces—cigarettes, notepad, pens, Mulligan's bio. Kelly reached over and grabbed her hand in a warm, tight grasp.

"You're a good girl, Annie. Now you also tell your friend Pisano to call me tomorrow for a little chat."

Annie impulsively reached up and kissed Kelly on the cheek. His skin was so soft that her lips, used to young complexions, pressed in hard against his face. She left the office feeling both scared and honored by the conversation, hoping she could find Pisano quickly. What an honorable guy Kelly was. And she had been honorable with him, as much as she remembered to be.

## SATURDAY, September 2, 1967

How funny, Annie thought, turning over to push her head deeper into the pillow. Pisano listens black.

Otis was followed by Martha, who was followed by little Stevie Wonder and his harmonica. Other invading sounds crashed through the pillow barricade, but it was the smell of a Camel that finally forced Annie to move her head. "You shit," she told Pisano, taking the newly lit cigarette and holding it gently, as if it were a joint. She pushed herself up on one elbow and took a few long drags, French inhaling, a trick that had taken her some six months to master along with freshman Latin. "You know, Pisano, that the first cigarette in the morning always reminds me of mass. No, really. We had to be at school by eight, unless we went to mass, and then it was seven-fifteen, so that we could take our places in the chapel before the nuns filed in. Now if you went to seven-fifteen mass, you wouldn't have had breakfast. So you could go down the block to Finkle's drugstore and have some coffee and a Drakes cake. And, of course, a smoke, because Mr. Finkle hated Mother Superior because she had made him take the prosthesis out of the window. He never turned us in for smoking in uniform. So I always went to mass. Never miss the chance for a smoke."

"Annie, why do you do that, always have some nutty reason for doing something? So you went to mass. I went to mass. Christ, I thought about being a priest. And I liked it. I wish I could get the same rush now. I'd go right back."

"Think about it. A couple years back, my greatest crime was smoking a cigarette in my nice little academy uniform. Or not polishing my saddle shoes. Or having a couple of beers using a fake ID. Or kissing some boy with my tongue in his mouth. That wasn't a crime. That was a sin."

"Did you always feel this guilty?"

"Pisano, I'm Catholic. Remember, only two kinds of people feel guilty enough about blacks, about Vietnam, about poor people, to do anything. That's Catholics and Jews. No, no, look around. Ninety percent of the people in this Movement, really in it, full-time, are Jews and papes. Now I think that Jews and Catholics are afraid that they also could be on the list of the most wanted minorities, but I also believe that part of the nice Protestant way of life, like *Leave It to Beaver,* just doesn't get what's happening. The government can't be wrong, Negroes can't be equal."

"You can change the subject faster than anyone I know. I'm talking about you."

"I know. But I don't want to talk about me."

"Then let's fuck."

Annie lay back in the bed and began to wiggle with laughter. "You moron, that's the most unromantic proposition I've ever had. And no, thank you, we are not going to fuck. Look, I liked sleeping with you, all curled up in your air-conditioned bed. And smoking and talking and drinking in bed. But, as I said to you, cuddling is good, it feels cozy, but fucking would just fuck this whole thing up. You are my real, true friend. I don't sleep with friends. I sleep with boys that I don't need to be my friends."

"That's what you used to do. I want you to do something else now. I want you and me, together, to make love. Although I really think of it as fucking."

"That would mess up our friendship, because I wouldn't be able to be with you like this."

"Why not? I'm figuring that you will like it so much, you'll want to be here, lying around my bed, all the time. I am, after all, an Italian."

"You are wonderful. It isn't you. It's me. It's goofy, but once I do it, sleep with someone . . . you know, sexually, well, I don't want to do it with him, that person, again. Never. And I really don't want to spend a whole lot of time with him, either. Like not at all. So there, my terrible secret is out. I only sleep with boys once. They're disposable, like Kleenex."

Signaling the end of the conversation, Annie started to swing her legs out of bed, the T-shirt she had requisitioned from Pisano showing the edge of her cotton underpants. Pisano sat facing her on the bed, holding his cigarette with one hand and her shoulder with the other. He had gotten quite a few good feels of Annie the night before, since "sleeping hobo" included a lot of grabbing and some kissing, but now he was careful not to let his hand drift down past her shoulder blade. Pisano had a theory about his redheaded friend, and if it were wrong and he brought it up, their friendship would be blasted apart in the explosion that followed. But why not try.

"You know what I think? I think you've never had a good time fucking, so you now believe that fucking isn't a very good time."

"That's wrong. What are you trying to say—that I don't come? Give me a break. You sound like some fraternity nerd. Hey, babe, I can make your insides tremble, I can make fireworks shoot off in your head and your toes curl."

"Did that ever happen? Fireworks and trembling and toes. To you?"

"This conversation is now at an end. And I think it's also off-limits. Okay? Over."

"Annie, I care about you. And I'm a sucker enough about you to say okay, I'll never bring this up again. But I want to sleep with you. And I'll make you happy. It's not so crazy if you don't like it, or if you haven't liked it. Look who you are and what you came from. You weren't supposed to be fucking everyone who bought you a cherry Coke or took you to a movie. And now you don't even get the soda or the cinema. You just get laid. That's right, don't tense up. You're always talking like some truckdriver. That's how boys talk. Getting some. Getting laid. Balling. Screwing. Fucking. But it's nice. It's swell. It's just terrific. And it's terrific to do with somebody you really like. And I really like you."

Pisano was getting ready to continue his speech when he realized his audience was crying, big fat tears rolling down her face.

"I guess," she finally gasped, "I guess I'm a kind of a virgin. Because I've done it, but it's just never been the way it's supposed to be. And I like you so much, and it would be awful if it made our friendship go away."

But her apologia was without an audience; so taken was Pisano with her metamorphosis from tough broad to timid child that his senses were overwhelmed and he knew he was suddenly in charge. "Oh, baby, you look like a giant three-year-old," Pisano said, hugging Annie to him, rubbing her back, pulling her hair, feeling at the same time the tender familiarity of old love coupling with the drugged rush of the new.

"Honey, it's all right. You'll like it. You'll love it. We're going to have a wonderful time. Shit, Annie, give me a little time and you'll like sex more than cigarettes."

■　　■　　■

Tyler impatiently shook the bottle, and the little yellow triangles spilled out onto the bathroom floor. Nothing was going right. Here these black bitches had him up against the wall, with goddamn Bitsy doing her bougie best to drain the last drop of blood from his body, and even though he had given in to all their demands, been a statesman about it, still his position in the peace movement was threatened.

On his hands and knees, feeling in back of the john for the little tablets, he thought of Marisa. He'd like to have her in front of him right now, the little bitch, like to do her right here on the bathroom floor. He stopped his search and shook the bottle full of the bright tablets. Magic potions, Tyler thought of the pink or yellow oddly shaped pills. Not drugs. Tyler would never allow himself the indiscretion of a drug, of pot or acid.

No, these were pharmaceuticals that sharpened one's wit, honed one's senses, clarified one's philosophy. Never, Tyler admitted, sitting against the tub to make his stay on the floor more comfortable, never would he lower himself to use drugs. But, thanks to Dr. Smithfield, these little yellow beauties, and the orange ones, too, helped to finely shade one's feelings. What a wonderful line. Tyler, the preacher, wished he had a pencil and paper here on the bathroom floor. Now he was feeling energized, and in a few minutes he would venture forth to find his wife. His beautiful, whorish wife. Now, as the little yellow triangles made their way to his gray matter, Tyler reflected, laughing at his own colorful pun, his exhaustion suddenly replaced with a feeling of purpose. He pulled himself up from the floor and, with a few gulps of cold coffee, bolted down one of the orange capsules. Six little pills were two more little pills than Tyler usually allowed himself.

Some little whore was answering the phone at the march headquarters. She refused to tell him where Marisa was. That was okay. He'd track her down today. He had lots of time. He'd get her, Tyler announced to the mirror, adjusting his bow tie. He'd put her in her place. Which was right on her face, the thought of which made him laugh a decidedly unpastoral chortle in the elevator, startling the visiting doyenne of Des Moines, Lucille Moore, who later told her friends that people did the strangest things in Washington hotels, even in the very finest places.

"You always take me to the best places, feed me the finest food, array me with the best clothes," Bitsy pronounced, sitting cross-legged in Kapinski's bed, which was really Kapinski's mattress on the floor. "This position is called the doughnut lotus," she said, reaching for another fat powdered pastry, gracefully avoiding both the paper cups filled with coffee and the bowl with the puddle of milk and mound of granola. Kapinski wasn't eating, or even remembering to drink his coffee, but instead was sprawled across the bottom of the mattress, his head on a pillow that he'd covered with Bitsy's slip.

"Don't you eat, white boy? Don't you need no nourishment to keep those hormones of yours goin'?" Bitsy asked in her best "po' black folks" accent. She punctuated the bites of doughnuts with spoonfuls of granola and with occasional nudges to Kapinski's prone body. "Are you dead? You didn't seem to work so hard to make yourself dead, dearie," Bitsy announced in an accent that had suddenly become properly British.

"I love your smell. I really do. I used to think I just loved it after sex, but now I realize that it's a general addiction."

"You are so radical, Kapinski. Here, most of America believes that I and my people have a peculiar odor." Bitsy had now assumed the even more practiced accent of the very upper-class West Indian. "But you, good God Almighty, you like it."

"I like smells. I like the coffee. I like the smells of food. Have you ever cooked, Bits, ever?"

"Never. No domestic service. But, boy, I do love to eat."

"You're going to get fat, Bits. And then your name will even be funnier. Bitsy Kapinski. Fat old matron."

"No way, my dear. Not fat, and not Kapinski. Though it is nice to be asked."

"We could do it, you know. We could get married."

"We could. But we won't. I'm not sure I want to get married to anyone, let alone you."

Kapinski never got to answer the gibe, which got interrupted by loud and authoritative knocking. The two men at the door flashed IDs that looked like check-cashing cards from the Georgetown Safeway but did prove that they were employees of the Immigration Service.

"Immigration Service," Kapinski said, holding the door almost shut while Bitsy dressed hurriedly. "You got the wrong guy. I have no desire to leave the country. I love America."

The shorter khaki-suited man started to explain that they were "*Im*-a-gration, people coming into the country," when his partner protected him from falling farther down the hole: "Why don't you cut the smart remarks, Mr. Kapinski. If you would, just give us a few minutes until we ask you a couple of questions about people coming into the country. Okay?"

Bitsy had somehow extracted herself from the mattress, pulled on jeans over her undies, and was sitting on the one easy chair like the Queen Mother by the time Kapinski asked the duo in. "I'd like you to meet Miriam Makeba," he said, pointing to Bitsy with a flourish. This time Mr. Short looked impressed. "No, really," Kapinski said, shaking his head, "she's really Princess Namumba Kaboomba from Central Africa. One of those recently liberated countries that keeps changing its name."

At which point Bitsy took over, introduced herself, and asked to see the agents' IDs. That done, she asked them what they wanted, apologizing first for Kapinski's sense of humor. "It's something all of his friends have to put up with, but he also inflicts it on strangers." She was in the tea-pouring mode, Kapinski realized, dealing with the two agents as though nothing would make her happier than to help them on their mission. In the South, Bitsy, in her smart little Lord & Taylor skirts and blouses, was always the one who convinced the sheriff that he should read to all those assembled the actual warrant or statement, thus providing the grist for a lot of follow-up lawsuits. It was that same tone of cooperation and alliance that Bits was now using on the agents.

"Look, we've got some very specific questions for Mr. Kapinski here," Mr. Tall was telling Bits, when she politely interjected:

"But, sir, I am Mr. Kapinski's fiancée, and I really do want to be part of this conversation." Thank God for Bits, Kapinski was thinking, for her knowing that having a witness to this conversation protected him more than these two jokers would ever know.

"We have reason to believe," Mr. Tall continued, "that a Vietnamese citizen, Troi Van Dong, is in this country, and that Mr. Kapinski has met with him, and even knows his where-abouts at this time."

"Troi Van Dong. Ummm, Troi Van Dong. No, doesn't strike a familiar note," Kapinski said, as if he were being asked if he knew a Jack Smith or a Joe Jones. "No, that's a new one on me. But, hey, good for this guy, getting out of Vietnam. You know, it's getting very dangerous there these days."

"We have reason to believe that Troi Van Dong entered this country illegally, that you know that he entered this country illegally, and that you know where he is hiding right now."

Kapinski smiled. "I would be willing to take a lie detector test that I have no idea where this Van Dong guy is. I would be willing to take a lie detector test that I have no idea how and where this guy entered the country. You guys know that I'm involved in the peace movement. What I'm concerned about is people who are getting sent out of the United States, not getting in."

"What I'm concerned about, Mr. Kapinski," continued Mr. Tall, "is finding someone who has illegally entered the United States, and both prosecute him and those who aided him. This is assisting, abetting in the breaking of a federal law, Mr. Kapinski—"

He never got to finish his sentence. "Ah, Mr. Kramer," Bitsy queried, "if you are accusing my fiancé of an illegal act, I think I should phone up our attorney. I am sure my fiancé hasn't done anything wrong, but I would like him to have all the protection afforded him under the U.S. Constitution. You certainly would agree to that, right, Mr. Kramer?"

"This is no legal proceeding, Miss Clark. We are simply asking questions."

"Yes, of course, but I don't think my fiancé should answer those questions. Without an attorney, of course. So perhaps it would be possible for us to come to your office, maybe Tuesday morning, after the holiday weekend, and then the four of us, and our attorney, we could just all chat about this. At your office."

Bitsy had won. There were some mumbled other sentences, some formalities, and then, just as it was about to end, she played a hidden ace. "Mr. Kramer, how do we reach you, if by any chance my fiancé or I come across this person? Or if we have any questions? Do you have a card?"

Mr. Tall was now fumbling, while Mr. Short looked tense. Shit, Kapinski said to himself, these bastards are really FBI. Or something. Must be working on their own. Had a little Immigration ID run up but weren't slick enough to have some business cards printed. Kapinski couldn't wait to get Bitsy alone to squeeze her, to compliment her.

"Ah, I'm sorry, Miss Clark, I don't have my cards with me. But let me give you my number. Okay?"

Bitsy, always gracious to the end, simply smiled and said,

"Mr. Kramer, why not just leave it that we won't call you? You'll call us." She smiled and, as if tea were over, showed them to the door.

There was not one ounce of graciousness, however, when she turned toward Kapinski. Her voice didn't betray the look of hostility, of anger, on her face, when she announced, "Honey, I'm really hungry. Let's head out to breakfast." Kapinski knew she was afraid this had gone so far that his apartment was probably already bugged. Not that he was bothered by that. "Just think of every call as a conference call," a friend of his had once told him. But this was no time for a philosophical discussion with Bitsy on how important freedom of speech might be. She was obviously pissed.

"Kapinski, I am really pissed," is how she began the conversation, walking down 16th Street toward the Cozy Corner, a leftover of better, whiter days in the neighborhood. "What the hell are you doing, anyway?"

Tea-pouring time was obviously over. Kapinski decided to do something out of character and, instead of engaging in thirty minutes of debate, simply told her the facts that she needed to know, ending up with his worry that Troi Van Dong had not shown up at his apartment last night and that there was no answer on the pay phone number.

Jefferson figured the best thing about staying in a really fancy hotel was the room service. The sheets and the wallpaper and the thick towels were great, too, but the idea that all you had to do was pick up the phone and ask and somebody brought you whatever you wanted, well, that was really something. This morning, at Marisa's urging, he was trying everything new, only ordering things that were completely unfamiliar, since she had said if he didn't like them, he could just order himself up something else. And she was so cute about it all, sitting with him in the bed, with the bed trays she had made the manager provide, and the waiter right there, with the big table and everything. It was going to end in a couple of days anyhow, since he either had to file for CO or head to Canada. The guy was serving up breakfast with quite a flourish, and as he dished up each portion, Marisa did her running commentary. "This is the eggs Benedict, and the eggs are poached and the ham and the English muffin and the whole is with the hollandaise, which is made from eggs also and is difficult."

Jefferson had gotten embarrassed the first day, when Marisa fussed over him so. First she didn't have the cash for the tour bus, but then she managed suddenly to have this hotel suite. She just signed for money with the people downstairs. Like that. He said that he didn't feel good about taking money from anybody, let alone a girl. But she said it was like the peace movement, everybody sharing. "Like a love-in, you know, we're just like a small-size love-in, with having such a good time and listening to music and generally just knowing about life." Of course, both of them wanted to work at the march office every day, but Annie had a long talk with Marisa, and she and Jefferson figured out that he had such a big decision to make that it was okay not to be leafleting or answering the phones. So they had done some more touring, which was what Marisa called sight-seeing. And gone to museums, which made Jefferson uncomfortable, but Marisa told him to look at the pictures and try to figure out what the people were like. That's all. And that was a lot easier. And they went to movies, lots of them, to new ones and to old ones showing in Georgetown. They stayed and watched *Casablanca* twice, and afterward Marisa kept talking about the beauty of Ingrid Bergman. But Jefferson told Marisa that she was the most beautiful woman he had ever seen, and he meant it.

Fredrich was clearing away the plates. Marisa had told Jefferson that all the best staff in hotels was Swiss, or German, or both because after World War II everybody pretended to be Swiss. But all the best places to go, she kept saying, were

Italian, and then she would talk about them. Jefferson would almost die from wanting to go and see these things. But he knew that in the next few days he had to make a decision that would mean that maybe he wouldn't go for the next ten years. Or maybe he wouldn't go anywhere but Vietnam forever.

"Now we've had such a nice time and we've eaten so well, now it's time to decide the agenda for this day," Marisa said, settling down in the pillows and starting to rub Jefferson's back. Jefferson was immediately horny, even though he had screwed her the night before and once again, about three in the morning. It was weird, really, that here she was, married three years and, at first with him, just like a virgin, scared and nervous. But Jefferson had had a lot of experience with girls like that, back in high school and at the Citadel, southern girls who wanted to do it and would fool around with you, but then back off, because they were afraid that you wouldn't be nice to them afterward, or that you would talk about them, or that maybe after you'd made love to them you just wouldn't think that they were any great deal or anything like that. How wonderful that, really, some of the very best sex had come with girls who were so religious and kind of fussy and especially Baptists and Methodists, because after all, they knew they were saved, so how much did a little thing like this matter anyway, one little slip, one little sin? So he was always careful with Marisa and never rushed her, not too much. But once they were started, it was always the same. He would start kissing her and feeling her up a little bit, kind of fooling around. And now she wasn't so nervous about her breasts, 'cause he was really gentle with them and touched them and rubbed them a lot until the nipples just came up hard. And then he'd keep on doing it, rubbing those nipples, and he'd do it with one hand, so he could use the other to rub her knees and her legs and inside her knees, and he rubbed them in the same pattern, and even though the first few times she'd pushed her legs together, he'd liked it when they opened up slowly. Which was one of

Jefferson's favorite moments in sex, when the girl's legs started to slide apart. He thought about it a lot, when he wasn't with a girl and was just jerking off, and it was that moment that was the beginning of the opening of the flower that was that girl, and he knew at that moment, each time, that all the other petals would fall back and she would be all blooming in the bed beside him, all open and ready.

Kapinski hated phone booths. What if the door was booby-trapped? What if, when he tried to push it open, it got stuck? And then if he couldn't get anyone's attention, and then if he was out of change? What if he absentmindedly scratched his cock, and that's the picture that wound up in his file? That would give some people a real laugh.

He couldn't shake his own paranoia, and it was bending him way out of shape. He took two pieces of paper out of his pocket. One held a phone number, which he dialed; the other was a credit card number, which he carefully read to the operator. "Yes, ma'am. That's a local number. For the Democratic National Committee. Yes indeed."

Some disgruntled DNC employee had passed the number on to the march about two weeks ago. By the time the bills came in, the Offensive would be over, and Mr. Lyndon Baines Johnson would have the job of paying for the phone calls for an organization that was going to put his war out of business. Kapinski figured it was the Democratic National Committee's contribution to the peace movement. This, on top of the Dow Chemical card number he'd given to Annie, telling her, "Better death through chemistry. Also better phone calls."

With Kapinski, a little ripping off seemed to come with the territory. "Look, these people see us as scum. As dirt. So let's give them exactly what they expect. Let's fuck 'em."

The number was ringing. It was in Baltimore, but that's all Kapinski knew. He let it ring three times, hung up, and went through the whole procedure again. It seemed a little

James Bond, and that's what he had told the guy from the church peace group who had set it up. But the guy, who had somehow gotten Troi into the country, insisted that this was what the Vietnamese wanted, and Kapinski knew that in dealing with the Vietnamese there was no arguing. It was their war, so it got to be their game. Just like what happened to blacks in the South. It was okay to have white folks help, but the struggle was theirs, so they decided that the decisions were theirs.

An answer at the other end was also the end of Kapinski's attempt at philosophical analysis. "Hello, this is your peaceful friend. I need to leave a message for the visitor."

Kapinski felt like a real ass. Here he was, in some phone booth in Cy's Coffee Shoppe, speaking in code to some moron who probably had a magic decoder ring to figure out secret messages. Now the fool was putting his hand over the receiver, obviously to talk to someone else. You idiot, I don't speak Vietnamese, Kapinski wanted to yell. The phone clicked. He called the other number. He needed help. The guy on the phone told him to have dinner at the Astor around eight and that he'd be in touch.

Probably going to send me a message in invisible ink, Kapinski complained to himself. He left the phone booth and the conversation feeling more than a little depressed, then realized that what he was feeling was hunger. He ordered two Wimpeyburgers and a black-and-white shake at the counter and was trying to decide if he should have fries when the guy on the next stool started a conversation.

"Food any good here, huh?" he asked Kapinski.

"Nope, but it's cheap."

"I don't have enough money for much. But then, after Tuesday I don't have to worry about that much. That's when Uncle Sam takes over."

"You've been drafted?"

"No, I enlisted. That way I got to choose the marines. I

figure that if I have to do this, it's better to go with a top fighting unit." The waitress came and took the kid's order.

He really was a kid, Kapinski realized. "So when did you turn eighteen?"

"Today. Today I'm eighteen. I had a big party at home, in Wheeling, last night. And I figured I'd come here to D.C. for the weekend, see if there is a little action or something. I have a buddy here, but he works for the phone company and gets overtime for Saturday, so I'm just hanging around waiting for him to get done tonight."

"Action, huh. Sounds good."

"Well, you know there's this peace march, and always these kinds of girls, you know, girls who put out. Well, we figured we'd just float around and see what kind of stuff we could pick up. Go to Georgetown or whatever. And hit a few bars. And then we'd go to the march on Monday."

"Before you show up for the marines Tuesday A.M.?"

"Yep."

Kapinski finished his Wimpeyburgers, drank his shake, wished the kid a lot of luck, both with the marines and with getting some action over the weekend, and then, in a gesture that surprised himself, he picked up the kid's tab.

Bitsy was thrilled that the federal government and Tyler's church were picking up the tab for this afternoon's session. Anyone paying for the legal idiocy on both sides of the table deserved what they were getting.

Lined up to represent the church were four representatives of Clayton, McWilliams, Schroeder and Hall. Gray men in gray flannel suits, only today they had turned up in summer mufti, two in blue and white seersucker, two in tan. All four had their hair clipped tightly to their heads, although the younger one, the Harvard guy who knew the Legal Aid lawyers, had just a touch of sideburns. His tie was just colorful enough to show that he probably thought of himself as a groovy guy.

On Bitsy's side of the table, things were not so well defined. The two federally funded poverty lawyers from NYC had on jeans, open shirts, and jackets that could have been part of their bar mitzvah suits. Then there was the freebie legal help, conned out of Washington's most prestigious firm. One was a long-haired radical who did both a remarkable amount of free work on civil liberties cases and a great deal of Supreme Court litigation. He was wearing a sport shirt with a psychedelic pattern, no suit jacket, and a plain blue tie. His colleague, young and very black, was a sartorial opposite, wearing the same uniform as the church's lawyers, including the oxblood wingtips that Bitsy always thought of as "Princeton pumps." Just take a black boy from Princeton, get him through a good law school, and buy him a pair of Florsheims.

Bitsy was bored. The ladies had won and headed back to New York to announce their victory to their troops. Now the lawyers would cut and slice and dice until the victory was in little pieces on the table. Yes, yes, she knew that they had to have legal protection and legal ownership, and that legal translated into having the agreement drawn up by lawyers, but she wished the cynicism created by civil rights didn't make her believe that every *if, and,* or *but* inserted into the settlement would chip away at the victory.

Whose victory was it, anyway, when she could see Tyler across the table preening like a scrawny old rooster? She stared at him and tried to make sense of what Annie told her Marisa had told Annie. Screwing that poor girl in the ass for three years, and her too young and foreign to figure out that the equation wasn't right.

We all know too much about each other, Bitsy thought, filling up the empty space in her head created by the meeting with a shopping list of people and their problems. Kapinski's father was a Commie. But maybe his real problem was that his father was an insurance salesman. She was black, but maybe her real problem was that she was rich, spoiled, and an embarrassed product of the Seven Sisters. Annie was just generally hung up on believing that her cause was right. That could be a leftover from Catholicism or simply that she wanted to avoid having a real relationship with anybody, and any cause could fill in the blank. Shit, Bitsy knew these people better than her father, who kept himself hidden behind his "Dr."

The lawyers droned on, and her mind wandered, from her father, whom she didn't know, to Burnett, who the longer she knew him became more a mystery. She liked him, but probably for all the wrong reasons; he just moved ahead with his own agenda and didn't let anybody else's vision get in the way. But she didn't know him. He was like the most popular girl in prep school, Angie Henning, who never had a "best friend" but was everybody's favorite. Burnett never really got close to anybody, but here they were, all strung out, trying to get him to give his approval. It was such a class thing, really, that no matter how they all decried it, they all wanted some pretty, preppy Ivy League boy with Weejuns and chinos and a Brooks Brothers shirt to lead them. Not that Burnett was that. No, he was really something special. She had known that right away, when she met him in the South, in 1963.

They were sitting in the back of church, going over voter registration lists from each of Mississippi's counties. What would become the Mississippi Freedom Democratic party was just a movement to get people registered to vote. Sounded so simple, Bitsy remembered, when you heard it in the living room of a professor's apartment or from some fire-and-politics preacher in a crowded college chapel.

But it was hot in the South, hot and mean, and everywhere you looked somebody was hating you. Hating you because you were black, because you were white, because you were from the North, because you were rich or you were poor. It just didn't matter, since the hate was everywhere.

No one was good or bad. Everything was mixed. Everything was mixed, and the smell of fear came right through the armpits of the county officials just as it did from the handful of sharecroppers Bitsy and her friends pushed and pleaded into trying to register. Bitsy was one of six college kids from the North working out of this one town, all the rest white. In the way she had in those days, Bitsy quickly separated herself from the Negroes they were going to help. In the first hour she mentioned her doctor father, her Ph.D. mother, riding dressage, prep school, and even how hard it was to get good theater tickets in London.

Even now, years later and aeons of self-awareness away from that strange time, the thought of how she had acted made her bite her lip. That apology for being differently black segued into the time of all black being the same. The bigger the Afro, the better. Get rid of those slave names. And for God's sake, believe that there is something called black culture, even if it's only kids who learned to dance before they learned to read or write.

Bits was moving away from that now. Perhaps her life with Kapinski meant she always kept one foot in the "white world." But that *was* the world. So you better read like a white person and talk like a white person. And if you want to make sure that poor black folk get their due, then don't put them in a situation that they can't handle. Like today, like this meeting. Get them the lawyers, no matter what color the lawyers were.

Bitsy had built her own idea of what black was, although it was a conversation with a white man that started her off, a late night talk with Burnett that summer of 1963. The Movement, which was what they were talking about, was fueled on these late night sharings, these singsong recitations of belief and braggadocio.

"So when are you going to get your shit together?" Burnett asked her, sitting across from her and stapling registration forms to the mimeographed step-by-step instruction they had written the week before with the lawyers. Seven dozen of the applications later got rejected because they had staple holes in them, but that night stapling was beautiful.

"You mean when I am going to learn to staple in a more neat manner?" Bitsy asked back.

"No, I mean when are you going to relax and not have to explain who you are to everyone who walks in the door? Like tonight, when you had to explain to the three new boys from Princeton that your brother had been accepted but had chosen Penn instead."

"That's just making conversation."

"No, that's you making your point that you are not like the field hands we're trying to help."

"I'm sure I'm not a field hand. Maybe you have problems figuring that out, though."

Burnett stopped stapling and looked across the table at her, freezing her in her own stapling frenzy, making her chilled, like when she'd eaten a Popsicle too fast that afternoon. She even found herself pressing her tongue between her teeth, to ward off the icy blast.

"I know you're not a field hand, but I also know you're a Negro. And I know that being a Negro does not make anyone a field hand. But you think that everyone white believes that it does. What do you think—that most blacks are slated for servitude and just a lucky few slide through the cracks, like you and your family? Well, that's not what it's all about."

It was the first summer that Bitsy hadn't had her hair processed or worn a wig. Instead she'd pulled it back tightly, slicking it down with Dixie Peach, and wore big hoop earrings and scarves that fought it out with her conservative clothes as to which would own her image.

"Look at you. You're like some damn African princess. No, your hair is great and your clothes are great and mostly they are just some combination only you could come up with. And you happen to be Negro. Now for most people in

Mississippi, being Negro is something more than a casual adjective. And that's true for you, too. But I don't have to keep telling you that I'm not a redneck. Okay, maybe I do occasionally point out that 'I don't hate Negroes.' But you shouldn't feel that you have to justify your color every single time you turn around."

Bitsy was still moving the pieces of paper, but Burnett had stopped a while before, sliding back in his chair and sticking his feet up on the table. Now she too stopped and glared at him across the grimy table.

"I don't think you have any idea what it's all about. When people look at me, they don't see me, the books I've read, the feelings I have, the person I am. They see the color of my skin. That's true, Burnett, no matter how you argue it. People do it without thinking. That's the painful part. Like saying, 'Ask the Negro over there,' or 'Maybe that colored girl will know where the store is.' They don't mean it sometimes, but the adjective is right in front of me all the time. Negro, colored, or a lot worse."

"You're nuts. Not nuts about what people think, but about what you have to do to change that perception. Screw 'em if they can't see the you of you. Let them go. Some of them will catch on, and some won't, and who wants friends who can't cut it? You can't spend your life trying to convince other people that you're okay."

Bitsy shrugged.

"Everybody in life has to make a couple of real decisions. Like, if you are going to live for other people or yourself. And that's a decision between being a giving person or being selfish. Then you have to decide if you're going to let your image, yourself, be molded by what other people think or are you just going to live your life, and that's who you are."

"Some of this sounds like you've been in too many training sessions."

"Maybe. But I decided a long time ago that I was going to

make my decisions and make my life on the grounds I decided on. Once again, I'm not going back to school this fall. I keep delaying my return, although I only have a couple of courses to get a degree. I guess if the time comes when I need a degree, I'll take a few months off and get one. Too much of our lives are run by other people—our families, our friends, our government. We should at least be allowed to have control over what we think of ourselves and how we see ourselves."

"I never thought about it that way. I just figured that it was me trying to explain who I was before people thought I was something else."

"To hell with people. You don't have to explain yourself to anybody. They might be able to tell you what you can and can't do, or what you must do. But they can't tell you who you are. That part you have to hold in reserve for yourself."

The talk with Burnett, the easy late night intimacy, never repeated itself. Last spring, at a conference on the New Left, she and Burnett wound up as the leaders in the same "small group experience," with some dozen student government types trying to deal with how they would play out their roles in the context of the draft and the antiwar movement. Bitsy tried to evoke from Burnett that same response, using his remembered words to spur on a reaction: "So your most important mission, after you define your work, is to define yourself. For yourself. It's important to have friends to support and affirm you, but it's more important that you know who you are, that you decide the image you project to the world. And even if people don't understand your image or your actions, you still know that it's the right thing for you."

But nothing happened. Burnett said and did nothing to respond to her, moving the group on instead to talk of tactics, confrontation, civil disobedience, and organizing.

The two incidents just didn't jibe in her head. Burnett had set up his life a certain way, had thought about it long and hard, and yet didn't want to share the valuable information with the kids who needed it most.

"The riots have nothing to do with what we are discussing here."

The Princeton pumps attorney had raised his voice, pulling Bitsy's attention back to the conference table. What they'd obviously been talking about was the state of Negro emotions, what with Detroit, Milwaukee, Newark, and, in the past week, even New Haven erupting in the streets.

What had sent Princeton pumps off was a gray man's comment about how this agreement would help keep a lid on emotions in New York, throw a little water on the passions that were flaming in the streets.

"You're not going to settle this by buying off people. You're not going to settle this by giving people poverty programs and food stamps," Princeton was announcing in a voice trembling with emotion.

Bitsy interrupted, her voice just as strident. "And what are you going to do? Tell us. Tell us all your plan. Give black people a better self-image? Make sure the top one percent gets into an Ivy League school? Allow everyone to vote?" Mr. Princeton was now turned toward her, the anger of a frustrated child in his eyes as Bitsy roared on.

"Don't dare to speak of people not wanting to be bought out of poverty or a dead-end life. Don't stick your nose up at food stamps, and then leave here and go to a French restaurant for dinner. Don't hold poor people to a moral standard that none of us could live up to. Are those people in these apartment buildings less likely to riot this summer with water that runs and electricity that makes a fan go round? You bet your ass. Are their kids less likely to burn the building down if their mothers tell them that it's 'their building'? You got it. Are these people entitled to live a better life, and do we all expect them to 'behave' better because we give them the stuff that lets them live at a slightly better standard? That's right. Amen. So please, unless you want to move into one of the buildings under discussion, or come and live in my neighborhood in North Philadelphia, where we've also got hot-and-cold running rats, don't make poor people self-righteous. Just make them winners."

Around the table, the consensus look was meekness, but Bitsy, never one to leave a victory half-laureled, sat back in the plush chair and pronounced the much quoted line that summed up her philosophy on social justice.

"There's only one solution to poverty, gentlemen, and that solution is money," she announced, waiting for the simplistic sense of her sentence to sink in. She then added, almost unnecessarily, "So let's see how much of that magic money potion we're going to be able to prescribe today."

It was probably the proximity to the pulpit that put her in such a preachy mood, she told Kapinski later. "After all, honey, you know how it is with us Episcopalians. We just start hollering and shouting and dancing with the Holy Spirit in the aisle."

Burnett was also spending a great deal of his afternoon in church, this one an African Methodist Episcopal outpost near 16th and R. The Reverend Elijah Brown, the fourth generation of preachers the Brown family had given to the world, sat with Burnett in a back pew. The dark church was unable to keep out the bright summer heat, and the sweat poured down from under the sleeves of Brown's pale blue polyester shirt, making silver rivers down the thick, deep brown mounds of his arms. The Reverend Brown was not happy.

"Tom," he said slowly, allowing the "o" to drift off into the "m," mantralike, "Toooommmmm, you peace people are going to start a war in my church."

Burnett sat in the deep afternoon heat, comparing the sweat on his own body, fragile-looking rivulets, like tears, making their way between his underarm paleness to the crisp tan that had grown permanent on his lower arms. A truckdriver tan; Burnett had gotten badly burned two years ago in Santa Marita, and now it seemed that a single hot day could bring back the bronze.

"I have it under control, Johnny," Burnett said, using the nickname that Brown had himself chosen as a child, when the Elijah proved too difficult. In later years the preacher would use his name as a stepping-off point for sermons that were more about tactics than about theology, homilies on courage, conversations with God and his fellowman about compromise. "With a name like Elijah, a kid had to be either a fast runner or a strong fighter. I was neither...so I changed my name."

Brown was always preaching about compromise and coalitions, about the church joining forces with other groups, not as a permanent commitment, but for a temporary lease on power. Big issues, like life and death, war and peace, freedom and slavery.

"Not sleeping bags, for Pete's sake, Tom. I can't believe I am going to have my entire congregation up in arms and yelling for my neck on a plate because of sleeping bags."

"I can't control every aspect of the antiwar movement."

"You can tell these college kids that when they are guests in the house of the Lord, they can play by His rules, which means that for a couple of nights they don't play at all. They come here and they sleep. And we make sure of that because we sleep the boys here, in the church, and we put the girls in the community hall."

"I'll try. I'm not going to play chaperon to some NYC grad students."

"Well, I'm going to play the servant of the master of this house. And they are not going to sleep together."

"It's the picky details like sleeping arrangements that keep the revolution from happening. Like today, the twenty-minute fight with the head of the Young Marxists for Peace, don't ask me who the hell they are, who wanted to hang a large picture of Lenin from the back of the speakers' platform. Or the druids—we've had these nuts in the hallway for days. I don't know what, but they sure are a pain in the ass. They're chanting all the time."

Johnny listened, as always sympathetic. What Burnett couldn't tell him was that all this petty, piecemeal stuff was nothing compared with the bomb that only he, Burnett, knew about, with the explosive that he had built and would light this afternoon. For a moment he thought about Mulligan with a bit of compassion; too bad that an adolescent inclination could so control an adult's whole life. Burnett had played prep school pool, keeping other boys' balls in his pocket. But that was just part of the system, like sucking up to certain masters so you could get the best college recommendations and having your parents hire a tutor for the summer so you could whiz through math.

Everything had seemed in its place until he went to the Caribbean. In the South, it was Simpson's advice, his sage counsel, that bound Burnett to him, that strengthened their mentor-protégé relationship. Sure, he knew that the talks he and Simpson had were not totally private. He knew that Simpson would use the information he passed on to further his own goals. But those were Burnett's goals, too. A shared world vision—that was their pact.

It all changed a few days before leaving for Santa Marita. In a meeting in Simpson's office, T. R., along with two other "advisers," had been circumspect when they'd talked about the "project," doing little to conceal the fact that there were details Burnett could not know.

When the other two left, Simpson told his young protégé that although there was general confidence in Burnett's judgment, some elements of the "project" were protected by law. It seemed so casual, so sincere, as T. R. pulled out the papers from his desk, explaining that it was a matter of "national security. Just a formality, really, since I trust you and you trust me. But for those of us who really care about America's place in the world, no precautionary step is too much."

Of course he'd signed the papers. It was a pattern of request and acceptance that had been used for twenty years. The "old boys' network" was what outsiders would see as the connection between Simpson and himself, ties of money and background. What outsiders didn't realize, what Burnett did not question, was what an easy step it was to replace the strings of similarity that bound him to Simpson with unbreakable cords of commitment. So easy that it was weeks afterward when Burnett realized that it was *the* national security oath that he had signed. He didn't think of that document then, or now, as a pact with the devil. Simpson had chosen correctly with Burnett. His protégé hated Communists. Just as despised were the right-wingers, the fascist generals and junta leaders, who gave the Left credibility in countries called by the misnomer "developing." What bothered Burnett about signing the oath was that the truth came only after the pledge. There was no way to make a decision on taking the pledge or not, since the very existence of the pledge was the real secret. T. R. Simpson that day had inducted him into this, the most secret society, assuming, of course, that it was an honor Burnett would not want to turn down.

At Yale, Burnett had been tapped for Skull and Bones in his junior year, one of only twelve who would receive the honor of this most prestigious secret society. But he had not returned for the fall semester and thus knew only secondhand and, he imagined, inaccurate reports of what had happened in the pyramid building. At Yale, the tapping was itself a mark of distinction, of trust, of achievement, selection by one's peers for a place of honor.

The tapping for the secret society Burnett now belonged to contained none of that pomp or circumstance, no black-tie meetings. What it meant was access to real power, to the magic and mystic movements of men who brought about the real change in government, men whose portfolio he now carried. Burnett was, he acknowledged to himself, a real patriot, one who would never receive the honor of his country or the understanding of his fellow citizens, but who nevertheless was engaged in the deepest battle to save and protect all that he believed sacred to himself and to them.

It was Johnny's hand on his shoulder that brought Burnett back, and the surprise of it, that big hot paw, turned the sweat on Burnett's body cool. "Sorry if I jumped. I guess I had floated away."

"Burnett, I've never seen you like this, all that time in the South, all those times when you were some lily white boy and all the other white boys were on the other side. Do you have something eating at you, friend? You look as troubled as I have ever seen anybody."

"I have a crazy colored pastor driving me crazy with his rules for separating the sexes. Didn't God pair off all those survivors by two, didn't he give the word to go forth and multiply?"

"He might've done that, indeed, but we ain't setting off the next generation in my church." Johnny laughed, then frowned. "Whatever it is, Tom, don't avoid it. Tell me what is eating at your soul. The look on your face is not from bad politics, but from feeling bad inside."

"Johnny, do you remember in the South, when we would have those late night meetings, and every once in a while, somebody would actually say it, that they were scared and couldn't figure out what they had done to get themselves in this place and how they wished they hadn't come south, or hadn't signed on..."

"Or hadn't been born Negro. That was the one I was always wishing. Sure, I remember it. I think all the time about what my life would have been like if, when Dr. Stendahl said to me that I could be a great religious studies scholar and that in six or seven years I could have a Ph.D., I hadn't just said to him, 'Right you are, Dr. Stendahl. Let me hide out here in Harvard Divinity School and let me send checks from my royalties to cover the costs of the struggle in the South.' Do I remember that feeling? I think of it every time I meet with the church committee and talk about a new roof or whether or not we should let the choir sing at a farmworkers' fund-raiser."

"Or field complaints about the peace marchers sleeping together?"

"Yes. My life is all tied up in the mundane. Christ was funny. He told us to go and feed his lambs and sheep and forgot to tell us how to duplicate the miracle of the loaves and fishes."

"Do you believe in miracles, Johnny?"

"I believe that people can be moved to do miraculous things. Like the loaves and fishes. Suppose, just suppose, that all those people, those thousands of people, showed up to hear Christ, and that a lot of them did have food, bread, and fish, which they hid because they didn't want to share it. So when the kid comes forward with his five fishes and two loaves, and Christ praises him, well, then the people in the crowd are ashamed, so they pull out their fishes and loaves and suddenly there is enough to feed everybody."

"That's the first plausible miracle I've ever heard of."

"All miracles are plausible, to God."

"Johnny, you really believe all this, don't you. Like it's not like you went into the family business or anything?"

"Like selling shoes? No. But do I believe it totally? From the pulpit, I have to say 'yes.' Or 'Amen, brother,' because I'm a Baptist, and what has held my church and my people together is believing the whole story. But do I, in the privacy of my soul, believe everything that I preach about? Depends on how good is the sermon. And whether or not that particular morning I've had my coffee, or a nice talk with the bride. Or if the kids were sick the night before. It's hard to keep your head in the big picture when you have to be so busy with the details."

"That's why I came here today. To deal with this detail. The Offensive is now running on its own steam. I've delegated everything. And I wanted something to solve, to fix. I wanted to be distracted from the big picture."

"Or from something else. Listen, it's been years since I took Psych 101, but you act like you are in great distress. And if you can't talk to me, isn't there someone you can talk to? Somebody that's like family? Who can help you, as we say in the God trade, who can help you heal your soul?"

"There's someone. But he's the last person I can have this talk with. Anyway, Johnny, can I use your phone for a minute? I need to check on yet another detail."

Mulligan had watched the morning tick away. On Kelly's advice, he'd skipped the steering committee meeting at the march offices. Kelly had come by and worked with Mulligan, not on the speech, but on the short statement that the congressman held in his hand. Kelly had printed out the several sentences in big block letters, clear and crisp, except for the place where Mulligan had held the sheet too tightly and the sweat from his hand had made the letters fade and run together.

In his head the thoughts were like the wet letters on the page. Everything was happening outside this room: that girl on the phone, Kelly back at the office looking for what Mulligan wasn't sure was even there, Burnett pulling strings that Mulligan thought had been disconnected years before. It was almost one o'clock. Burnett would soon call, expecting Mulligan to tell him that he, the young and brave congressman, could not be a party to the Offensive Against the War. It was, he was to tell Burnett, too radical, too polarizing, too much outside the mainstream of American politics.

"But why do I have to say these things to you on the

phone?" he'd whined at Burnett the day before. "Why do I have to carry out this pretend surprise?"

"Because it is likely, since there's been the announcement of your participation, that there's a tap on your phone. And with the FBI, you never know how many people will get to listen in. As a friend of mine says, 'Every call's a conference call.' So for all the possible members of the audience out there, we will both play our parts. I will call up and ask you how your speech is coming along. You will ask me if I have control over some of the real crazies who you now understand will also be speaking. I will tell you no, that they are still hanging in there, and you will get nervous and back out. Finally and forever."

Mulligan pushed himself down in the covers. He kept the air conditioner going all the time so he could always sleep with a quilt. It was so cozy, so comforting. If only he didn't feel so tense. Mulligan was playing a Barbra Streisand album. He'd gone to New York just a few weeks ago and caught her Central Park concert, he and this cute airlines ticket agent he'd met on a previous trip. Such a nice guy, and sophisticated, too, for that kind of job, what with the travel and everything. Thinking about the evening had Mulligan's cock pushing hard against the weight of the quilt. And, for the first time since the nightmare had begun dozens of hours before, Mulligan laughed. At himself. "You stupid ass," he said out loud. "Here is your entire career and life on the line, and you're getting a hard-on thinking about some pretty little fairy in Central Park. You're acting like some goddamn old queen."

The phone rang. But it was not Burnett. It was the Offensive's press girl, Annie. Kelly had been so goddamn vague with him about her role in all of this, evasive, really, saying that once the march was done with, he would fill in Mulligan on a lot more detail. But she did sound like a friend on the phone.

"Congressman, I just want to tell you that there's been terrific response about your role in the Offensive Against the

War. Some reporters have been calling up the House leadership and getting some reaction about what this really means."

"Annie, the only thing that the Speaker is going to say is that I am one congressman out of four hundred thirty-five, and that's not a hill of beans."

"That's not what one of the guys from the AP said to me. He said that there had never been such a big crack in the 'we're all together in this war' image that LBJ likes so much. It's one thing to get up and give a speech about tactics or about negotiations, but that standing up and saying you are against the war, that's something else."

"I didn't get that feeling at the press conference Thursday. I guessed, maybe I was wrong, that if it had been Bobby Kennedy there, then it would have been news. But I'm just some backwater hick congressman."

"Naw, sometimes it just takes reporters a little while to catch on. Jerry Kelly was exactly right. The focus of tomorrow's stories on the Offensive shouldn't be the more traditional peace groups turning out to protest once again. No, the news is that you signed on, and that means the antiwar movement is broadening. People all over the country are going to stand up and applaud, and then they're going to be part of the Movement."

"I hope you all move to my district so you can vote for me next year," said Mulligan, who was starting to enjoy his own jokes.

He felt strange, putting the phone back in the cradle, waiting for Burnett to call, scrambling under the bedcovers to find the Kelly-printed page. But strange good. For these two days he'd lost the sense of purpose and, yes, the courage that he'd had when he'd made the decision to speak at the Offensive. Sliding out of bed, he searched on the floor of his closet and came up with a new pair of bell-bottomed jeans, which he pulled on with no thought to underwear. He went into the bathroom, washed his face, combed his hair, and by the time

Burnett's call came, just ten minutes later, Mulligan's hand hardly sweated at all.

"Hi, Congressman?" Burnett queried. The son of a bitch, Mulligan thought, him and his upper-class formality, so if there is a tap on the phone, they know it's really me.

"Yes, Tom. How's it going?"

"Great here, Mark, although we are still having trouble finalizing the speakers' list."

Mulligan stared at the paper in his hand. "Have you been able to get the more radical of the groups to have just one speaker, rather than have several repeating the same strident stuff?"

"I'm sorry, Mark, and I hope this won't in any way affect your decision, but I think we're going to be stuck with the same lengthy and repetitive list that I showed you in the office."

Mulligan paused. Kelly told him to say a Hail Mary to himself, to get the right setup on the phone, "and the prayer won't do you any harm, either."

So now here goes. "Burnett, I guess you've tried your best, and I'm really sorry because some of these groups run so counter to what I believe." Pause for effect. "But you and I know, Tom, that the really important issue here is the war. We know that it's important to show how wide and how deep dissatisfaction with this immoral war is in America. And that's why, no matter what happens with the speakers' list, I'm with the Offensive to stay."

That was all Kelly had written, so that was all Mulligan said. He sat holding the receiver, listening to Burnett's breathing. After another moment, and still nothing from Burnett, Mulligan announced cheerfully, "Well, I've got a lot of work still to do on the speech. Thanks for your concern, Tom."

"Okay, Congressman. Well, it's good to know where you stand. Good luck, and, as they say in Hollywood, see you in the pictures."

Mulligan's hand was sweating now, but his head was clear, and into it popped something that Kelly had said that afternoon.

"You know, Tom, I hope there are a lot of pictures, and I hope people know that I'm standing up for what I think is right. And I hope they understand that this is despite placing my career in jeopardy, because I think the American people are fair and I think they'll judge me fairly, and not take to character assassination or innuendo. What do you think, Tom?"

There was no response, just heavy breathing.

"I have some other words for you, Burnett, and for your friend Mr. Simpson. Because I know just what you and he are all about. You want me to pull out of this protest because you and T. R. Simpson think you can run the country better than anybody else, that you have some kind of a God-given right to decide what the hell the future should look like. So don't you tell me about pictures. There are lots of pictures. And maybe you and Simpson weren't lying nude on some balcony, but when you were in Santa Marita, honey, you two were fucking the country."

Burnett slammed down the receiver, and Mulligan just as quickly dialed Jerry Kelly, then burst into tears at the first "Hello."

"Mulligan?... Mark, talk to me. What happened?"

"I did it. I read the paper. Then I probably screwed up, because I told him I knew about him and Simpson. And about Santa Marita. You shouldn't have told me. I just lost my temper. That's dumb, right?"

"Maybe. Maybe not," said Kelly, who had never made a slip and said something to a congressman that he didn't want the world to know. "Maybe it's an insurance policy, one you never have to pay on. Whatever, that's not important, kiddo. What is important is that you told him clearly that you were going to participate in the march, right? And now I'll be over in about an hour, and we'll write up a great little speech. I've had three press calls this afternoon about what a major role you're playing, so we're doing just fine on that front."

"Jerry? Thank you. I don't know what I'd do—"

"Let me tell you what you're going to do. You're going to be one great fellow. You're going to be a member of Congress who votes his conscience and who stands up for what he believes in. And I'm going to do the wheeling and dealing to keep you in that seat."

Kelly got off the phone and reached in the top drawer to grab yet another cigar. What the hell, he thought, succumb to temptation, and, lighting up, he waited for the phone call that would help him complete what he thought was the whole puzzle.

"Why do we eat here, anyway?" Pisano asked more of himself than of Annie, yelling over the noisy crowd in the Astor's doorway.

"It's cheap. It's ethnic. It's here. Because if everyone we know eats here, it must be good."

"I hate this place. The only good thing are the forty-nine-cent martinis."

"You'll go blind. They're probably made from ethyl alcohol."

"Maybe it's a plot. Wipe out the entire movement. Dead by overdose on moussaka."

"Three, please. No, the third guy is here. He's just peeing."

"Why do you do that?"

"Lie about being all here? So we get a table."

"No, say something like 'He's peeing.'"

"Because 'pissing' doesn't sound as elegant."

"Thank God you're good in a bed."

"Do you really think that?"

"That 'pissing' doesn't sound so elegant?'"

"Screw you."

"Yes. Let's skip Kapinski and go do that."

"So you do mean it? That you like doing it with me."

"Well, 'like' is a strong word. How about delight, relish, crave?"

"Here's Kapinski."

"Why did the guy at the door ask me if I was pissing in the street?"

"Forget it. Annie's got a weird sense of humor."

"A martini and the moussaka. Why do we eat here all the time?" Kapinski asked after ordering.

Annie sat smoking as Pisano slowly and carefully walked Kapinski through the story they'd cooked up together earlier, carefully pointing out that Burnett had some "power, some information," over Mulligan, but that they weren't privy to any details.

Kapinski drank his martini down in one gulp and waved the waiter over to order another one. Annie could never get over his capacity for booze and, when he still used it, how much grass he could smoke in an ordinary day. She knew from Bitsy that two years ago, when Kapinski's paranoia had hit a high point, he'd sworn off getting high, saying that if he was going to jail for something, it wasn't going to be for smoking a joint.

"This is really heavy shit," Kapinski finally said. "Don't worry. I'll protect the ass off the congressman, although getting a little ass is what probably got him in trouble, huh?"

"Who's to know? What we have to figure out is what Burnett is going to do."

"Shit, Annie, I can't figure out what the hell Burnett is doing screwing around like this." Kapinski was ignoring Pisano. "Does this mean that everything he did has just been leading up to screwing us up? All the time in the South. All the meetings. Everything."

"You're making too much of this." Pisano was being "reasonable," a pose that always struck Annie as fake. Nobody was "reasonable" about things they felt strongly about. People should yell and scream and fight. Reason had nothing to do with it.

"Let's be reasonable," he continued, bringing a knowing nod from Annie. "I'm the one who got the story. I'm the one who's working on the story. But, give me a break, what was Burnett? Teenage agent? The madras spy? Did he start in short pants?"

"You don't get it, Pisano," Kapinski shouted, banging the table and just missing his plate.

"I just don't have the same conspiracy theory of life that you do. That's all," Pisano yelled after him as Kapinski marched off to the bathroom.

The reporter turned to Annie. "I just don't think I can play into Kapinski's, or Harold Sams's, paranoia. Between you and me, I do think these are big-time players. I'm not naïve. I know that. And I thought enough about the Offensive to tell you and not to break this story too early. But being a committed liberal instead of a radical does not mean that Burnett is in the pocket of the government."

Kapinski returned, and ordered up yet another martini, shrugging as if he were going to drop the argument. Then he started on another tack, this one directed at Annie. "So, are you going to tell other people about Burnett, other people in the Movement?"

"I don't know." Annie seemed vague, lighting cigarettes and forgetting to smoke them. "Yes, I guess. I don't know. What do I tell them? I mean, Pisano is going to have this story in the paper on Monday, the morning of the Offensive, stressing the connection between Burnett and Simpson, raising the question of who is really deciding where the peace movement should go. That should thoroughly ruin Burnett, I mean as far as any involvement in any other peace stuff. Maybe he'll go back to Central America. Maybe he'll go to law school...."

"And then he can get a job in the White House dealing with youth and civil rights organizations." Kapinski was relentless.

"But in civil rights, Burnett was terrific. I know that. I was there," Pisano said, wondering how he'd wound up in this conversation defending Burnett.

"Sure, Pisano, you were there. You were at the Democratic National Convention in Atlantic City, with the Mississippi Freedom Democratic party. And you were there when we got sold out. We got nothing for all our work. We got two seats, two lousy votes out of a whole delegation, and nobody who worked down in Mississippi for two years got to participate in the decision."

There was another round of drinks and a quick good-bye on M Street, with Annie and Pisano heading off to Georgetown and Kapinski saying he was going to make the rounds of a couple of the churches where kids were sleeping.

Pisano and Annie walked along, holding hands.

"Kapinski is really dedicated," Annie finally said.

"I'm a reporter. I'm not going to change."

"I'm just saying I admire his commitment."

"You can admire him all you want. Just as long as you come home and sleep with me."

Kapinski was pissed. "I hate all this 'peace and love' shit. I hate these hand signals, like a V-for-victory sign. I hate the fact that every sicko in America has some plan to end the war."

"I think you had too much to drink and you should get some sleep."

Bitsy was sitting at the table, wearing only a giant T-shirt and writing in her teeny spider scribble on yellow sheets of paper. As Kapinski watched her, she seemed to be scratching out more than she was writing in, but he knew that Bitsy would trim and fix and tidy up her speech until it looked ironed, like everything else she owned. Even her T-shirt.

"I need to talk to you."

"I need to write, so I don't sound like a fool. 'Sorry, Dr. King is busy in Chicago at the big people's meeting, so we've brought you the third-string Negro to speak out today for peace and justice.' I would like to not make such a fool of myself."

"This is about the Offensive."

"I didn't think it was about modern playwrights. *This* is about the march. My speech. It might not be a bad idea for you to work on what you are going to say, rather than ranting and raving the way you sometimes do."

"I'm not going to speak."

"Say what?"

"I'm going to introduce Troi Van Dong. That's the plan. He's going to be in the crowd, and when I get up to speak, I bring him up on the platform."

Bitsy took everything in, calmly and quietly, like the perfect graduate student in Romance languages that she should have been, only asking a couple of pertinent questions. The agents with the fake IDs had rattled her, despite her demeanor.

"It's really weird. All this time, all through the South," she told Kapinski, "we were always talking about agents and taps on the phone and spies. And even when the stuff came out about the National Student Association and the Agency, well, that was something else. Something far away. But these guys were here."

"I knew it. And everybody thought I was a crazy lefty."

"You are. You're crazy, with this Dong thing. You have no idea what the guy is going to say. Suppose he calls for armed insurrection. Suppose he calls for revolutionary steps. What will you do? Stand there and say that you believe in peaceful change?"

"Maybe I don't. Maybe a lot of people are getting impatient with everything being done by the book. This summer, every riot, every single city where young Negroes rioted—hell, why is that different than countries where there was a revolutionary takeover?"

"Because you can't charge the riot to your air travel card.

Get straight, Kapinski. We have a lot of weekend radicals, a lot of summertime protestors. And hopefully we will be able to stir up enough shit to get out of Vietnam and get back to helping poor people again. But the reason we have all these kids upset is that most of them are draft bait. And the girls are upset because the boys are going. It has nothing to do with the war in that smelly little country. It has nothing to do with *giving* people anything; it has to do with some people *keeping* what they've already got. Staying alive and not dying in some rice paddy. Giving Negroes some jobs so they don't burn down the whole city."

"That's the most cynical bullshit I've ever heard."

"Kapinski, what's pure enough not to be cynical? Bringing some wanted-by-the-South-Vietnamese-government revolutionary to make his D.C. debut on a speakers' platform that we all will share? You're not cynical. You're just crazy."

"What about the way *you* feel about the war?"

"I feel that I don't really give a shit about people I don't know. I feel sorry, really sorry, when I see the network news. But not the way I felt when I saw kids in the South with rickets. Or in North Philadelphia with rat bites or brain damage from eating paint."

"Maybe that's because the kids in the South and in North Philly are black kids. Maybe you can't feel that way about yellow kids."

"Don't put any Third World stuff on my head. It's not the color. It's that they're American kids. They aren't supposed to be bitten or beaten or done in or watching some screaming redneck pig spitting hate. They're supposed to be watching *Mr. Rogers.*"

"What you're saying, Bits, is ugly. And it's wrong. You're choosing American kids over Vietnamese kids. What I hear you saying is that the only reason to save Vietnamese kids is to save American kids."

"Well, I wouldn't have put it that way, but, yeah, that's what it comes down to. If I have to choose, I choose mine."

The neon street looked too much like Saigon.

Even though he knew the man would be angry, Dong had wandered the streets of Washington through the early evening hours. To have come this far and see nothing, that would be stupid. So he stood like a tourist in front of the White House, watched the guards carefully ignore the antiwar pickets, then strolled up 14th Street.

And here, at the corner of 14th and H, it was so very much like Saigon, at least the city of the never-ending war. Girls were in the streets and in the bars, black women with abbreviated shorts and white boots, their pink lipsticks like neon slashes against their dark skin. He walked slowly, careful not to make eye contact, since that would be an invitation for a sexual encounter. Always the Americans in his family's restaurant had told him that the sex in their clubs was nothing like what happened in Saigon. There, in one club that the soldiers liked, they could stand up close to the bar, and, through holes cut in the wood and plastic, girls would reach out and take the cocks out of their khakis and pull the instruments through the holes and work them off to a state of climax, even as the men were drinking and joking with their comrades.

Prostitutes and camp followers. That's what the Americans had made of his country's women. Whores and pigs. All Americans were the same, ugly and pale like fishes. And now he was an instrument of the Americans. He had no thought, no belief, no trust, only a love for his family and for his sister, hooked on heroin and in that bar, crouched down like an animal and servicing men who would never even see her once beautiful face.

## SUNDAY,
## September 3, 1967

Jefferson Talbot stretched out and stared at his feet, all pink and smooth, propped up on the pillow at the foot of the bed. He had thought Marisa's idea was crazy, an "afternoon of being taken care of, of being pampered, a new experience." A visit to a beauty parlor, that's what it was, only Marisa kept calling it a "salon." And it had been something, sitting in the mirrored room, on a pink chair that was like the one at the dentist's, only softer; one woman doing his fingers, another his feet. Then the "herbal wrap experience," which he thought was just fine, only he wouldn't do it again. But the massage, boy, that was something, the man and the woman coming right here to the hotel, setting up their tables in the parlor of the suite and he and Marisa wrapped up in big white towels like kids at the beach. They lay on the tables and talked a little, but mostly just enjoyed the rubbing and the pulling and the hurting. And then they had a long nap, and when they woke up they made love and then got dressed and went downstairs to dinner, and then they went to the nightclub and they danced, but mostly slow dances, like an old married couple out for their anniversary. And they drank brandy, only Marisa called it cognac, and when they got to bed, too tired and too drunk even to make love, they had wrapped themselves around each other and fallen asleep. And that was very nice, too, Jefferson decided.

"Another wonderful day, huh?" Marisa said, coming out of the bathroom, drying her hair with a towel. Every day Marisa washed her hair, wrapped it up in a neat widow bun at her neck, then took it down in the afternoon, letting it fall into deep waves down her back. "Wet hair or not, here I come,"

Jefferson yelled, standing on the bed in what he hoped looked like an attack pose, his cock straight out like a knight's lance.

"No, no, not yet. Now we must talk."

"We talked last night. Now we must make love."

"We didn't talk about the war or about what we are going to do with your draft."

"I don't want to think about it. Maybe I can file for CO. They ask you some questions about whether or not you would have fought in World War Two. I guess I would say 'yes.' I would be denying everything I believe in if I denied some of the things I believe in."

"Sometimes we believe different things at different times."

"That, Marisa, is called 'situational ethics.' You have an idea of right and wrong, but you can change it, depending on what the situation is. Now some things that I used to believe I've let go, but not my ideas of honor or duty." Jefferson reached down and gently grabbed Marisa's right breast before he finished the sentence: "And other things that I used to ignore I just hold on to real tight." Both of them laughed at his bawdy joke, but Marisa quickly returned to being serious.

"I am mixed up. My husband, he talked about good all the time, but what does it mean when he acts the way he does?"

"He's just one sick cookie. Maybe he's on drugs, or maybe he's just crazy. No man could do to you what he's done, not to mention not doing to you what he refused to do, and not be crazy."

Marisa swung her wet hair around, half shaking her head no. "Okay, so what are you to do?"

"I could go to Canada. But that's like running away. I can fake a little and get a CO. I don't know which would hurt my family more. I could go back to my draft board and tell them I am crazy, and probably everyone in my family would back up that statement. Or I can stand up for what I believe in and do something that's really nuts and burn my draft card. A couple dozen people have burned their cards this past year. They become felons. The law says you have to carry your draft card with you all the time, until you are twenty-six. But, hell, Marisa, I believe this war is wrong, and maybe I should just do something about it."

"We could run away. To Italy."

Jefferson curled his newly buffed toes under, then wrapped his legs around Marisa and pulled her toward him on the bed. "You are Italian. I am American. Maybe you didn't notice, but this is my country. I have had my father and uncles and grandfathers and probably even great-greats fight for this country. I think they were right. I would fight for my country. But this war is not my country, and I don't believe in it. If I step away from this, walk away from this war, then I have to do it in such a way that I don't dishonor them. My ancestors."

Marisa had trouble with the concept. First, that anyone who was American could think about having ancestors was just crazy. It wasn't as if Jefferson came from a noble family or anything. And then, couldn't someone be paid to make whatever arrangements were necessary that he wouldn't have to go? He was so cuddly and warm, his long, tight body so wonderful to rub against. And as soon as she did, the amazing reaction from his wonderful thing.

In another minute they would have been too engrossed to notice the knocking at the door, but Marisa peeled herself away from her lover and, despite his protests, padded across the room, pulling on her robe as she went. "It's probably a little something from the director. I was calling to him yesterday about a brunch."

She opened the door, and Tyler pushed past her into the sitting room, then into the bedroom itself. Jefferson was too confused to react to the entrance, looking like a broken wind-up doll all crumpled up in the wrinkled bedclothes.

"You whore. You slut. I'm going to kill you," was how

Tyler began, but he didn't get much further. Jefferson jumped
up in bed, oblivious to the fact that he was naked.

"Sir," he announced to Tyler, "don't start any of your
nonsense here. I demand that you immediately leave this
room."

"I'll leave the room, you son of a bitch. But I'll take this
whore with me." Tyler grabbed at Marisa, who was trying to
get through the doorway, past him to the bedroom and Jefferson.
He held her by her upper arm, shaking her so violently that
her wet hair and head bounced like a rag doll.

"Paul, please, no. Please, stop. I'll talk with you. I'll
explain."

"What would you say? That you violated your marriage
vows? That you are cheating some ordinary prostitute out of a
living? That you have made a fool and a cuckold out of your
husband?"

Jefferson could never remember in what order things
happened after that, only that Tyler first spit in Marisa's face,
then, holding her head with one hand, smacked her across the
face with his other. And Jefferson could remember that Marisa
yelled out only one word. Not for help. Not for Tyler to stop.
Not an apology or a curse. Only one word.

"Jefferson!" she screamed.

Generations of Talbots had fought for honor and glory.
Years of Citadel training had sharpened his skills, and his
youth gave Jefferson even more of an edge. But it was anger
that arched his back, that curled his hands into fists, that had
him jump off the bed and throw a perfectly manicured kick
that reflected top grades in three summer courses in guerrilla
warfare.

Tyler yelped with pain as the foot bashed into his neck,
but he didn't release his hold on Marisa's hair. "You bastard,
let her go!" Jefferson shouted, and whether through pain or
through sheer stupidity, Tyler crashed to the floor and pulled

his wife on top of him, her hair falling over his face just as it had crested over the pillow just minutes before.

Jefferson grabbed Tyler's hand, pulling the fingers back from his lover's hair, and then scooped Marisa up and onto the bed with one hand while holding Tyler flat on the floor with his foot.

"Let me up. I'll kill you..." Tyler started on a rampage. But that was his last threat.

Jefferson grabbed the minister around his neck, and slowly, gracefully, like a father hoisting a child, he lifted the now stiffening body until Tyler's eyes were level with his own, leaving the preacher's feet dangling several inches above the carpet.

"No, Reverend Tyler, you will not kill me. But I can and I may kill you. I can do it with such ease that a quick squeeze here"—he pushed against Tyler's Adam's apple to demonstrate—"or a thin knife pushed in here"—raising his knee against Tyler's groin—"and you would be gone. Forever. And I could do it without a second thought, because you have harmed her."

Marisa, gasping big, deep breaths, was bent over on the edge of the bed. Jefferson, still holding Tyler aloft by his neck, turned the hanging body a little to the left to give him a better view of his wife.

"Look at her. Look at her this once and then never look at her, or for her, again. I'm not saying don't touch her, or don't talk to her. I'm saying you can never see her. I'm going to have Marisa call her father today. Now I don't know what you think about Italian politics, but I know that any Italian worth his pasta knows about bodyguards. And then, Reverend Tyler, it's one-platoon football. They not only protect the client, but I'm sure they can remove anybody who might harm the client."

Tyler was straining for breath, so Jefferson let him down but still kept one hand on the minister's throat. The other he used to pinion one arm behind Tyler's back.

"Now let me give you my oath as a man and as a gentle-man that if you ever do harm to Marisa again, I will kill you. That if you ever see her again, I will kill you. That if you don't let her go, graciously, from this marriage, I will come and I will kill you."

He whipped Tyler around to face him, smiling his soft, southern smile, and he pulled the minister's face close to his own.

"Look, you bastard. You are getting off easy, with your reputation and your cock and your life intact. So do you agree?"

Only for a second did Tyler hesitate, and then he nodded. "Speak up," Jefferson insisted. "Let there be no doubt in Marisa's or my mind as to what your intentions are. Tell us that we have your word."

"Yes, yes..." The words came out, raspy and broken like an old man's. "Yes. Yes."

"Then say good-bye to her. And get the hell out of here."

Tyler did not speak, but like a young child he raised his hand and waved, his fingers looking soft and pasty slowly making the sign of farewell.

And Marisa followed suit, holding her hand palm up and squeezing the fingers in, Italian style. She was still making the babyish gesture when the door slammed behind Tyler in the next room.

"So, there you are. He's gone. You're okay. He's really gone."

"But if he's gone, why am I still afraid?"

"Because you think he's coming back. But he won't. Because he really wants to live and he's afraid of me. And maybe, just maybe, he's sorry for what he did."

"He didn't say he was sorry."

"I could have made him say that, but all I wanted him to say was that he would go away. And that's what he has done."

"Am I having to tell my father? Do I tell everything?"

"Not everything. But you have to tell him that Tyler was cruel, that he struck you, and that it is too awful to talk about. Your father should come here and see you, and your father should also talk to Tyler, to let him know that he is forbidden to be near you again."

"Oh, my God, Jefferson. We could be dead, killed."

"No, because I would have killed him. Really. Just killed him. When I had my hands on his neck, I knew that with one little movement, one little extra push, he was gone. I wanted to do it, to get rid of him forever. But there was no need for him to die. I could accomplish what I wanted without killing him."

"You are so good. You wouldn't hurt anyone."

"No, Marisa, that's just what I'm not saying. I could hurt him. And if he came near you, I would kill him with no second thought. Just kill him. So, how can I think about not going to war when killing comes so easily to me?"

"But this would be killing to rescue me. In a war for Marisa, you would be my army."

"Honey, I am your army. But I am not going to be in anybody else's army, at least not in Vietnam."

"So what are you doing?"

"I'm going to serve up the best little ol' protest that I can cook up against the war. I am going to serve up my draft card, fried to a crisp, just like a piece of Carolina chicken."

Elvis Presley was Burnett's guy. There was no end to how far Presley could put on the world. Planting his teenage sweetheart at Graceland and convincing the world that despite his gyrating hips, he was virginal with his honey and that they were constantly watched over by chaperones. Burnett could never believe how middle-class, intellectual America kept putting Elvis down. This man had pulled off one of the greatest political coups of the modern era. Not since Chamberlain got off the plane and announced, "Peace in our time," had anybody so fooled everybody. Sure, chaperones. And Elvis stands around and plays for her and them after dinner. Elvis was blue-collar and greasy and a little too funky even for the white boys and girls who loved rock 'n' roll and thought there was nothing better than dancing late at night in Small's in Harlem or in a hundred other juke joints where the white girls thought they were oh, so cool if some big black buck would come by and ask them to dance or have a beer. Or a Scotch on the rocks, that's right. That's what Negro boys were always offering girls with long hair and tight blue jeans so they looked suave and sophisticated. But not Elvis. He wasn't cool. He was just sexy. And not for those white girls and boys of a certain class. They had to have some black boy or black band or the Supremes or something to get it on and then get it off. Damn, Burnett thought, I'm getting uptight, having some fight in my head about Elvis.

The narrow studio apartment near Dupont Circle had been home to Burnett for some six months. No one had ever come to visit, so no one but Burnett could enjoy the pile of pro-am AR stereo equipment that, because of the absence of any competing sights, was the apartment's major focus. Right beside his bed was his record case, a professional-looking leather box that Burnett had copied from a deejay he'd met several years ago. The box held sixteen LPs, held them separated and scratch free. That's what Burnett had with him these days, sixteen LPs. The rest of his collection he kept stored in T. R.'s basement—more than six hundred LPs, plus the dozens and dozens of 45s that he'd hoarded since high school.

In a few weeks he'd have the whole collection. In a few weeks he'd have everything. Mulligan sticking with the Offensive would make the next few days tougher on Burnett than he had hoped, but now there was a schedule, now there was a plan.

Burnett liked plans, liked keeping things orderly and

straight. Like his records. He had almost every record he'd ever purchased. The only records missing were the sixteen he'd taken to Santa Marita two years ago that were lost when the building he had left them in exploded. What a laugh. Blown up by "friends" of the United States. His friends from the Movement thought those nine months were spent in a "Peace Corps kind of organization, only privately funded. By a couple of foundations in New York." And, if anybody had checked, that's exactly what they would have found out. Two old supporters, the Liberty Goals Foundation and the McCorkle Family Fund, both familiar to civil rights activists, were nominally the underwriters of "Mission to Santa Marita—Establishing Secondary Schools in a Semi-Militarized Area." World War II would be classified as semi-militarized by Santa Marita standards, Burnett decided on the first day. Hundreds of thousands of dollars were pumped annually by the federal government into Liberty Goals, McCorkle, and at least a dozen other smaller New York–based foundations, all with solid credentials and connections. Most of the money got spent overseas—for facilities like the "training camp" where Burnett spent most of the time in Santa Marita, or to bring "potential student leaders" to the United States, for study and to make the early connections so necessary for advancement as a liberal alternative to the communistic liberation movements.

Notable persons lent their names to the boards of such foundations—high-quality people, most of whom would have stalked out of the boardroom if anyone suggested that they were pawns of the federal government or of the Central Intelligence Agency.

In an Evelyn Waugh cleverer-by-half twist, those in the know called themselves "witting." The other board members were kept in the dark by dry-cleaned financial statements, carefully crafted proposals and reports, and had the opportunity to respond to such careful coddling with judiciously cast votes during annual meetings orchestrated by that maestro of manipulation, T. R. Simpson. Board member, founding member, legal counsel—it didn't matter what Simpson's role was named, he was happy as long as he got to play the part.

T. R. would not be happy this morning, Burnett knew, but there would be no harsh words, no recriminations. Mulligan had refused to back out of the protest. Worse, Mulligan knew about T. R. And there was still the Offensive to run, so Burnett had had to go over and be the happy little peacenik all last night, meeting with the march captains, the first-aid directors, the organizers of the bail bond fund, because peaceful or not, somebody would get arrested somewhere along the line of march. He'd had a late night call from Simpson, who'd told him that he would call this morning with a new plan, that they could recover from this setback with Mulligan, that nothing was written in stone.

It was the first morning in a long time that Burnett had just hung out, making coffee in the Chemex from the beans he'd bought last week on Wisconsin Avenue. Such luxury. And so few of them. When he came back from Santa Marita a little more than a year ago, he had spent a few weeks on the Cape, in Touro, at Simpson's home. The Simpson girls were all married and had seven kids between them, so there was constant happy noise in the house and the overflow of the good things that money and time together could bring. Jokes at the dinner table and stories and great steaks that got barbecued just right and fresh fish cooked up for lunches that ended with too much wine and long naps afterward.

"I'll never have what you have, and it's all your fault," Burnett sparred with T. R.

"What are you saying? You mean you want the dull, uninteresting life of a Washington corporate lawyer, his nagging wife, his nasty children, and their little brats?" When Simpson finished he swooped up the toddler who was walking very near the edge of the porch and yelled out, "Some mother or another had better rescue this child."

The back porch of the cottage had been built up several feet from ground level, to allow T. R. the pleasure of stretching out on a faded green-and-white canvas lounge and still catching a good look at his precious ocean. The Cape was a string of pearllike spots, all understated, all a little shabby. One identified the location of one's house by one's neighbors: "I live across Slough Pond from the Schlesingers." Or by longtime dead owners of the cottage: "We're in the old Cannon place. We've had it now about twenty years."

Simpson had inherited his cottage from his parents, and the faded photographs that lined the walls, the saggy furniture, the almost matching pottery were all testament to how much he belonged here. "My favorite time, my favorite place, and you, Tom, one of my favorite people."

"It is terrific. I love the ocean. My parents keep asking me to go down and spend some time with them in North Carolina. I think my father feels a lot better about my 'scattershot' life since you spoke with him. No degree, no law school, and no job prospects. With my one brother at Penn and the older one on Wall Street, hell, he figured I was just the runt in the litter."

"I didn't tell him anything. You have to understand that, and of course, you can't tell him anything. I just said that you were doing exactly what I would be doing if I were your age, and that things were different. That there were people, like me, who would look out for your future. Who would make sure that ten years from now you wouldn't be standing in a mud hole urging people to go vote or strike or organize."

"That was good of you, T. R."

"Good, but not enough. You deserve more. You deserve to have your contributions and your smarts seen and appreciated by more people than your set and mine."

"I just feel strange because I keep holding back. No close friends, although a lot of people probably think that there are. The men I went to school with are far away from me. And I'm always on guard with people in the Movement. Afraid I'll say something that will get people thinking. A lot of people think they are my friends, but of course they're not. It's all kind of bullshit."

"Well, it's going to end. You need to go on to school. I think Harvard, the Law School, would be a good idea. Now I am a little worried about this antiwar movement, so I don't want you backing out just yet. And, yes, I know, you will always be available. But let's see what we can work out to get you through this phase of your life and on to one that is more personally satisfying."

So two years after going to Santa Marita, less than a year after his chat on the porch with Simpson, Burnett was called into T. R.'s office with the plan for the Offensive. Sap off some of the radical antiwar energy while setting up a scenario that would split liberals off from the peace effort. When Simpson somehow got the word that the Conference on New Politics was going to be set for Labor Day weekend, and that it aimed at uniting disparate antiwar groups and the fragmented civil rights movement, he immediately sent Burnett into action. No formal announcement of the CNP had been made, so Burnett was first into the ring with the Offensive Against the War. And he rounded up just enough second-level people so that when the conference was announced, too many egos were already enmeshed in the Washington protest plan.

Simpson hadn't let him in on the coup de grace until a few weeks ago. Then he had brought him the photos of Mulligan and urged him to begin the process of "baiting the hook, catching the fish, announcing the prize, then letting him get away."

Burnett had not been comfortable. His own sexual history with Mulligan (not part of his conversation with T. R.) was only the first layer of anxiety. It just seemed too cruel, too unnecessarily controlled, to add Mulligan into the Offensive mix. And the war itself. He was having more and more doubts about what the hell the United States was doing there. In the South, it was much easier to understand. Everyone accepted the problem. What he and Simpson were offering were simply different solutions. But the war was another story. In or out, that was the question.

"We've already turned the antiwar movement into two warring camps," he had told Simpson when the Mulligan part of the plan had been advanced to him. "People can't figure out what to do—the conference or the Offensive. Some organizations think that they'll cover both bases, but then there is a hell of an internal fight, since the representative they send to Chicago is going to address just the other Movement faithful, while here in D.C. we are going to have television cameras and tens of thousands of protesters. It's like there are two great parties on Saturday night, you've been invited to both, and you're real angry because you're sure you're going to miss the one with the best band."

"I don't understand your objection to Mulligan."

Simpson was showing no trace of his usual paternal patience, Burnett realized. Yet the younger man wasn't going to back down on this. He was no kid, no child, to be sent on an errand without understanding the why and the wherefore.

"I feel strongly about this, T. R., I just don't want to do this."

"Feelings and 'want' have nothing to do with this business. There are lots of things I don't feel and I don't want. But I do what has to be done. Now, it's too bad for Mr. Mulligan, although I doubt that he was a new Sam Rayburn in the making. He seems to be rather secondhand goods, Tom. But he's a live congressman, one who is building up a small reputation; he's opposed to the war, and he's getting restless for a real role. I want to give him that role. I don't want him to write the play, just act out the part. And so we do a little stage managing."

"He's ruined after we do this to him."

"This country is ruined unless these left-wing crazies are put in a box. Lyndon Johnson put out the Goldwater fire, but there are a lot of people out there who think it's just fine to hate Jews and Negroes and Catholics and anybody who's not them. Think of us as the middle. Caught in the middle. And believe me that the Left is pressing in on us. That's the next true crisis that this country faces. How can we tell emerging nations that they must put down the communist factions when we have those same revolutionary groups in our own country? How can we tell some small, primitive African country that they can be free and democratic when we've got lunatics marching down Fifth Avenue, opposing the policies of the United States?"

"T. R., I have kind of a crazy question for you. I understand how big the problem is, and how small Mulligan's political future is when it's weighed against the good of the country. But the war, I mean, do you believe in the war? Do you believe in what we are doing there?"

"I know that the Communists can easily take over Vietnam. It's an easy prey. Do I believe that the goons running Saigon are anything but goons? Hell, no. But they are our goons. They belong to us. And, for that, we belong to them. We are committed, as a country and as people, to fight for the right for South Vietnam to continue on its own rocky road to democracy. We hope it will get there. But we found, with China and with Cuba, that once the Communists are in, there is no longer an alternative. That's checkmate.

"And, of course, there's one other point. The biggest country in the world with the baddest regime, China. What if the domino theory isn't just a metaphor? Vietnam falls, and then all of Southeast Asia, one country after another, all the way to the borders of India and the waters that lap at Indonesia. You can't be a great power and worry about every little life that's lost."

Simpson paused and then concluded: "Do you know what

Harry Truman said about Hiroshima? About the guilt of dropping the bomb, of burning hundreds of thousands of people to death in a flash of light? That he never thought about it, never worried about it, never lost a second of sleep over it. Never looked back. And, Tom, if we're not tough enough now, if we're Adlai Stevenson and not Harry Truman, then we're going to end up with some nut like Nixon in the White House. Because I know this in my political bones ... America isn't going to agree to lose a war. So it isn't a matter just of believing in this war. There's a lot more at stake, and frankly, Mulligan is just a political grunt who's expendable."

Burnett knew Simpson was right. It was just his exhaustion.

"Tom, you sound like a seasoned soldier who has been on the front lines for a full tour of duty. That might seem a little fancy, but look what you've done. All those years in the South. Always on the watch. How could we have been so effective in breaking up this black power thing, how could we have so effectively used one group against another? How, without your knowledge, your insight, your firsthand reports? And look how much you, in many ways, influenced decisions that had such far-reaching results."

"But Santa Marita! Christ, T. R. That was such a bust. And when I realized that our groups, the future leadership that we were supporting, were dealing in drugs, it just knocked me for a loop. And the random violence. Just for no reason."

"It's cultural, Tom. It's a non-Anglo society." Simpson laughed. "We WASPs, we Yalies, will never figure it out. My grandfather went as a missionary to China. My father was born there and spoke fluent Chinese before he spoke English. But do you think my father *knew* the Chinese? Not on your life. We have a job to do outside the Western, industrial world, but let's not pretend that they're going to throw their culture away, any more than my grandfather could pretend that his converts had actually stopped burning incense to their ancestors. We are the missionaries of the latter half of the twentieth century, just as my grandfather and his colleagues were the missionaries of their time. We just bring truth and salvation in a slightly different package."

Then came the exchange that finally brought some relief from Burnett's exhaustion and doubt. He'd thought of it several times in the last few days, not lingering on the architecture of the argumentation for the destruction of Mulligan but relishing the final piece of information that Simpson imparted. "And then, I think it's over for a while for you. For a good while, really. I've called up a friend who is at Harvard, and they are arranging a special admission for you at the Law School this year. Papers have been filed; it will appear as though you were accepted there seven years ago, before you went south. And that you simply delayed your admission. All very clear-cut. The transcripts have been sent from Yale, with letters dated seven years ago from the master of your college and several professors. They note that you qualified for your undergraduate degree three years ago, by finishing up some independent papers."

"T. R., that's really something."

"For God's sake, Tom. We are here, moving countries and changing destinies. The least I can do is get an Old Blue into Harvard."

The last was said with the intimacy of peers without all the complications of family, just the two of them in their own private Skull and Bones.

Burnett took off Elvis and put on Buddy Holly. So young, and so dead. Two years ago, before Santa Marita, Burnett went on the road, visiting some twenty campuses. At some schools he spoke about civil rights, about the South, about voter registration. At others he watched. These were the campuses that Simpson thought would explode if the antiwar movement kept heating up. Near the end of the summer, Burnett watched a rally on Sproul Plaza at the edge of the University of California campus in Berkeley. One speaker, looking several years beyond his undergraduate education, started giving the usual simplistic argument for radicalism, the usual catechism against the war and racism. What pulled Burnett up short was when the man started quoting not Mao or Marx, not even Bob Dylan or Pete Seeger, but Buddy Holly.

Holly, the speaker said, had died young and perfect. His music was intact. Untouched. Virginal. Simplistic. Like Holly's lyrics: "If you knew Peggy Sue, then you'd know what I've been through." And somehow, skillfully, the speaker made the slide to Vietnam, to the fact that thousands and thousands of young Americans, "with their politics as untouched, as pure as Buddy Holly," would soon be going into the streets to fight against this "imperialistic war." And then he said something that resonated with Burnett, that distilled his life better than his own thoughts had ever done: "Better to die like you want to live than to live as though you are afraid to die."

Several weeks after Burnett heard him, the speaker, a grad student in math named Frank McLoughlin, was a mainstay in the massive antiwar demonstrations that closed the campus for almost a week. Having heard him once, Burnett could understand how kids stood there, getting beaten over the side of the head by the Alameda County sheriffs (almost all of them imported to the Bay Area from Alabama and Mississippi).

Buddy Holly got interrupted by Simpson's phone call. There was, Burnett heard with relief, no anger or even anxiety in his voice. It was as if everything were going according to plan. And, of course, there was a new plan, containing just the actions, the elements, that so scared Burnett.

"I'm sorry, Tom. Now a lot of the burden will be directly on you. I hoped that Mulligan, if we could have persuaded him to withdraw, would have allowed you to play a much more passive role."

"Let me tell you, I just don't feel up for it. I know how

much we've invested in the Offensive, and in getting the right results, but I don't know if I can pull it off."

"Tom, you must pull it off. Let me just run through it with you. It's a simple enough scenario. You make sure that you speak last. No matter what. You must be the last speaker. Now I will have young Rich Elkins run off a sample of what I think you can say. You remember Rich. He helped with your speech for Selma. You could probably put together just as good a speech as Rich, but we want it to be just right. And you're going to have enough pressure with the march itself."

"And just what am I going to say?"

"You're going to say that you are concerned, worried, about the future of the peace movement. That you found out this very morning that certain antiwar organizations have been meeting with the North Vietnamese, taking their direction from a foreign government. Now this is very important: that you want to end the war, but you only want to do it by peaceful, legislative means. And that you now understand that there are people in the antiwar movement who advocate violence. This is key. We have to brand people as radical via their tactics. These people advocate violence, while you embrace the theories of Dr. King and Gandhi. You believe that the entire peace movement must be on guard against these alien forces. Then you give your speech condemning U.S. involvement."

"I don't see how you think I can pull this off."

"You can pull this off because we have no other means to fragment the antiwar movement. You can pull this off because you can't stand up there and say that these bastards are Commies, but you can brand them and their tactics. If we don't do something, we are going to have a million college students in the streets by next spring, just in time for the presidential primaries. And once these demonstrations start, there is no telling where they will end. We can't have revolutionaries deciding American foreign policy in the streets."

"I'm sorry if I don't sound thrilled about this, but, Jesus, T. R., I'll be this century's top pariah. I'll get to Harvard and no one will sit in a classroom with me."

"Tom, I'm not asking you to publicly back the war. You are simply recognizing that there are elements in the antiwar movement which are not peaceful, which do not allow for orderly change, which in many ways tend to rip apart the fabric of American society."

"But I'm going to get ripped apart in the meantime. And that's not all. I don't believe that a lot of people involved in the march are crazies. I don't think Kapinski is crazy, and his father's a Communist. Maybe we're throwing the good away with the bad?"

"What the hell do you know about Kapinski? What do you know about what anybody believes? We're certainly not going to throw away years of working hard to keep the radical fringe just that—a fringe movement in this country. We both know that it's one thing to be a liberal. I pride myself on my politics. But going to the left of liberalism doesn't mean you simply take a step left. It means you cross the greatest divide in politics. Being a Communist is as opposed to what you and I believe in, Tom, as if we compared ourselves with plants."

"Maybe I'm just chicken. Maybe I'm afraid."

"Tom, once you start moving, you'll be fine. Just fine. I'll get Richie working on some words, and we'll talk again, at length, tonight. About ten or so. I'll stay home and wait for your call."

"I don't know how late this meeting will end. But as soon as it ends, I'll call. And, T. R.? I'm sorry. You know how I defer to you in these matters."

"I do, Tom. And you know how much I care for you. Don't worry. Richie will put together what we want to say in exactly the right way. And it won't sound like a speech. It will sound like an antiwar activist who is suddenly concerned that the movement is getting away from him."

"Okay. That seems good. Tonight."

Buddy Holly had played himself out during the phone call. For a minute Burnett thought about putting on another album, but instead he sat at the plain wooden table that served as his desk.

In front of him was one of the lined notebooks, pages numbered, that undergraduates used for science classes. The numbered pages meant you had to record everything, every experiment. Mistakes and all. Nothing went unwritten.

It was past 9:00 A.M., and he knew he should be heading to the office. But, first, his morning ritual had to be finished. Just as he had for the past seven years, Burnett took his fountain pen (the one his father had given him for high school graduation), noted the date at the top of the page, and, after signifying that this was the morning entry, began to write about his conversation with Simpson.

As he did, he made himself write about his personal agony. He realized that he no longer knew the line between game and reality. Was he against the war? Simpson wasn't, of course, but he wasn't a hawk, either. Just a sensible man, a committed man, trying to keep the country sane. But that was Simpson. What about himself? Which was he against, the war or the radicals who were running it?

Hell, what was politics anyhow? All politics was personal. The Harvard academics now coming out against the war; they were JFK cronies, all of them. Where would they be if JFK were still president, and Vietnam was his war? Where would they be if it were a Harvard war, not a Texas war? Politics didn't matter. What mattered was personal relationships. What mattered was Simpson, his trust in Simpson. Burnett knew he would go along, take Simpson's judgment on this, his life, as he had for such a long time.

Burnett put his pen down and rose from the desk.

He had lost count of the notebooks over the years. He figured there must be a few dozen, full of his dreams and hopes, beliefs and concerns. And actions. Why and how and when he did things. His life in numbered notebooks.

These he did not store in Simpson's basement. No, the notebooks were in safekeeping with his old Yale roommate, Jimmy Bronson, now just ordained Right Reverend James Bronson, curate of Holy Angels Episcopal Church. Jimmy knew what to do with them.

Pisano had finished writing his piece. Rewriting, really. He'd cleaned it up, added a few more facts, and hyped the lead a little.

The story was simple and clear, perfect as an advance to the Offensive Against the War. It would run tomorrow morning, and people would be reading it in Washington just as the march began; a tale of a government that operated on two levels: as the antagonist, in this case the peace movement, and as the protagonist, the war machine. The piece in no way condemned the Offensive. It simply pointed out that the organizer of the march, one Thomas Burnett, was tightly tied to well-known Washington forces. One powerbroker, unnamed, was a veteran of the cold war, adviser to presidents, and acolyte of containment, of the notion that communism could not be permitted to expand. It also revealed that Burnett had spent almost a year in Santa Marita doing God knows what on the payroll of a program underwritten by two foundations, one of which had been fingered as a CIA conduit by the news media revelations last February; that Burnett attempted to get Representative Mark Mulligan to denounce the Offensive, and this after convincing Mulligan that he should be part of the antiwar demonstration; and that the march itself was acting as long-term nuclear reaction in the peace movement, fragmenting and defusing the tentative links between student and civil rights organizations, between antinuke and antiwar groups.

Kelly had spent a long time with Pisano the night before. It was Pisano who at first wanted no mention of Mulligan in the story; why take a chance on opening a pipe that would flood out and drown Mulligan's career? But Kelly had a different tack: don't ignore the one-two Burnett tried to pull on Mulligan. Instead, just let it be noted that Mulligan was placed under pressure. Intimate that the pressure took the form of threats.

"There will be a million guesses as to what the pressure was. Everything from one-night stands to cheating on an entrance exam. Just keep it vague. Spotlight what Burnett did, not what he knew. Anyway, there's just no one in Washington who doesn't have a one-night stand hidden somewhere," Kelly explained. "Everybody will think it's about broads, he's too young for a booze problem, and the spooks will back off. They don't like engaging in hand-to-hand contact. They want to meet you in a dark alley and drive a thin shiv up your gut."

"Kelly, how are you sure, really sure, that they won't retaliate by releasing the photo?"

"Nobody's totally sure in this town. But I have friends. Even friends in Langley. And your snooping around and Mulligan's refusal to buckle under have called into question Simpson's effectiveness. Remember, Simpson plays both sides of the street. He has influence over Burnett, but he has to translate the power into results, or some of the professionals out there might think he's just old hat."

"But he's a professional, he's been around a long time."

"No, not a professional. A pro-am. A guy who probably got involved in a serious way in the war and stayed around for a little OSS work afterward. Hell, some of the best guys around were in the OSS. Even before McCarthy came along, they were too liberal to make it in the federal government. When the right-wingers said the U.S. had 'lost' China to the Communists, then the Hollywood Ten stuff and McCarthy made being a liberal a crime, well, these guys ran into the woodwork and linked up with the Agency. No formal joining, mind you. Just a bunch of guys who all wore the same school tie. After all, what was the Agency, anyway? Just the guys from the OSS."

"When you talk like that, they seem like the guys in the white hats."

"They have no hats, Pisano. That's precisely the problem. They are secretly deciding things because they think *they* know better. And they don't. They are screwing around with foreign policy. These enemies of McCarthyism at home will support almost anybody abroad. And let me tell you, that includes the Fascists." Kelly grinned when he saw the expression on Pisano's face. "Don't look so rattled that I know that word and that I can use it so easily. The Fascists and the torturers and the despots. Kill off popular movements in emerging nations if any of the leaders looks remotely like Fidel."

"How do you know so much about them, Kelly, if they are so secret?"

"Because they're not as smart as they think they are. Christ, these are the guys who gave you the Bay of Pigs. Some people think they gave you Dallas. I don't believe that."

"And you think they'll stay away from Mulligan now?"

"Pisano, nobody's making any promises. But if this poor bastard doesn't stand up now, they own him forever. It's worth a bet."

It was a delicate job of writing, trying to give the impression that the pressure being applied to Mulligan was because of a youthful indiscretion with a girl; the impression that Burnett's unnamed friend moved in high places, but not as an official member of this administration; that the speakers at the march were more left than Mulligan, not conventional liberals, but not violent revolutionaries.

Pisano liked the story. Tight and clean, it cast doubt on Burnett without torching the entire peace movement. He had spent an hour the day before talking with the news editor, Skip Renfrew. They had several strong pieces of evidence against Burnett: the photo of Burnett with Simpson, which probably couldn't make it into the paper, Burnett's double cross of Mulligan, Burnett's spooky history. Pisano and Renfrew decided to use a well-worn Washington journalistic gambit and wait until an hour before deadline before calling Burnett. Then Pisano could put him on the spot: "We're going with the story, Burnett, and you can either say something about the accusations or we'll run a 'No comment.'"

Pisano pulled the last copy book out of his typewriter and walked across the city room to drop the story on Renfrew's desk. Behind Renfrew, enclosed in his glass cubicle, Harry Armsteader presided over the city's second-best newspaper. Several years back it had looked as though Armsteader would be editor across town at the much more prestigious *Washington Post,* but a few rough spots had slowed him down, and he had contented himself with stepping down a notch and running his young, aggressive staff, a suitable complement if not a challenge to the preeminent *Post.*

Pisano dropped the story on Renfrew's desk. Renfrew said he would give the story a quick read, then Pisano could call Burnett. But before Pisano was back to his own desk, Armsteader emerged and asked Renfrew for a copy of the story.

Usually Armsteader held off on reading a piece until it was through the first editing, but it was Sunday and he probably had a golf game somewhere, Pisano thought.

He called Annie on the phone at the march headquarters. "I can barely hear you. What's the background noise?"

"Some kind of goddamn monks. Not the druids, but Hare Krishnas, a dozen of them. They showed up here an hour ago and said they wanted to see someone in charge of television. One of the teenies sent them in to me. Their leader, who by the way is Hare Krishna via Shaker Heights, announced that he and his other believers were going to chant us into peace. 'Great,' I said. Then this fool announced that they were starting right then and there. I suggested they go out in the hall. They're out there with the druids. All chanting, only one of the new ones has a little drum. The better to keep the beat. Then two of the Women Strike for Peace people complained that they couldn't hear with the chanting in the hall. So I've moved them into my office. If we start getting coverage on this, if a TV crew shows up, the Offensive is going to look like a Smothers Brothers routine."

"Why not just shut the door and go work someplace else?"

"This is *my* office. I am not giving up my office to a bunch of sari-wearing sissies."

"Annie, you're nuts. You are going to be getting press calls all day."

"Think of the chanting as background music. Any interview I give will sound like a voice-over. Or I can tell members of the fourth estate that these are Vietnamese monks, angry at the grinding down of their native land."

"I gotta go. Armsteader is waving at me from across the office."

"Wave back. Give 'em hell. Break a leg. Call me when you get your Pulitzer."

"Good-bye, you nut. I love you."

He hung up. What an asinine thing to say, Pisano thought, shaking his head, then got worried that Armsteader would think he was refusing to enter the glass box. So he did what Annie had suggested: he waved and headed across the still, Sunday-empty newsroom.

"Yes, Harry," he said, entering his editor's office. Following Armsteader's hand signals, he closed the door behind him. Armsteader had spent two years in Paris after the war and had brought back both an extraordinary ability to read a French menu and an addiction to Gauloises cigarettes. He stank of them, his office stank of them, and if a reporter spent more than ten minutes with Armsteader, the reporter picked up the scent.

Armsteader was lighting one of them at the moment,

using an antique silver matchbox to strike the flame, sliding an antique silver tray over to Joe, for him to use as an ashtray, even though a Marlboro was a little tacky for these smoking accoutrements. Mrs. Harry Armsteader was constantly purchasing such delightfully extravagant gifts for him, the editor would tell old friends and colleagues. Only a few of them knew that for the past several years, Mrs. Armsteader had been carrying on a semiclandestine affair with Robert de Marais, who owned Washington's most expensive antique store.

Pisano had no such knowledge. It didn't matter. The meeting was not about Armsteader's private life, but about his.

"I understand you're banging the press secretary of this so-called March for Peace."

In the fifth grade, Pisano got caught with his fly down and his cousin asked him, "Someone die in your family, Joe? Is that why your fly is at half-mast?" Only then, and at this moment, did he feel complete nausea, a total loss of physical control. Now, at least, he could take a drag on a cigarette.

"Yes, yes, I am. Your spies are good."

"Not my spies, Joe. My 'sources.' That's how we talk in the news biz, Joe. We have 'sources.' And, Joe, we never fuck our sources. Never."

"It didn't influence the story. It just didn't. She was a terrific help. I mean, she really helped me put some of the pieces together."

"What did they, this understated 'they,' threaten Mulligan with? Is he taken to wearing dresses? Did he kiss his mother? Or did he just screw the homecoming queen? Wait a minute. I forgot. Screwing doesn't count as a reportable offense."

"Harry, I just can't tell you. My sources, and I have two of them, my sources told me some things, but not others."

"Did you screw any of these other 'sources'? Shit, Joe, if you substitute the word *sauce* for *source* in your story, this piece would read like an Italian menu. Sauce this, and sauce that.

Where are the facts, the who-what-where-why? The old-fashioned stuff that newspaper stories used to be made of?"

"I have hard facts. Burnett is the head of a peace march, only it seems he has ties to the Agency. He is supposedly fighting the Establishment, only he is like buddy-buddy with them. He got funded by a CIA conduit foundation to go to Santa Marita. He tried to get a congressman, whom he convinced to join the protest, to then pull out, so it would look like the march was very radical. Like the whole peace movement is very radical."

Harry tapped his next cigarette on the end of his silver envelope opener. "Where are you coming from, Joe? The peace movement is radical. It's got all these long-haired misfits and revolutionaries and weirdos. These are not apple-pie people. Now maybe the little girl you're banging is a nice all-American type, but most of these characters are misfits."

"But that doesn't change Burnett."

"If Burnett is the story, Joe, you've done a lousy job of reporting it. Where is your interview with him, huh? How can we run a piece on a guy, take his whole future into our hands, and not give him the common courtesy to ask him a few questions?"

"I talked about it with Renfrew, and he said we'd wait to ask him until just before deadline. That way we really have him on the ropes. Either he would talk to us, or we could run the story as it stands."

"Renfrew is not the editor of the paper. I am. And I say that this piece is never going to see the light of day. If you want to break what you think is big news, find Burnett today, interview him. Give him a fair shake. Let him respond to all the allegations. We'll run the piece on Tuesday, or Wednesday. If this guy is really tied in with the spooks, nothing much is going to change in two days."

"The protest, the Offensive will be over."

"The war won't. It's not going to go away, Joe. Look,

you've only been in D.C. for six months, right? For years you've been away from home base, in the South. You were writing about something we all knew nothing about. And you knew about it. And so you got your way with a lot of stories. But this is different. This is Washington. This is my hometown. I know how stories like this, unless they are handled carefully, can wreck someone's career. You go a little too far, push your thesis a little too far down the road, and suddenly there's no more road in front of you. You're history. And you know what, kid? You're much too good a reporter, you have much too big a future, for me to let this happen. I want you to succeed. I want this story to be the best damn story anybody has ever written about spooks and their friends. I want this newspaper to be the first to carry it. But first, I want us to be accurate."

Joe was tapping his cigarette on Armsteader's polished desktop.

"And about the girl, Joe? I don't know if this is serious or just a roll in the hay. Hell, one sometimes turns into another. But we have a saying in this business. And it's a good one to live by: 'If you're covering the circus, just don't fuck the elephants.'"

Pisano tried to light another cigarette, then realized that his time in the glass box was over, that Armsteader had saved his prep school precept for last, a little truth to carry with you into the world. For a minute Pisano thought about telling the stuffy old bastard where to stuff it, but he liked his job, liked reporting, and, with Annie, he knew he had broken what should have been a cardinal rule.

"Thanks, Harry."

Armsteader didn't answer, just nodded his head as a sign of dismissal.

The walk back across the newsroom was painful, Pisano bent over slightly like a pitcher pulled out of a tied game. Armsteader watched the young reporter, then picked up his telephone and dialed the unlisted number at Simpson's house.

263

"It's done," he said. "The story is killed for today. But you will be undone on Tuesday or Wednesday. I've beaten him down, made him think his story was horse shit. But he'll get out of here in a couple of hours, he'll go see Kelly, he'll talk to his lady friend—and he'll report like a madman tomorrow at the march."

"I'm not worried about Tuesday. Or Wednesday. Or what he'll find out about Burnett tomorrow or the next day. I was worried about tomorrow. But you've taken care of that, Harry. I thank you. As a friend. We share a complex history and a lot of loyalty, to each other and to the country we both believe in."

"Don't start your patriotic bullshit with me, T. R. I've known you too long. I did this as a favor. Everybody deserves one favor. You'd never asked for one before, so here it is. But let me give you fair warning. On Tuesday or Wednesday, this kid is going to come up with a story. He's going to know a lot about Burnett. From what he's already written, and it's flimsy in its current state, he'll have one terrific read. Probably make it to the top of the fold. Nobody else has a lead on this Burnett, so maybe I'm just assuaging my guilty conscience, but I think we'll get a good story in the end anyway."

"Harry, you might get a better story than you have right now. But again, thank you. And, trust me, I'll never ask a favor again. And I, and you, can forget that we ever had this little exchange."

It was late afternoon by the time Annie evicted the Hare Krishnas from her office. One television station had gotten wind of the Krishnas' visit, but Annie fended off coverage by saying that the chanters were currently meeting privately with several ministers.

"Just toned the little blighters down," she announced to Bitsy after waving the chanters into the elevators. "Made it sound like it was a pleasant ecumenical get-together. Let me tell you, the arrival of the very exemplary and reverend Elijah Johnny Brown, praise Jesus, didn't hurt too much, either."

Annie's phone rang, and Bitsy wandered into the next office, where Kapinski was staring out the window. Outside the room, in the Pit, the internal politics of the march minions was erupting. The New York Women's Strike for Peace was insisting on carrying a banner that identified their group and also proclaimed that they were the New York delegation.

"'New York Delegation. Women's Strike for Peace.' That's what it says, and that's what it means," one peace advocate was screaming.

"And everybody will think that you're it. That you're the leadership," Sam Bornstein shouted back at her. "You're not it. You're only part of it."

Bitsy reached out and hugged Kapinski. "Speech done?" she asked him.

"Yes, I'm done. I've done everything. Only now I'm out of contact with Dong again."

"Kapinski, I can't figure out how you got yourself in this mess. Whatever, he'll show up. He'll show up and steal the show, although I think a lot of people are going to be real mad about you doing this on your own."

"He's gone. What can we do? We can't say that we brought the student opposition in from Saigon, and then we lost him. 'Hey, I misplaced one Asian revolutionary.'"

"Call the number again."

"Why bother? There's no answer."

"Did you have a backup plan, someplace to meet if something happened?"

"You mean like shopping with your mother, 'If you get lost, meet me at towels and sheets'?"

"Don't get cute. *I* didn't lose him. And if you hadn't been so smart-ass and wanting to keep everything to yourself, I would have told you to make a backup or something. Or get somebody's name to call."

"I could call the Vietnamese embassy. I could say I was looking for one of their student leaders."

"Maybe we should tell the other members of the steering committee. We have to all sit down in about an hour and decide the order of speakers. Then, at least, if something has gone wrong, we will be united on what to say."

"Right. Everyone will be so happy to help me, since I was going to pull off the biggest coup of the antiwar movement and leave them all out in the cold. Sure, they will all say, 'Kapinski, even though you tried to one-up every one of us, we're all on your team.'"

"You can be as smart-ass as you want. You have to tell these other people—Burnett, Tyler, Annie—the whole schmeer."

"No. I'm not telling anyone. And you can't tell anybody about Dong. He could have been picked up by the FBI. He could have gotten scared and is just hiding out. He could be dead, or he could be on his way back to Vietnam. You know these Vietnamese. He could show up tomorrow at a news conference at the embassy and denounce all of us, but I can't really believe that. Whatever, we can't tell the steering committee. Promise?"

"Is this just to save your ass? Don't lay any trip on me that I have to do something for a greater good, when it's only your greater good."

"Bits, I give you my word. And that's always been good. You just can't tell anybody about Dong. Especially Burnett. Okay?"

"Okay, although I am remembering that you were the one who got me into this mess."

"Bits, it's the dumbest thing I ever did."

The Reverend Elijah (Johnny) Brown could move real fast for a fat man, his wife liked to say, especially fast for a black fat man. He was hustling so fast out the front door at 1029 that he almost missed the Reverend Paul Tyler hurrying inside.

"Brother, how are you?" Brown asked like a reflex action, then noticed the bruised face and the sunken eyes. He knew that look. Once, when he was little, he went to visit his uncle in Baltimore, his mother's brother who worked for the post office, a widower with no children. The visit ended three days later when Elijah saw his uncle whip his dog, beat him with a stick. The violence sent the child running to the train station, where he begged a porter to lend him the money to call his mother. He sat on a station bench, his dangling legs too short to reach the floor, and he waited the three hours for his mother to come fetch him. She never questioned his truthfulness or tried again to have him visit his uncle, whom he saw afterward only at family gatherings and on the holidays. But the look of that dog stayed in Elijah's head. It was the look of old black people in the South before the civil rights movement. And it was the look on Paul Tyler's face this bright, hot Sunday.

"How the hell do you think I'm doing?" Tyler finally answered, his eyes darting around as if checking out a crowd, although Sunday had emptied the streets in front of 1029. "I'm going to a meeting of the steering committee. I'm going to see what the hell is going on with this march."

"You look as though you need some sleep more than a meeting. Why not come back with me to the parsonage and we'll have a cup of coffee and a little cake or something?"

"The entire country is going to the devil. My whorish wife is encamped with her lover at a hotel. He beat me up. I'm going to have him arrested. My entire career is being burned down by riotous Negroes who forget what I did in the South."

Johnny Brown put his heavy sweaty arm around Tyler's shoulder. "Son, this Negro remembers. And loves you. Loves you like my Christian brother. You are in bad shape. I don't know why, and I'm not sure what to do for you. But you are falling apart even as I'm looking at you. Now you don't want to make such a crazy fool of yourself that you never can walk

with these people again, do you? 'Course not. So let's just take
an hour off. A rest stop. My car's right here. Get in, get in.
And we'll go to the parsonage for an hour's rest and a cool
drink. And maybe something to soothe your soul, too."

"I don't want to go, Johnny. I'm really mad at all of you,"
Tyler was protesting, not like a man, but like a child who had
grown too tired and was fighting sleep. Brown gently guided
him to his Corvair, easing him onto the seat, then hustled to
the other side, jumped in, and started the engine. Tyler made
soft sounds of protest, then bent his head down to his chest
and stayed silent on the short journey to the parsonage.

T. R. Simpson was tired. Here it was Sunday, the day of
rest, and work loomed ahead of him. He thought of a Thurber
cartoon, a tiny, tired man walking down the path to his home;
the lines that define the house are drawn up in the rear to
become a large, menacing woman. There was no such woman
in Simpson's life, but the work seemed to press down heavier
and heavier.

Now this complication with the Offensive. It had been
such a simple plan, and Burnett had done such good work in
the past. Obviously he had misjudged Mulligan. He'd have to
have a closer look at the young congressman in the next
months; his refusal to buckle under to pressure meant he was
someone worth knowing, although Simpson believed that ho-
mosexuality was an abomination before God.

His wife was still at the Cape. The girls and the grandchildren had been so disappointed when he got stuck in
Washington this weekend. Such a wonderful family. Such a
good life. Simpson counted himself among the blessed.

"Yes," he answered when the ring came on the private
line. Simpson had long ago discovered that "hello" invited
casual talk; a "yes" set up the limits on conversation. It was not
an underling on the line, but a peer, a close friend whose

presence, even on the phone, instantly raised the temperature of Simpson's tone.

"I talked to Harry. He killed the story, although he's going to be furious when events unfold."

"T. R., are you sure you want to go through with this? It seems so drastic."

"Drastic needs require drastic means. I don't need to tell you, Frank. You're in and out of the White House. You see what happens to him every time one of these protests are held."

"But the kids are right. Goddammit, if I had any guts, I would walk into the Oval Office tomorrow and just quit. Tell him that this war is a cesspool, a bottomless pit. That everything we wanted out of this administration is going to be tubed."

"And then who would be left in the inner circle? Nobody, nobody but those who want to bomb the North, level it. Turn it into a vast parking lot. If what you and I want is to get this country out of Vietnam, then we've got to keep the president under control. Every protest, every picket line, just drives him farther and farther into the corner. He is one stubborn SOB, and we've got to close down the dissent in order to keep our options open."

"But, T. R., aren't we out of bounds? This man got elected with the biggest landslide in American history. He's got to have some sense of what voters want, and if he thinks voters are unhappy, then he'll change his foreign policy."

"Frank, this man does not listen to pollsters and he doesn't listen to advisers, unless they tell him what he wants to hear. Who knows? Maybe Bobby will come forward and announce that he's going to run for president next year. Stranger things have happened in this past decade. What I do know is that any protests, any marches, are red flags in front of Johnson's face. So we have to discredit the antiwar movement in order to get on with our own efforts to end the war. He's not going to listen to what we say if he hears it first from an antiprotestor, screaming at him from the front of the White House."

"I hope you're right, T. R. I don't feel comfortable playing around this way in domestic policy."

Simpson took a deep breath and picked up a toy soldier that one of the grandchildren had left on an end table. Strange to have boys' things in the house after decades of dolls and nurse kits. "Ah, Frank. We're fooling around in domestic policy because the Moscow boys are fooling around in domestic policy. No, before you erupt about FBI reports and all that other crap, I do not believe that the antiwar movement is a Soviet-inspired creation. I do believe that the Soviets encourage and foment a lot of specific antiwar activity. And I believe that to have liberal students, good kids from good American homes, becoming part of these Red-tinged protests, well, it's just unraveling a piece of the fabric of the American society that will take a long time to weave back together."

"So you're committed to running this duplicitous march and, now, to following through on the alternative plan? I mean I felt okay when we had Mulligan backing out, but putting this burden on Burnett and then having to carry through—I just don't like it, T. R. At all."

"Is it better to destroy this antiwar movement as an alternative to liberals and moderates, and to do this by any means necessary, than to have the man who is our president wreak havoc with everything? We can keep him under control, Frank, I know we can."

Frank Pederson didn't answer. Simpson just heard the click of the receiver on the other end of the line.

He sat quietly, playing with the toy soldier, wondering which one of his boys would call him next.

The Offensive headquarters was filled with people, hundreds of people. Faith in the creaky air-conditioning had given out around six P.M., and the windows in the offices had been opened, their doors propped open to the Pit, where rented fans were doing little to dispel the heat. Two old New York Socialists kept moving through the crowd, announcing that everyone who had no important reason to be there should leave the building.

"Sure," Annie shouted to Bitsy as she made her way to the press office. "Sure, there are a lot of modest types here, who will just stand up and say, 'I'm not important.' Just don't hold your breath waiting."

In Annie's office, three requisitioned teenies were putting together the press packets: the program; short biographies on all the speakers; a page of statistics, including how many Vietnamese had been killed in the war, how many Americans; a list of regional coordinators for the Offensive and their location during the actual speeches, so that the hometown papers could talk to a hometown protestor; finally, a short statement from the committee stressing that every effort had been made to maintain a nonviolent and peaceful demonstration against the U.S. involvement in Vietnam.

"We should have a little order here," Annie said, then looked like a mother hen over her teenies. "Great. These all look great. Now don't let them out of your hands until you put them in the paws of an actual working reporter. And I don't mean some slime from the *Berkeley Barb* or the *East Village Other*, although their officially credentialed representative should get one, count 'em, one press packet. Every fool that ever went to NYU apparently has a press pass and wants to come to this march and take my press kits."

The teenies, Annie had told Pisano, were the best people to give out things like credentials or press kits. "They're like Hitler Youth. You tell them what the rules are, and they don't care if it's David Brinkley. If he doesn't fit the reporter profile, no kit and no credentials. That's because these kids just don't have any heroes. They've got stars and they've got antiheroes, but if you are fifteen years old, the only clear thing you remember about JFK is that he got shot in the head on your television screen. No heroes."

One had been in charge of taking messages while Annie was out in the Pit. There were several names and numbers listed on the yellow pad and, beside Pisano's, three asterisks. Annie blushed, thinking that teenie had figured out Pisano's importance, but cooled down when the teenie explained that he had called three times.

She waved the teenies out of her office and, with the door shut, got Pisano on the phone.

"How's our Pulitzer?" proved to be the worst choice for an opening line.

"Annie, you are not the coauthor of this piece. I have just left Armsteader's office, and he kept talking to me about how I was banging somebody I should have been covering."

Suddenly the room was very hot, hotter than the temperature, and Annie's head began to sweat and her hands got soaked. "Sorry about that, Joe. I wouldn't want you to compromise your principles."

Silence.

"I'm sorry. The story got shot down. We're just going to run a regular advance. It's short, with a speakers' list. Hey, you got a helluva press kit here."

"I gotta lot of them here that I have to make sure get given out."

"I'm sorry, Annie. I didn't mean it. I'm just so angry, and you're like the one person I can bitch to."

"That's a real compliment."

Annie put out one Camel, soaked through with the sweat from her hand, and took another one out of the pack. The matches on her desk had pictures of lavish fruity drinks. She wished she had one, to soothe her where the cigarette smoke burned her throat and hurt her chest.

"This place is crazy. I gotta go."

"No, no. Let's talk. Just because I made an ass of myself is no reason to blow this whole thing off. Hell, Annie, I'm sorry."

"Look, I really gotta go. And, hey, I'm just going to stay at my place tonight. You know, you covering tomorrow and everything. It'll make everything easier for both of us tomorrow."

The steering committee meeting was in the back room of the Rathskeller on 15th Street, scheduled away from 1029, since that avoided the problems of telling self-important peaceniks that they were not invited to participate.

On the walls were shelves of beer steins and implements of Hun-like war. Mimeoed agendas were on the big plank table, sandwiched between the schnitzels and the sausages. Now there was little left to do except bicker over the details of what little was left to do.

Tyler arrived late, and with Johnny Brown, who was not a member of the committee. Instead of taking the one empty chair at the table, he walked to Burnett, tapped him on the shoulder, and whispered a few sentences in his ear. Brown did a little casual glad-handing down at the other end but made no attempt to take the empty chair. Burnett then followed the other two out into the hall.

"What's going on?" Kapinski stage-whispered to Annie, who shook her head in reply.

"Maybe Tyler feels like he's got to make new friends among the Negro population," Bitsy said.

Her voice was too loud, and her comment, along with the sudden absence of Tyler and Burnett, pushed an uncomfortable silence on the table.

In less than five minutes the trio came back into the room, Tyler having left his anxiety in the hallway and Johnny Brown looking for all the world like a daily-double winner. Burnett motioned to the empty chair, and while the table watched to see which one would sit down, a waiter appeared and dropped the chair he was carrying at the Kapinski end of the table.

Tyler sat there, while Brown slid his bulk between Burnett and Bitsy.

"Have I missed something?" Kapinski asked. "Some vote or something taken in the hallway?"

Before Burnett could reply, Tyler answered, "Sorry, Ed. And my apologies to all of you at this table. I'm sure that you've been following the news media and realize what a week this has been for me and my church. If not, Bitsy here"—he motioned down the table—"can fill you in. I asked Burnett if I could change my role on this committee, and because I want everything to be open, I have asked him to permit Johnny to sit in while I make my request."

Tyler smiled. Bitsy watched him and realized that even after this week of threats and then negotiations, he was good when he was talking. There were better preachers around, but Tyler could get you, that voice could just send shivers. Annie watched him with not quite the same reaction, having spent several hours through the week with Marisa on the phone, the last conversation following Jefferson's decking the son of a bitch that morning.

"I had envisioned my role at this march as a preacher, as someone who could bring a moralistic and spiritual slant to this Offensive and to its participants. But I feel as though my activities this past week"—he nodded, smiling, to Bitsy again—"have cut down a little on my stock of moral righteousness. And so, like all good clergy, when I am afraid my words won't have impact, I decide to use someone's who does."

"Does this mean that you want the Reverend Brown to speak tomorrow?" In his frenetic impatience about Dong, Kapinski's limited listening ability was shrinking fast.

"No, not speak. Pray. I want Johnny to pray, and I want to pray with him. Don't look like you're going to have a communistic collapse, Kapinski. And I don't want to hear anything about atheistic supporters of the antiwar movement. The Movement always wanted the clergy up front, wearing our collars, getting arrested in our full garb, like Father Groppi out there in Detroit. Well, for once, I want to play on my playing field. And to make sure it's the biggest playing field possible, I have asked Johnny Brown to quarterback it. We will take the ten minutes allotted to clergy, but we will simply pray. Together. From the entire body of Scripture."

Great, thought Kapinski, now I'm going to have some goyim reading the Psalms. But no one else seemed to take offense.

"But where in the lineup of speakers will such a moment take place?"

Bitsy asked the question gently, but she could have just as easily thrown a firecracker on the table.

"Is that what we are now discussing? The order of speakers?" Sam Bornstein from the Socialists asked, then answered his own question, launching into a diatribe about putting forth one ideological line only limiting the attractiveness of the antiwar movement.

"Sam, it's not like you're going to get people signing up to be Socialists. And we are all against the war."

"Don't be so sure that young people aren't beginning to understand how much socialism offers them."

"And just expect a workers' revolution by Friday," Kapinski kidded.

"No, but you expect the Socialists to come through with the money, don't you?"

Burnett stood up, slowly, Annie thought somewhat majestically, like a young prince, here with the aging courtiers and rabble. Pisano would never be able to write about Burnett, not really about him, because he never saw Burnett's talent in these meetings. Leave it to the spooks to figure out who were the best and brightest people in their generation and then steal them away.

"I'm going to make this real short. We are going to do it alphabetically, and, like in the Bible, the first is last, the last first. So that means that the Young Socialists League is first, Women's Strike for Peace is next, followed by the Vietnam-American Friendship League. Okay, Kapinski? He's followed by SANE, by Physicians for an End to the War, by New York Mobilization, by the guy from the National Student Association, and by Bitsy. We agreed in our invitation to Congressman Mark Mulligan that he could speak last. Except for me. I bat cleanup. The clergy can pray at any time they think fit. And I think if it's not an imposition, Tyler could do everybody's introduction. And I don't really give a good goddamn where Peter, Paul, and Mary sing. And I have a tough night ahead, and if there are no objections, that's the order."

Each member of the committee had come with his or her agenda and argument for placement; all would have sounded logical and ideological, but their soapboxes had been effectively overturned by Burnett's short speech.

Bronstein hemmed and hawed a little, looking as though he were warming up for a diatribe, but Kapinski turned to him and said sharply, "Sam, it really would be crazy to make an argument against this kind of approach. And, in the spirit of fellowship and peace, I will even volunteer that in my speech I will urge all members of the audience, regardless of politics, to become Socialists immediately."

"Thanks, with help like that..."

"Okay, so let's move along on getting the final version of the press release. Annie?"

He never liked guns.

He could remember, as a young boy, his father and his father's gun. His brother wanted to touch it, to see how it worked, and once he was even caught playing with it.

He never had to be warned against touching the gun. He never tried. His father was so surprised when he turned out to have a facility with weapons. He shook his head and realized the train station guard was looking at him strangely. He tried to fit in. He had the key and had directions on where to find the locker.

Too many damn directions this week. And too complicated. All these cat-and-mouse tricks. Like a paperback detective novel.

The locker was just where the directions had said. At least the directions were direct.

The gun was there, wrapped in a T-shirt. He slipped it into the green bookbag he was carrying. His father loved books.

He loved his father. His family. He hoped they would understand. He hoped they would remember many things about him. Especially that he had never liked guns.

## MONDAY,
## Labor Day, 1967

Four colored boys walked by the corner of Vermont and K, heading to the bar at the next corner. They didn't worry Jefferson. He'd known colored all his life in Georgia, and they'd known him. He did think it strange that almost everybody at the march offices, people who had worked in civil rights in the South, were just practically all white. Everyone.

Jefferson leaned against the building, waiting, liking the cool of the cement against his back. The Washington heat was still holding at one in the morning, just like any southern town in summer. The heat at the march would be a killer for sure.

The office upstairs must be almost empty. The two high school kids who worked for Annie had come out about an hour ago, then returned with big bags from Dart Drugs and Orange Julius.

"We're staying all night, here at headquarters," the blond one offered.

"Annie says it's imperative to be on time at the Memorial tomorrow—no, I mean today. Five-thirty A.M. We've got a lot of stuff to do," the other one added.

The girls must have lied about where they were spending the night, Jefferson thought. Probably telling their mothers they were staying at each other's houses. He could remember doing that, four, five years ago. Staying out to drive around country roads and drink cheap liquor and get laid. These kids were staying out to make the goddamn revolution.

The music carried down the street from the bar, Martha and the Vandellas singing "Hey There, Lonely Boy." Not me, Jefferson thought. No lonely boy here, with Marisa waiting on him back in the hotel. She'd wanted to come along, and she'd have liked it, just standing outside and listening to the music and feeling the heat. She loved everything. And boy, did that include sex. That woman just couldn't get enough of it. The thought rattled Jefferson. Maybe it was disloyal to think that about your girl.

Thoughts of Marisa took his mind off his mission, and he almost missed Burnett, who was out the door and around the corner by the time Jefferson shouted out, "Hey!"

Burnett turned to see the kid from the march headquarters mimeo room who'd followed him around the office most of the summer like a pet puppy. "Jefferson. Hey yourself. Can't talk. Got to get some sleep. Big day, huh?"

"Yeah, I know what a big day it is, but I really have to talk. To you. I tried to find you earlier. After the steering committee meeting."

"I had to run a quick errand. Now I've got to get some sleep."

"Maybe we could get an Orange Julius or something. It's like a matter of life and death. Almost."

Burnett laughed. In the middle of a maelstrom, and this kid wanted a life-and-death conversation over a soft drink.

"What the hell! I won't be able to sleep, anyway."

They went across the street, where Jefferson insisted on treating to the giant Julius specials, and they sat in the dark on the picnic benches for a couple of minutes, listening to the music from the bar. Burnett liked the feeling, even though he wasn't sure how to even start a conversation with the kid.

"Shit, Jefferson. Is that Martha and the Vandellas singing 'Dankeschön'? No wonder this country is falling apart."

Jefferson didn't understand. Burnett was probably saying something sophisticated, and he didn't get it. It was probably a joke. He didn't get jokes. Maybe it was that they were singing in a foreign language. But, what the heck, he nodded at Burnett, slowly, like he was enjoying the remark, and clearing his throat a couple times, he started his almost rehearsed speech. He felt in his pocket to make sure the object was there.

"Tomorrow—no, today, is a big day. I'm really sure it's going to make a big difference. Really start to turn it around."

Burnett reached across the picnic table and grabbed Jefferson on the shoulder. "Thank you, sir. I needed that. I think something important's going to happen, too."

"I'm going to do something. Something I think is important."

"I heard. Annie told me, and I told her, and I hope you understand, that if you're going to go ahead and burn your card, you have to do it early, before the program starts, before the speakers get on the platform. I can't have a U.S. congressman standing there while somebody commits a felony."

"Crazy, huh. Burning my card is supposed to make me a criminal, but if I did what I was supposed to, go and kill people, then I'm a patriot."

"I'm telling you, Jefferson. The country is falling apart."

"Now I get it."

"Get what? Don't take me literally. The war is just a lapse, really, a minor mistake in a long history. Like when there's a tiny scratch on an album and the needle skips. You don't have to believe everything I say."

Burnett was joking, but Jefferson's conversational baggage was serious and heavy.

"I believe everything you say, Burnett. I came here tonight to tell you that if I had just listened to you two years ago, I mightn't have ruined my life. Really."

"Jefferson, we just met this summer."

"No, that's how long you've known me. I've known you a lot longer. I've known you since the summer of 1965, when you came to the campus in Albany. A bunch of high school buddies and I were going to go over just to listen. We didn't believe in a lot of the stuff that you folks from the North were doing, but we figured we'd go listen. There was a party, so I was the only one who went to hear you talk. I came up afterward and stood around as people were asking you all sorts of questions. But I didn't have much to ask, or say, myself, so all you did was say good night to me as you left. And you told me to 'keep the faith.' Shit, I didn't have any faith then. I was pissed off at all you white boys messing around with my state and with revving up the Negroes. But when you talked, it made it seem like something else. And I was just trying to say that, and you went off with a couple of Negro boys for supper, and I was so afraid that my parents or somebody would see me. So I just headed home. But I took your words with me."

Burnett tried hard to place the speech. Fall of 1965 would be right before Santa Marita. He had given so many speeches that summer on voter registration, on nonviolent action, on keeping whites and blacks working together in the civil rights movement. If only he could remember this speech, the room, anything.

"I knew it was too much that you would remember me. I was just a kid, just listening. But I thought about your speech, and when I went back to school, I tried to follow what was going on. I would read the newspapers in the library. And I would watch the news on TV. And I would try to figure out how your motto applied to my life."

The bar had closed, and the pleasure of the music and booze down the street had become the noisy pain of people shouting good-nights. Burnett lit a cigarette. His mouth was somehow dry after the drink, and the bitter taste of the smoke reminded him of the first drag when you hit the beach after a long time in the ocean.

"See, this is going to sound corny, but you're like the Beatles song, one of the beautiful people, the people who turn other people, like me, turn them on to life, and that's what you did." Jefferson knew that what he was saying made him sound like some kid, but he didn't know how else to get to the point where he could do to Burnett what he knew he had to do. "You just told me that we all had to live as though we were going to die and that we had to be ready to die to save the way we all wanted to live. When I heard about you and the Offensive Against the War, well, I had to come. Because this is the way I want to live. I'm here tonight to show you how I feel about how those words changed my life."

There was little Burnett could say to applaud Jefferson's statement, the convolution meaningless when countered by the pure and crystal commitment, as intricate as a showman piece played by a prodigy.

"Jefferson, you really touch me with what you say. But I'm just not worthy of your speech. You can't make decisions based on what I believe or what I say."

"I can, Tom. You are my mentor. I choose to follow you."

The "Tom" startled Burnett. T. R. was just about the only person who still used his Christian name. He shook his head.

"You're giving me power I just don't want. No one person has the answer to what anybody else should do—to live his life, to end the war. Making decisions for you is a head trip I don't want to take."

Jefferson stirred his half glass of Orange Julius with his straw. Like the kid he still was, Burnett thought. Just twenty, the same age that Burnett had been when he met T. R., and with the same puppy-dog happiness at placing his fate in his master's hands.

"I made my decision. Jail is better than Vietnam. I just wanted to thank you for your inspiration and your leadership."

Burnett stood up. The kid leaped up beside him, immediately erect, the well-learned military response. He yanked the cold, hard object out of his back jeans pocket and startled Burnett when he thrust it forward, like a bayonet.

"It's a medal. It's my medal. For being the outstanding first-year cadet. I wanted you to have something that meant a great deal to me, and I don't have that many things."

Burnett stopped shaking his head and took the thin metal box. Inside, in a velvet coffin, lay the medal, large and gaudy like something favored by a South American dictator.

"Jefferson, I can't," Burnett finally mumbled, holding the medal out for a better inspection.

"You don't have to wear it or anything. Just keep it. Like my award to you for changing my life or something."

The two young men stood near the Orange Julius stand, and one watched as the other pinned on the medal. Then, mumbling something about having to sleep, Burnett hugged Jefferson, not with the touchie-feelie style of the Movement, but with the deep and manly embrace that players give to each other at the end of a particularly tough game.

Walking home alone, the medal bouncing on his chest, Burnett thought about what he had told the kid, about independence, about the power of deciding his own future. That power Burnett himself had ceded long ago to T. R., when he'd signed his goddamn life over. Made his pact, sold himself before he had any idea what he was worth. Now how much could he expect his life to bring, who would pay for a secondhand, slightly used agent, a traitor to his generation and maybe to himself?

A few blocks from his apartment, Burnett found himself running, faster and faster. He reached his building and bounded up the steps, two at a time. Inside, more stairs, and when he got to his apartment, he fell against the door, suddenly exhausted, not from the run, but from the great release. The medal pressed into his chest, a cold, sharp reminder.

Kapinski got to the Lincoln Memorial just as the sun was coming up. He counted two dozen, no, maybe three dozen people all acting too busy, doing last-minute additions to the sound system.

The new elite, he complained to himself. All these electronic freaks who made their money being rock 'n' roll roadies. Can't have music without them. Can't even have politics unless everything was wired for the best sound. Nobody was sure what would be said here today, but it was damn certain that everyone in the crowd would hear every word.

The crowd might hit fifty thousand people. At least that's what the committee thought, adding up the buses rented and the locals and just people driving in to be part of it. Only somebody had leaked that number to a TV reporter last night, and now if the cops said fewer protestors showed up, the march would be a failure. Burnett must have done it, since his job was to screw up everything.

So the papers had that number this morning and also stories from South Vietnam on yesterday's election. Big surprise, right, that Ky and Thieu were swept right in. And all the stuff from LBJ's boys on the Hill about how it was important to give democracy a chance. Then those three southern congressmen, who condemned the march as being the work of traitors and Communists. And that shit about American boys dying so that these college kids could march. The opposing sides were getting farther and farther apart. Thinking about it made his head hurt, as if he had some college-boy hangover.

"Hey, my main man!"

Groovy, Kapinski thought, waving at the blond sound man. Here's another dope-crazed white boy trying to sound like some ghetto black.

"We're all getting too good at this, too much practice," Annie announced, coming up behind Kapinski. She had two young volunteers in tow who had managed, they told her, to be at the office by the required 5:30 A.M. by not leaving the night before. One of them carried an armful of press kits; the other toted Annie's big African bag, her walkie-talkie, an envelope with $1,000 in cash, and her present from Pisano. It was after 1:00 A.M. when she had gotten home and found the Safeway bag full of Snickers and Camels. The note was reasonably mushy, "Here is your CARE package. I hope you have a good time at camp. Please take care of yourself, and remember that having an Italian in your life is not always easy."

Annie slowly unwrapped a Snickers and stood with Kapinski a little left of the Memorial, watching the guys from Berkeley finish the TV platform. The pale light made Lincoln more three-dimensional, and the shouts and yells from the sound crew couldn't begin to fill up the vast silence that set around him and his building and floated over the Reflection Pool. The water at once both connected and separated the Memorial from the Washington Monument. In a few hours what would connect the two would be tens of thousands of protestors, cheering, shouting, demanding an end to the war.

Annie thought this time of morning, this half sunrise, exotic and somehow wondrous. This was the time when her high school girlfriends, exhausted from pajama party talk, would collapse on the pink rug in her bedroom. This was the time when she finally stayed out all night, partying at Somers Point, then climbed through her bedroom window so as not to

wake Jennie. This was the time in the South when she and
Burnett would arrive at the Friendship Baptist Church and
begin the days that only ended long after dark.

Wavvy Gravy and the Hog Farm had set up their tent off
to the side of the Memorial's giant steps. Hippies, Diggers,
crazies all of them, really, but so sweet, Annie thought, with
their free food and help at any huge demonstration. Especially
important today with the expected heat, since they would pass
out water and juice, but no salt tablets, which could be interpreted
by the D.C. cops as acid.

"Is he going to screw us, huh?"

Annie waved away the kids with the press kits and turned
to face Kapinski, the anger on her face clear even in the dim
morning light.

"I thought we agreed not to talk about this in front of
anyone."

"Annie, don't give me a lecture. Answer my question."

Annie shook her head. "You don't get it. We're all going to
have to figure out what to do after this march, after today,
to make sure we don't look like CIA dupes. How are you going
to say you signed on to this set-for-failure protest? Did Burnett
dupe you? Or are you part of the plot, huh?"

Kapinski began to sputter out an answer, but Annie
shushed him, like an impatient mother. "Kapinski, I don't
know what the hell you believe in, but I want your word that
you will never, and I mean *never*, talk about Burnett or any of
what's happened until we all agree. You and me and Pisano.
All of us."

"Don't put this trip on me, Annie. If Pisano could have
gotten some of this stuff in the paper, it would all be public
right now, today. So I'm not signing any blood oaths or
anything."

"If Pisano could have gotten this stuff in the paper, it
would have exonerated you and me. Taken us out of the
shadow. Sure, we would have been taken in, but it would have

been by professionals, by the guys who really run things. Kapinski, I want your word."

Kapinski looked around. Secrets and pledges and things that went bump in the dark. "Sure, Annie, sure. My word. But I also have to have your word, and you have to promise that you'll get Pisano to agree that if other questions get raised, well, you won't talk without talking to me."

"Like what? Like what kinds of questions?"

"Great. You want me to sign the goddamn loyalty oath, but you won't give a little back. Like anything, that's like what."

"Fine. I don't know what you're talking about, but fine. Okay."

Annie motioned to her teenies, and the trio headed to the roped-off area, leaving Kapinski standing like some tourist from Skokie, staring at the Memorial.

Burnett finished writing the note and slipped the last notebook on top of the pile already in the box. He'd stuck five dollars in stamps on it, figuring that if it wasn't enough, the postman would just collect the postage due. After all, it was going to a clergyman.

Maybe a prayer, Burnett thought. Maybe a small prayer. Oh, God, I made choices that I thought were right. I thought my motives were right. His prayer was too rich. Fucking self-righteous pharisee prayer. He'd dressed carefully, wearing the yellow-and-green-striped tie his mother had given him on his birthday. Oh, God, what will I tell them? Oh, God, who will love me? Who will be my friend? Fucking self-pitying prayer. His khakis had come from the cleaners, and as the early light refocused the room, defusing the brightness of the overhead bulb, his freshly cleaned pants shone, glimmered. He'd read some book, some book with large color illustrations, so it must have been when he was very young, about knights arming themselves to go into battle. Prayers, prayers for each piece of clothing, of armor. He stuck his "Off the War" button on his shirt pocket, then pinned Jefferson's medal right below it. Battle ribbons. He slipped the belt through the loops and looked at the man looking back from the mirror. "Dear God, let me do what's right," he mumbled, and then watched as the young man in the mirror stained his crisp shirt with the tears that kept running down his face.

Marisa had changed her clothes three times and now was judging the effect of her fourth outfit on Jefferson. The object of her endeavors was stretched down the bed, smoking a cigarette and sipping coffee.

"I know this seems silly, but I want to look just right. I'll probably never do anything this important again."

Jefferson pulled her toward him as she pirouetted for approval, grabbing her on the arm. "Don't wrinkle me, please," Marisa said, smoothing down the print shift, her hand meeting his as it headed under the fabric. "Jefferson, you are crazy. We have to be there in just an hour. We don't have time. This is too important."

Her lover had maneuvered Marisa onto the bed and, despite her protests, was starting to remove her dress. "Honey, nothing is as important as the way I feel about you. Maybe men went off to other wars because they loved women, but, honey, you're the best reason I can think of for not going to fight in some dirty little jungle in a war I want no part of."

As Jefferson rolled her over onto the rumpled bedcovers, a small part of Marisa's brain managed to disconnect and reassuringly remember that she still had the green-and-pink Pucci print hanging in the closet.

Representative Mark Mulligan waited at the front door to his apartment house, trying hard not to sweat in the heat that was already building. He thought it was crazy, but Kelly had insisted on picking him up.

When his AA's black Buick pulled up, Mulligan thought it was just a shadow, but, no, there was someone else in the car.

"Congressman. Good morning. Great morning for a demonstration. No, you get in the back. Let me introduce you. This is Maureen Kelly. No, no relation. Maureen is the assistant dean at Trinity. My wife's known Maureen for many years, right, dear? And so, when Maureen was having dinner with us last night, well, it just seemed so right. You know, she's against the war, too. And working with young people and everything."

Maureen Kelly waved her hand. "Enough, Jerry. Look, Congressman, the last thing you need along today is extra baggage. But Jerry was insistent, and I must tell you, I didn't resist. I am against the war. And I think what you're doing today is, well, simply wonderful."

At the end of her speech, the antiwar Miss Kelly folded her hands on her lap. Too long with the nuns, Mulligan thought, but he launched into a long discussion of the war and how grateful he was for support like hers, all of which she drank in gratefully, like a cocker spaniel praised for wagging her tail. She was pretty, Mulligan admitted, in a boyish, sporty way. And in the ten-minute ride to the Memorial, it turned out she was athletic, playing tennis, swimming, skiing in winter. And she made him laugh, some story about taking her mother skiing.

Kelly waved some pass, and the car went through the barricades and into the VIP parking area behind the Memorial. "What the blazes are these hippies doing? Setting up housekeeping?" Kelly complained. He eased the car into a somewhat illegal space, too close to the platform, and, motioning Maureen to get out on her side of the car, took a moment for a hurried conversation with his congressman.

"Nice, huh? A nice girl."

"Yeah, Jerry, but we're going to an antiwar demonstration. Not to the prom."

Kelly held the congressman by his shoulder and stared

like a nearsighted old lady trying to see the small print. He then yanked him close and fiercely whispered a rule that Mulligan would live by forever. "Mark, from now on, you're not going anywhere without a date. Not to the revolution. Not even to the bathroom. Especially not to the bathroom."

"I'm having a problem with the body count."

Annie stood at the back of the roped-off VIP press area and smoked what she figured was her fiftieth cigarette of the day. The guy from the police department kept claiming that the crowd was under twenty-five thousand, and she'd spent the last hour showing the TV guys the list of buses, the supposed square feet of the Ellipse, comparative footage from the 1963 civil rights demonstration, all to back up what she knew was a shaky claim that more than fifty thousand people were demonstrating against the war. Exhaustion had overcome excitement, and Annie leaned against one of the sound trucks and tried to keep track of the speeches. Pisano patted her on the head.

"Body count? That's the problem the army has. They keep killing more people in Vietnam than the country has. What's your problem? Nobody believe that the crowd of protestors is at three million?"

The chants from the crowd buried Annie's response. "Hey, hey, LBJ. How many kids did you kill today?" was repeated over and over, like jump rope rhyme, Annie thought. She tried to focus in on Kapinski, who was having a hard time keeping the crowd's attention.

"We won't go back to our campuses. We won't go back to our homes. We will stay and fight," he was proclaiming. "Not fight Lyndon Johnson's dirty little war. But fight for peace. Fight for the true freedom of the people of Vietnam."

Pisano turned to Annie with a cynical look. "Kapinski gave that same speech in 1963, only then he was staying and fighting for the true freedom of the people of Mississippi."

"So he's not Clarence Darrow. How do you think it's going?"

"Nobody's burned an American flag. Nobody's thrown a bomb at the White House. Even the bit at the beginning with Marisa and that kid went well. Although it might have helped if the hand that held the burning draft card didn't have a new manicure."

Annie reached over and hugged Pisano. "You're such a cynic. And now, with your paper down on you, what's going to happen? You gonna get tougher?"

They sat on the fender of the truck, and Pisano lit a cigarette, passed it to Annie, and lit another one before answering her: "No, I'm going to get better. I could have gotten at least part of the story in the paper this morning, only I didn't do the basic stuff. Armsteader was wrong, too. What the hell, maybe that's what happens working for a newspaper. Maybe not everything you write makes the paper, but you keep doing it because most of what you write makes the paper."

One of the teenage volunteers came by carrying a box full of Cokes. The day was not quite as hot as had been predicted, but the demonstration had been under way for almost five hours, the march and now the speeches, and it helped, Annie thought, to be in the VIP section and get a cold drink.

The singing had begun, led by some folksinger whose name she kept forgetting. The crowd swayed back and forth, their arms linked, singing, "All we are saying is give peace a chance...."

Annie kept trying to gauge the crowd, how many students, how many older people, how many who looked radical, how many who looked middle America. In the VIP section, the five hundred badges had been given out: members of the steering committee, "honored guests" from the antiwar world, staff people from the offices of congressmen too afraid to show up themselves, news media types, activist richies from

New York, and the fifty-plus student body presidents from across the country who were supposed to represent American youth. Several of the antiwar types who had tried throughout the summer to torpedo the Offensive, whether from real ideological differences or from plain competitiveness, had shown up and were milling around, somehow given full access by the VIP passes they'd managed to score.

After all the aggravation about who would speak, nobody in the VIP section paid much attention to what was being said. These were the cognoscenti of the Movement; it was only the masses, beyond the roped-off VIP area, who had to heed the words of wisdom issuing from the podium. Annie could never get over the Movement caste system, defining who was in and who was out, but she was glad she fell inside the ropes.

Mulligan had taken the podium after a long, prayerful introduction by the Reverend Paul Tyler, who'd snapped everyone to attention when he'd intoned: "Heavenly Father. Brothers and sisters, this is the one elected official who deserves not just our attention, but our prayers, our support, our eternal gratitude, and, for those of you from his home state, your votes."

"Does that mean God is registered to vote in Michigan?" Annie asked Pisano.

"Maybe this is Tyler's best role," Pisano offered. "As emcee. The Ed Sullivan of politics."

"He doesn't strike me as funny."

"What do you think of Mulligan's speech?"

"He could stand up there and say, 'How now, brown cow,' and as long as he was a congressman and against the war, I don't give a damn, and neither does the Movement."

A radio reporter came up, stuck a microphone in Annie's face, and began asking questions. "How many have been arrested today? Did the members of the New York State Communist party contribute to the violence? How much damage do you think was done at the Justice Department?"

Annie reached over and flipped the on-off button on the reporter's tape recorder. "What outfit are you from? Hitler Broadcasting? Seven people got arrested, none for any violent acts. I assume that violence means some bodily harm to somebody. Two of our marshals got hit by bricks thrown by some punks. We've done no violence. And if you want to know about the paint at the Justice Department, ask J. Edgar Hoover."

"The paint? What was that about the paint?" Pisano asked as the radio reporter walked away.

Annie shrugged. "A few people, not as part of the official plan of the Offensive Against the War, spilled red paint, you know, like blood, on the Justice Department's door. It's apparently a bitch to get off."

They stood listening to Mulligan, leaning both against each other and the truck. Annie watched distractedly as the congressman finished, shook hands all around while acknowledging the claps and yells of the crowd, then made his way to the side of the platform. Kelly was waiting for him there. Mulligan took Kelly's extended hand, jumped down, and walked quickly out of Annie's line of vision. She just as quickly forgot that they were gone. The crowd chanted, impatient with the short delay that kept the next, the last scheduled, speaker from the microphones.

"Just Burnett to go," Annie announced to Pisano.

"Did you talk to him?"

"No. I was afraid I'd say the wrong thing. Like begin to yell that he's a creepy traitor. Anyhow, I don't care what he says or what he does. All I want to do is get through this day. We have all these people. It's peaceful. We have a black speaker. We have a congressman. Nobody has set fire to himself, or to the White House. And tomorrow we'll get up and the war will be over."

Burnett was taking the mike. This was it. Annie took the slight delay to wave her teenies over and remind them that they had to stay at the platform until all the sound equipment was packed, making sure that they got signed receipts for everything before it was hauled off. When she was done, she finally noticed Burnett, at first not what he was saying, but how he looked. Here in the middle of this hot, sweaty Washington day, with the smell of people mixing with the occasional whiff of dope, Burnett looked preppy and almost perfect, the one wrong note sounded by his "Off the War" button and by the gaudy medal on a blue-and-white ribbon that hung from his shirt pocket.

As scheduled, he was telling the crowd just how many of them had turned out, how effective the day had been, and then, as his wrap-up, was starting to tell those who wanted to lobby the next day just where to meet.

Annie watched him reach forward and grab the sides of the podium. His hair flopped down on his face, and he shoved it back with the back of his hand. Annie was close enough to see the wet spots his hands left on the flag that hung over the podium, and she thought, just for a moment, that he looked her right in the eye. Burnett was breaking away from the schedule and had started on the true theme of his speech.

"When I organized this march, this day of protest, I wanted it to be a time of peace. Not just a move toward peace, but a move toward the peaceful acceptance of others in the antiwar movement. We have all hidden too long behind our self-imposed ramparts. We have too long built ideological and tactical barricades."

Pisano turned to Annie, but she shook off any conversation. Kapinski was hanging off the platform, waving to her in the crowd, but she ignored his signals. Some Asian kid pushed past her and blocked her view of Burnett for a minute, but before she could tap him on the shoulder to move, he was edging through the VIP crowd to the platform and Kapinski was pulling him up.

"There is only one question: How can we stop the war and bring the boys home? There are many answers. Everyone here today believes they have the right one. Protests like this. Yes. We all believe that. We are all here. Lobbying tomorrow. Sure. Let's give the elected officials a chance to represent us. We watched as three young men burned their draft cards today. Is that effective? If it is their moral stand against an immoral war, who are we to condemn them? Who are we to condemn any person who speaks out against this war, who fights for what we believe in?"

Burnett paused, and Pisano and several other reporters surrounded Annie, asking her what the hell the speech meant. Did it mean that Burnett believed that violent tactics were okay? Was he condoning the bombing of draft boards?

"For God's sake, just listen to him. That's what I'm going to do."

The crowd listened, too, and even in the VIP section only applause broke the silence that surrounded Burnett's speech. For the crowd, this was the activist whose vision had brought them here to Washington. But for both seasoned protestors and virginal activists, there was the expectation, the yearning for greatness, that came at the end of every rally, of every protest. Would this last speaker raise them up, the hush of the crowd asked, to heights where emotions finally met expectations?

There wasn't much more of Burnett's speech. A couple of good lines that would become memorable in the aftermath of the afternoon: "When we called this the 'Fall Offensive Against the War,' I thought it was a great way to say 'Kill the war. Off it. End it.' Now I wish I had named this day of protest something different. I wish I called it an 'Offensive for Peace.' Because if we don't start working for something, peace, and not battling against each other, then the dark forces that are at work in this country will once again be deciding not just our destiny, but also the future of a nation ten thousand miles away."

A pause again. Shit, Annie thought, how far is he going to go? She never knew the answer to the question.

The Asian kid had pulled away from Kapinski on the platform and moved to Burnett's left side. He put his arm around Burnett, who turned and faced him with what Annie thought was a look of surprise. Later, when she watched the film, she realized the expression was one of acceptance.

The Asian kid held Burnett in a lover's grasp, his arm tight around Burnett's shoulders. The kid leaned forward to say something in the microphone, and it looked as if he would pull Burnett closer still, for another sign of affection, a kiss of passion.

"I am Troi Van Dong. I am an elected leader of the Student Union of South Vietnam," he announced, and the crowd went crazy, screaming, cheering. The chants started: "Get. Out. Of Vietnam. Now." It was so powerful, Annie thought there was no stopping the crowd, but the kid whacked the mike and the screech quieted everyone. The crowd would have done anything he asked. He was the oppressed person they wanted to free; he symbolized his country, a country the crowd saw as a prisoner of their own government's power. So ready for admiration were the tens of thousands of protestors that it took a moment for his actual words to cut beneath their euphoria.

"I am here to condemn your protest as an effort by the international Communist conspiracy," he started, and pushing Burnett forward, closer to the mike, he continued, "And to condemn this man as a tool of the Soviets."

"No, no," the shouts started from the crowd. "Get him off the stage. He's not from Vietnam." Scattered boos and hisses erupted.

"We must support democracy in South Vietnam. We must wipe out the Viet Cong forever. We must save my country."

It was all moving too fast. Annie started to push toward the platform, but Pisano held her back. She watched Kapinski shove his way toward the microphones, but before he could get there, it happened.

Troi's left hand slipped into his windbreaker and pulled out a gun. One of the policemen would later tell Annie that it was a Colt .45, what he called "the preferred sidearm of the army since it was introduced in 1911."

Troi put the gun to Burnett's chest, right below the Outstanding Freshman Award, dangling on its blue-and-white ribbon. He pulled the trigger, once, then twice again, moving the gun slightly each time, so that in a few seconds he had destroyed any chance Tom Burnett had to live.

The noise from the gun was louder, thicker than Annie could have imagined, the microphones echoing and magnifying, sending the sound back to the platform from across the Ellipse.

Annie tried to yell out, and when her scream couldn't break free, she took her fist and beat Pisano on the arm, almost a pantomime for her rage.

The force of the shots broke open Burnett's body. His hands somehow still draped over the podium, but the gunfire shook him like a broken puppet. In the seconds it took for Burnett's body to slump over the platform, the blood and life poured out of him, coloring the American flag–draped podium that half caught his body.

People jumped from the platform, fled the platform, fell to the ground. Around her Annie watched as hundreds of those close enough to see exactly what was happening dropped to their knees, many of them covering their heads like the fifties children they once had been, practicing what to do in case of nuclear attack.

A great gaping space had opened up around Troi at the podium, his only companion the body of Burnett, slipping slowly to the platform floor.

Only Tyler stepped forward. He grabbed Burnett's body, stopping its slide. He dropped with it, cradling Burnett in a strange, bloody pietà.

The prayer that rose up came not from him. It came from Troi.

"Oh, my God, I am heartily sorry," he began. Then, after a rush of Vietnamese, he put the automatic in his mouth and pulled the trigger for a final time.

Pieces of his head burst over Tyler and Burnett. Troi's body twisted backward, collapsing beside them. Tyler reached out to Troi's face, his hand attempting to caress the assassin's forehead in some instinctive gesture of caring. But when the minister touched the murderer, the forehead collapsed under his hand, its supporting skull blown away by the shot.

It was at that moment that the horror was large enough to break the scream from Annie's body.

T. R. Simpson listened as the events of the afternoon were reported to him, his face showing no emotion.

He would miss Burnett, miss him terribly. And he would think, many times, he knew, of how he'd helped make the decision to take Burnett's life. It had to be done. They were all getting too close, asking too many questions.

There were still minor details to be worked out. No real worry about Pisano and Annie. A few dropped hints in the next few days, references to how a mention of the real story could hurt the peace movement. That would take care of those two. Mulligan and Kelly would want nothing of Burnett's story revealed. It could cut too close to a story about his and Mulligan's adolescent relationship. And Kapinski—that was easy. Just too loyal to say anything, ever.

The decision had been difficult, but this was the second time Simpson had made it. He had taken Burnett's life twice. Once, today, in a crucial battle in the war for world domination. And once, years ago, when Burnett stood out from the crowd of students, all of whom wanted to be his protégé, all of whom wanted to walk in his steps.

"Send the cable back channel," he said to the man who

waited for the order. His voice was as vibrant and careful as it had been on that sunny spring day when he'd first spoken to Burnett crossing the Yale campus.

"Release Troi Van Dong's parents. Get them to the Philippines and give them new identities. Also make sure the sister is placed in some sort of hospital to get her off the heroin, although I don't believe that anyone we've started on that stuff really gets off it, really cleans up."

Simpson reached down and fed the last of the afternoon's cookies to his dog, who licked his hand in thanks.

"And make sure that Troi's family understands that Dong is the agent of their freedom. He loved his family more than his political beliefs. A very dangerous thing to do."

Only after his young associate left the office did Simpson sit down. The dog rubbed his head against Simpson's leg, in an unfounded hope that more cookies were coming. But the simple act, usually taken by Simpson as one of affection, was suddenly annoying, and he shoved the dog away.

It was late, hours after Burnett's murder, and Annie and Pisano sat on the bench at the 30th and M bus stop. They had walked from march headquarters and were almost to Pisano's when Annie announced that she needed to stay outside for a few minutes, to talk.

"Afraid the apartment is bugged?" Pisano asked her, only half kidding. Her lap was crowded with the bags she had been carrying: her African purse, her Harvard bookbag filled with whatever papers from the office she could stuff into it, and the brown Safeway bag that Pisano had left at her front door less than twenty-four hours before.

In the first hour after the shooting, they had managed a moment of privacy in the chaos around the speakers' platform. And in that moment they had agreed to stay silent about the intricate and dark details of the day, about Burnett and his links with Simpson.

"Do you think we'll miss Burnett?" Annie finally asked.

"You will. You knew him a long time. And, today, he really lived up to what you thought he was," Pisano said, offering her a cigarette.

"You think that's why he died? Because he did what he thought was right?"

Pisano took a long time answering, and when he did it was only a question.

"Do I think this was all some massive government plot? Hell, no. This isn't some spy movie. Once I start thinking that way, then I have to blame myself. My story, my digging around, that's what would have helped do him in. Listen to me, 'do him in.' Now I sound like a movie. No, this was some poor crazed kid, with more anger than he knew what to do with. Probably thought of himself as a patriot."

"Do you think Kapinski will say anything about Burnett?"

"No, I trust him. He's a good guy. There's no reason for Kapinski to screw over Burnett's memory. He's as shook as we are. And he's involved in bringing Troi Van Dong into the country. He kept hinting at something big early in the week, and I just got so intent on the Burnett stuff, I forgot to follow up on Kapinski. Anyway, he won't talk."

The streets were fairly busy for late at night. The Georgetown students were back on campus, the stay-overs from the protest were in the cheap restaurants and bars. An almost empty bus pulled up to the corner, but Pisano waved the driver on.

"Are you ready to walk home? Do you want anything to eat?"

"No, not for another couple minutes. What does your story say?"

"My story? It's a cooperative effort. A half dozen 'experts' got called in, to get the White House reaction, State reaction, congressional reaction. The events will probably be so buried that it will be hard to tell that two people died. My story, my paper's story, says that some crazed Vietnamese student, with a history of opposing the government in South Vietnam, somehow got into the United States and, in a bloody act of sacrifice, killed off the all-American activist. Armsteader talked to me for a moment on the phone. Said we should hold back on the 'stuff,' that's what he called it, 'stuff,' that I tried to get in the paper this morning. He was going to 'pass along my information' to the experts at the paper who deal with such things. And what a great job I was doing."

"So it's all going to just die out, right?"

"In some ways, it's best that way. Let Burnett die. Don't kill off his image. Let him be a hero. 'Cause he was a hero, wasn't he?"

"Are there pictures? With your story?"

"The photograph is Tyler holding Burnett, with Troi holding the gun and praying. We had a shot of Burnett being shot, but the old men decided it was too gruesome for people to have with their coffee."

Annie stood up, a silent announcement that she was ready to go home. Pisano took her Harvard bag, and she cradled her purse and the Safeway bag as they walked along.

"Too gruesome? How do we wipe it out of our heads?"

"We don't. The Offensive stays. Today stays. It never goes away."

"I hope my head holds on to the good stuff, too. And, this sounds crazy, I guess I really hope I remember everything. Every detail. All this, all that happened has me so mixed up. I want the confusion to clear away. I want to think about things, sort them out, so that someday I can figure out what really went on. Make some sort of peace with myself."

BOOK THREE

# THE
# CONVENTION

Kapinski had scored a delegate's credential and smiled his way past the guards into the convention center. Pisano was on the down escalator and managed to look to the left just as Kapinski went up, his hand raised to his golf hat in a formal salute as the journalist passed by.

"You joining the Establishment?" Pisano yelled.

Kapinski smiled, his salute melting into a babyish bye-bye. If asked, he would have no reason to be inside the convention center. Entry was not even part of his plan. But when the Teamsters official from Detroit said he was heading out to an expensive restaurant—"Like do I need this platform shit?"—Kapinski had been happy to relieve him of his delegate's badge.

Wandering down the hallways as if he had nowhere to go, Kapinski window-shopped the issues: a little black caucus, some second-rate phone companies, prolife, proabortion, and, not too surprisingly, Bitsy surrounded by a dozen cameras and twice as many reporters.

"The platform is important because it says what we as a

party stand for. It allows minorities to be heard. It sepa-rates us from the other side."

The guy from ABC, whom Kapinski thought looked a lot like Thomas E. Dewey, wasn't going to take Bitsy's answer at face value.

"But really, Miss Clark, is the platform worth the paper it's written on? Really, isn't it just a symbolic stand by the party?"

Uh-oh, Kapinski thought. Don't tell that girl she's fight-ing over some symbol.

"Sir, I don't know if you happen to notice it, but I happen to be black. And a woman. And if this political party didn't take the stands it did in previous platforms, in previous elections, I wouldn't be here, either in this hall or as part of this political process. Sure, the platform has symbolic value: so does motherhood and the income tax. But motherhood, income tax, *and* the platform are symbols because they mean something and they stand for some-thing. If we're not willing to state and defend our princi-ples, then what really are we all about? This platform, the one that the delegates *will* hear debated tonight, signals the battles we are going to fight in the future."

"But, Miss Clark, don't a lot of elected officials just ignore the platform stuff when they go home to run?"

Bitsy seemed to stretch herself taller, like some flower reaching for the sun. By God, Kapinski thought, she was made to fight these battles; she grows to fit the role.

"There's a lot of what you call stuff that professional politicians would like to get rid of. They'd like to get rid of poverty, but they don't want to raise taxes to do it. They'd like the abortion question to go away. Also the environment would be nice if we would just look at the trees and not see the forest and the planet melting away."

Umm, Kapinski thought, Bitsy talking about saving the

environment was like Karl Marx talking about good hygiene: you just knew she had something more on her mind.

The reporters scattered, and Bitsy and Kapinski were facing each other across several feet of indoor-outdoor carpeting. She smiled, and suddenly the girl inside the matron came out, like a child peeking around a doorway.

"So, what did you think of my performance?"

"It's women such as you, Miss Clark, who make me happy to be a delegate here, at the national convention," Kapinski announced, waving his borrowed credential.

"Delegate? From what state?" Bitsy asked, playing along.

"From a state of mind, and it happens to be the same as yours." Kapinski's voice had the tinny edge of the perennial outsider.

But he drew from Bitsy a thought she usually kept to herself: "Time doesn't really pass, Kapinski. It just keeps turning back on itself. We think a battle ends, but it really doesn't. It's the same fight, over and over, only the battlefields change."

"But sometimes we gain some ground," Kapinski said.

"Is that going to happen tonight? Are we going to win? I mean, are we going to be able to stop Mulligan from pushing this claptrap empty-headed platform down delegates' throats?"

"Well, my dear Ms. Clark, let me tell you that those are two separate questions. And, as you know the rules of the 'Ask Mr. Kapinski' game, you can only ask one question."

"You fool. All right. Will we win?"

"As I have told you many times in the past, Ms. Clark, you will if you are pure of heart."

"Kapinski, you can just go to hell."

"Ms. Clark, I probably will."


"Do you remember that woman who had all the pictures of herself in her apartment?"

Pisano looked up from the floor, where he sat cross-legged reading a notebook. "What woman? What are you talking about?"

"You know the woman. The fund-raiser in New York. It had to be like sixty-five or sixty-six. You were covering us doing voter registration in the South, and you finagled a trip to New York to cover a fund-raiser we were doing in a big Central Park apartment. It was the first time you told me about Mr. Penis. Remember?"

"Your memory is totally selective. Okay. I remember."

"The woman who was giving it was married, and she had three or four grown kids. But almost all the photographs and even a couple of the paintings were of her—as a baby, with her parents, at her wedding, at birthday parties. Just of her."

Pisano closed the notebook and put it back in the canvas bag. "This is great. I'm here to talk about what we should do about putting the squeeze on Mulligan, about how far you are going to get in your piece for tonight, and you want to talk about some rich broad who had a lot of pictures of herself."

Annie swung around on the anchor chair.

"I'm tired of everything getting co-opted. Granola you get from Kellogg's, and they take all our songs and make commercials. And now there's that bread machine, where instead of making it by pushing around the dough and watching it rise and stuff, you just put it into some overnight piece of Formica."

"Annie, you never made bread. You hardly ever ate granola. And the commercials pay for your job. What does this have to do with the platform or the convention? Or with the goddamn lady with the pictures of herself in the New York apartment?"

"Everything." Annie hit the switch under the desk and told Ralph in the trailer that the piece was just fine, that he should hold it out in case of any last-minute changes, but she thought it would stand. She said it in a calm, everyday voice, but Pisano erupted:

"Great. That's how I find out you've made up your mind, that you're not going to wreak vengeance, not going to tell the whole story. You're not going to tell about the manipulation of the Movement. Not going to tell about Simpson or Burnett, not tell the stuff you found out from Burnett's notebooks. Not tell about Mulligan. That's great. What the hell have we both been going through all this agony for? You've made this past two weeks purgatory with your indecision, and this past day has been hell."

Annie shrugged and started to clean up the anchor desk, throwing empty Diet Coke cans and Snickers wrappers into the trash.

"I made my decision. Purgatory's over. The Movement is over. It's just breaking too many promises. First you and I promised Kelly that we wouldn't tell about Mulligan. We kept that promise, even when we had the notebooks. We even put the squeeze on Kapinski not to tell about Simpson and Burnett, to let Burnett be a pure martyr for the Movement. Of course, Kapinski was so blown away about helping Dong get in, we could have gotten him to agree to anything. I can't remember if he was more upset that Burnett was killed, or that he had made such a tragic strategic mistake."

As she talked, she was sweeping the Sixties memorabilia into one of the canvas bags. She absentmindedly stuck one of the raised-fists buttons on her credential.

"They were our first secrets. Taking care of everybody. Protect Mulligan, because he was being courageous. Protect Burnett, because he was dead. Protect Kapinski, because he was a tragic dupe. Everybody bought the story of the extraordinary young peace leader killed by a deranged

Vietnamese. Even you didn't push your own story, about the tie-ins between Simpson and Burnett."

"My story had too many blanks, and I was dealing with an editor whose main concern was to cover his ass. Good old Harry Armsteader, who was obviously sitting right in Simpson's back pocket. Pretty hard to get a story in the paper when your boss has a deal with the spooks. Now, *if* you had let me see the notebooks when you first got them, I could have written about it. Or if you had even let Harold Sams have them. Maybe his 'big book' wouldn't have turned into such a self-conscious diatribe. Spooks behind every closed door."

"I felt funny for the longest time letting you see them. Burnett had been so clear in his note to me: 'I know you keep your word. Please keep my words. Come forward only if my loyalty, my patriotism, is questioned. I trust you.' And I kept that trust."

"So, here we are. Two nice middle-aged people who share a secret, oh yes, share it with a self-promoting U.S. senator who just could be president one day. You and me and Mulligan. But, just to play devil's advocate for a minute, make sure, Annie. You won't get this shot again. Set history right."

"The lady with the photographs. You know what made me think of her?" Pisano tiredly shook his head. "Years later, I found out she wasn't rich to begin with. Her husband had a lot of money. She was like Orson Welles in *Citizen Kane*. Where he wants his childhood back with Rosebud and everything. Only the lady didn't want her exact childhood—she wanted a better childhood for herself. She made it up. Had all these old photographs put in fancy silver frames, had portraits painted from the photographs. She made herself into a woman of wealth who had always been a woman of wealth. She made peace between what she had been and what she had become."

Annie had stood up and was digging in her other canvas bag for a Snickers. Pisano got up from the floor and, grabbing the bag with the notebooks, blocked the door.

"You are not leaving until you make some sense of this."

"It's simple. You just aren't listening. The most important thing for her was to make her life all one piece. Not that she had been anything bad growing up. She was just a child, but a poor child, not the right kind of child, one who would turn into the woman she had become, the woman of established means."

Pisano didn't budge. "Keep going."

"Mulligan has created himself. Most politicians do. And what he's made himself into is a very proper senator who could be a very proper president. Nice and clean and neat. So he screwed some boys when he was young. I'll bet you he's faithful to his wife. So he took some radical stands when he was a novice on the Hill. He made damn sure he never broke with the pack again. He's made a lot of peace, between what he was and what he is now, and, on the whole, he's turned out to be a pretty good guy. And if he's messed up on this one issue, it's not my business, or your business, to tear down the person he's created."

Pisano was still blocking the door and, at Annie's attempt to go past, held up his hand like some visiting pope about to impart a blessing. "I don't have to hold back. There's no reason I can't tell him I'm going to use some of the Sixties stuff in my piece tomorrow morning. See if that brings him to his senses. Killing off the platform could be a real victory for the kinds of people who burn books and kill off dissent."

"Back off, Joe." Annie was adamant. "Mulligan already gave at the office. He stood up there, Labor Day 1967, and put everything on the line. You're probably right. Abolishing the platform is a very wrong move. But I owe him one. And so do you."

Annie sat down on the anchor chair, her canvas bag pushed together on her lap like a kid cuddling a stuffed toy. But she didn't sound like a kid when she started to talk.

"I used to be in the business of saving the world. I'm not in that business anymore. And you never were. Now I'm just in the business of telling people what's going on, or, in the case of my piece tonight, telling them *some* of what's going on. A long time ago, when we didn't tell the truth about Burnett, we played at being God. We were like Simpson. We gave ourselves the power to decide what was right and what was wrong. We covered up for Kapinski. We protected Mulligan. Now, as I sit here in the professional observer business, I don't think I've got that right anymore, to start screwing around with history, to play God."

Pisano walked over to the anchor chair and put his hand on her shoulder, rubbing softly as the two of them shared the silence, broken only when Annie announced she was going to get a Diet Coke and would treat him to one.

"So you're not crazy. I'll admit it," Pisano announced as they started down the stairs for the second time in ten minutes.

"Crazy is to think that I should screw around with this. Look, we shouldn't destroy anyone's vision of their own bravery. Every person who marched, who protested, was courageous. They went up against the system. They helped end the war. Do I want to tell them they've been manipulated, used? Mulligan had the courage to go against Burnett, against Simpson. How much courage is one person supposed to have?"

"If you're elected to the U.S. Senate, you're supposed to have the courage to stand up for what you believe in."

"Maybe Mulligan is just a guy trying to get along, just a guy who is just who he is."

"Or who he wants to be."

"Pisano, for an Italian, you sure are smart."

"Not so smart. I still can't figure out the bread machine."

"The bread machine?"

"The bread machine you were talking about, when you were talking about granola and rock 'n' roll. That goddamn bread machine."

"Oh, that bread machine. I was just thinking about buying one. The bread machine has nothing to do with Mulligan or any of this. Why would you think it does?"

Mulligan always liked a couple of minutes before any public presentation to do what he thought of as "focusing." That's what Kelly used to say, "Focus. Get your mind on it, kid. Just pull it together."

The hearing had ended in the shambles that Mulligan had known would come, with Bitsy announcing a few minutes before he banged his gavel down that the issue would be decided "by all the delegates on the floor of the convention, not by a few men in back rooms."

He had been ready, Mulligan reflected. He had stood up at his table and, pointing the gavel at Bitsy, answered that the deciding had taken place over the past six months.

"You are not going to push this convention into a corner, using thug tactics," had been his perfect line. "Blackmail" would of course have racist connotations. "I am the chair of this committee, and my responsibility is to the convention and to the party, not to a few dissidents. This meeting is ended." Bang.

Focus, he told himself, just gosh-darn focus. God, he missed Kelly in moments like this, although he knew exactly what his mentor would have wanted him to do. It was too perfect, really, when not just the presumed nominee, but also three of the other hopefuls had come to him last spring, urging him to get rid of the platform. "It's like a noose around our necks," Governor McClintock had said.

McClintock was not complex; neither was his plan. Let the hearings progress. Let every special-interest group, women, gays, the other ragtag hasslers and hustlers, testify and protest and denounce. And then either get them to agree to a platform that paid only mild homage to their demands, which was highly unlikely...or, when attempts at a compromise platform failed, put forward the Mulligan plan for party unity. The Mulligan peace plan, that's how he thought of it, a peace that could bring victory to the presidential candidate in the fall, while allowing a Senate or congressional candidate to take any stand on any issue that his politics and his pollster thought was relevant to a victory.

"Never an idealist anyway," Mulligan told himself with a detached stare into the dressing room mirror. "Never much of an ideologue. Not like some people."

A sad smile spread over his face. His wife called it his faraway look. Jennifer had been so perfect, really. A great partner in his career and a wonderful friend. He had never betrayed her. Never, certainly, slept with another woman. And, except for an occasional cocktail party conversation, never even flirted with another man. She'd have to wonder, surely, why the sex was so infrequent. Once, but only once and in the early years of their marriage, did she suggest that something might not be right, that they needed a vacation, more time alone, a romantic spot. But they were so busy. It was the first time he had run for the Senate. Then the two little girls seemed to take all their attention when he was home. Mark carefully deflected the request for more togetherness into a suggestion, one that he prompted Jennifer to make herself, that she work part-time in the office as a volunteer. And, although his pretty, slender wife would never be a strong voice in issue or policy

matters, she handled a crisis with the staff or with a constit-
uent with the same loving patience she gave to the girls'
requests for a special birthday party or a trip to the zoo.
Nothing was too much, as Jennifer funneled her bank of
energy and excitement into Mark's career.

It had really been quite successful, and now he would
get what he wanted out of his party's presidential contender,
not the second spot on the ticket, but, if his party's ticket
won, the promise of the job of secretary of state. That way,
if the ticket went under, Mulligan was still sitting clean and
pretty in the Senate. If the ticket won, he had four or eight
years to sharpen his foreign policy skills, and then no one
could touch him in the primaries.

Just a little careful planning, a little focusing, and he,
Mark Mulligan, would wind up in just a couple of years as
president of the United States. If only Kelly could see him
now.

"I can't figure why anybody would want the job."

Kapinski had found Annie and Pisano as he wandered
through the folding chairs and the early-arriving delegates,
those not important or rich enough to be at the special
receptions hosted by the *Los Angeles Times* or Sprint or the
Oil Producers Association of America.

"That's because you've never had a real job, Kapinski.
You just make the revolution," Pisano answered him.

"I saw Bits."

"She's really turned into the star of this convention,"
Annie said. They were camped out near the curtain that
blocked off the back of the podium, Annie claiming that
they needed to sit there so she could watch for her crew.

"Bitsy was always a star. She just took a little time to
figure it out."

Annie stood up from the folding chair that marked the
end of the New York delegation and the beginning of

Minnesota, allowing a very large woman with maroon hair to get to her seat.

"That's what you're going to look like if you keep fighting nature and don't let your hair go gray," Pisano kidded. "And the Snickers! You're turning into a regular little butterball." Annie ignored him and stepped close to Kapinski.

"Did she talk to you about the kids?"

"We don't talk about anything. I put the three of them on a plane to her every June. And I get them back every September. Two years like that. Also, now we each get every other Christmas."

"You can't do this. She's got to be able to discuss the kids with you. You two are all your kids have. This has got to stop."

Kapinski sat on Annie's recently vacated chair, happily settling down, like some old butcher, tired from being on his feet all day, taking some small joy in getting a seat on the bus home. His suit, which the guy at the May Company swore wouldn't wrinkle, did.

"Annie, we're doing just fine. Bits needed to feel very far away. And successful. She needed to feel powerful and important. And black. The kids are okay. Maybe we eat too much McDonald's, but we're all doing just fine."

Looking at Kapinski, it hit Pisano that despite the furrowed brow, the wrinkled suit, the baseball cap, and the life of small victories and big defeats, here was one happy man. Kapinski had done in the Sixties exactly what he'd wanted to do. And he had just kept on doing it.

"So, as I was saying, why would anyone want the job?"

"President? It's like anybody who plays baseball; you always think you have some shot at making MVP."

Kapinski took off his golf hat, his bald head cliché shiny in the convention hall glare. "Why the hell is it so cold in this cave?" he asked Annie.

"So the speakers don't sweat on national television. The conventional wisdom is that if Nixon had kept his upper lip dry, he would have beaten John Kennedy. So sweating is a sin."

"I don't know much about these nuances."

"What do you know, Kapinski?"

Pisano surprised Annie with his question.

"I know Mulligan is in big trouble if he keeps screwing around with Bitsy," Kapinski said. The sentence sat like the fat delegate, uncomfortable on the folding chair. "You know, I never met Mulligan. I shared the platform with him the day of the Offensive. And, years later, when I testified at the congressional hearings on the MIAs, I spent a long afternoon with that guy, the older guy, who worked for him."

"Kelly," Annie volunteered. "Jerry Kelly."

"Which is how I found out. I guess you two knew all along, knew about Mulligan and how he liked boys." Kapinski paused. "Now about the other stuff, I kept my word. I never spoke about Burnett and Simpson, never told about how Burnett was just an establishment tool, as we used to say in the good old days. But the stuff that this Kelly guy told me—boy, that's really some story."

"It doesn't have to do with anything now, Kapinski. Doesn't have to do with what he or you or any of it is about," Pisano said.

"It's about Mulligan pretending to be something he's not. I couldn't have figured him for liking boys. Shit, he wants to wipe out the gay rights plank in the platform. What kind of a hypocrite is that? I had never figured it out, back in sixty-seven. I almost fell off my chair when this old guy, Kelly, starts talking to me as if I were in on the secret of something. You guys never said a word."

"We didn't need to," Pisano said with a edge in his voice. "When Burnett was shot it was a moot point. And it should stay mute."

"I never told anybody, Annie, never told about Burnett," Kapinski said, directing all his words at her, as if Pisano had left the hall. All around them delegates were shouting and yelling and wearing the silly hats and buttons that they always seemed to want to put on at conventions. Nobody could have figured out, Annie realized, that these three people were talking about death, and whether they would let at least one life continue on its present path.

"I let Burnett's legend stand. I don't know if you made the right choice, Joe, when you decided to forget the story about Burnett and Simpson. I fought you then. I probably would fight you now. But I let you and Annie make the decision. Burnett stands in history like a good guy."

Kapinski rocked on his chair, and somewhere in Annie's crowded memories there were half a dozen other pictures of Kapinski rocking his way through other conversations. The labor organizer pulled his cap low, shielding his eyes with the visor, as if the brightness of the memory were too much to bear.

"But then, here I was, Mister Radical, going to testify before Congress three, no, four years after the U.S. pulled out of Saigon. You remember. I went over as part of that reconciliation effort. Then some liberal congressmen ask me to testify about what was going on, especially about the MIAs and stuff. Well, Mulligan's guy couldn't be nicer. Brought me lunch and we had a long talk about the march. I almost said something about Simpson and Burnett. Like I couldn't figure it out, but I just trusted the guy. Kelly."

"He could do that," Annie said. "He could just get you to tell him almost anything. He was that kind of a guy."

"Well, at least I'm not totally nuts. And then we were talking about the Offensive Against the War and about Burnett and Dong, and Kelly said the strangest thing. He said maybe Simpson was smarter than anyone knew. He wasn't taking any chances. He plans the march to confuse and diffuse the peace movement. Then you, Joe, started asking questions and threw him and his friends at the Agency into a real panic. But you weren't the big problem. Burnett was. Simpson had to do something. He had the weapon, Dong, he just had to reprogram him. Only I guess we didn't know about programming then, huh? So they got Dong to wipe out Burnett. From what Kelly said, they just weren't sure of what Burnett was going to do next. And then Kelly asked me how did I feel about bringing Dong here, anyway? So I think to myself, 'Well, how the hell does he know about me and Dong?' And, if his theory is right, it wasn't just one whacked-out Vietnamese, but instead it was really spook city."

The band off to the side of the podium was playing "Happy Days Are Here Again," and Annie, no matter how hard she tried to concentrate on what Kapinski was saying, couldn't stop the words from running through her head.

"We thought it could be that way, remember, when we talked right after it happened. That's when we promised not to say anything. Remember?" Annie asked a little too pointed-ly, a look of adolescent sadness on her face.

"Hey, I promised never to say anything about Burnett and Simpson. I kept my word. You two kept yours. But, shit, think about it. We were practically kids. We used to think we were paranoid. In a million years, we couldn't have figured out just how manipulative these guys were." Kapinski kept on rocking.

"Kapinski, how did you feel when Kelly said it? I mean, you were so nuts after it happened. And bringing Dong here and everything."

The rocking stopped.

"I might have been nuts for a little bit. And, I admit, I felt a whole lot better after what's his name, after Kelly told me this scenario. The only way he could have known about Dong and me was that he spent some time *after* the march talking to his buddies in the Agency. And if he knew about Dong and me, then he had some decent insider stuff to put together the story about Simpson wanting to get rid of Burnett."

Annie thought that if there had been room for it between the lines, Kapinski's face would have shown some of the remorse he still carried. How goofy they all were, believing in everything, especially the power of their own beliefs. And how they had all gotten used.

"I always figured it was my story," Pisano finally said. "The one the paper wouldn't run, that tipped them off. What the hell would they have done with Dong, anyway, if they hadn't decided to kill Burnett?"

"Had him denounce the antiwar movement. Stir up general shit. Don't look so surprised. How many of these antiwar Vietnamese kids have suddenly turned into right-wingers, especially after they got out of Saigon and got their Harvard MBAs?"

He was used to bullhorns and crowds, and Kapinski's voice was too strong for this tiny audience of two. Annie shrank down on the folding chair, but her voice was as strong as the union organizer's: "So it's all fake, isn't it. We were dupes and fools. I could handle it, after the war, when the bastards that brought us the war all had their books and their theories and their first-person stories about how they stood up to Johnson, how they argued with Nixon. Their lies I understood. But this I hate. I hate being part of the lies because I just didn't know the truth. I'm so upset, I wish I had a cigarette."

Pisano stood up and walked behind Annie's chair, the better to rub her shoulders, his tenderness eventually bringing her head down to rest on his right hand. Kapinski sat alone on his folding chair, facing them. Pisano and Annie fit so well together after all these years, and he was so very alone when he was with them.

"You might feel like a dupe. But not me. I'm one of the guys who ended the war. I made all this shit happen. And if some of the stuff that happened was Agency stuff, spook stuff, things I knew nothing about, that doesn't mean I didn't end the war. I pressured the boys in the White House. I took their war and stuffed it right back in their faces. And they are just not going to take it away from me. Or you, either, Annie, unless you let them."

The senator sent word out that he had no time now for Mr. Kapinski. That got changed when the funny-looking, bald-headed labor guy sent the aide back with word that he was bringing an old message from Jerry Kelly. Then the aide returned with a different attitude, and Kapinski was led backstage, behind the podium.

"Hello, Senator," Kapinski began. "I'm Edmund Kapinski. You've only seen me a couple times before. And, if this conversation goes right, you'll never have to see me again."

Mulligan swung around, his dukes up like a Dead End Kid. His face was a funny color, blotchy, separating like rancid butter.

"I don't know who the hell you are, mister. Or what kind of a joke this is. But Jerry Kelly was a very great friend of mine, and you shouldn't be knocking his name around."

With a shrug, Kapinski slid down on the counter under the long mirror and, motioning Mulligan onto the chair, started what seemed to be a rambling monologue in his singsong voice.

"People send messages in different ways. Maybe I should have said that Kelly gave me a message a long time ago. But then that wouldn't have gotten me in here, would it? No, you would have had some flunky tell me I should write you a letter or something. Or sit for a couple days and wait my turn and say my piece in front of your platform committee. But then that's why my wife did—oh, yeah, Bitsy Clark is my wife. She and I don't live together anymore, but we're still married, so she's still my wife. Bitsy played it fair, dealt with your committee, but it just doesn't seem to be doing her any good. No, I think you're going to use her arguments, and everybody else's who complained about the platform, and you're just going to say, 'Hey, let's just get rid of the goddamn thing.' And especially tonight, with the delegates juiced to get out of here and on to the parties, well, it would be so easy to get them to forget any kind of commitment."

Mulligan was looking at Kapinski more carefully now, like some insect found on a pillow in the morning. Could it bite? Had it already bitten?

"But, Kelly, he was really something, right? And not only was he a big help in giving you the support to face down Burnett—that's where you know me from, Senator, from the Fall Offensive, way back when. But Kelly was also a big deal in getting us people who went to Vietnam after the war to come and testify and say whether we had seen MIAs or what. Yeah, that's where you know me from, too. Small world, huh."

Mulligan sat back in his chair and lit a cigarette. He still hadn't responded to anything Kapinski was saying, but he was still sitting, listening.

"So Kelly and I had a talk, the afternoon after I testified. And we reminisced about our struggles against the war. I always thought it was unbelievable all the people who turned out to be against the war, after the war ended."

"Jerry was a good and honest human being who probably did more for the issues he thought were important than almost anyone on the Hill."

Mulligan looked around for an ashtray, but before he could get it, Kapinski reached around him and served it up, like a waiter at a fancy party. He leaned over until his golf cap was almost touching Mulligan's forehead and said in a loud whisper, in what his kids knew was his best Peter Lorre imitation, "He vas your friend. Such a good friend that he was still trying to make your role in the antiwar movement even more impressive, more important, than it was. That's why his hearings after the war ended were such a smart idea. Now I would have been the first on the block to tell you that having a congressman speak at the Fall Offensive wasn't my idea of big time, but you were real important. And when I found out how they were screwing around with you, the Agency threatening you with what they had, well, I thought you were great."

Kapinski paused. His kids knew that pause. What was going to follow, depending on the length of the pause, could be rated from a four to a ten on the explosion scale. This was a ten.

"But Kelly talked too much. He was so proud. And, I guess he was getting a little old and not so careful. So after lunch, when he was on his second cigar, he got really into it. Okay, maybe I pushed him a little, too. But he wanted to tell me the true story of your courage. Not only did you tough it out with the Agency—and, hey, things just weren't so open about sexual stuff back then, were they—but you were doubly brave. As Kelly told it, maybe a day before the march, Kelly had found out from his buddies in spookland all about Troi Van Dong. Now he wasn't sure of the kid's name, but he knew there was something happening with a crazed Vietnamese kid. That just maybe somebody was going to get killed."

The door opened and an aide started to say something, but Mulligan waved him away.

"Kelly knew you weren't the target," Kapinski continued. "You were okay. But he told you, and you both knew some-body on that platform was in danger...big danger. That's why you made such a swift exit as soon as your speech was done. Kelly had even gotten a timetable on it. Nothing would happen until the end of the speeches. And you didn't tell anybody. And Kelly didn't tell anybody."

Mulligan had the rancid butter look again, but his voice was firm when he finally began to speak, "Why am I supposed to sit and listen to you, mister? Who the hell are you to come in here and tell me about some supposed conversation you had with Jerry Kelly more than ten years ago? What does this have to do with today, anyway? Making threats about how I knew something I wasn't supposed to about the Offensive, about the guy who killed Burnett?"

Kapinski stood up, looking a lot taller than he would measure out. It wasn't lost on him that the senator had focused on the assassination, not the assignation.

"This has to do with making one sweet mess of your career if I start to talk about it. There are several reporters, people you and I both know, reporters who just can't seem to get over the sixties. This is a story that these reporters would just love. The brave and courageous congressman, who let everyone else on that platform take the chance of getting their brains blown out. How do you think that would read, Senator? And where did the brave congressman get his information? Well, from the spooks. Not such a popular source, either, in those days or now. And, hey, I'm not even saying what the tabloids would do about the sexual stuff."

Mulligan didn't answer but just stared straight ahead, his arms folded across his chest like some piece of armor.

"Now let me tell you something else. And then I'm leaving. You don't do one goddamn thing about this platform. You be a good little chair and you let the convention decide on what this party believes in. You take your platform and the minority planks to the floor; and if a little blood gets shed in the voting tomorrow night, who gives a damn, huh? That's what it's supposed to be all about."

Mulligan dropped his head into his hands. Kapinski reached out and put his hand on the senator's shoulder, in a reprise of the move he'd watched Pisano make with Annie just an hour before. He was surprised at how beautifully cut Mulligan's hair was, how gracefully it fell on his perfect cotton collar. The senator looked very clean.

"So it's simple, Senator. You play the game the fair way. You give the convention delegates a chance to decide on their platform. Who knows? Could catch on. Democracy could be like a happening thing. And, trust me, Senator. I'll never talk to you again about your history, about Dong, about anything. Trust me, Senator. I know how to keep a secret."

The anchorman stressed that Senator Mark Mulligan had taken himself out of the running for the vice-presidential nomination this year.

His speech, throwing the platform open to the entire convention, also contained Mulligan's refusal to be part of this year's ticket. He was clear that he would work for the ticket and for whatever platform the convention decided on. For many political observers, however, Mulligan's move made him a future friend to both conservative and liberal forces, the kind of politician who bridges differences in his party. Nothing short of approval by acclamation of Mulligan's proposal could have put him in a stronger position for a presidential run four years from now, although for this year's presidential contenders, Mulligan's move brings new burdens and concerns. Deep differences on issues have divided this party for a long time, as we showed you tonight in our documentary piece on the history of activism in the Sixties.

Pisano stood beside Annie outside the control booth, watching the network sign off. He hugged her, saying, "By God, that anchorman is a brilliant analyst. Who wrote those words, huh?"

"Not you, you half-assed pundit. Who, by the way, had no idea what Mulligan was going to do."

"That's because Mulligan didn't know what he was going to do. At least I don't think he did. Until he thought about it. Or maybe until somebody talked to him. But I don't want to know that. Maybe he's just the guy we always thought he was in the Sixties. Maybe all your analysis about him creating himself was just a little leftover psychobabble?"

"Or maybe we don't know who got to him last," Annie said, sounding more cynical than usual.

"A Senator Who Makes a Difference. Sounds like a campaign slogan. Maybe presidential, huh?" Pisano reached over to grab the last Diet Coke from the portable refrigerator. "How much longer do you have to stay?"

Annie looked at her watch. She hated having to wear one, but as she got older and the days got more crowded, the little place that kept time in the back of her head kept getting more and more jumbled. And so she'd succumbed to middle age and watches, fearing that bifocals were just around the corner.

"I can leave now. I have to be back early in the morning, by the time the morning show ends. I tried to book Mulligan, but he said he had his moment in the sun and I should get Bitsy. Unbelievable the stunt she pulled with the 'We Shall Overcome.' Although I have to tell you that it was never one of my favorites. So I've got Bits and somebody from the platform committee. Pretty strange, huh?"

"Not so strange," Pisano said. "Let's eat something real expensive. By ourselves. The restaurants are staying open late to accommodate the happy delegates. I'll put you down on the expense account as a source."

Annie walked beside him, carrying her two large canvas bags. "I have to change. I can't get in anywhere good wearing a Hard Rock jacket."

The guard nodded to the two of them. The heat from the southern city put a flush on their faces as they walked through the parking lot.

"So we'll go back to the hotel. You can change. Maybe we should just get room service and fool around. Think about it. I can call the boys. I don't understand why this crazy camp won't let us talk to Bobby during normal hours. We're paying two weeks' salary so he can work as a theater hand for four weeks. Something's wrong somewhere."

Annie looked at her husband as if he had grown two

heads. "Because it's a learning experience, sweetie. It's good for him. Challenging, new. How else do kids ever grow up?"

Pisano shook his head.

"I don't know. Maybe they go off and try to change the world?"

Kapinski stood outside the convention center, trying to catch Bitsy to congratulate her on her victory. But, as the crowd thinned out, he realized he must have missed her. Even the reporters and TV crews were leaving. For a minute Kapinski thought about hanging around and having a meal or something with Annie and Pisano, but he was tired. It had been a long day.

Some of the younger delegates, for no particular ideological reason, had pulled hundreds of yards of the bunting outside with them, leaving it scattered along the sidewalks, draped over bushes and cars and the big orange trash cans. What had looked fresh and new hanging in the hall was suddenly tired, torn, and worn.

"The party's over," Kapinski sang to himself. "It's time to call it a day." Politics itself always looked worn out at the end of the day, but the system managed to pull itself back together again. Like America. Not without a little help from its friends.

"It's quarter to three..." Kapinski sang, warning himself not to get depressed. Sinatra either picked him up or put him way, way down. He'd always liked Frank Sinatra. Sinatra had lost a lot of hair, just like Kapinski. But neither of us guys have lost our pizzazz, he thought to himself.

The pay phone was at the end of the parking lot, near the police barricades where Kapinski would take up his picketing duty at ten tomorrow morning.

He reached in his pocket and pulled out a handful of change. Pay phones left no record, but only if you had enough change. Just remember, he told himself, what T. R. said long ago, "Every call's a conference call."

The Washington number rang twice, and then a familiar voice came on the line. Every once in a while he would almost expect T. R. Of course, it couldn't be. Shit, he was dead now six, seven years. He missed him. There was a real patriot, someone who committed with his whole life to preserving what Kapinski knew was important. The American system. T. R. was one cold-blooded son of a bitch who did what he had to do to serve and save America. Just like Kapinski. Freedom. By any means necessary.

"How did it go?" the man who took Simpson's place asked him.

"You saw him on television. Your Senator Mulligan is now nice and clean for the next presidential go-round. The current presidential nominee wants the senator's head on a plate, which means that they'll keep him at arm's length for the campaign. Then when you break the investment stuff in October and kill off their chance of retaking the White House, well, Mulligan will look like the white knight we always knew he was."

"What was the reaction at the convention to his speech?"

"The liberals love him. The conservatives love him. And he thinks that once again he lucked out."

"Any problem? What did you finally wind up doing?"

"I was great. First, a little allusion to the sexual stuff, so he would think I was in the know from Pisano and Annie. Now he'll never go to them to try to check out my story. Then I told him the bullshit stuff about the phony conversation with Kelly. Oh, yeah, I also ran part of the fictional Kelly conversation story by Pisano and Annie, just to make sure that it had no holes. They bought it all. What would be more logical than I would have had a deep, moving conversation with Jerry Kelly? So when I laid it on Mulligan, how was he to know that I never met Kelly, except to say hello at the hearing? All Mulligan knew was that I not only knew what he had done, I also knew what he had known. Got him nervous."

Kapinski took off his golf hat and stuffed it in his pocket.

He would head back to the hotel and call the kids. Tell them what a star their mother had been. He loved his kids, Martin, Victor, and Eugene, as his father had loved him. Both the Edmund Kapinskis, Sr. and Jr., wanted for the three kids every bit of the good life, every piece of freedom that America had given to both of them.

Kapinski, Sr., was a true patriot, one of Hoover's heroes, as he told his son, who was then just a year older than Martin was right now. Kapinski had followed his father into the family business after all, but, no, that wasn't for his kids. And it had been everything his father had told him it would be. And nothing that he could ever tell his sons.

He was getting a little tired. He could feel the tension in his back, between his shoulder blades. He wished there was someone to rub it out.

"Okay. That's it," he said to his friend on the phone. "You got it all. I'm turning in. Another job done."

"Kapinski, what can I say? You can always pull it off."

A big smile flashed across Kapinski's wrinkled face. This would be the only honor, the only praise, the only credit, he would receive. Kapinski gave himself the title that he gave to T. R. and to his father, "a real patriot." He was one who would never receive the honor of his country or the understanding of his fellow citizens, but who was engaged in the deepest battle to protect all that he believed to be sacred. The public acclaim, the respect of his fellow citizens, the honor to his family, none of this was his. But, then, that was the deal he'd cut with Simpson, so many years ago. There were times when he questioned Simpson's methods, but never his motives. For, after all, he too, like Simpson, had served his country and his set of ideals. They had triumphed, so he had won.

"Hey, what can I tell you?" Kapinski said, signing off. "As my old man told me, there is nothing more important than working for what you believe in. And I've always been a patriot. That's how I made peace with myself."